# Lord of the Horizon

Now that the corrupt government and religion of Egypt have been overthrown, the work of reconstruction begins. This is not as easy as it might seem to be. The new Pharaoh, Amenemhet, marries the daughter of the Pharaoh he deposed, thereby enabling her mother, a Babylonian by birth, to retain influence. Like a spider, she spins a web of intrigue and manipulation which threatens to plunge Egypt back into darkness. Her prize is Amenemhet's son Senusert, who will one day be Pharaoh himself. Slowly, cleverly, she pulls Senusert into her sphere of influence, alienating him from his father and his principles.

Finally, Pharaoh realizes what has occurred, and calls on his friend Ra-ab Hotep, hero of the revolution, to take Senusert to his home in the Oryx and help him grow up properly, so he will be ready to fulfill his duties as Pharaoh.

But the Babylonian is not yet defeated. She continues to challenge Amenemhet's rule and authority, leading inexorably to the final showdown.

''During the last twenty years, seven books of mine have been published as historical novels which to me are biographies of previous lives I have known.''

— Joan Grant

# BOOKS BY JOAN GRANT

*Far Memory Books:*
Winged Pharaoh
Eyes of Horus
Lord of the Horizon
So Moses Was Born
Life as Carola
Return to Elysium
Scarlet Feather

———

Far Memory

———

The Scarlet Fish and Other Stories
Redskin Morning

———

The Laird and the Lady
Vague Vacation
A Lot To Remember
Many Lifetimes *(with Denys Kelsey)*

# LORD OF THE HORIZON

## by Joan Grant

**ARIEL PRESS**
Columbus, Ohio

First published in Great Britain
by Arthur Baker Ltd. in 1944

First Ariel Press edition 1989
Second Printing

This book is made possible
by an anonymous gift
to the Publications Fund of Light

ISBN  0-89804-147-3

WITH LOVE
TO
MY MOTHER

# author's note

Ra-ab Hotep, whose autobiography *Eyes of Horus* described the first part of his life, is twenty-one when this book opens. His father, Khnum-hotep, has just abdicated in his favor, so he is now the Nomarch of the Oryx. The Oryx is one of the eighteen Nomes into which Egypt was divided, and it was there that the Watchers of the Horizon, under the leadership of Roidahn, prepared for the Dawn, the day when they would be ready to overthrow a tyranny which shadowed the Two Lands.

The Dawn is come. Amenemhet, Vizier under the Old Rule, has been declared Pharaoh after the decisive victory of the Battle of the Six Hundred. Prince Men-het, last of the dark XIth Dynasty, was killed in this battle against the men of the South, who were led by Ra-ab Hotep.

The wife of Ra-ab Hotep is Meri-osis, daughter of Ramios, Keeper of the Royal Treasure. His sister, Kiyas, has recently married Hanuk, son of Roidahn and Nomarch of the Jackal.

The tombs of Ra-ab Hotep's family can still be seen at Beni Hasan. The Nome of the Oryx was bounded on the north by the Nome of the Jackal, and on the south by the Hare. The Royal City is known historically as 'Ithtowe,' and the site, not yet discovered, is probably about twenty miles *north* of Cairo.

# LORD OF THE HORIZON

# PART ONE

# Ðawn In Egypt

Mist was swirling like pale smoke across the smooth water of the Nile, as my rowers bent to their oars to take Meri and me on our homeward journey to the Oryx. We stood together in the stern, watching the walls of the Royal City slowly recede in the distance.

"It is Amenemhet's city now," said Meri. "But this is our dawn: the dawn of days when we need fear no parting. Did you ever realize how difficult it was for me to think as one of the Eyes of Horus, instead of as a woman who shared in plans which would send her husband into danger?"

I smiled down at her, "That fear has joined those centuries of fear which we have helped to send into exile."

Another Nomarch's Barge was following in our wake: Kiyas and Hanuk, returning to their Nome of the Jackal. "I wonder if Kiyas remembers our wedding journey...when we passed the funeral barge of Men-het's 'Beautiful Unknown.'"

"Stop thinking of Men-het," said Meri. "He died in battle, as he would have chosen. He died for Egypt, for he was the last of his dark dynasty."

"So many died with him."

Her hand tightened in mine. "Do you think I have forgotten that? If your wound had been even more serious I might be returning to the Oryx...alone. We must go to the Hare to tell Sebu how her husband died. She will know that his death was magnificent, but she will need your reassurance that he died in the heat of battle without pain. Will Sebu rule the Nome until her son grows up?"

"Sebu's brother, Tet-hin-an, has been appointed to

3

rule for Nehri until he is considered ready for authority.''

''I hope Sebu will often bring Nehri to stay with us,'' said Meri. ''He is only two years older than Ameni and they will soon be old enough to have adventures together.''

Ameni, who had been sleeping on a cushion beside us, woke with a sudden wail, as though protesting against having his friends chosen for him. Meri picked him up and comforted him with the inarticulate noises which women use to babies. Either paternity had blunted my critical faculty, or else Ameni had greatly improved in looks during the last month....No, it was less than a month since I had first seen him: he was then eleven days old and this was his thirty-third day. Niyahm, who had once been my nurse, came to fetch him....I think she considered Meri and me quite incapable of looking after our son.

When the sun grew warmer, we went to the shaded platform above the deck of the rowers. It was good to be able to let time slide past, quietly as river water. Scenes from the last few days unrolled to my drowsy thoughts like the unfinished drawings of a scribe....Myself, sitting in judgment on those whom the Eyes of Horus had condemned; sending some into exile, decreeing that others should remain to make reparation to fellow Egyptians whom they had wronged. Amenemhet, in a litter inlaid with gold and turquoise, carried by forty bearers, entering the City for the first time as Pharaoh. Crowds lining the broad avenues to watch him pass; some cheering, others still disbelieving that any of the promised reforms would be carried out.

Then came other pictures, more sharply defined....The young noble whose estates I had confiscated to the Royal Treasure, reducing him to the rank of field-worker on land which his family had owned for five generations. His voice, cold as the hand of a dead man, ''Had I known, Ra-ab Hotep, that you came to the Royal City as a spy, I should not have shared wine with you.'' Then, making mock obeisance, ''But I forget, I am not speaking to Ra-ab the leader of

4

rebels; I address the Nomarch of the Oryx, the close friend of the Usurper, whom the more credulous of my fellow countrymen call Pharaoh!''

So many faces I saw; the face of Amenemhet, strong and quiet as granite. Another face, glimpsed for a moment between the drawn curtains of a litter...Men-het's widow, Kiosostoris the Babylonian, going to his tomb with offerings.

Toward evening the North Wind filled the sail, and the rowers slept beside their idle oars. Slowly we overtook a trading-barge, thronged with people who were being taken to one of the Southern Nomes. They crowded to stare at us as we passed; a few of them cheered, but the rest kept sullen silence.

''They don't look very pleased,'' said Meri. ''I thought they would all be rejoicing because they have left their filthy hovels in the Royal City and are having a holiday until new homes have been built for them.''

''They will take time to believe in the New Egypt. They have been oppressed for generations, and to many of them Pharaoh is still the ultimate source of fear. They have been told, 'Pharaoh is dead; Pharaoh is born again.' How can they recognize, until it is proved to them, that Amenemhet will become the symbol of *their* peace, *their* happiness?''

Meri sighed, ''It is going to be difficult to help them if they won't believe in our promises.''

''They will do so only when they have learned that they are all to share in the New Egypt.''

''Why didn't you take me with you to the stone quarries? I wanted so much to hear you declare to the slaves that they were free..it must have been one of the great moments for which we have worked so long.''

''I am thankful that I went alone. You thought they would be wildly excited, that their cheers would cleanse the quarries from the echoes of whips and the shouts of overseers. But it wasn't like that, Meri. Some of the slaves had labored there since childhood, day after day, year after year, until

5

they had become apathetic as blind oxen. The few who realized what freedom meant, were too awed to rejoice. I told them that they were all being taken to Nomes of the South, to rest until their health, both of mind and body, was restored. To them it was only another order which must be obeyed without question: in weary files they trudged down to the barges which I had brought to carry them to freedom.''

At first, few of the people who were sent to Hotep Ra would believe that they had come there to find happiness. They were furtive and suspicious, and it seemed as though a miasma had fallen on this contented village, where for fifteen years the Watchers of the Horizon had been trained by Roidahn to take over the new authority. They were pathetically obedient; some even sang at their work because they had been told that the children of Ra are happy...and often I wanted to cover my ears to shut out the sound of their joyless voices.

The younger of the freed slaves began to improve with great rapidity, but those in whom hope had flickered out seemed to have lost the energy to live. They had breathed, eaten and slept in fear, the only driving force they recognized. They reminded me of a donkey I had once seen near the Royal City: it was plodding along under a heavy load, followed by the owner who beat it whenever it faltered. I took the stick away from the man, and when he would not listen to me, broke it over his back. The donkey plodded on, stumbled, and stood waiting for the blow with which it was so familiar. It moved forward a few paces, stumbled; moved forward again, and then fell on its knees. It was dead when I reached it.

Before the Dawn, I had lived for a time in the Royal City, and had often been to the poorest quarters; yet I now realized that I had gained no adequate conception of the depths of squalor in which some of my fellow Egyptians had lived. They had always been hungry; even on a day when the

6

food bowl was full it was held by the ghost of famine. Lice and scabs; children whose joints were swollen and tender; children who cried because they were too hungry to sleep; children who begged for alms and were not surprised when instead they received a blow...all these were commonplace to them. Yet it was also a commonplace that when a child was very ill, neighbors would give up what little they had so that the puny body might have a chance to bid death wait a little longer.

They had even been denied the right to wash in the river; having to go far beyond the city walls to a disused canal. The old Pharaoh had decreed that the Goddess of the Nile would be offended if her waters were polluted by the common people.

Nearly every night a little procession could have been seen going through the narrow alleys: a man or a woman carrying a child to the burial place; or two men carrying between them a corpse covered with a white cloth which had been used for this purpose many times already. They were generous even to the dead: few there were who did not put some grain into the food bowl which was all that could be spared as funerary furniture.

Many of them had once held land of their own: they had not been able to pay tribute during a bad year and now a stranger's hand held straight the plow behind their oxen. They had drifted to the City, seeking refuge in the rabble of hovels which adjoined the quays. Sometimes they found work unloading the trading-barges, or earned a handful of food by carrying a merchant's pack. The children ran errands in the markets, and, if they were fortunate, they were rewarded with spoiled vegetables or fruit.

I remember giving lettuces to a child who had just come to us. He thanked me; then he examined them carefully, leaf by leaf. His lips quivered, ''You have made a mistake,'' he said sadly, ''they are quite fresh.'' I told him I knew that, but he tried to give them back, saying, ''Please take them, otherwise people will think I have stolen.''

None of them wished to live on charity but were eager to be given work. Each was allowed to choose to which caste he wished to belong, and few decided to return to the Royal City. I had twenty men taught how to make mudbrick, so that they could build houses for the others. Every evening I used to talk with them, drawing, with a stick in the soft earth, the homes which were to be their own. It was like telling a story to children and seeing them gradually coming to believe in it. The Gods had given me the powers of a magician, for I was able to make their dreams come true on Earth.

## amenemhet phaRaoh

Amenemhet was making a Royal Progress to the Oryx, there to invest Roidahn, the leader of the Eyes of Horus, with the title of Lord of the Horizon.

On the evening before leaving Hotep-Ra, where I had spent most of my time since returning to the Oryx, Roidahn said to me, ''In three days Amenemhet will reach here to confer honors on the Oryx, and on those of us who have helped to make him Pharaoh. Except to the warriors who went with you into battle, the Royal Progress will seem to be the climax of many years' endeavor. For the first time in their lives our people will have nothing to fight for, because they will have achieved the ambition which for so long has united us. The darkness is at an end: there are no longer whip-men in Egypt, and the followers of Set have been killed or sent into exile.''

''You speak almost as though it were a tragedy instead of a triumph,'' I said with a smile.

''It could become a tragedy...if in peace we were to forget the need for leadership.''

''But why should we? The Watchers have given the peo-

**8**

ple a new Egypt: from Headman to Vizier there are links of authority trained in our laws.''

''They have learned enough wisdom to take on their present obligations, but, unless the wisdom is daily increased, it will soon become inadequate. Will granaries keep forever full if no fresh corn is sown? How then can a man keep his wisdom unless his thoughts are fertile? There will always be evil which we must conquer, and there will be evil until all men are Gods...and what will then happen is a problem with which we need not concern ourselves! Fear is not only the weapon of tyrants, Ra-ab. It can be used by mother against son, by wife against husband. As long as there is a family which is not in harmony, both in itself and with its neighbors, the seed of conflict waits in the hand of Set; and he will scatter it wherever the soil is ready. It was easy for us to lead our people, because we could show them a positive enemy, the tyrant who called himself Pharaoh, and his dark brood of ignorant officials. Whether it was a headman or an overseer whom he saw as the immediate symbol of false authority, a man could say to himself, '*He* is my enemy; when power has been taken from him I shall have nothing to fear.' Now that has happened, and soon the man will find that there is always something to fear, unless wisdom is his spear and courage his shield.

''We have prepared new fields, but it is not enough to sit and watch the grain spring from the furrow; we must keep constant guard against the weeds of inertia and the blight of ignorance. In each of us there is conflict; between what we have attained, which is of Ra and eternal, and that which we still lack, which is of Set and is transient. That conflict can be like the dual pressure of wind and water which sends a sailing boat on its course; or it can be like the upper and lower grind stones, which crush everything between them into dust. Release the energy latent in that conflict, direct it into the right channels, and it will help to create an Earth which is a reflection of the Fields of Ra. It must be used to overcome those

9

ordeals which Ra has sent to teach strength to mankind; to drive out famine and to bring fertility to the desert; to catch the wind in the sail and to guide the waters to replenish the fields; to overcome pestilence, and the fear of death. Only then shall man grow strong in his Father's image, and find contentment on Earth.

"The water in an aqueduct is man's servant, yet, if the stones have been carelessly placed, many may die in a time of flood. If we do not continue to build aqueducts down which men's energies can be directed, they will use it not *for* each other but *against* each other. We must make them realize, Ra-ab, that the trumpets which sounded the death of the Old Rule, were also the call to battle for the future. There is work for the Watchers while there is jealousy or cowardice, fear or hunger, ignornace or cruelty, in any part of Earth. There is work for the Watchers while even one of all mankind does not love his brother—and himself. Only when each knows his own heart, and loves all that he finds therein, can mankind say in truth 'The Dawn is come.' And on that morning they will see that the Gods are brothers in their own likeness.''

So that the great multitude, even those to whom his voice could not carry, should be able to see Pharaoh, a stone platform, like the plinth of a god-statue, had been built on a wide, level space where Hotep-Ra joined my own estate. Almost every man, woman and child in the Oryx had come to honor Pharaoh: like the encampment of a great army of peace, stretched the pavilions of the overseers and headmen, the thatched shelters of the fieldworkers; and in the evening the smoke of their camp fires rose in the still air as the pillars of a mighty temple. So that their hearts might be as a stele on which the words of Pharaoh were inscribed, to every overseer and headman, a scribe's copy of his speech was given; to be a well of sweet water for the refreshment of the weary.

The stone platform was like a boat in a sea of people; and Amenemhet was the steersman who set their course to the horizon. He looked remote as a god-statue: his face, under the White Crown, calm and enduring as the crossed hands which hold the Crook and Flail. Yet to each who heard him, he spoke with the voice of a friend; each felt that to them he was as a rock in a desert of shifting sand, and that once again, Pharaoh was a link between his people and their Gods.

Thus did he speak to them:

"People of the Oryx, who in the darkness called on the name of Ra: the long night is ended and the Dawn is come. I greet you in the Name of Ra and of Egypt. By the Crook and the Flail, which in your name the Gods have put into my hands, I pledge you my word that Set shall remain in exile while there are Watchers in Egypt.

"As the light in your hearts drove out the darkness from the Two Lands, so shall that light show us the firm causeway which leads to the horizon, and not let us fall into the marshes of tribulation. Remember that the light of your own hearthstone is the child of Ra: let that hearthstone be the symbol of peace in which neither hand nor voice is raised against friend or kinsman. Strive for happiness as lesser men strive for power: and remember that love is both the seed and the flower of joy.

"Let your actions be such that if they were done to you they would increase your happiness. Love others that they may love you; and love yourself that you may love others. That is the First Law of the Watchers: the imperishable rock on which the New Egypt must be built.

"If this law be kept, there will be no need for other laws; yet so that you may know what the First Law shall give you, I will tell you what harvest will spring from that single furrow if you are wise husbandmen.

"You will be born without fear; for your mother and your father will rejoice that Min has given them fertility.

"You will learn the speech of kindliness: so that the rasp of anger, and the sound, harsh as splintered bones, of

11

quarrels, shall be as a foreign language which holds no meaning for you.

"Your body will grow strong: for there shall be no fear to poison the food you eat; nor shall the specter of famine come near the house in which you live.

"If there should come a pestilence, then will you go to the temple and be healed. If you should ask a question which a kinsman cannot answer, then shall you go to a priest, so that that which is obscure will become known to you.

"Your work shall be according to the needs of your soul: though you are born in the house of a fisherman, you may become a scribe; though you are born in the house of a potter, you may become a warrior; or from the house of a field worker, you may become a noble. You shall be measured according to the weighing of your heart; neither being wearied by a field too large for you to till, nor restricted by boundaries that are too narrow.

"If your neighbor's ox should stray, then will you help him to find it; and if there be fire in your straw stack, then will he carry water to quench the flames.

"The man of many fields will not feel arrogant in the presence of him who has but a hundred cubits: does the elder brother despise the younger because five years separate them from the same womb?

"You are bound to no one save by the gold link of affection. Should brother and brother be kinsmen only by blood; then will they say farewell with the usages of courtesy and take different roads—rather than travel together in hostility.

"If the weary should come to your door, you will give them rest: and to the thirsty you will give water, both in the cup of clay and from the Jar of Truth. Then may you travel without fear, knowing that though the road is long it ends at the door of a friend, and that the man of peace shall not thirst even in a desert.

"You must always remember that Set may come to your door in disguise. He may offer you gold which is not yours by right. He may offer you the rod of authority when you know it is too heavy for your hand. He may offer you the strong wine of flattery which you know you are not old enough to drink. You must recognize him as your enemy; and if he will not leave you when you bid him go, then you must call upon your friends to help you drive him again into exile.

"In obeying the First Law, you will have broken many of the arrows in Set's quiver:

"You will not fear solitude: for you will never be friendless.

"You will not fear your husband or your wife: for you will have taken them in love and not for expediency.

"You will not fear your child: for no enemy can be born of love.

"You will not fear any kinsman: for blood cannot bind you unless it be to another child of Ra.

"You will not fear idleness: for all are needed in the New Egypt.

"You will not fear work: for it will be congenial.

"You will not fear famine: for in the granaries there will be bread for the lean years.

"You will not fear flood: for the water-channels shall be maintained, and the aqueducts be mighty in their cubits.

"You will not fear to grow up: for the years will show you new horizons.

"You will not fear to grow old: for in each new horizon you will find further wisdom.

"You will not fear death: for you shall remember the Fields of Ra.

"You will not fear Set; but conquer him by the Light in your own heart.

"I, Amenemhet, Pharaoh, have spoken."

# allegiance of the north

Pharaoh made known to me through his Vizier that, before continuing his Progress, he would for three days be the guest of Roidahn at Hotep-Ra, and that he wished the Nomarchs of the Oryx and the Jackal to accompany him there.

In sharp contrast to the Pharaoh of ceremonial, was the Amenemhet who shared the meal that evening with Roidahn, Hanuk and Kiyas, Meri and myself. As Eyes of Horus we were friends and equals, and he was not separated from us by the Crook and Flail. The plans for the new Egypt had long been made, so we talked of trivial things. It was not until Roidahn and I were alone with him beside the lotus pool that Amenemhet said:

''There is news I have not yet told you, and it is my wish that you should hear it before it is announced to the people. Remember that we are speaking as brothers, so you must say without question what is in your hearts.''

''I think you have never found me lacking in honesty,'' said Roidahn. ''My tongue has always been a faithful messenger of my thoughts, even when the news it carried was bitter.''

''The news I bring you is that Pharaoh has chosen his Royal Wife.''

''That is glorious news!'' I exclaimed. ''As a man I rejoice that you will share the happiness of a husband; as an Egyptian I rejoice that there is to be a Royal Heir; as one of the Eyes of Horus I rejoice tenfold that Pharaoh shall again be man and woman ruling in unity.''

''May your rejoicings prove to be well founded: that I may come to love my wife, so that I rejoice in her company; that the Gods grant her a child, so that Egypt has an Heir; that I come to honor her wisdom, so that she shares my authority.''

''Are you afraid that as a lover you may be biased as to her qualities? Surely the woman you choose must be your complement, or you would not be giving her the title of Royal Wife?''

''I have no doubt that the Gods have arranged for me to marry a woman suitable to the role she must fill. But, until from personal experience I come to know her qualities, I cannot give judgment on their worth.''

''Is she then a stranger to you?'' I asked, almost incredulously.

''When I was the Vizier I frequently saw her on ceremonial occasions, but I cannot remember that we ever spoke to each other except to exchange the phrases of formality.''

I thought that he must have grown to love her in dreams, as I had first loved Meri, so I said, ''It is a rare love that needs few words to build it to certainty. Mine was like that; and each day the link between us strengthens to our joy.''

''I have not used the word 'love'; nor, to my knowledge, have I met my future wife in a dream. I have seen her because she was brought up in the palace...being the elder daughter of Men-het.''

I was glad that Roidahn saved me the need of making any comment, for I was deeply disturbed to hear that Amenemhet intended to marry a girl for whom he felt no affection; a girl whose father would have been Pharaoh if he had not died in battle against the Watchers of the Horizon.

''If you speak as Pharaoh, it is not for us to question the wisdom of your actions,'' said Roidahn, ''but as your friend I must speak, even though it angers you. The Eyes of Horus have condemned marriages of expediency, saying that such a relationship, if undertaken without love, ranks as the commerce of foreign concubines who welcome any stranger. You, Amenemhet, are a symbol of Egypt, the new Egypt in which men and women shall love each other so that Ra lives in their homes. Had you found the golden link with the daughter of a fisherman, or even with a foreigner, Egypt would have known that she was worthy to be her Queen.

But you will betray your people if you offer them an heir who is not born of love.''

A pulse beat in Amenemhet's temple; had I not seen it I should not have known that only by an effort of will was he able to control himself; yet there was no emotion in his voice as he said:

''Do you remember, Roidahn, that once I called you an impractical idealist? The Gods rejoice that you have proved me wrong; for without your dreams Set would still rule, and men might yet wait centuries for the Dawn. You yourself have told me that, just as there must be Watchers of every caste, so there is a place for men of many types of character in the pattern of the Two Lands. You are a man of ideals, Ra-ab of action, and I—the Master of Expediency. Ra-ab and Hanuk, under your command, united the South, but we had no warriors in the North. There was only Amenemhet with a small bodyguard in the Summer Palace. The North call him the Usurper. They would have killed him had they not been afraid that if the South conquered, and set up another Pharaoh of its choosing, his murder would be avenged. After the Reed joined us they treated me with greater deference; because they were uneasy, and feared to show their hostility so openly. Yet they would not support us in rebellion, for they feared to shed Royal Blood lest it bring down upon them the anger of the Gods—*which* Gods they never bothered to ask themselves! Then the five Nomarchs of the North came to me, saying that if I would agree to marry Men-het's daughter and so make valid my claim to the throne—to which I would then be entitled by inheritance—they would support our cause. They added that should I refuse, they would acknowledge as their rightful Pharaoh any man whom she might choose for a husband. Would you have had me pay so great a price as the happiness of thousands of my people, merely to provide myself with freedom to choose the Royal Wife?''

''Only the future knows whether you have made a wise decision,'' said Roidahn. ''You cannot give to others what

16

you do not possess; therefore you must be contented in your own heart, and know peace in your own household, before you can give these gifts to the Two Lands.''

''If the contentment of a man's household can be measured by the quality of his friends, then surely I shall be at peace, Roidahn. For as long as you rebuke me, Pharaoh need never fear to find only the brittle reeds of flattery when he needs support!''

''Isn't she very young for marriage?'' I asked. ''I never saw the princess when I was in the Royal City, but I thought they were still children.''

''Nefer-tathen is thirteen. It would have been better if she had been a year older, but I promised the North that the Oath of Marriage will be taken on the day of the Festival of Min, that is, a month hence. I may find it necessary to let no more than the Oath bind our marriage until she is older; I may even consult the physicians before deciding when it would be propitious for her to bear a child.''

''But there needn't be a child...'' I began, and then realized that it was not for me to comment on such aspects of Pharaoh's life.

''Is it the Princess's wish to become Queen, or was she persuaded by the North?'' asked Roidahn.

''You do me an injustice if you think that I would take a woman who was unwilling. I did not even trust to an emissary, and insisted that I had her consent in person before I gave mine. She was already in the North, with her mother, so it was easy for a meeting between us to be arranged.''

''Do you think you will come to love her?''

''How can I tell? As yet I only know that she is beautiful, with a beauty which shows no trace of her mother's foreign blood. It is unnecessary for me to describe her to you in greater detail, for you will soon have an opportunity of judging her for yourselves. I wish Roidahn, as Lord of the Horizon, and the Nomarchs of the Oryx and the Jackal, to come to the Royal City some days before the wedding, so

17

that an opportunity can be made for her to meet you without formality.'' He smiled. ''At least Roidahn must admit that I have not forgotten one of the Watchers' rules of marriage… that a man shall give his wife every opportunity to share his friends.''

## Royal Wife

At Meri's suggestion, I arranged for us to stay with her father, Ramios, Keeper of the Gold Seal, while we were in the Royal City, instead of going to the House of the Two Winds, which had come to me on the death of my kinsman, Heliokios. We made the journey by river, and Kiyas and Hanuk joined us on the way north. I loved to see the two of them together, for it was obvious that each day of their marriage brought them increasing happiness.

Though in the Jackal there were fewer changes necessary under the new rule than there were in other Nomes, Kiyas had found many outlets for her intense vitality. She was building a Children's Village, where the orphans would be cared for, and this would adjoin a village for people who were too old to look after themselves, to which they could go as an alternative to living with their families.

''Each village will be a small estate,'' said Kiyas, ''with its own gardens and herds. The children are to be allowed to take a share in the administration of their community, instead of having always to do what grown-ups tell them. Hanuk thought that too much responsibility would make children unhappy, but I told him that there must be many children who are like we were, Ra-ab, who are only rebellious because they are bored, and who only resent authority when it seems to them stupid. Some of them have their own plots of ground and grow food which is shared among the rest; and soon they will be given looms so that they can learn to weave their own clothes, and one of their scribes is a skilled potter who is teaching them his craft.''

Kiyas and I were alone in the prow of the barge: I understood her so well that I knew she was only talking to hide her real thoughts. ''What are you thinking about, Kiyas? I'm quite sure it's not only about your orphans.''

''Dear Ra-ab! I've never been able to deceive you, have I?''

''No, so I shouldn't waste time in trying.''

''I don't want to; I want to talk...usually I tell everything to Hanuk, but this might worry him.''

''Most husbands are used to being worried!''

''Oh Ra-ab, I wish we weren't making this journey!''

''Why? Because it reminds you of Men-het?''

''Because I don't want to meet his daughter. She knows that we all belong to the Eyes of Horus, and that it was because her father fought against us that he was killed. But no one except you and Hanuk knows *why* Men-het came out to battle; that it was because Kiyas whom he loved tricked him into believing that the Warriors of the West mocked him for a coward. I'm not sorry I did it; I'd do it again, a hundred times if necessary, for it helped to bring peace to Egypt. But the part of me that knows this is Kiyas the Nomarch of the Jackal, not Kiyas the woman. *She* betrayed a man who loved her, and is it so surprising that she dreads to meet his daughter? For I betrayed her too, Ra-ab. If it were not for me she might be ruling Egypt in her own right. She would be able to choose a husband she loved, instead of being married for expediency...for *our* expediency, to a stranger twenty years older than herself.''

''You take up a burden that does not belong to you. If there is guilt to be borne, it is mine as much as yours...and if you had the choice would you take the greater burden of giving Egypt a Pharaoh we could not trust?''

''I have said that I know it is foolish of me...but I have

never kept my thoughts from you even when I knew them to be foolish.''

The servants were setting out cushions under an awning in preparation for the evening meal. ''We must go back to the others,'' said Kiyas. ''Never let Hanuk know that I have kept hidden from him this small anxiety, will you? It is never strong enough to matter when we are at home, for then I've got so many things to do.''

''Building an Orphans' Village...to make you forget another orphan?''

''Sometimes you are almost too discerning, my Ra-ab... but I love you for it.''

Tall, gilded poles, set like racks of spears on each side of the pylons, flew pennants of scarlet and yellow, Amenemhet's colors, at every gateway of the Royal City. Masts, roped to each other by garlands of flowers, had been set up in the streets between the rows of shade-trees. As Ramios's litter-bearers carried us towards his house, I saw how different were the crowds to those which had been here when I was in the City before the Dawn. A few people still looked anxious or furtive, but for each of these there were a hundred who smiled as did the people of the Oryx. The eighty ram-headed sphinx of the great avenue, set up during the Dark Dynasty, had been allowed to remain; but the cartouche of the tyrant had been erased from the stele which each held between its fore-paws.

Ramios welcomed us as though we had been away for only a few days. Acting on secret information from us he had absented himself from the Royal City during the time of siege; but his action had not been considered suspicious by those who upheld Men-het, and when Amenemhet became Pharaoh he had returned to find his possessions undisturbed. I expected him to be eager to hear details of how the Watchers had come to power...or at least of the part we had played in it, but I found that he considered such news irrelevant. He had disapproved of the old regime only because the officials were corrupt, and so had greatly increased the difficulty of his keeping a faithful record of the tallies of the Royal Treasure. Now that he could rest assured that the men who acknowledged his authority would neither take nor offer bribes, he took little interest in reforms which did not personally affect him.

"You will be interested to hear," he said as soon as greetings had been exchanged, "that I have made further improvements in my barter-system. People will still be allowed to exchange their produce for grain, but also, if they wish, they may receive barter-tokens, which may be taken to storehouses maintained by the Nomarchs, and there exchanged for anything they require. Pharaoh has approved my plan, and has agreed that a grant shall be made from the Royal Treasure to enable each Nomarch to equip the new store-houses."

"Father, you are so beautifully unchanged," said Meri. "You haven't seen me for more than two years, and yet you don't ask me whether I like living in the Oryx, or whether Ra-ab has proved himself to be a congenial husband, or whether your grandson has cut his first tooth."

Ramios looked rather embarrassed. "In my position as host I considered it my duty to give news instead of asking for it. You must be weary after so long a journey, so let me give you wine before I demand that you increase your thirst by conversation. As to the news for which you think I should have asked...the discerning eye of a father showed me that these questions need not be put into words. I would even be prepared to state that my grandson has several teeth; for only a lusty baby could result from parents so obviously contented."

As I watched him greeting Kiyas I wondered what he would think if he knew that she had once been the "Beautiful Unknown" who, through Men-het's love for her, had been a favorite topic of conversation in the City.

"It is a great joy to welcome you to my house," he said,

''for I have long regretted that I had not the opportunity of meeting Ra-ab's sister.''

Something in the inflection of his voice made me curious. Had he perhaps seen the Prince's concubine, and recognized Kiyas? I was sure that unless it suited him he would never satisfy my curiosity.

Later that evening, he said to us, ''Pharaoh has informed me that tomorrow we are to have the honor of receiving the future Queen as our guest. He wishes the meeting to be informal, and they will come here after sunset so that the other officials of the Court shall not consider themselves slighted in not receiving an equal mark of the Royal favor.''

''Father, do you approve of Amenemhet's choice of the Royal Wife?'' asked Meri.

''It is not for me to question the decisions of royalty,'' began Ramios. But Meri interrupted him, ''I didn't ask you as the Gold Seal. I asked you as my father. Do you think that any of us would betray you if you should be so daring as to say something indiscreet?''

''Since you put it like that I will tell you what is in my mind. Naturally you will respect my confidence.''

''You can be sure that we will,'' said Kiyas. ''All of us are well used to guarding secrets.''

He looked at her, the shadow of a smile in his eyes, and then replied with emphasis, ''Of that I am confident.''

He cleared his throat, and took a sip of wine before continuing. ''Of the Princess Nefer-tathen I know very little, though I have seen her on several occasions when I have been at the Palace. She is mature for her age, and I hear that the scribes find her a willing and intelligent pupil. I have never heard it whispered that she is vain or ambitious, and even when a small child she was exceedingly docile. One might almost describe her as clay in which the potter has not yet set his thumb.''

''Poor Amenemhet!'' said Kiyas. ''She sound most terribly dull.''

22

"That is not necessarily an unfortunate quality in a Queen," said Ramios severely. "The ceremonial of court life is not particularly diverting, and one who, shall we say, required a wider scope for her exceptional talents," here he paused and sent a piercing glance at Kiyas from under his heavy eyebrows, "might find it difficult to fulfill her obligations with dignity and discretion."

By now I was almost sure he had recognized Kiyas, and smiled to myself as I wondered whether he would ever bring himself to admit it even to Meri or me.

"Then if it doesn't matter her being dull, why don't you approve of her?" asked Kiyas.

"It is not that I disapprove of *her*, indeed I regret it exceedingly if anything I may have said should lead you to believe I hold such an opinion. I am doubtful of her suitability because her mother is a foreigner, a *Babylonian*; a race whose creation ably demonstrates that the Gods have a secret purpose which is beyond man's understanding. Though, since the Gods found it necessary to make scorpions I suppose that mankind should have been prepared for Babylonians!"

"Is it quite fair to condemn Kiosostoris because she is a foreigner?" suggested Hanuk. "Men-het must have had some good reason for marrying her, or he wouldn't have made her the mother of his heirs. After all, she can't help being a foreigner."

"If she attempted to help it I might find some compassion for her, but she *glories* in being a Babylonian!" Ramios's voice was more colored by emotion than I had ever heard it. To be born a foreigner and yet not to regret it had for him the stink of blasphemy.

"I was always rather sorry for her," said Meri. "Though I don't think I've ever spoken to her. Everyone knew that Men-het didn't love her, and she seldom went outside her own garden, or attended even the Palace entertainments. She was very pretty in an odd sort of way—if one likes the Babylonian type."

23

"I cannot say that I consider her handsome," said Ramios, "but then, being Egyptian, I am hardly in a position to judge. No doubt a tortoise finds pleasure in the appearance of another tortoise, in fact if this were not so, those admirable animals would have defeated the purpose of their creator." He gave a small, dry chuckle, rather like a cough, and waited for us to appreciate his little joke. When we had done so, he said to Meri:

"If you considered Men-het's wife to be of retiring disposition, one deserving of pity, then your ear for gossip was not so excellent as I should have expected. She remains in her own apartments as a spider remains motionless in its web... knowing that without further effort her prey will become enmeshed. The women's quarters of the Palace have always seethed with intrigue, but I had hoped that one of Amenemhet's first reforms would have been to send that woman, and all those who are close to her, into exile. It would have been to inflict no hardship to send her back to her own country...a country which she considers to be so vastly superior to our own. That she is to be allowed to remain here is in itself a disaster; but that she should be about to assume the title and privileges of Royal Mother, is, I consider, almost too horrible to contemplate."

While I was discussing the events of the day with Meri before we went to sleep, I said, "How much reliance do you think we ought to put on your father's estimate of Kiosostoris?"

"I don't know, Ra-ab, that's what I've been wondering all the evening. He has always disliked foreigners, but none as vehemently as he does the Babylonians. He was a friend of Amenemhet's father, the old Vizier, and tried to persuade him to oppose Men-het's marriage. It was arranged because an alliance with the Asiatics was considered expedient, and I don't think that Men-het was given any choice. I have always thought of her as stupid, and terribly shy...certainly it never occurred to me that she might be a sinister influence.

24

Do you think it's our duty to tell Amenemhet what we have heard...we needn't say it came from Father.''

''No; he would never listen to us. Now that his decision to take Nefer-tathen as his queen has been announced, it would be as bad as though he broke his oath if he withdrew it. The poor child has done nothing to deserve such an insult, and surely Pharaoh is wise enough not to be disturbed by a scheming woman.''

''But he'll never be happy: the mother is evil and the child is a fool...if we are to believe what we hear. And Father is much more shrewd in his judgment of character than one would think to hear him talk!''

''If Nefer-tathen changed her mind about the marriage, then the Royal Oath would not be affected. Couldn't you convince her that no woman is happy who marries a man she doesn't love?''

''I could try,'' said Meri thoughtfully, ''tomorrow, when they come here, would be my best chance. You don't think Amenemhet would be sorry if she changed her mind?''

''I think he would be enormously relieved.''

For Kiyas's sake I was glad to see that the Princess Nefer-tathen did not resemble her father. She had black hair, and eyes of a curious dark gray, spaced very wide. She wore a head-dress of gold and turquoise flowers, and a dress of blue mist-linen, elaborately pleated and embroidered with gold bees. She sat between Ramios and her betrothed husband, and two fan-bearers stood behind her chair during the meal. Amenemhet was old enough to be her father, and he treated her as though he were. She only spoke when she was asked a question, and even then I felt that she had been trained in the correct answer, that her words held no spontaneity.

At the end of the meal, the women, on Meri's suggestion, went out into the garden. I hoped fervently that she would find a way by which the little Princess would escape a marriage which promised so little happiness to either of them.

Amenemhet turned to me and said, ''Now that you have met my future wife, do you compliment me on my choice?''

''She is beautiful; and her beauty is of a type which will increase with the years. Her grace and dignity are already remarkable.''

''With that I must be content,'' he said with a smile. ''Until you have had opportunity to judge her other qualities.''

''You spoke truly when you told me that she shows no trace of foreign blood. I presume that when she is married, her mother will no longer continue to live at the Palace?''

''That has not yet been decided...in any case it is not a matter of importance.''

''It is not for me to comment on your decisions, but parents are not always propitious company in which to build from marriage the first rung of a ladder leading to the stars.''

He laughed. ''I shall remember your advice; and should I fall into any errors from which your experience as a husband might rescue me, you will receive a summons to the Palace.''

The Royal guests left early. As soon as they had gone I asked Meri, ''Did you succeed? Is there any chance that she will release him?''

''None. I begin to believe that Father is right about the Babylonian: that poor child dare not think for herself. Her mother has decided that she is to marry Pharaoh, and it would never occur to her to question the decision. I asked her if she loved him, and she said, 'Of course; it is the law to love one's husband.' I told her that love does not recognize any laws except its own, and, as though she were repeating a lesson, she answered, 'Children cannot know their own hearts until they are grown-up. If I obey my mother I shall be happy, and if I obey my husband I shall be content. I am very fortunate to be Queen of Egypt. Even the rebels dared not break the line of succession, so it is through me that Amenemhet will rule. I shall be Pharaoh, though by my generosity I shall allow him to hold the Crook and Flail. One day

I shall have a daughter, or even a son, and when they rule I shall be the most important person in the Two Lands, for the Royal Mother is even more important than the Queen.'

"Then I asked her, 'Haven't you ever dreamed of meeting someone whom you loved very much, loved because your heart told you he was your dear companion...not just because your mother said it would be expedient?' She wasn't offended, but I could see she was puzzled. 'What an odd thing to say! I'm going to be Queen of Egypt. Unless I marry Amenemhet, he will no longer be Pharaoh, and then there might be another war and many Egyptians be killed, as my father was killed...and it would be as though they died by my hand. How could I wish to murder thousands of our people because I was so foolish as to allow my heart to lead me away from the man I am intended to marry?' "

# horizon of horus

Tet-hen, who on my previous visit to the City I had known as the only clear flame in a dark temple, had now been made High Priest, and it was he who officiated at the Royal Marriage.

The day before we left for the Oryx, Meri and I went to see him. "I am glad to have this opportunity to talk with you both," he said, "for it is easier to ask a favor than to send it in cold writing-signs by the hand of a messenger."

"If there is any favor which it is in my power to grant, you have only to name it."

"Make no such promise until you have heard for what I am going to ask," he answered with a smile.

"The man who must haggle over favors acquires no merit for generosity. You are building additions to your temple: do you wish for gold or fine building-stone?"

27

"I want something more valuable than either...the man who can fashion them. In the Oryx you have the greatest living goldsmith, the sculptor who has no equal in Egypt. Once he came to this temple to take measurements for a statue; but when he found it was to be made in Set's image he suffered mutilation rather than debase his art. Would it not be fitting if Neku the Goldsmith were to create god-statues here and that our new offering-vessels were made from his designs?"

"In that request it is I who receive the favor, for nothing would give us greater joy than for Neku to be so rewarded for his steadfastness. He shall start on the drawings immediately I bring him your instructions and, if you wish it, he shall bring them to you when they are completed."

I was interested to see that wherever Set or Sekmet, or any other symbol of the Shadow, had been depicted, the stone had been cut away. Sometimes the effect of this was curious, for, as on the entrance pylon, where Set and Ra had been shown as brother Gods, Ra was now facing an outline which showed where his traditional enemy had once been honored.

"Amenemhet at first thought to have the building razed to the ground," said Tet-hen, "but I advised him to let it remain, as a reminder that though Set has been overthrown he must be continually kept in subjection. It is useless to tell men that evil does not exist, for, until they are strong enough to know and withstand its power, they will not have the strength to receive the radiance of the completed light. Were they to be told that nothing exists save beauty and divine compassion, they would be like small children who require to be protected from danger because they have not yet sufficient strength to guard themselves."

"Was I unwise to order that the Temple of Sekmet at the Old Capital be destroyed? Ptah-aru told me that evil might live even in a grain of dust, so not only did I cause the structure to be demolished, but said the ground on which it was built should be set apart for fifty years."

"A wise precaution; and very necessary unless your priests cleansed with power the evil from the stone. But why did you set fifty years as a measuring rod for evil?"

"I thought that by then the evil done there would have been forgotten, and so no longer have power to capture men's imagination."

"The years may rob a copper knife of its keen edge, but millennia do not diminish the power of evil; for it is not compassed by time as we know it. The good that a man does lives after him, for it shares eternity with his spirit; so does evil live, until the spirit which gave it birth has been cleansed. Power is continuous until its direction is changed. Good is the current which carries the Boat of Millions of Years on the river of eternity; and 'Evil' is the name of the eddies in that river, which for a while drive back against the flow."

"Then why didn't you destroy this temple?" asked Meri.

"The burning of certain herbs can cleanse a building after a pestilence, and there are ways by which more subtle evils may also be rendered harmless."

"What happened to the priests of Set when Amenemhet came to the throne? Where they all killed, as were those I condemned at the Old Capital?"

"They were taken before Pharaoh for judgment. The only one of them who had real power was Kepher...and him you saw destroyed by the Hawk of Horus. The priests here had no right to be given the priestly privilege, so they were judged as ordinary criminals...which they were, although they wore the robes of a caste to which they did not rightfully belong."

"Are any of them still alive?"

"None. Men almost as corrupt as they have been sentenced only to exile; but had these men gone to a foreign country they might have found fertile soil in which to plant the weeds we have uprooted. They had accumulated vast treasure, and this has been given into Pharaoh's keeping, except for such part as is required to rebuild this temple and make the changes necessary under the rule of Ra. The rest is being distributed throughout Egypt for the building of new temples, thus benefiting the people from whom it has been stolen. I understand also that Ramios is using it for his reform...to build store-houses for the exchange of produce. You will have already heard that the Oryx is to receive sufficient to build a temple worthy of its great position in the new Egypt.''

As soon as we reached home, Meri and I spent several hours each day working on the plans for the temple, which was to be built on land bounded by my estate and Hotep-Ra; land henceforward to be known as the Horizon of Horus. It soon became obvious that the ground-plan would have to be much larger than had originally been contemplated, as we thought of many additional requirements for which provision must be made.

There were to be five sanctuaries, the largest dedicated to Ra, the others to Ptah, Horus, Min, and Nut, opening off a large central hall of sixty pillars. Beyond this hall would be an open court to which led twelve small rooms, where temple counselors and healer-priests could attend those who came to them for assistance. These rooms would also be used for the pre-initiation trials of temple-pupils who were training in some aspect of Anubis.

We decided that pupils of either sex should occupy the same courts, even though we knew that in the early dynasties, when the light flourished, it had been customary for them to be segregated until after initiation, when they became free to marry. Each pupil would have a small room; the window high up, the walls four cubits in thickness so that no sound should awake the occupant until he were ready to return to his body. This was especially important for those who were developing the faculty of memory; but in all lines of temple training it is well for a smooth return to Earth to be assured whenever possible.

There was to be a large swimming-pool, surrounded by lawns and flowering shrubs, and beyond this a pavilion, open during the hot weather and closed by painted, wooden shutters when it was cold, where the pupils would take their meals together. Beyond this again were the kitchens, and the quarters for the temple servants. Each initiate priest would have a small house of his own, and those who wished to marry would have houses built for them adjoining the temple enclosure.

Although in the Oryx the people had always been able to ask for the services of a healer-priest, there was no place for the sick to be cared for save in their own homes, though in case of grave emergency, such as an outbreak of pesitlence, they were taken into the temples and, if necessary, even allowed to sleep in the sanctuaries. Now a row of forty small rooms were provided, opening on a long, narrow garden down the center of which flowed a wide water-channel to give coolness in the hot weather. They were the same size as the pupil's rooms, but without the extra thickness of wall, and with larger windows through which the garden could be seen from the bed-places. It had originally been suggested that fewer and larger rooms should be built, in each of which several people could be accommodated; but Ptah-aru decided that in privacy they would regain their health more rapidly. Women who had a difficult delivery of their first child might, if they wished, come to the temple for subsequent births; and if a seer-priest thought that a girl would be likely to have considerable trouble with her first-born, she too would come here. While a woman was away from home, a temple servant would be sent to look after her family if no member of it was able to undertake this task: for it was recognized that freedom from anxiety is a necessary factor for uninterrupted recovery. If pupils were found to be unsuitable for further training, they might either return to their families or remain in the temple as servants.

Meri and I had been to see the progress of the temple buildings, and on reaching home I was told that a stranger had
arrived from the Royal City and asked to be received by me.
To my surprise I found it was Yiahn, whom once I had wit-
nessed practising his skill as the Royal Embalmer. For a
moment I thought he must have incurred the anger of Pharaoh
and come to me for sanctuary. My thought must have been
obvious to him, for he smiled and said:

"You are right in thinking that I come to ask a favor, but I
have the Royal Permission to do so."

"Then you have only to ask, for it to be granted. Even if
you could not call on me in the name of friendship, am I not
already indebted to you? Therefore the merit of any favor I
grant is yours, for giving me an opportunity to repay part of
my debt. But the pledge of friendship should be sealed in
wine, though I am afraid that in my storerooms there is not so
rare a vintage as once you gave to the young kinsman of
Heliokios."

After we had taken wine together—wine which I think
gave honor to our vineyards, he told me why he had come to
the Oryx.

"As you know, Ra-ab Hotep, the motive which caused
me to become an embalmer was that I might learn more of the
body of Man. Because the healer-with-the-knife was not
recognized, I was only able to use my skill among the very
poor, who are more willing to judge by effect than by tradition. I know there is much of which I am still ignorant, but I
know also that for me to continue to make dead men look as
though they were still alive would be as though a Healer-
priest should be content to pass his life as a fisherman. To fish
is admirable...but not if the God's have found a more subtle
use for one's energy! I went to Pharaoh and told him that it
was my wish no longer to practice as an embalmer, saying
that two of my pupils are now as skilled at the preservation of
man's outward semblance as I am myself. Pharaoh asked me
the reasons for my decision, and on hearing them he reminded

me how difficult I should find the overcoming of prejudice. I then told him of the cures I had effected; of women who had not died although their unborn children were dead; of growths which I had removed so that the flesh surrounding them was no longer polluted; of festering sores which I had incised and cleansed. He then told me to come to you, saying that as it had been in the Oryx that the Watchers created their new authority, there also might an old craft be restored to its rightful heritage.''

''We are building a new temple, and when I planned it I must have known you were going to join us! Come to the Room of Seals and I will show you the scribes' drawings of the buildings. You must choose where you would like your house to be built, and how many rooms you will require for your pupils.''

''Then I am to be permitted to stay here?''

''Yiahn, my friend, you are not only permitted, you are implored to stay.'' I laughed, ''And should you leave us, I shall try not to forget that our laws give to every man complete freedom of choice; for, if I did so, I might be so discourteous as to send soldiers to bring you back: only of course, in order that I might once more implore you to stay!''

''And if you want to get rid of me, your soldiers will have to carry me across your boundary...and watch every cubit of it to prevent my return!''

''Then we are agreed. You will remain here as my guest until your house is ready. How excited Meri will be! And Kiyas will come from the Jackal to bring you her greetings.''

''She is beautiful, your sister. How happy I was to enjoy the company of the 'Beautiful Unknown,' who came to my house in a sarcophagus, yet who was alive to my greeting!''

''You have not yet told me what more I can do for you.''

''You have given me wine, and hospitality, and the promise of a house...and, so much more than that, the chance to practice my skill.   Do you wish to grant me yet more favors?''

''Of course.''

''Then may I learn as much as your Priests of Ma-at are inclined to teach me?  I know that I am too old to become their pupil, and that I must continue to work without the benefit of their sight.  But from what Tet-hen tells me...did I tell you that I knew Tet-hen?''  I nodded, and he went on, ''I feel sure that the seer and the healer-priest could find a use for the man with the knife, and for the physician.  They are all working to the same purpose in different ways: they are brothers fighting against Set, though using different weapons.  In the new Egypt these two branches of the Tree of Knowledge must recognize their mutual roots.  It would be unseemly for the priests to continue to regard us as butchers and to look on the healers-with-herbs as cooks who falsely claim magic: and it is unseemly for us to look on priests as magicians, who must be believed or disbelieved but whose powers are beyond the understanding of ordinary men.  That is one of the bridges which must be built in the Oryx; between the priests and the men of temporal skill.  They are as important to each other as soul and body....''  He laughed, ''Perhaps I express myself too strongly, but it is a subject very near to my heart!''

''This is magnificent: tomorrow we will go to Roidahn, and you will find him as eager as I.  The priests of the spirit, and the priests of the body; together they shall work what men call magic.  And what is magic, except the action of forces whose natural laws are not yet fully known?  Together we will understand them!  Yesterday I saw a woman walk who had been brought here in a litter and had not moved hand or foot for nearly a year.  I will not bother you with the details of the story: she had allowed her only child to swim in the river after its father had refused permission.  It should have been safe enough, for the bathing place is protected by a row of stakes; yet there was a crocodile, and it took the child.  The next day the woman was unable to move.  A Priest of Anubis found that she was so terrified of accepting responsibility that she wished her body to be helpless. He freed her from the thongs of guilt and she is now cured.''

Then I went on, ''I have always known that the soul affects the body, and most of the cures wrought in our temples have been due to healing the soul and leaving the body free to heal itself. I now realize that when the body has long suffered, it needs power on its own level to set it free. It is not enough to say, for instance, that when a woman has a growth in her womb it was caused by her longing for a child which for some reason she was unable to conceive; not only must her longing be re-directed, we need your knife to remove the growth.''

''We must not forget that there is also a place for the physicians.''

''My father has an old papyrus which describes many plants beneficial to man. To please him, I have arranged for these to be grown in a garden adjoining the temple; but I have always thought of such things as being expedient only when there are not sufficient healers. Now I know that Khnumhotep is right: they have an important role. They are necessary to us, just as food is necessary. Some of the plants of which he has record are still unknown to us. I shall send men in search of them, to Punt, to the Land of Gold, to the Far South, across the Northern Sea; searching for more of the gifts which the Gods have given to man, and which we have been too foolish to accept with gratitude.''

# nome of the Jackal

On the day that Amenemhet completed the first year of his reign, a daughter was born to Kiyas; and a few days after receiving the news, Meri and I went to visit her in the Jackal.

When Meri told Hanuk how greatly the baby resembled him, I was amused to see him display the same self-conscious pride as I had felt for Ameni. Kiyas treated the baby as though it was a puppy, and I noticed that she had chosen a nurse who would never attempt to oppose her wishes as Niyahm frequently tried to oppose Meri's.

After spending three days at their House of the Nomarch, they took us on a progress through the Nome to show us the improvements already effected.

"We have not yet so many priests as you have," said Kiyas. "For although the old Nomarch never permitted Set-worship, he had very few real priests. Most of them were men who repeated the ritual prayers to Ra in complete sincerity, but they could make no real link with the Gods. Yet they were kindly, and since the people were fond of them, we are letting them continue in office until sufficient new pupils are initiate."

"How many pupils are there?"

"Twenty training to be healers, three whom the Priest of Ma-at expects to pass the second degree of seership within five years; five who follow Anubis, but who may take several years before they pass their final initiation; and one who is rapidly developing the faculty of far-memory. Father is very excited about her work, for she may be able to fill some of the gaps in his records; it seems that she has been on Earth during periods in which he is specially interested. He agrees with me that far-memory is the only really accurate way of knowing the past, for a papyrus, however faithfully scribed, gives only the bones of history and not its living reality."

"We are building a temple," said Hanuk, "or rather, enlarging one already in existence. But you know that already for you have seen the plans. We followed your example and built in plastered mud-brick instead of in stone, for it is so much quicker, and less laborious for the workers."

"Are you having much trouble with the people who were deprived of office at the Dawn, and yet who were not

*past lives*

36

bad enough to be sent into exile?''

''Some of them *have* been rather difficult,'' said Kiyas. ''We found that many of them were too frightened to speak freely when we received them in Audience, so Hanuk had the excellent idea that we should both act privately as Temple Counselors.''

''That's a very good idea,'' I said, ''and one which we might well follow should the need arise.''

''But you don't need to, for the people of the Oryx aren't afraid of the Nomarch. Even those whom the Watchers condemned are learning not to be afraid of us, but you can't blame them for being a little apprehensive at first. It's so difficult to make them understand that we are not punishing them, but only trying to cure them of being unhappy. Hanuk, tell Ra-ab about the Overseer you saw yesterday.''

''He was a man whom I knew had been for a long time taking bribes, and unless the people gave him what he demanded he used to threaten them with whip-men...that, of course, was before the Dawn. Yet I think he was only corrupt because he considered it a legitimate perquisite of his office, and so he must have been amazed when on the day Kiyas and I returned here as Nomarch, one of his own goat-herds came to his house to say that their positions had been reversed. He thought the man was mad until he saw that four soldiers had been sent to see that the order was carried out.

''When I explained to him that he had been deprived of his right to collect taxes only because he had shown himself to be unready for temptation, he wouldn't believe me, and remained convinced that the change had been made solely to humiliate him. I assured him that just as the previous goat-herd had risen to the rank of overseer, so should he rise if he showed himself to be more valuable to the community in a wider role. He went off grumbling that he had been wronged: yet in less than a year his herd has doubled, his wife makes the best cheese in the Nome and his daughter is such a good milker that it is said she could persuade a sphinx to give a copious yield! Yesterday I offered to reinstate him, but to my surprise he flatly refused my offer. He said that he hoped in a few years to earn the title of Keeper of the Nomarch's Herds, and that if I wished to do him a favor I could barter for a foreign ram to improve the strain.''

''Did he give no reason for his remarkable change of ambition?''

''Yes, he did...and I had to admit that he was justified. He said that under the Old Rule everyone wanted to gain wider and wider authority because the higher their rank the fewer people there were whom they need fear. Since fear has lost its hold, a man is free to seek contentment along the path best suited to his talents. People are no longer divided into overseers and those who have to obey them, for they know that they are all threads necessary to the weaving of the pattern. He said to me, 'While I was an overseer, my wife never enjoyed having guests to our house, for if they were of the same rank they disliked us as rivals, and if they were less important than ourselves they hated us because they were afraid. Now that she is the wife of a goat-herd, she knows that the people who share our food do so only because they value our friendship. So I am most fortunate, for I enjoy good company, and my wife has turned out to be a better cook than she who once served me. And I no longer have to worry lest my daughter's husband should choose her only because he hopes for advancement.' ''

''Having so small a priesthood,'' said Kiyas, ''means that we have to undertake some of the duties which would normally be theirs. For instance, we have had to decree that the Nomarch has power to pronounce a marriage at an end. Now that the Watchers' three grades of marriage have been introduced, there will soon be little need for the exercise of this authority: but there are still a lot of problems left over from the Old Rule. So many people seem to feel *guilty* because they are not happily married...it sounds very unlikely, but it's quite true. We always see the man and the woman separately before giving judgment: sometimes they both feel guilty and sometimes each blames the other. And I have often heard people say, 'We used to love each other, but somehow I feel quite different to what I did five years ago. It is a very terrible thing to admit, but I've *changed.*' They say it as though 'change' and 'betrayal' were two words for the same thing!

"We explain to them, and sometimes it takes a great many words before they believe us, that all living is constant change, and that without change there can be no growth. I said to a woman only recently, 'If you lost the power to change, your soul would be stagnant. Think what would happen if even your body was no longer influenced by the growth-principle of Ptah: you would soon be bald, for your hair would cease to grow, your skin and nails would wear away because they could not renew themselves, and soon the bones would pierce through flesh that was shriveled and decayed. What an unpleasant prospect! Yet you wish that your soul should cease to grow! Only those who fear to change pluck out the first white hairs, or see tears in the eyes under which wrinkles begin to appear. To fear growth is to fear age, and to fear age is to fear death. Do you fear the beauty of the sunset because you do not believe there will be another dawn? Do you shut your eyes to the stars because you fear that Ra has forsaken Earth forever?' She thought for a moment before replying, and then said, 'It is easy to talk like that when you are still young; but wait until you are as old as I am, with your children nearly grown-up, and neither you nor your husband want to have any more. Then you will ask yourself why he should stay with you when he could find a younger wife to please him.' So I said to her, 'If I were offered linen from a weaver but recently apprenticed, or linen from a weaver of twenty years' experience, which do you think I would choose for my tunic? Have you learned so little during your fifteen years of marriage that you need fear competition from the inexperienced? Is there so little friendship between you and your husband, that you must rely on your body for a link to hold you together? Has your companionship proved to be so much less pleasant than he hoped?'

"She said reluctantly, 'He has always been good to me in his own way; but he's lazy unless I scold him, and at festivals he has a great thirst for beer.' 'Did you scold him so much before you were married?' I asked, and she exclaimed, 'I thought you said *you* were married, but you can't be if you ask such a foolish question. No woman scolds a man before she is married. For one thing she doesn't want to—not having found out how tiresome he can be at times; and for another, it might turn his eyes to someone else.'

"I pretended to be very surprised, and said, 'What a pitiable thing is marriage! For it appears that it can turn a smiling girl into a shrew, and a desirable man into an idle drunkard. But let us pretend for a moment that you and your husband are two people who set out to climb a mountain together. It is steep and smooth as a pyramid, save for a long flight of steps wide enough for two to walk side by side. Perhaps after a time he grows weary; if you go on alone instead of waiting until he is rested, is it surprising that soon you can no longer speak to each other in ordinary voices, but have to shout...and that the words are often carried away by the wind? Or it may be that you become weary of the climb and seek another road, forgetting that the mountain is so steep. When you leave the steps you slide down the smooth slope, unless the other, who has still a firm foothold, stretches out a hand to help you scramble back to safety. Perhaps you forgot to stretch out a hand when your husband stumbled, and even mocked him for sliding downhill. Or was it he who was proud that he could climb so much faster than you? The one who leads must always help the other to follow, and the one whose foothold is secure must always help the one who stumbles; if they do not, their progress is slow, for life is a journey which cannot well be undertaken without a dear companion.'

"She said grudgingly, 'I suppose you mean that I ought to have been more tolerant, and not so quick to notice his faults?' And I answered, 'It would have served much the same purpose if you had appreciated his virtues. Either he has virtues, or else you were a fool to be so deceived in his character...for surely you were too pretty not to have had the choice of several men?' She said indignantly, 'I *was* a pretty girl...not that you'd believe it to see me now.' So I told her, 'Beauty changes not in degree but only in kind—unless you refuse the gifts of the years. A baby has its own kind of beauty, but if when it becomes a girl it is still bald, still has such short legs that it can suck its toes in comfort...would the girl be considered beautiful? What is suitable to one age would be a mockery if it did not grow into another aspect of beauty. Why do you deny the value of maturity? Would you forgo the pleasures of a grandmother just because you are bitter that you are no longer heavy with your first child? A woman who sorrows because she is no longer young is as tiresome as a child who always wails for the toy which is out of reach. For sixty days I want you to try to rejoice that you are no longer young and foolish; to remember that, although your husband is free to take another wife, he will not wish to do so if you take as much trouble to please him as you did fifteen years ago. If after those sixty days you find there is no longer a link between you, then your marriage shall be decreed at an end.' ''

"Did you find that your people were willing to accept the Watchers' law of marriage?'' asked Meri, as Kiyas finished her story.

"It wasn't such a startling reform here as it probably was in the other Nomes, because many of our people have kinsmen in the Oryx, and have seen for themselves that it leads to happy marriages. The only people who grumbled against the new law were those who have long been unhappy in their family life. They seem to think that through enduring misery they acquire merit, and that they will somehow have been robbed of their right to a reward unless the next generation goes through similar unhappiness. Hanuk and I found that a useful guide to character is to ask people whether they approve of the new marriage, or the new law which decrees that a parent must relinquish all authority over a child unless that authority is the product of mutual affection. It is surprising that most people are so much more proud of their ignorance than they are of their virtues. You never hear a woman say, 'How meritorious I am to have stayed with my husband for twenty years...and I did so because I loved him and should have been miserable if we had been parted from each other.' Yet they frequently boast of having continued to live with a man they dislike!''

''That's going to be one of our most difficult problems,'' said Meri, ''to convince people that there is no merit in misery. They must be taught to fight for happiness as we fought for the Dawn, real happiness, not the temporary anodyne of self-delusion. Happiness is never negative; it can only be achieved by an effort of will.''

''It's not so easy as it sounds, Meri,'' I protested mildly. ''To be happy you have got to canalize your energy into the right channels. For a man who loves the soil to become a linen-weaver would be to throw away his happiness. For a woman to have a child if she is not by nature maternal might be misery; yet her sister might find barrenness a terrible deprivation. We shall have to modify the caste system before men are free to follow their talents. The son of a fisherman should not be expected to be a fisherman, nor the warrior to be the father of warriors.''

''But in the Oryx they don't have to,'' said Meri.

''Nor do they in other Nomes; yet the tradition is so strong that only the most virile characters ever rebel against it. Why did the man Hanuk was telling us about become an Overseer? Because he was the son of an Overseer. By a fortunate chance...or perhaps in calling it chance I underrate Hanuk...he was made a goat-herd, and, for the first time in his life, was happy. No one must expect their children to follow, of necessity, their own example."

"I shall remind you of that," said Meri, "if Ameni shows no talent for being Nomarch."

"I shall be sorry if you have to remind me, for I hope that parenthood has not robbed me of all understanding. If, as a drawing-scribe or a fisherman, he would find better soil in which to grow, I hope I shall have the charity not to starve his talent."

And, turning to Kiyas, I asked, "What do you hope for your daughter?"

"That she shall be lucky enought to find *her* Hanuk while she is still young."

Her husband smiled down at her, "If she resembles her mother, then indeed he will have cause to be thankful to the Gods."

# Summer Palace

Towards the end of the second year of Amenemhet's reign, Egypt rejoiced at the birth of a Royal Heir; and when this child, Prince Senusert, was six months old, I received word that Pharaoh wished Meri and me to attend him at the Palace. Though the message was in formal terms, such as is usual between Pharaoh and Nomarch, I was surprised that while it stipulated that we should bring Ameni with us, it gave no hint of the matters which were to be discussed.

"I wonder why he wants us to stay in the Palace instead of in our own house, or with Ramios," said Meri reflectively, then added, "And it is curious that he wants us to bring Ameni."

"Perhaps he considers it wise to judge the worth of the

Young Oryx at an early age, so as to decide whether he is a suitable future Nomarch.''

''I don't think that is very likely...and anyway he would take Roidahn's word about Ameni, even if he thought we might be prejudiced.''

''What does Niyahm think about our prospective journey?''

''She is delighted, of course; and so busy cultivating a manner which she thinks will impress the royal nurses with the importance of the Oryx, that she is almost too grand to speak to me! She has insisted on my having twenty new dresses, and Ameni is to have so many new kilts that even he will find it difficult to get all of them torn or muddy!''

In spite of Niyahm's anxious forebodings that Ameni would manage to fall off the barge, or into some even more grevious danger, the river journey passed without incident, and on the sixth day we reached the Palace.

In the private apartments, the ceremonial of court life seemed remote; yet from Amenemhet I sensed a constraint, a withdrawal from human contact, which I had not seen in him before. Not until the little Queen had taken Meri to see the Heir, leaving me alone with her husband, did I learn the reason for our summons.

''I want you to remember, Ra-ab, that rank can make no barrier between friends. Many times have we spoken as Eyes of Horus, sharing an equal authority; but now I want you to forget that we have *any* rank. We are both husbands, and does it matter we are soldiers, or fishermen, or rulers?'' He paused and then said slowly, ''I have never had the power to make close friends....''

When I would have protested, he shook his head and went on, ''No, Ra-ab, I am not asking for sympathy, I am stating a fact. I have often felt for others admiration and loyalty; and in my turn I have received both; but I have always found it very difficult to open my heart...perhaps because no one has ever wanted me to do so. Many give me respect, and to some of my people I am even an object of veneration; but no one has turned to me when they were in sorrow, and no one has ever wished to share with me their joy.''

''What of your wife?''

''It is of her I wish to speak; for though I am Pharaoh I at least have the courage to admit my limitations. You and Roidahn were both disappointed when you heard I was going to marry Men-het's daughter. You spoke the formal words of well-wishing, but your eyes were too honest to echo your lips; and though Roidahn told me that what I was going to do was foolish, I would not listen to him. By this promise of marriage I had gained the allegiance of the North; and Pharaoh does not break his promise. I had never loved a woman, so I betrayed no one when I took a wife who would help me to unite Egypt. And she was willing...very willing, or so it seemed to me: though I still do not know how much she was influenced by her mother, nor how much of her father's ambition she has inherited. I forgot that she was too young to know her own heart; or that it is difficult to be wise for a lifetime at thirteen.

''I tried to be gentle with her, and for nearly a year after we were married I did not take her as my wife; for I thought her body too immature to bear a child without hardship. She shared her own apartments with her mother, and we seldom saw each other except in company. I tried to see that she acquired the knowledge necessary to a ruler; I appointed scribes to teach her how Egypt is administered...naturally they tell me that she is a pupil of genius, but to me she displays no interest in anything she may have learned from them.

''Then it came to my ears that the people were beginning to wonder why there had been no Heir. I told Nefer-tathen that it was my wish that we should have a child, and she seemed pleased. I did not realize that her foreign mother considered ignorance in such matters to be an ornament to a bride. When I tried to take her, she looked at me with

45

horror...as though I were possessed by a demon. I left her immediately, and did not see her again until I had ordered Kiosostoris to give her daughter the necessary instruction as to what she should expect from a husband.

"It is not a happy augury for a child's birth when at its conception, the mother tries to conceal her tears, and the father his self-disgust. But an Heir was born: and his parents, with smiles which might have been painted on their mouths, received the gifts which our people brought as a sign of their rejoicing.

"I have tried to compensate her for the loneliness of being married to a man she does not love...and who does not love her. I have taken no other woman, and so am considered a most devoted husband: nor does she desire any other man; so well did I sicken her of love-making. Nearly every time I see her I bring her a gift: a necklace, a jar of ointment, a tame gazelle, some rare plant for her garden. She thanks me for them very prettily, and so conceals what we both know... that we can find nothing about which to talk.

"It is a bitter jest, Ra-ab, that I, Pharaoh, who swore to bring happiness to Egypt, to bring peace to the Two Lands, have brought no happiness to my wife and can find no peace in my household. Roidahn was right when he said there cannot be peace in a home, whether hut or palace, save when those to whom it belongs are joined only by love. We are joined by nearly everything else: by Egypt, by the Crook and Flail, by the blessings of a great priesthood, by an oath made before the Gods, by our blood mingled in a child: yet we are entirely alone, more alone than is a solitary traveler who even in a desert has the stars for company.

"I have always recognized that between you and Meri there is a link which to me has the mystery of divinity. Because I lack its secret I am less than other men, and fear has entered into me that as Pharaoh I may fail Egypt. That is why I have asked you to come here, asked you to forget that I am Pharaoh, and to remember only that I am a man who desperately needs to learn that which seems to you so natural. I want you to regard me as a most ordinary host. You will see my wife and me together many times; the four of us will share our meals without ceremony, go wild-fowling, watch the sunset from the river-walk. I want you both to study me very carefully; to tell me how I can learn to love my wife, so that she can love me. Think of me not as Pharaoh, but as a prisoner who thrusts his hand between the bars to beg for alms.''

Meri was already in bed when I went to our rooms, and as soon as the door closed behind me, she exclaimed, ''Oh, Raab, I was so *sorry* for that poor child!''

''What is wrong with him? You told me he looked very healthy.''

''I don't mean the little prince, I mean his mother.''

''Why call her a child? She has the presence of a woman twice her age.''

''Yes; the presence of a child pretending to be grown-up, pretending so hard that she over-acts the part. You only saw her while she was with her husband, and at first she was the same with me. She told her attendants to bring the caskets in which her jewels were kept, hoping to impress me with their magnificence. She reminded me of Ameni when he heard us say that a lion had come down on the herds. Do you remember how he picked up the stick he pretends is a throwing-spear, and ran up and down the room shouting. 'I'm not afraid of any old lion! I'm a mighty hunter! If it doesn't run away quick I'll stick my great sharp spear through it until it dies dead and can't hurt any more cows?' When Nefertathen was showing me her possessions it was as though she were saying, 'Look at all the things I have been given: look how fortunate I am! I am the Queen: every woman envies me: every woman wants Pharaoh, and he has chosen me as his only wife!' She is so unsure of herself that she wants to be praised all the time, so as to keep herself from knowing how miserable she is.

47

"When she took me to the nurseries, she only wished me to see how clever she had been to give Egypt an Heir. Ameni ran to me, and when I took him in my arms she looked surprised...glancing at Niyahm to see if she would object. The Heir was lying on the chief nurse's lap, and Nefer-tathen, looking almost like a child who expects to be rebuked, went and picked him up. By the way she held him I knew she had not often done so before. He cried, and I could see that she wanted to give him back to his nurse but was too proud to do so while I was holding Ameni. I wanted to get her away from the nurses, so I said, "Shall we take them out into the garden? I think they would enjoy being in the sun, and it is no longer too hot.'

"Ameni trotted off by himself to investigate a flower-bed, and the baby lay in his mother's lap and sucked his toes. She was so absorbed in him that she forgot she was the Queen... yet she was more like a child playing with a doll than a mother with her baby. Ameni found some lovely wet earth under the wall, and he enjoyed it so quietly that I never noticed what he was doing until he was as muddy as a little hippopotamus in its wallow. Then he grew bored with his game and came back to find me; and when Nefer-tathen saw him she gave the first real laugh I have ever heard from her, a warm chuckle like a contented baby. Then she asked, 'Won't your nurse be angry that he is so dirty?' and when I told her that Niyaham wouldn't mind, and that if she did I should tell her not to be tiresome, she sighed and said regretfully, 'You are very lucky to be able to do what you like with your son; I hardly ever see mine...because he is the Royal Heir, and has to be looked after by very special people who know all about babies.' So I told her that if people interfered between her and her baby she had better send them away. She looked startled and said in a shocked voice, 'But I *couldn't* tell them to go away! My mother chose them, and she would be very angry with me.' So I suggested that she tell her mother that it was by Pharaoh's order that they were to be dismissed. For a

**48**

moment she brightened, and then said despondently, 'That wouldn't be any use either. He would say that Mother was much more experienced in such matters than I. He doesn't look on Senusert as a baby who needs to be played with...he is only the next Pharaoh, who unfortunately needs a few years to grow before he can become Co-ruler.' ''

''What did you say then?''

''I didn't say any more, but I believe that if we are wise we shall be able to teach her to look on Amenemhet as the father of her child, the child they both love, and so build a bridge which they can cross to find each other.''

We had arrived at the Summer Palace after nightfall, and it was at dawn that I saw the sea for the first time. I woke Meri, and we left the sleeping house, and ran together across the beach of fine, white sand. The water was sharp and cool, quite different to the smooth caress of river water. We swam far out, then turned on our backs and floated, like two gulls resting after a long flight. I noticed a small rocky islet, its flat top nearly level with the water. I called to Meri to race me to it, and climbed out of the water just in time to help her up beside me.

''I feel like a young God who has just been given one of Nut's daughters in marriage,'' I said.

''Nut's daughter replies that she thinks she will enjoy her wifely duties, but, being inexperienced, requires that they be shown to her!''

I took her in my arms. And a little while later I said, ''Only the daughter of a Goddess could show perfection without requiring practice in its attainment; you are indeed the daughter of a Goddess!''

''I wish I were Nut, so that I could pick up the Oryx in my hand and plant it beside the sea. I should like the river too, of course, but there seems to be something in this new element which makes you even more desirable as a husband than you have always been. Dear Ra-ab, I love you! Do you think the

sea will have the same influence on the two whom we are
trying to teach to be lovers? I have prayed to Min so hard for
them, Ra-ab! Pharaoh and his Queen, yet we see them as
they see themselves; two people who cannot find happiness
either together or apart.''

''They will have a better chance of finding it here than
they had in the Royal City,'' I said. ''Amenemhet didn't require much persuasion to come here; though, unless I had en-
couraged him to be firm, I believe he would have allowed the
Babylonian to come with us and spoil all our plans.''

''Did she show her anger when she was told that she must
stay behind?''

''To me it was obvious; but then I was watching for it. I
was in the room when Amenemhet told her we were coming
here, and she said, 'I shall not find that inconvenient, for the
Summer Palace is pleasant at this season.' He replied, very
graciously, 'I regret that you cannot be spared from the Royal
City. I like to feel that one in authority is always here to
represent me.' She was half flattered, half suspicious, and
asked, 'Does the Queen go with you?' and he answered,
'She does, and bring with her our son.' Then the Babylonian
protested that the Royal Heir required the attention of his
grandmother, and that the nurses might grow careless unless
she were there to supervise them. Amenemhet said drily,
'You will have no cause for anxiety, for the Queen and I will
be accompanied by the Nomarchs of the Oryx. I think you
have seen Ameni, and so will be able to rest assured that his
mother is wise in the care of children. Niyahm, their nurse,
will look after Senusert, and should the need arise, she will be
advised by Meri-osis.' That made her really angry, but when
she began to argue, Amenemhet said, 'Pharaoh has
spoken!'; and even she dared not say any more!''

Meri laughed, ''Oh Ra-ab, I do so wish I had been there to
see her discomfited! She is a loathsome woman, though it is
difficult to explain just why she arouses in me such a profound
distaste. She has great dignity, and has always treated me

with every courtesy; she appears to be devoted to her daughter and to have no thought except for what she considers to be her welfare: yet I believe there is hatred between them...though the girl cannot recognize it.''

''Hatred? Why?''

''I think that Kiosostoris endured the humiliation of being neglected by Men-het only because she lived for the day when she would be Queen, and in a position to revenge all real or imagined slights. I am sure she hated Men-het, though she has only twice mentioned his name in my presence. She expressed the conventional grief of a widow, there was a note in her voice as though she gloated in the knowledge that she had at last triumphed over him...because she was still alive and he was dead. If Amenemhet had not sent for us she would have turned her daughter into a puppet. Already she chooses every dress that Nefer-tathen wears, decides how her hair is to be worn, selects the necklace, the head-dress...and then discards them for others...she may put twenty in succession on the poor girl before she is satisfied. She watches while the Queen's attendants carry out the ritual of her toilet, while her nails are painted and her skin smoothed with scented oils. The girl herself displays no more interest than if she were a statue being decorated for a festival. Her wishes are never consulted; it is macabre, as though she were dead and being made ready for the tomb.''

''Not, I hope, by the embalmer!'' I said in jest.

''It's not funny, Ra-ab. And it may lead to bitter tragedy for Egypt. You believe that Amenemhet is in no danger from a scheming woman like the Babylonian, but she is very dangerous; even though she is quiet, and smooth, and careful of tradition. A snake is also quiet and smooth...and no less deadly.''

The Summer Palace was admirably suited to our purpose, for it had none of the formality of the residence in the Royal City, and might have been the house of an ordinary couple. It had no second story, and was of plastered mud-brick colored

51

a dusty pink. On one side was the sea, and on the other a large walled garden, planted with orange and lemon trees that shaded wide terraces on which stood jars of flowering plants.

Only our personal servants attended us, and Amenemhet was free to forget that he was Pharaoh. Gradually the little Queen lost her shyness. Meri taught her how to bathe her baby, and she used to carry him down to the beach and let him roll in the hot sand. At first she tried to avoid being alone with her husband, and always asked us to join them, when on calm days the rowers took us out to the fishing grounds; or, on days less calm, we sailed the boat which had been built to Amenemhet's own design. But to our delight, we found that after a time, she and her husband began to make excuse to be alone together, and after the evening meal would often wander off along the beach. Amenemhet treated us as though we were kinsmen in whose company he rejoiced; he let Ameni ride on his shoulders, and spent hours carving a boat for him out of a piece of driftwood.

One evening, when he and I were basking in the sun while our wives were putting our sons to bed, he asked:

"Ra-ab, I shall have to give you a new title, 'The Son of Ptah,' for you have created a man out of a statue. I had almost begun to forget how it felt really to be alive. I carried out the ceremonials necessary to Pharaoh, and probably continued to give excellent judgments to petitioners; but I was only the shadow of a man. Even Senuseri was conceived as a duty...for I was such a fool that I never realized that I loved my wife. I *do* love her, Ra-ab, and what is far more miraculous...she loves me! I will now admit that I was afraid to come here, because I thought that seeing the happiness between you and Meri might make me bitter that it had been denied to me. But I learned that your happiness was something I could share, until suddenly I found that it had become my own.''

He laughed and said with a catch in his voice, "I'm *happy*, Ra-ab! I thought happiness was a thing I should always try to give to other people yet myself never experience. Our next child shall be given the heritage which should be the right of everyone...to be born of love.''

A year later, three days' festival was declared throughout Egypt in honor of the birth of a Royal Daughter. Yet on the second day the pennants of the triumphal masts were furled. Nefer-tathen, whom Amenemhet loved so dearly, had returned to the Fields of Ra.

# the Babylonian

On hearing from my steward, in whose care I had left my estate of the Two Winds, that there were matters which required my attention, I decided to make the journey north, and was glad that it would provide me with an excuse to see Amenemhet. We decided that Meri should remain at home, for as the river was in flood and I should have to travel by litter, the journey would have been tiring for her. She was expecting our second child before the end of the year.

In the Royal City I stayed with Ramios. When I asked him for news of Pharaoh, he became evasive, saying that he seldom had occasion to see him, and then only on official business. But later in the evening he was more communicative, and when I again mentioned Amenemhet, he said:

''I find it difficult to understand why a man who took a wife for expediency should allow himself to become so immersed in grief when the Gods decide to separate them. It is proper that a husband should show regret for the death of his wife, and this is even more necessary when his mourning is shared by Egypt; but now that the Forty Days' Lamentation are long since ended, he owes it to the Court no longer to remain in seclusion. If it were only that he was too preoccupied with his children to have time for anything else save his official duties, his attitude would be easier to understand; but I hear that he leaves them in the care of their grandmother, and seldom visits the women's quarters of the Palace.''

''You misjudge him, Ramios, if you think he did not love the Queen. As you know, Meri and I were privileged to be their friends, and I can assure you that the link between them was very strong.''

He looked embarrassed, as he always did when questions of emotion were under discussion. ''No doubt you know much more about it than I do, Ra-ab. But I consider that my long connection with the Household has given me certain insight into the unofficial obligations of Pharaoh. How can he have opportunity of judging the worth of his nobles if he never sees them except on ceremonial occasions?''

''Are not the entertainments of the Court always ceremonious?''

''You misunderstand me: there are no entertainments, not even banquet days of festival. He did not even attend the ceremony of Thanksgiving to Nut on the first day of the Inundation. The people expect Pharaoh to share in their pleasures...or at least to pretend that he does so. Certain human aspects of character serve to accentuate the Royal Divinity. The people no longer fear Pharaoh, but he is giving them little opportunity to love him. For many days he does not go outside the gates of the Palace; nor does he hunt lion, or go wildfowling with those nobles whom he used to honor with his company.''

''Do you think he will see me?''

''If you claim the Right to Audience he will do so: that is the most which has been granted to anyone since the Queen died.''

Yet Pharaoh did agree to see me; and not in Audience.

At first I thought he had changed very little; then I realized that only by a great effort did he maintain his outward composure. He gave me no opportunity to speak of matters near to his heart until the servants had left us, alone in the little pavilion overlooking the river.

"Ra-ab, do you think that the Gods are jealous of man, in that they never give great happiness unless it is shadowed by the fear of its loss? If I had known what the future held for me, should I have sent for you and Meri? Should I have agreed to go with you to the Summer Palace? Had I not done so I might not have deeply regretted that there is no longer a Queen...I might even have been wondering who would be suitable for the second Royal Wife. Yet I have known love, and now, because it has been taken away from me, I am desolate. I am more alone than I have ever been."

"You have Senusert and your daughter. Cannot your love for Nefer-tathen find expression in loving her children?"

"I have tried to love the baby, but I cannot do so. Every time I see her I am reminded that if she had not been born her mother would still be living. The physicians told me that if the baby had not been so strong, fought so fiercely for its own life, it would have been still-born, and the mother would have had a better chance."

"What physician told you that? A foreigner?"

"Yes; how did you guess? It was the foreign physician who came to Egypt with Kiosostoris."

"His motive I do not understand; yet I can tell you that the man lied. No child has ever killed its mother by being too strong, though a sickly baby has been known to affect the womb which gives it shelter. If you doubt my word, consult your Priest of Ma-at; and if he cannot satisfy you, allow me to send to you the man who was once the Royal Embalmer, and who now in the Oryx teaches pupils to heal with the knife."

"I am grateful for the friendship which makes you try to give me reassurance; but I cannot take the comfort you offer. I know that it was because my love was too warm, too carnal, that my wife was sapped of her strength. She seemed to glory

55

in my caresses, as I did in hers...yet through them I killed her. Had I realized what I was doing, I would have killed myself, rather than she should suffer because I lacked austerity."

I was appalled to hear him so falsely accuse himself, and cried out, "Whosoever made you think of your love like that should be destroyed! They are not only cruel; their tongue is the child of Set!"

He looked puzzled. "I don't understand you, Ra-ab. Do you think I am likely to be influenced by anyone in my judgment of myself?"

"You must have been. Amenemhet is revered for his wisdom; yet in judging himself he has lied, and suffered the innocent to be persecuted."

"I never thought that our friendship would be polluted by flattery. Why call me innocent when you know I am guilty?"

"If you are guilty, then Set is the Lord of the Morning! You know that love is the law of Ra; are you a coward to deny love because through it you have suffered?"

"I should be a coward if I tried to plead innocence. I forgot that my wife was little more than a child, and treated her as though she was not only a woman but a beloved concubine."

"Is not every wife glad to share the pleasures which you seem to think are the right only of concubines?"

"I should be sorry if Meri were to hear you say that."

"You need not be, for she has often said it herself. We rejoice that we are lovers as well as husband and wife."

"What shall I do if my daughter's heritage from me is a body which is dominated by desire? She and her husband may rule Egypt at my death. How can she be guided to choose a husband worthy to be Pharaoh if she seeks a man whose body is summoned by her own?"

"Why should those two things be incompatible? Do you find that Meri and I fail in our duties as Nomarch because we rejoice in the powers vouchsafed to us by Min? Physical love is only unfortunate when it is not echoed by other levels of the spirit.''

''To be preoccupied with desire is to become an animal.''

''Do you consider that Ptah and Min betrayed their divinity when they made our younger brothers? I have never understood why it pleases some men to despise the pleasures afforded by their bodies, just because those pleasures can be shared by those who are on a different rung of the ladder of eternity. Do you despise flowers because they too have seeds; or call a lion ignoble because it seeks a mate? Though saying this may anger you, all that you have told me this evening shows that instead of thinking as a Watcher, seeing the truth clearly without distortion by false sentiment, you are thinking as one deliberately self-deluded...or as a foreigner.''

''I am not angry with you, Ra-ab, though I see that we cannot reach agreement. If you could see the devotion with which Kiosostoris cares for my motherless children, you would not speak so bitterly of foreigners. I know that you dislike her, and it grieves her that neither you nor Meri have been able to extend to her the friendship you gave her daughter. It is not for me to order your friendship. I only regret that this should be so, for had it been otherwise I would ask you both to come often to the Palace.''

''You have only to ask, and it shall be our joy and honor to come to you.''

''I must put duty before my pleasure; and I must let nothing add to the grief which Kiosostoris has already suffered through me. I was the cause of her husband's death, and of her daughter's. She asks only to live undisturbed in her own apartments, and that the children be left entirely in her care. I am afraid she has never forgiven Meri for letting Senusert be put in the charge of Niyahm and taken away from the nurses which his grandmother has chosen. She might have been able to forgive what she considered to be a gross

57

infringement of her privileges as Royal Mother, had I not been so tactless as to stress how much Senusert had benefited by living like an ordinary child. Now that Men-het's younger daughter has returned to Babylon, Kiosostoris has nothing with which to fill her life save her grandchildren; and I can only be grateful for her devotion.''

"Are you trying to tell me, Amenemhet, that so long as Kiosostoris remains here it would be difficult for you to welcome me as your guest?''

"I hope that you will always make occasion to see me when affairs should bring you to the Royal City.''

"I understand. But never forget that when your circumstances change, and it is again possible for you to share your life with your friends...we shall be waiting for you.''

On my way home I stayed a night at Hotep-Ra, hoping that Roidahn might be able to think of some way by which we could release Amenemhet from his prison of imaginary guilt.

"You are right,'' said Roidahn, ''in fearing that he has come under the domination of Kiosostoris. While I was staying in the Palace at the time of Pharaoh's marriage, I took the opportunity to meet her whenever possible. Her calm, formal demeanor is a mask for one of the most powerful personalities I have ever encountered. Had she, instead of her father, been King of the Babylonians, we should have needed a great army to defend Egypt. Hers is the character of a ruthless tyrant, possessing a terrible singleness of purpose which drives her on to dominate everything with which she comes in contact. Foreigners do not treat their women as do Egyptians, and it must have been bitter for her to undergo the restrictions imposed on a princess at the Babylonian court. She would have been allowed power of life and death over her servants—and no doubt exercised it whenever it suited her. But her sphere of action would have been strictly limited, and in her father's eyes her value was to be counted only through her husband. That is, no doubt, why she was so eager to be used to strengthen the alliance with Egypt. She knew that in Egypt it might be possible for her to exercise her powers more widely, and as the Queen...providing that she was able to dominate her husband, she could at last realize her ambitions. Because she desires to dominate, she would expect others to try to guard themselves against such influence. That is why she played the part of the meek wife who wished only to be allowed to live in seclusion with her children. She was like a captain who, while he trains his warriors for the attack, hopes to lull his enemy into a sense of false security.''

''It was a pity that the blow to her ambitions caused by Men-het's death was not sufficient to kill her!''

''Why do you think it was a blow?''

''Surely that is obvious: it destroyed her hope of becoming Queen.''

''It is power which she desires; not necessarily the out-ward sign of it. I have little doubt that her influence played a large part in getting the North to declare that unless Men-het's daughter became the Royal Wife they would not give allegiance to Amenemhet. Once her daughter was Queen—the daughter whom she found it so much easier to dominate than her husband had been; she thought that she would virtually rule Egypt. She was very subtle: she told her daughter so often that it was her duty to marry Amenemhet, that, had it not been for you and Meri, Nefer-tathen might never have come to realize that she loved her husband. For the power of the Babylonian to be complete, she had to domi-nate not only her daughter and Pharaoh but also their chil-dren; therefore it was part of her plan that the Royal Heir be estranged from his parents. It was easy for her to act behind the pretense of grandmotherly devotion. At most she could be accused of being over-anxious for the child's welfare. She chose the nurses—women who would be obedient to her wishes and no one else's. She made Nefer-tathen believe that if she interfered the child would suffer, and so further estranged the parents by making them feel that they were bound to each other only by their duty. Even the conceiving of the child was a duty, performed faithfully but with repugnance.

"Then Amenemhet remembered his friends, and because the call he made to them was in the name of love, she was powerless against it. Her hatred for you and Meri must have had something in it of the hatred of Sekmet for Ra. Only a woman with almost superhuman strength could have concealed her feelings so cleverly. It was a brilliant stroke to make Amenemhet believe that she sorrows because you will not extend to her your friendship. It was essential for her plans to isolate him from his friends, and now that she cannot influence him through his wife she is making him destroy his own will."

"Even she could never do that!"

"Is she not already doing so? A man's rightful power comes from the knowledge of his strength in Ra. By making him believe that he is guilty, she is causing him to deny his own strength. Had he not always been troubled by austerity, the weapons she is using would have been blunted. He has always tended to forget that vitality must have its rightful outlet through *all* vehicles of the spirit before the heart can attain perfect balance in the Scales of Tahuti. She has made him think that physical love is lust, and that for the body to refuse companionship is to show itself superior to ordinary flesh. I think that was very cunning of her, Ra-ab, though it is a weapon which Set has often put into the hands of his pupils. Make a man feel guilty and he will soon believe that he is evil. And when he believes that he is evil, it is not difficult for him to give Set the title of Father. When Amenemhet is sufficiently convinced of his guilt, Kiosostoris will pretend to reassure him, for in doing so he will come to look upon her as his only comforter."

"Is there nothing we can do, Roidahn? I would take upon myself the responsibility of destroying that woman; and I should consider myself honored that she died by my hand."

"You and I are Amenemhet's closest friends, and for the moment he has chosen the Babylonian in our stead. If we were to kill her he would neither trust us nor any others of the Eyes of Horus; therefore I am afraid that your plan, though courageous, is impracticable."

"Then what *can* we do?"

"Nothing: except pray that he will remember our friendship and call to us in its name. Even Ra can do no more for mankind until they remember him."

## Seeδ of the Earth

Although the birth of Ameni had been so easy for Meri, I grew apprehensive as the time of her second ordeal drew near. She laughed at me when I voiced my fears, and said that I should have received sufficient proof that she was skilled in such matters.

"I believe you are seeing yourself as Amenemhet," she said, "with a dead wife he is convinced he murdered."

"Don't say that, Meri, even in jest."

"Then don't think it, when you know you are a fool to do so! If I died—though I am sure I'm not going to—it would only be because my time as Meri is finished. The baby would only be a coincidence, not a cause. And what a pleasant coincidence that I should die doing something useful, instead of through a pain which was productive only of death!"

"I know you are right. I wish Amenemhet could hear you talk like that."

"It's a pity that lots of respectable husbands murder their wives," remarked Meri reflectively.

"Do they?"

"Oh yes. Very seldom in the Oryx; but I expect they do in other parts of Egypt...and thousands of foreign wives are murdered every year.''

I had a mental picture of wives stampeding across the plains of Babylon, pursued by husbands who brandished dripping knives. I smiled, ''Isn't that rather a highly colored account of family life among foreigners?''

''Oh, I don't mean that they murder them deliberately—though it's really just as deliberate as if the husband put poison in his wife's drinking cup; and it doesn't break any laws.''

''No doubt my knowledge of foreign customs is deficient; but I think among most peoples you will find a rigid law against murder...even it it's done by mistake.''

''Nothing is ever done by mistake, as you know as well as I do. I have often heard you tell petitioners that every action has a motive, and every motive a cause. When I said that thousands of wives are murdered every year, I meant it, and they are...by having children they don't want. If your body says, 'Don't disturb me, I'm busy making a child,' and the soul says, 'Stop making it!''...is it so surprising that the spirit desires strongly to leave a house where there is so much quarreling. *I* want a child, and my body wants a child; and so do you and your body...so we've got nothing to worry about. When the baby is ready it will be born. This time I will stay in bed as long as you like, for you will be with me instead of laying siege to the Royal City. I shall be able to enjoy all the special privileges; and people will come to tell me how clever I've been, and will bring me presents, and there will be three days' rejoicing throughout the Oryx. I think it is going to be a girl: Ameni said he wanted a sister. But if it isn't we can have another later on; so it doesn't really matter.''

I tried to comfort myself with the memory of this conversation, when, less than a month later, seven days before the fourth anniversary of Ameni's birth, Meri woke and announced that she thought the baby would be born during the morning.

I had insisted that a healer-priest, and a priest of Ma-at, as well as Yiahn, whose skill had already proved invaluable to many women who had undergone difficult delivery, should be in the house in case they were needed. Meri said that their attendance was unnecessary, and that she only required the attention of the birth-woman, who had assisted at the coming of so many babies, and who had been with her when Ameni was born.

The birth-chair, which had been used in our family for four generations, was brought into the room, and I tried not to look on it as an instrument of torture. Meri was very cheerful, but a little later she caught her breath whenever the pain clutched at her. I realized that by showing my agony of mind I was only adding to her burden, so I made a great effort to appear casual.

"You don't mind my staying in here, do you?" I asked.

"No, of course I don't, I'd hate you to go away. At least I would unless it is horrid for you."

"Nothing about you can ever be horrid; and if you send me away I'll fuss much more than if I were here. Are you *sure* I oughtn't to call Ptah-aru or one of the others?"

"Of course I'm sure. I'm getting on very well. Besides, the birth-woman is waiting in the next room and she will come when I call."

"Hadn't we better have her in *now?*"

"No, Ra-ab. Please don't fuss. There's nothing she can do until the last minute. And unfortunately there are going to be a lot more minutes before that one comes."

The pain got worse after a time, but she still went on talking unconcernedly. I held her hands, and when the spasms were at their height, the thin fingers dug into my palms. I wished that I believed, as do some of the primitive tribes of the far south, that by slashing my body with a knife and rubbing salt into the wound, I could take upon myself some of her pain. But I was unable to have even this meager consolation.

"Dear Ra-ab, you look as though you were having three babies covered with spines, instead of me having only one. We shall have to add some more rooms to the temple, where fathers can be attended while their wives are in labor."

Her face glistened with sweat, although the room was not too warm. Her words came in gasps, as though she had been running a long way. "I don't think we'll have to wait much longer...it seems to be ...a very impatient baby. I think I'd better go over to the chair: you can call the birth-woman now."

I shouted for her, and she came running.

"You'd better wait outside," said the birth-woman firmly. "There's nothing more you can do, and you'll only get in the way."

I started to tell her that nothing would induce me to leave my wife, but Meri smiled, and said, "You go...and tell Niyahm that the baby will be...ready for her in a minute.... And don't come back till I call you. I shan't be long."

I found Niyahm waiting in the ante-room. She brushed past me and went into Meri's room.

In an agony of indecision I walked up and down outside the door. Did Meri really want me to stay outside, or was she trying to save my feelings? Was I betraying her by staying away, or would it only make things more difficult if I went back?

I prayed to all the Gods in turn, so vehemently that I think the Fields of Ra must have resounded with my pleas.

I heard a shrill wailing, and for a moment I thought that Meri's magnificent courage had at last been forced to bow to pain. Then, with a surge of unspeakable relief, I recognized it as the yelling of a new-born, and apparently extremely vigorous, child.

I realized that in the pillared hall at the end of the ante-room were people who were also waiting for news. Khnum-hotep, looking very old, was among them. I went up and put my arm around his shoulders. "It's all right, Father; the baby is born. It must be all right, it has such a loud voice."

"How is Oyah...How is Meri?" And I realized that for a moment he had slipped back to Kiyas' birth and that he was asking for Oyahbe.

I concealed the agitation the absent-minded word had aroused; for Oyahbe had died soon after Kiyas was born. At the door of Meri's room I met Niyahm carrying the baby in her arms. "It's a daughter," she said proudly, "and every bit as fine as her brother was."

"How is my wife?"

"She had it as easily as though she had worked in the fields all her life. Don't go in till they've finished clearing up in there. She's back in her bed already, but she wants them to finish washing her before you see her."

I didn't have to wait very long. Meri was pale, and her body looked very long and flat. Otherwise she showed no sign of the terrible hours through which she had just passed.

"Dear Ra-ab: I feel so happy! And I've been so clever: it's a girl. Aren't you sorry you didn't believe me when I told you not to fuss? Having a baby is nothing at all when you are good at it as I am."

"Nothing at all!"

"Ra-ab, what's the matter with you? You look absolutely exhausted. You aren't ill and hiding it from me, are you?"

Her voice was sharp with anxiety. I began to laugh, and she joined in.

"I'm not ill," I said. "I only look tired because I'm not so good at having babies as you are!"

We called our daughter Beket, and Ameni soon became as devoted to her as I had been to Kiyas. When she grew old enough to be able to crawl, Ameni always went on his hands and knees when he was playing with her, for he said it was unfair for us to pretend to be superior just because we could stand.

65

Beket had very decided opinions of her own, and if people were too stupid to understand what she wanted, she would yell until they were forced to bring sufficient attention to solve her problem. One day, hearing delighted chuckles coming from the nursery, I went in, to find her petting a young rat which Ameni had just given to her.

"You had better take that rat away from her before Niyahm sees it," I said. "It was silly of you to give it to her; she might have been bitten."

"I didn't mean to give it to her. I brought it in here because I thought she'd like to see it, and it jumped out of my hands and went to her by itself. She wasn't at all frightened, so I'm sure it won't bite her."

I tried to pick up the rat, but Beket clutched it and howled. It cowered down beside her seeking protection, but, as she stroked it, gradually lost its fear.

"She'd let me take it away if I promised to bring it back tomorrow," said Ameni. "She always understands what I say, even though she can't talk properly yet. She likes animals better than humans, because they can speak the language which doesn't need words. I often bring her animals to play with. Yesterday it was a beetle, and the day before it was a baby frog. Don't tell Niyahm, though, will you? She'd only be cross."

It seemed that twenty years had vanished, and I was hearing myself say, "Don't tell Niyahm!"

"I wonder if Beket will lead you into adventures as Kiyas used to lead me?"

"It will be very exciting when she is old enough for adventures. She'll be able to learn to swim soon, won't she? I should think it would be easier than walking, and she is such a very good crawler."

"Let's take her down to the pool and see. You carry the rat and I'll carry Beket."

Meri had had a shallow pool made for the children, where they could sit in the water and splash as much as they liked, but this was the first time Beket had been in the large swimming pool. I supported her on my hand and let her rest on the water. She shouted with pleasure, and, after Ameni had explained to her in their private language, she began to kick her arms and legs like a frog. After a while I put her down, to dry in the sun, on the warm stones, while Ameni showed me how much his diving had improved since the day before.

I heard Meri's voice in conversation with Roidahn, who was staying with us; and they came through the opening in the white wall which led from the garden, where they had been sowing seeds that Roidahn had brought from Hotep-Ra. Meri was laughing and looked very young. She saw Beket, and cried out, ''Quick Ra-ab! There's a rat attacking her!''

Ameni scrambled out of the pool and ran to his mother. ''It's not an *attacking* rat, it's a *tame* rat and she loves it. Don't frighten it or it might run away.''

''Are you sure it's safe, Ra-ab?'' asked Meri anxiously.

''Quite sure: but if you're worried, I'll tell Ameni to take it away from her.''

''I'm not worried...but perhaps Ameni had better take it...anyway it's time for Beket to have her milk, and Niyahm will be waiting for her.''

Beket decided to accept this interruption amiably, and Meri took her off toward the house, while Ameni walked beside them, carrying his rat. Roidahn joined me in the water, and after swimming for a few minutes, we lay in the sun to bask.

''Your daughter is a remarkable child, Ra-ab,'' he said with a smile. ''Watchers seem to make excellent parents, for Hanuk's children are as exceptional as your own. I wonder who will become Lord of the Horizon at my death? No, I do not think I shall die soon, but I hope that before my work is finished, there will be someone ready to take over my particular authority. That is why I have not yet appointed my heir; for the one whom I shall recognize as my Son in Horus need not be linked to me by blood.''

"Do you think Ameni will be a priest?"

"By the time he is seven years old, our priest of Ma-at will tell you whether he has had any previous temple training. In any case I should not advise you to send him to a temple, for as the future Nomarch he already has a great heritage."

"Perhaps it will be one of Hanuk's daughters, or Beket, or a child not yet born."

"The Gods will send my successor in their own time, and I do not feel undue curiosity as to their plans."

"It must be strange for people who do not think as we do, Roidahn, to find they have so little influence in the shaping of their children's ways of life. Ameni and Beket are both born of love, brought up in the same surroundings and by the same ethic...yet there is no reason why they should have any resemblance of character."

"In recognizing that, you may save yourself much future anxiety. I fear that I showed very little understanding of my daughter: only a year separated her from Hanuk, yet they were almost strangers. She married a man whom I thought exceedingly dull, yet he has succeeded in bringing her great contentment."

He sat up, wrung the water from his dripping hair, and then went on. "Sometimes I receive parcels of seed from a man whom I once befriended and who now lives in the Land of Gold. He sends them to me because he knows that I have always taken great pleasure in my garden, but he is not a methodical man, and he never remembers to separate the seeds into varieties, nor does he tell me from what plants they were collected. All I can do is to sow them in what I hope is suitable soil; but, until I have learned their peculiarities, some suffer because I water them too much, and others because I water them too little; some have to grow in the shade when they would prefer the full sun, and others wilt because the direct rays are too strong for their tender shoots. Fortunately I have some experience as a gardener, so while my plants are still young I can usually make an accurate guess as to where they should be transplanted and what conditions they require for their flowers to reach perfection.

"That is all a father can do...to try to provide the right soil in which his seed can reach maturity, but he must be ever watchful that the plant receives the treatment it requires. Our seed also is from a foreign country, from the Land of Ra. We must not think of ourselves as a sycamore, which knows that from its seed another sycamore will grow; for we have lost the need for that continuity, and we must always remember that from the loins of a most ordinary man may be born a child who is worthy to be Pharaoh, and that from a man who is venerated for his wisdom may come forth a fool!"

## Sanctuary

For the fifth evening in succession Ameni had taken me down to see whether his puppy was old enough to leave its mother. Both Meri and I had assured him that at least another twenty days must pass before it could sleep in his room, but he found it very difficult to be patient.

"You are *sure* that he is not ready yet?" asked Ameni anxiously. "He looks *much* bigger than he did yesterday, and see, his eyes are open!"

He picked up the puppy and held it carefully in his arms. The bitch watched him, a little worried, and thumped the straw with her tail when at last the puppy was returned to her.

"You will have to go back to the house now," I said, "or Niyahm will scold us both."

"Couldn't she wait just a little longer? Just long enough for us to see if the new calves are all right?...or while we have a *short* paddle in the water-channel?"

No doubt Niyahm would have had to wait, if a servant had not come to tell me that the overseer of a town on the southern boundary asked for permission to speak with me.

"Take him to the Room of Seals, where I will join him; and see that he has everything he requires."

I turned to Ameni, "So we shall both have to go: you to bed and I to work."

"What has the man come to see you about?"

"I don't know yet. Climb up on my shoulders and I will give you a ride back to the house."

He wrapped his legs round my neck, and clutched my hair with both hands. Today he decided that instead of being a cow plodding patiently along, I was to be a very fierce galloping lion, which would be sure to throw him off if he didn't hold on very tightly. When I put him down at the entrance to his own room, he asked again:

"What does the man want to see you about?"

"I still don't know; but if it's exciting I'll come and tell you about it before you go to sleep. If it's a long and dull kind of thing I shan't be able to come, and Mother will say good-night to you for both of us."

He hugged me, and then trotted off to find Niyahm.

The overseer was a man in whose house Meri and I had spent a night only three months previously. He had given admirable decisions on various points of administration, so I was rather surprised that he had made this sudden journey unannounced.

After we had exchanged greetings, I asked, "I hope that you are not the bearer of bad news? But if the news be bad, then let me hear it; for a burden is less heavy when two men carry it."

"It is neither good nor bad."

"Yet it was sufficiently important for you to come to see me?"

"It seemed so...I had to make a decision which I did not feel justified in giving without first consulting you; for the case does not come within the framework of the ordinary laws which I administer. Now, there are only three people whom the decision will affect, yet tomorrow there may be more... and again tomorrow.''

''If someone has broken the laws and you were undecided what sentence to impose, why did you not send them to my Audience?''

''Because you told me that all questions affecting a change of policy must be brought to you. Three days ago, two men and a woman crossed our boundary and were brought to me by a farmer who had found them hiding in his strawstack. By their clothes he could see they had been banished from their Nome; and, though at first they lied, when they realized that he was friendly toward them, they told him their story. They came from the Leopard, but the Nomarch, using the new authority recently given by Pharaoh, had decreed their banishment from Egypt. According to the law, he had given them the token which authorizes the headman of any village through which they pass to give them sufficient food for a day's journey, provided that they cross the boundary out of Egypt within forty days. They appealed to me for sanctuary, saying that they had been denied their right of appeal to Pharaoh, and that though they deserved some punishment they were not unworthy to live in Egypt. They asked to be allowed to undergo such retribution for their crimes as you considered fitting, and then to be given the chance to prove themselves worthy to live in the Oryx. Is it your wish that their petition be granted, or that the decision of the Leopard be upheld?''

''If the Leopard decreed banishment from Egypt he exceeded the exact wording of the new law. The Nomarchs have been granted the right to banish from their own Nomes...that this in fact may mean banishment from Egypt may have been taken for granted, but it was not specifically stated. What had these people done?''

''One of the men is a thief, though his theft need have caused no injury. He borrowed the bull of his neighbor,

71

without asking that this favor be granted and without offering payment. The neighbor claimed that the calf subsequently born belonged to him, but when he tried to take the calf by force, this man, Bena, set about the owner of the bull with his fists and knocked out three of his front teeth. The other man, Rus, was a friend and kinsman of Bena's, and when he heard that the owner of the bull, who was also the headman of the village, had ordered Bena to be taken before the Nomarch, he set fire to the headman's rick. The bull, frightened by the smell of fire, broke its tether, and galloping away in terror, fell into a deep irrigation-ditch and injured itself so seriously that it had to be killed. Frightened by what he had done, Rus drank a great quantity of new mead, and then went roaring down the village street shouting for anyone to fight him... and reviling as cowards all who refused his challenge. He got his fight too! Most of the village joined in: three men had broken bones, and one was unlucky in a wrestling throw and broke his neck! They were convicted of theft, felony, fire-raising, and disturbing other men's peace. They were lucky that murder was not added to the list of their crimes!''

''And what had the woman done?''

''It appears that she is the sister of one man and the wife of the other. When she heard that they were to be sent into exile she went to the chief city and demanded the right of Audience with the Nomarch. He had to grant it to her: to refuse would have been to break the law. It was a crowded Audience that day, and one of the Eyes of Pharaoh was the guest of the Leopard, who was, no doubt, specially anxious that all should go smoothly. The woman began by being courteous, pleading that the decree of exile had been made without full knowledge of the facts and should be reconsidered. Her plea was refused; and it seems that her tongue is as agile as an eel and sears like hot copper! She called the Leopard most of the 'eighty malodorous names,' and was just beginning on a detailed, and most pungent, criticism of his ancestors when the guards dragged her away.''

72

The overseer beamed. ''From the little I know of the Leopard,'' he added appreciatively, ''he is not a man to carry off such a scene with dignity. He has inherited from his grandfather a tendency to fatness without also inheriting the humor necessary as a compensation!''

Before replying, I poured wine for the overseer and myself.

''Your story deserves this vintage to accompany it,'' I said, ''yet it appears unfinished, for you have made no mention of the sentence imposed on the headman for being so grudging over the services of his bull, nor have you mentioned what judgment was given to those who accepted Rus's drunken challenge. Surely the whole village did not need to defend itself from one man?...And they should have remembered that the roarings of a drunkard ought to arouse the same compassion as the cries of a baby whose belly is distended with wind: both being childish afflictions which those of us who are more mature should do our best to relieve. As for the Leopard...being alone together and both men of discretion, it is not improper for me to discuss a fellow Nomarch. Had the Leopard been wiser in his choice of a headman—for surely to be a good neighbor is the first quality necessary in a headman, he would not have found himself discomforted before his distinguished guest. I think that Amenemhet will enjoy the story when it is brought to the Royal Ear!''

''Then I was right to come to you?''

''How could you think otherwise...without crediting me with less wisdom than the Leopard?''

''And I am to let them stay?''

''Certainly, if that be their wish after the laws under which we live have been explained to them. Should they agree to accept our authority, then they may settle here...and may they flourish. To what caste do they belong?''

''The men are both husbandmen; and the woman has a special skill in caring for bees.''

''Now that I am bringing new fields into cultivation, I can

73

find work for them on my personal estate. You still look worried? Don't you consider they deserve a second chance?''

''I do: but in giving it to them you will establish a precedent. May not the new authority given to the Nomarchs often be abused? It is more difficult to cure people than to send them away. Other Nomarchs may not be willing to take outcasts into the Nomes: news of Hotep-Ra traveled throughout Egypt before the Dawn; and again the news of sanctuary will spread.''

''Those who have been misjudged will amply repay us with their loyalty.''

''But what of those who were not misjudged? In time you may find the dregs of Egypt here.''

''Have you forgotten that I also am a Nomarch? If I find that they do not deserve a second chance, then they shall go: and I shall see that they are sent beyond the boundaries not only of Egypt, but beyond those lands which pay tribute to Pharaoh. They can go on one of the barges which take grain to the Land of Gold.''

''It will be a great risk.''

''*Not* to take it would be to become like the beggar who saw a gold bead lying in the mud...and starved because he dared not pick it up in case he got his fingers dirty! Smile, man, and have another cup of wine, in which to drink to a new Hotep-Ra!''

## trampled Vineyard

Meri and I were walking through the vineyards in the cool of a summer evening, when she gave a startled cry and pointed to a small field which lay to our right.

''Look, Ra-ab! What's happened to the vines?''

Some of them were uprooted, and the rest so savagely hacked that it would be a long time before they again bore fruit. These vines were the private property of one of the gardeners, a man who had been in the service of my family for nearly forty years. They were his special pride, and I knew that their destruction would give him great sorrow.

"Whoever has done this to Yek shall be severely punished!" And, as I saw the further extent of the devastation, my anger increased in intensity. Not only the vineyard had suffered but also the garden beyond it: vegetables had been trampled down; most of the flowers which edged the path had been uprooted. The petals of a clump of Lilies of Ptah showed like drops of blood among their bruised leaves. The main stem of a trumpet-vine which covered the roof of the store-house had been cut through, and the scented, waxy flowers were already wilting. Then I saw that the door of the store-house had been broken; and, obeying a sudden impulse, I pushed it open. The scent of spilled wine flowed out to meet me: twenty wine-jars, which had been a present to Yek from my father, had been thrown from their stands and all that remained of them was a welter of broken shards.

"Yek!" I shouted. "Yek! Where are you?"

My voice sounded very loud in the confined space, but only an echo answered me. As I strode out, leaving the door swinging on its leather hinges, I had a sudden desire to feel the weight of a whip in my hand; a whip which sang through the air to wheal the back of whoever had destroyed the work of careful years.

I thought the house was deserted, for the shutters were closed, and again my shout of "Yek!" had gone unanswered. It was Meri who noticed that the door-string was not sealed. She lifted the latch and went inside; I followed her.

It was dark except for a few rays of light which came through the chinks in the palm-leaf thatch. The outer room was empty, and I should have turned back had not Meri gone

75

forward to draw aside the curtain which concealed the entrance to the inner room. Yek was sitting on the bed-place; his head sunk in his hands. Only when Meri touched him on the shoulder did he look up; for he was so absorbed in his grief that he had not heard us.

"We are so very sorry, Yek," said Meri gently. "We have come to help you."

"We have come to do more than that," I said. "We have come to punish the man who did this. Tell me his name; tell me which of my people has betrayed the Oryx."

"It was not one of us," he said. "Your people would never have done such a thing to me, your servant."

"Tell me his name."

"Bena, who came here for sanctuary from the Leopard. But it is not only for my broken vines that I grieve, it is because that through Bena I also have betrayed you. He told me that you had decreed that in his own village it was the headman, not he, who was guilty...the headman who would not lend him the bull. When Bena had broken everything I have built, he said that by your laws it was I, not he, who would be judged guilty....Perhaps I should have given him the wine...."

"Wine...what wine?"

"The wine of the first pressing, that I hoped you would accept on the anniversary of your marriage. Bena said I was a fool to want to give it to you, and that your winestores were filled with rarer vintages than any I could offer, that my best I should keep for myself and my friends. The next day he returned with a basket of duck eggs and four pieces of honeycomb, and offered them as barter for the wine. Perhaps I was too hasty with him: I grew angry, and said that what I would not give him as a free gift could not be taken from me by bribes...and then we exchanged words to which courtesy was not even a distant kinsman. That same evening his sister came to me, saying that she wished to apologize for her brother. 'I told him,' she said, 'that he was a fool to misunderstand you. *I* understand that you dared not sell the wine. Had you done so the Oryx would have taken your land away from you. Naturally, though the ''law of the tribute of the tenth part'' is outwardly upheld, a man in the Oryx does not keep his land unless he buys private favor. Will you tell me how much honey-comb I should send to the Nomarch on his anniversary, so that I shall be allowed to continue to keep my bees?''

Yek sighed; and paused a moment before continuing.

'Again I failed my Nomarch,'' he said sorrowfully. ''Instead of trying to make her understand that *our* laws are not corrupt, and that in *our* Nome no one need buy their peace, I told her that she had a spirit which would befoul the body of a toad, and should she again utter falsehoods about our laws and those who upheld them I should try to persuade my dog, amiable as it is, to hurry her departure! I passed that woman's husband this morning; he spat at me and cried out, 'If you were not too dry and wizened even to be acceptable to the vultures, I should break your miserable carcass...which dared to call my wife a toad. Hurry, old man! Run fast on your spindle shanks, or I may forget to be tolerant of your obscenity!''

''I pretended not to have heard him, and walked on, careful not to hasten my pace. He stood there, roaring with laughter and jeering at me while he spattered me with filth from a midden. I considered it my duty to report their conduct to the overseer under whom they are working. Their reply to this action of mine you have already seen....''

I seemed to hear the overseer from the town in the south saying ''It will be a risk''...and the memory of my confident answer increased the bitterness I already felt toward the three who had betrayed our hospitality.

''Tomorrow I shall choose among my best vines those which at the right season shall be transplanted to your vineyard. Full wine jars shall replace those broken in your storehouse; and every reparation shall be made for the damage

**77**

done by those whom I unwisely made my guests."

"It is I who should make reparation," said Yek. "I know that in every man there is both good and evil, but from these three it was only the evil which I called forth. For this I am ashamed and in sorrow; and a man so foolish as I does not deserve the pleasures of a vineyard. Leave my possessions as you see them now, so that they may serve to remind me if again I fall into pride. When I with my own hands have made whole again that which is broken, perhaps, I shall have become wiser...or at least not so stupid."

"The guilt is not yours but mine," I said. "If I bring a wild leopard into my house, do I blame my son when it bites him? It was I who brought destruction to your vineyard, and I who must make it whole again. It was I who was proud, thinking that I was more wise, more just, than the Nomarch of the Leopard. These three shall go into exile: I shall send them on the grain-barge which is even now being loaded for the Land of Gold."

On our way home Meri said, "You are going to send them away, Ra-ab? You are going to admit that you have failed?"

"At least I am not so blinded by pride," I said bitterly, "that I have not the courage to admit failure. Pride made me bring them here. *Pride*...do you understand, Meri? I believed, and I still believe, that there is good in every man if only one can find the voice to quicken it. I found it pleasant to believe that *I* had that voice. I might have been justified in bringing them here if they had been able to injure no one but myself. That was the argument which my father used when I wanted to keep a leopard cub when I was eleven. He said it might bite me, and I replied that I shouldn't mind for it would be *my* cub. Then he reminded me that it might bite Kiyas too. I had to admit that, for I knew she would insist on playing with it. I have not the decency which I had at eleven, for now I let my friends suffer at the claws of a leopard's cub I could not tame. I never thought either of us would have to hide behind pretense, Meri, but now you will have to pretend...pre-

78

tend that the Nomarch, your husband, is not a failure.''

''Ra-ab, my husband, is going to sit under that palm tree, and listen to me instead of talking a great deal of nonsense!''

It is difficult to go on being dramatic, even to oneself, when the audience will not accept the play as tragedy. I sat down, feeling miserable and something of a fool.

''If you send them into exile,'' said Meri firmly, ''you will lose confidence in yourself. I shan't lose confidence in you, for you can't be successful all the time, however great a person you are. The next time people come here asking for sanctuary you might turn them away if you'd lost confidence...which would be a pity if they happened to be our kind of people after all; and if you didn't turn them away you would be much more anxious about them than was necessary.''

''You don't want me to *keep* them here, do you, Meri?''

''Yes, I do...at least until they have had a third chance. I think it was really our fault as much as theirs. You and I believed that if only one was nice to people they would always be nice back; but I think people have got to grow used to niceness...as people who are starving have to be fed gradually. We forgot that these three had been brought up to believe that kindness is only prompted by expediency, and that the strong man always forces others to obey him, and that those who do not demand obedience are weak and should be despised. They had never been taught to make their feelings obedient to their will. You don't blame an animal for having less power of reasoning than a man, and yet we blame these people for not seeing the same truths to which we have been accustomed since we were children.''

''What would you do with them?''

''I'll tell you in the morning: I'd like to think about it in sleep before deciding. In the meantime I should send soldiers to go to collect them. They could be put in the old prison for tonight, and it won't do them any harm not to have anything to eat, or only water and stale bread.''

She stood up, smiling down at me. "We'd better go home now, Ra-ab. You promised to tell Ameni the quail-chick story before you said good-night to him."

I felt much more cheerful. "Do you think we shall be able to cure them?"

"I expect so...After all we haven't really tried yet."

"And if we fail?"

"We'll think about that when it happens."

## Exiles' Village

Before the end of another year I saw that I had not been too ambitious in planning the Exiles' Village on such a compara-tively large scale, for it became necessary to build further accommodation for those who came to the Oryx for sanc-tuary. Until I had given judgment on the new arrivals, they were lodged in the House of Petitioners: in a few cases I con-firmed the sentence of their Nomarch, and, after being pro-vided with food sufficient for three days, they were con-ducted to the boundary of the Oryx. There were others whom I judged to be fit to mix freely with our people, and they were given work to do, or else began some training which would enable them to be of use to the community. It was only those in whom I hoped to effect a cure, but who in their present state would be uncongenial companions, that I sent to the Exiles' Village, where they would remain segre-gated from the rest of my people for as long as I deemed necessary.

At each end of the Village there was a large house where lived the men and the women who had come to the Oryx alone, and in between was a row of smaller houses in each of which lived a family. Within the boundary of the Village were fields where they could grow their own produce, and which provided grazing for the herds I had given them in order to make them so far as possible self-supporting. A healer-priest and a priest of Anubis were in attendance on them, and in addition there were also Watchers to give them instruction in craftsmanship. Four temple pupils, two men and two women, saw that our instructions were carried out. It was seldom necessary to employ force, but, as people sometimes require to be taught to accept more subtle authority, twelve soldiers under a Leader of a Hundred, were also available.

Everything had been done to make the surroundings as pleasant as possible. The houses had been color-washed in blue, pink or yellow; some of them had simple frescoes in the main room, and each had a small garden, planted with flowers and a shade-tree. The single street was lined with sycamores, and a large swimming-pool had been built near the canal. The fields had been plowed and sown before the first exiles arrived, so that they should not be disheartened by the difficulties of breaking new ground; and, as the number of inhabitants increased, so were additions made to their fields and herds.

Acting on my father's suggestion that the experience we gained there might be of value in the future, a record of each exile was kept, this being the sole duty of three scribes. Every seventh day these records were brought to me, the scribe adding such details as the priest in charge of the case thought necessary for my information. Twice each month I went in person to the Village.

The first time that Kiyas heard the monotonous drone of the scribe's voice coming from the Room of the Seals, she told me that for a moment she feared I had become as preoccupied with the past as was our father. I laughed, and told her that, had she listened more closely, she would have found that the subject to which I was attending belonged to our most immediate present. This is what she would have heard....

"A woman, age twenty-three, from the Nome of the Tortoise, exiled for killing her new-born child. She was brought here by her sister, who left her in our care and returned to her own Nome. The woman at first refused to eat unless someone fed her. She had to be constantly watched and tried to mutilate herself. She tore her nails and her hair. For the first ten days she refused to speak except to answer 'yes' or 'no' to the Temple Counselor when he questioned her. In her sleep she repeated over and over again, 'Blood will wipe out blood. I have killed and I must be killed. I cannot wipe out my own sin. I must make someone hate me enough to murder me. Hate me! Hate me! Hate me!'

''Away from Earth she told the priest of Anubis that the child she killed was not her husband's son but the son of a foreigner, a small merchant who had been trading in the Tortoise. She said that immediately the child was born she recognized that it was an Asiatic, and she killed it before the fact became obvious to everyone. She said she hated the baby because it was trying to take her husband away from her. She thought that people would believe the child died naturally; but the marks of her hands could be seen on its throat, and, under questioning, she admitted her crime.

''She was condemned only to exile because she pleaded that the foreigner had forced her submission. The foreigner has now returned to his own country, but she is terrified that one day he will return and be able to prove that she lay with him in exchange for a bracelet which she coveted.

''The Temple Counselor, having heard these facts from the priest of Anubis, spoke to her while she was awake. She no longer refused to talk, but claimed vehemently that she had been raped, and that in killing the child she had only been defending herself against its hated father. When at last she was convinced that it was useless to lie, she admitted that what the priest of Anubis had said was true.

''It is very easy to see the motive of her wish to die. She hates her body because she considers that through vanity it tempted her to take the bracelet: in reality she hates it because

**82**

it tempted her to take the foreigner. Her marriage was arranged by her family: she had no love for her husband. On her condemnation to exile, the marriage, at the husband's wish, was declared at an end.

"She is to be taught that to find expiation she must cherish a child of foreign blood, but that before she is ready to do this she must learn to honor her own body. She already shows considerable improvement: she no longer tries to mutilate herself, takes food when it is given to her, and is making an effort to keep herself clean. She has been given an orphan lamb to look after. It sleeps in her room and she gives most scrupulous attention to all its needs. It is expected that within three months she will be ready to leave the Village, and arrangements will be made for her to look after an orphan of foreign blood."

The scribe unrolled another papyrus and began:

"Husband and wife, aged thirty and thirty-five, exiled from the Nome of the Ibex. The man killed another in a brawl and the woman came with him voluntarily, not because she loved him but because she had no kinsmen and was so unpopular that no one would give her shelter. They have three children, the eldest nine and the youngest four, whom they nagged and bullied, though were not seen to inflict on them any physical cruelty. As soon as it was recognized that there was no real affection between parents and children, the children were sent to the House of Orphans. The parents were very indignant, and claimed that this was a violation of their rights. They were told that in the Oryx parents had no rights over their children save in virtue of the link of affection between them. As this did not exist in their case they were judged to be unworthy of authority over anyone.

"They refused to collaborate in any communal activity, nor would they cook their own food or attend to their house or garden. It was explained to them that if they wished to stay in the Oryx, they must learn to abide by our laws. They claimed that it was their right to have the children work for them; and, had they not been taken away, the house would have been properly looked after; adding that it was the privilege of older people to make use of the young.

"By decree of Ra-ab Hotep, Nomarch, they are to live as children for three months, the place of their parents being taken by two of his soldiers. One month is now past. They wear clothes suitable to extreme youth, she a kilt which reaches from her waist to half-way down her thighs, and a necklace of two beads on a cord; he, a breech-clout. They are made to get up before dawn and do all the work of the house. Even when they are working as fast as they can, the soldiers nag them, and if they are not immediately obedient they are whipped...Old wheals were discovered on the bodies of their children.

"When trying to rest, they are frequently wakened and told to do some meaningless task; for it was also found that their children were not allowed to play without being frequently interrupted. They never know when they may expect their food: nor did their children. Sometimes they are forced to eat that which is particularly distasteful to them. The woman dislikes garlic, but she was never tolerant of the preferences of her children, so she is given garlic at every meal, a clove of it even being rubbed round her bowl of millet porridge. He has been made to help clear a new water-channel. At night he is washed by the soldiers, and they scrub him so hard that the skin is sore, and when he protests he is told not to be naughty.

"Sometimes they try to run away. Then they are brought back, shut in their room and go without food for a day and a night. For this was the treatment they accorded their children."

"Woman, aged sixty, exiled from the Nome of the Sycamore, because she refused to obey the laws of cleanliness. On being told that unless she submitted to being cleansed of lice she would not be allowed to live in the Oryx, she agreed under protest to her head being shaved and her clothes burned. She was provided with a wig and fresh clothes. She was shown how personal and household garbage should be buried, but she refused to do this and threw it into the street. It was repeatedly explained to her that filth is the breeding-ground of pestilence, but she continued in her habits and made no effort to change them. She was told that if this occurred again, she would be given the work of cleaning out the ox-stalls; and this she was put to do. But she still continued to throw refuse into the street, although it was noticed that she took a certain pride in her house, and the room was always swept clean. It was explained to her that no private possession has any value except it be held in trust for the community; and therefore it was as much her duty to maintain the street uncontaminated as her own house.

"This instruction having produced no results, by decree of Ra-ab Hotep, Nomarch, the occupants of the adjoining houses emptied their garbage on the floor of her room. She was told that each time she failed to comply with the laws necessary to health, this should be repeated. A marked improvement has since been observed in her habits. She was found to have some skill in pottery and has been provided with the necessary materials. And now that her behavior has become more attractive, she is finding that the neighbors are not so unfriendly, as had been her previous experience. She has asked for some flower-seeds for her garden, and has put a pot of convolvulus on her window-ledge. These signs are so encouraging that it is hoped she will not long have to remain in the Village."

"Boy of fifteen, exiled from the Nome of the Reed for cruelty to animals. His actions persisted in spite of repeated punishment. He was watched, but without his knowledge. On his second day in the Village he was caught burying a cat alive. He showed no shame, and said defiantly, 'You can

85

beat me, but I won't mind. I'm used to being beaten, but they can never make me scream.' He pulled off his tunic to display a back deeply whealed. He was told that he would not be beaten, but that he would remain in his room until judgment was given. He looked disappointed, and it was noticed that he did not eat the food given him that evening. To the Temple Counselor he boasted of the number of animals he had tortured and of the pain which had been inflicted on him in return. But while asleep he was more frank with the priest of Anubis: it is probable that when awake he has no memory of the following incident of his childhood.

''His mother died in giving birth to him, and when he was three years old his father accused him of having caused his mother's death. The child soon afterwards fell in the fire and burned himself; but the father, instead of showing sympathy, said, 'It is well that you hurt yourself, for your mother died through the pain you caused her, and every day I suffer because I have no wife.'

''A few days later the child grabbed a cat by the tail, not intending to hurt it but to stop it running away. The cat scratched his hand deeply, and a neighbor hearing him cry ran in to comfort him. He thought to himself, 'I am guilty because I gave pain to my mother, therefore I must suffer before I can be cleansed of my guilt. Through hurting an animal, I suffered pain, but I also received the sympathy for which I long.'

''On waking, the priest of Anubis knew that it would be useless to inflict on the boy the pain he had given to animals; for to do so would be to fulfill the object of his cruelty. The infliction of pain was a quest for pain through which he might receive sympathy. The priest decided to take drastic steps, which have proved very effective.

''Next morning, in the boy's food was mixed a draft compounded of Poppy Drink and a violent purge. As soon as the gripping of the bowels commenced, the boy was told that he was afflicted by a pestilence, and warned that unless he was both brave and obedient he was likely to die. He was drowsy with the poppy fumes, and so became less influenced by the memory of the immediate past. In his food he was given other drafts, which kept him intermittently in pain and made him sufficiently weak to prevent him from having any desire to exert his independence. Exactly as though he were really suffering from a pestilence, he was cared for by one of the temple-pupils, a girl of twenty, beautiful and compassionate. She held his hand to help him bear the pain, and smoothed his forehead until he fell asleep. She washed and fed him as though he was a baby, and when he grew stronger she told him stories of the way of peace.

''He conceived a deep devotion for her, and asked that he might be allowed to serve her in however humble a capacity. She told him that one of her duties was to look after the geese, and that it would be a great help if he would do this for her. Her words caused him to remember his many cruelties: he wept bitterly, and said he dared not do what she asked, for sometimes deliberately, and sometimes almost against his will, he was cruel to animals, and that if he attacked her geese it would be almost as bad as though he did her personal injury.

''She said to him, 'You were so ill that you might have died. I asked the Gods that you might be born again: they listened, and you recovered. The cruelty which you once inflicted, and the pain you suffered, are as though they had never been: they are dead, but you are alive. Because of the link between us, you will never again forget the link between you and our younger brothers.'

''He was filled with hope, but even so he did not entirely believe her. She brought him a kitten, and left them alone together. When she returned, he was asleep with the kitten curled up beside him.

''He has asked to stay in the Village so that he can work for the girl who brought peace to him. He is learning how to look after sick animals, and he is so gentle with them that he can drive out their fear.''

# Return of Nekht

Though I was far from being a Priest of Anubis, I had sufficient true-dreams to recognize which were records of actual
experience, and which were only a product of hopes and fears
clothed with a semblance of reality. Now that Meri and I
shared our waking day, we did not so often remember the life
we shared during sleep; for the effort of memory absorbs
much vital energy unless one is fully trained in the use of this
faculty. To Meri and me the Gods had been so generous that
we were seldom parted, and when we could exchange our
thoughts in words there was no need to use a more subtle per-
ception.

So I was surprised when, three times in seven nights, Meri
and I shared the same dream, describing it to each other in
detail when we woke. It was a familiar type of experience,
talking with someone we knew to be a close friend on matters
concerning the lives of the people under our care. To talk
with someone whose name on Earth I did not know was also
familiar, for all of us have links with people who are not born
in our century, or who live in distant countries. Yet, just as a
vivid flower stands out against quiet foliage, so did Meri and I
know that the fourth person who took part in these three conversations, which she and I shared with Roidahn, was of vital
importance to us both. We agreed that it was a man, mature
in both mind and body, yet younger than ourselves in years.
We even remembered that Roidahn had called him
"Nekht," "the one who has power"; and that Roidahn had
said, "He is my son."

"It wasn't Hanuk," said Meri, "and Roidahn has no
other son."

"He must have meant that the man was the child of his
spirit. He once told me that the one who inherits from him,
the second Lord of the Horizon, will be known as his son."

"Nekht..." said Meri thoughtfully, "we both remembered his name is Nekht. I wonder when he was born and when he will come to the Oryx. Will Roidahn recognize him at once, or will even they take time to renew their friendship?''

''You think he is already on Earth?''

''Don't you? He looked twenty; but his authority may have made him seem older than his years.''

''If his name is in truth, Nekht, he would wear the body of maturity away from Earth even though he were still a baby while awake. He may be newly born, or still a boy...or even a man who is very old, yet who is wise enough not to be encumbered by years when he is free of their limitations.''

''You don't think he could be Ameni, do you?'' said Meri. ''I remember that when I saw him I wished that he was my son.''

''No; he wasn't Ameni. We should both have recognized him no matter what form he happened to be wearing.''

''Of course we should...I hope Nekht comes soon to the Oryx. I have never seen him except in a dream, and yet in a sense I am lonely for his company. I can never really be lonely now that I have found you, my Ra-ab; but perhaps we are both a little lonely for him.''

A year later we were no longer lonely for Nekht: he was born to us as a son.

When Nekht was fourteen days old, Meri and I took him to stay at the house which Roidahn had recently built at the Horizon of Horus.

Instead of an outer courtyard there was a small formal garden, where grew many of the rare plants which had been brought to him from foreign countries. As Meri, carrying the baby in her arms, walked up the central path, she looked young as on the day when she had brought Ameni to my tent, the day of the Dawn over Egypt. Roidahn stood looking down at the sleeping child; then with his forefinger he touched him on brow, eyelids and breast.

"He has returned to us from another day's journey," he said. "To you and Ra-ab, and to myself. And, though he called us by other names, the love between us will be as familiar to him as the rays of the sun, which do not change with the centuries."

"You are sure that he is...Nekht?" asked Meri.

"Quite sure: and so are you. Why do you question your integrity?"

"I don't question it in my heart," she answered with a smile. "But when I am asleep he is so much wiser than I... even you and Ra-ab sometimes accept his counsel. Yet he cries and kicks, and pulls at my breast just like my other babies. He likes his back patted, and sometimes he complains when he is washed. At such times I try to forget his name is Nekht, in case he should feel humiliated by being taken at a disadvantage!"

"As he is in truth Nekht, he can suffer no humiliation, for he has already passed those of the Forty-two Assessors who ask, 'Hast thou seen thy shadow on the wall and thought it mighty?' and also, 'Hast thou a vision of thyself in thine heart in honor?' He will not think of himself either as more or less than he is judged by the Scales of Tahuti. He will neither be blinded by conceit, nor refuse to accept responsibility which is rightful to him. Is not humility knowing one's own place on the ladder which reaches to the stars?"

Meri laughed. "I am content, Roidahn, to know that even the most lowly rituals of the toilet could not embarrass Nekht the power-bearing."

"A man cannot be humiliated by anything, unless he has seen himself as though in a wind-ruffled pool, which distorts the true image. To suffer humiliation one must judge oneself by the opinion of others. If one says, 'This act will make people think less of me,' one has become influenced by fear: and if one says, 'Surely this act must make men admire me,' one tries to grasp something which does not exist. The wise man knows that though the multitude acclaim him, his stature

90

will not increase even by a thumb-joint; and if all the people of his country call him traitor and fool, he will not be diminished by so much as a grain of dust.''

Roidahn smiled, ''If you were to say that I am an inconsiderate host for engaging you in conversation when you must be tired after your journey, you would speak the truth...But I would not be humiliated, for I know that the love between us is too strong to be affected by my discourtesy.'

''There is no refreshment so welcome as hearing you talk,'' said Meri. ''Nekht can go to Niyahm, while we, who are older though perhaps not so wise, can talk of his future, and to it drink a toast.''

Before we returned home, Roidahn said to us:

''Though you have already proved yourself to be most admirable parents, and advice from me might sound presumptuous if we were not such close friends, I want to remind you both that until Nekht himself recognizes it, you must not tell him of what we believe to be his future. Nekht must not feel he is weighed down by destiny, for though you and I know that with a little training he can again become a priest, the choice lies with himself. He may, of his own wisdom, decide that his character would find more fertile soil in which to grow if he chose the way of a soldier, or a fisherman.''

''But surely,'' said Meri, ''it is his duty to become a priest.''

''His first duty is to himself...to continue to grow toward the sun. We think of ourselves gifted with foresight because we know that he has been a priest and could be again; but the man of integrity knows his own heart better than even those most close to him can ever know it. It would be foolish of us to think that we can foretell the future because we can see the probabilities conceived in the past. When Nekht has chosen his role, we may be able to show him how it can most easily be fulfilled, so that he will waste little energy on paths which branch from the road he wishes to follow.

"It is probable that to him dreams will always be very vivid. Let him tell you about them, show that you are interested...but no more so than if they were waking adventures. Never let him think that his experiences are different, or in any way remarkable. Do not display undue curiosity; for children, like animals, require and guard their privacy.

"Remember that though away from Earth he is mighty in magic, on Earth he will for several years continue to be a child. He will be subject to the fears of a child, and, at least in part, to the limitations of a child's mind. Many potential priests choose a different road because of the fear which the memory of certain experiences aroused when the body was not yet strong enough to accept them. Always be very gentle with him. If he wishes to sleep with a lamp in his room, never tell him that he is too old to be afraid of the dark. Remember that for a body not yet mature to contain so great a spirit is often an almost intolerable strain. It may make him nervous or shy; or perhaps, to hide this even from himself, he may appear absurdly daring, or even tiresomely aggressive.

"Away from Earth he is as a great river; but his body is an aqueduct of which all the stones are not yet in place. Until he is skilled with the sluice-gates of his Will, sometimes he may allow too much power to flow, sometimes too little. One day he may appear too wise for his years: perhaps you will feel worried that he concerns himself with matters in which he seems too young to deal. The next day you may be impatient because he seems such a very ordinary boy; absorbed in making a fish-trap, with sailing a boat, or, should he share Beket's tastes, with catching frogs in a muddy water-channel. But gradually those sluice-gates will work smoothly: he will achieve balance on both sides of the River, and thus become the man who is also the priest, the priest who is also the man.

"One who claims that he is more than ordinary men because he cannot be influenced by pleasures or discomforted by pain; who must be over-particular about his diet lest the fibers of his soul become coarsened; who must either remain immobile so that his vital energies may be conserved by meditation, or else must take excessive exertion so that his body is too weary to make any claim on his attention: such a man is not a priest, even though he may possess certain powers by which the credulous are unduly impressed.

"But when you meet one to whom you can say, 'You are my brother; you are a man as I am. Yesterday you were weak as I am weak, but now you are a little stronger than I and so can tell me how I too can grow.' If you can say to him, 'If we were to drink wine together we should both name the same vintage as the best; and if there was a choice of twenty meats, we should both fill our food-bowl from the same dish; and the women we love might be twin sisters.' If you can say to him, 'That which I suffer you have suffered also. You are close to me: you are my friend. You are ordinary as I am ordinary, and that is why you can understand why I am unhappy and know what has caused my unhappiness. Yesterday you were in sorrow, as I am now: but you found a cure for sorrow and that cure shall be mine also—for are we not brothers?' And if he, whom you call brother, is given that name also by the thief and by the cripple, by him who is betrayed, and by the betrayer; by the concubine, by the wife, by the Overseer and by the beggar. Then he has another name as well as Brother....That so ordinary a man is a True Priest.' '

# PART TWO

# Net of Intrigue

My estate near the Royal City was most ably administered by my steward, so that each year I spent there no more than a few days. I always arranged that this visit should coincide with one of the festivals on which Pharaoh entertained his nobles to a banquet, hoping that Amenemhet would take the opportunity to renew the link between us. On such occasions he always greeted me with every courtesy, but it was not until the tenth year of his reign, six years after the death of his wife, that he asked me to come informally to his private apartments.

I took this as an indication that he was ready to forget our estrangement, so I was disappointed when he limited the conversation to impersonal matters. Even when the meal was finished and the servants had left the room, he discoursed at length on the advisability of building a new aqueduct in the South...a plan which did not personally concern me as it was outside my Nome. It became increasingly obvious that he was talking to conceal his thoughts, and at last in desperation I said:

"Amenemhet, I know that it is not for me to choose for the subject of our conversation; but in the name of friendship I ask why you have sent for me."

"The years have not changed you, Ra-ab." And for the first time that evening he smiled. "Another man might resent my long silence...yet I am confident that you have not forgotten the promise you made when last we sat together in this room: that you would return when I needed you."

"You know that to aid you is my greatest honor."

"Once I appealed to you as a husband: now I do so as a

father. It is Senusert who needs your help, needs it most urgently. Unless you can teach him to judge his own heart, he will never make a Pharaoh fit to carry on the traditions of which we try to be worthy. His grandmother treats him as though he already wore the Double Crown; she surrounds him with scribes and attendants who treat him with a deference which is unjustified by his character. He is eight years old, two years younger than Ameni: yet already I wish that it was your son, not mine, who will rule Egypt at my death. Had his mother lived, things would have been different.'' He hesitated, ''No Ra-ab, the fault is mine: I have left him too much in the care of women; who praise him when he is stupid and call him hero when he is only a braggart. As a father I have betrayed him. You warned me against Kiosostoris, but pride closed my ears.''

''Why don't you send her away?''

''Because the boy feels for her an almost fanatical devotion. If I were to exile her he would never forgive me: it would destroy my last chance of ever establishing the link of true affection with my son. What I am about to ask, you have every right to refuse: I promise that it will make no difference to our friendship. I want you to take Senusert to the Oryx, and bring him up as though he was your son.''

''I am greatly honored that you think my household the right background for your heir.''

His face softened. ''For nearly a year you and Meri made of a lonely Pharaoh a man who was happy. Perhaps now you can save Senusert...though it will be difficult, for he must be an intolerable companion—even to himself. Bitter words for a father to use, Ra-ab, but I fear you will find them fully justified. I should never ask you to take this disturbing influence into your house if it were for myself alone: but it is for Egypt. Unless Senusert can prove his right to so great an authority, he shall go into exile...Even though he is my son, and I dearly loved his mother.''

For a moment I came near to disliking Amenemhet. He

95

had left his son in the care of a woman against whom he had been warned by his closest friends. His own sense of guilt had prevented him sending Kiosostoris back to her own country, and now he blamed the boy for accepting her authority. Perhaps I did not conceal my thoughts as well as I imagined.

"Ra-ab, do not condemn me unheard. I have suffered perhaps even more than you realize, from having no one to whom I could give intimate affection. Senusert seemed to love his grandmother...at least I took it for love. I was afraid to break the link between them lest he experience a little of what I felt at his mother's death."

"Why then are you willing to do it now?"

"Because I have at last recognized that she is deliberately trying to destroy him. She does everything possible to protect his body from danger. He is not even allowed to climb trees, or go on the river except when I take him with me. But she is trying to dominate his will so that at my death she can rule Egypt in his name. That has always been her consuming ambition...to rule Egypt. Twice I have been the unwitting cause of removing the channel through which she hoped to find an outlet for her lust of power. Her husband died; and I am Pharaoh in his stead. Her daughter became my wife; and died because I loved her too well. Now, for the third time, I shall spoil her plans. She shall never see the boy again; or not until such time as you can assure me that he is in truth one of the Eyes of Horus, who need not fear the schemes of Babylonians."

"So you *are* going to send her into exile? It is obvious that she will never be willing to relinquish her hold on Senusert."

"I prefer her to remain under my roof. To send her away would be to give her the satisfaction of thinking I fear her. She cannot harm me, and I am able to protect my son. And there is another reason why I prefer her to remain; it suits me to know her plans, and though she has many spies in her pay...I pay them better.

''The strongest current of her life is her hatred for me; but I am protected against it because she is no longer able to deceive me. Recently it came to my ears that she had received certain curious remedies at the hands of her foreign physician, remedies likely to cure a man—only of the troublesome necessity of continuing to breathe. One of her servants died soon afterwards: he may have incurred her displeasure, but it is more probable that his death was a preliminary test. I thought it wise to tell her that, should I die before Senusert became Co-ruler, she was unlikely to live to see the ceremonies attendant on his accession to the throne. I explained that, knowing the depth of her affection for me, the shock of my death was sure to hasten her own. She does not lack subtlety; she can recognize a threat even when it is concealed in smooth words.''

''Not only foreign physicians have a remedy for living too long. May I assume that should Kiosostoris die you would not be—displeased?''

''I do not wish to be deprived of one of the few amusements which I permit myself to enjoy...outwitting the Babylonian!''

''You, who have sworn to live for Egypt, have not the right to indulge in so perilous an entertainment.''

''Of that, Ra-ab, I am the only judge.''

''How can you prevent her following Senusert to the Oryx? How can I deny her entry to my house if she demands it as her right?''

''She will not know where he has gone; no one shall know save your own family. I suggest you say that he is the orphan of a distant kinsman, whom you have had the charity to take into your family. He will, of course, not be allowed to claim any royal privilege, and should he say he is my son, that can be ascribed to a delusion following a severe fever.''

''How do you wish him to make the journey?''

''In your barge: it may be necessary for your personal servants to share the secret, but I know you can rely on their discretion. I shall inform his grandmother that I am taking him with me on a Progress to the North. Senusert will be told the same story; which will put him in good humor, for he enjoys standing beside me when I receive homage. You will arrange for your barge to join us at the end of the first day northwards: then you will start immediately for the Oryx.''

''You think he will go with me willingly?''

''He has often heard of Ra-ab Hotep...what child has not, for the Battle of the Six Hundred has already become a legend. He will be flattered if you ask him to be your guest...perhaps for a day or two he might even be obedient. Should he refuse to go with you I give you my full permission to use any means you choose to enforce obedience...*any* means, do you understand, Ra-ab? If when I next see him there are scars on his back, they will not be questioned. The Eyes of Horus chose me as their Pharaoh: now they shall decide whether this child of my blood shall hold the Crook and Flail, or be condemned to exile.''

# Royal heir

On the following morning I saw Senusert for the first time since he was a baby. He was making writing-signs on a clay tablet, under the instruction of a scribe. They were sitting in a small pavilion on the embankment at the end of the palace garden and, as I was hidden from them by some closely planted shrubs, I was able to watch them without being seen.

So long as the scribe had nothing but praise for the boy's work he seemed absorbed in what he was doing. Then the man leaned forward to point out some fault. Senusert sprang up in fury, flung down the tablet which shattered on the stone pavement, and rushed out of the pavilion. He ran in my

98

direction and I stepped out on the path, so that he would have to stop or run into me.

He saw me and stopped abruptly, and looking up, said furiously:

"How dare you stand in my way! When Pharaoh goes out in the City the streets are cleared for him. How dare you stand in the way of Pharaoh's son!"

I laughed. "You had better not let Pharaoh hear you claim to be his son. He is not tolerant of liars."

"How *dare* you say I lie! I'll tell my grandmother, and she will have you whipped for being so impertinent."

"What a fierce little wild-cat it is! But if you want to be a liar I'll teach you how to be a more convincing one. If you want to pretend that you are Pharaoh's son you had better learn how to behave like Pharaoh...then you might get someone to believe in your foolish tales."

He lowered his head and tried to butt me like an angry goat. I picked him up and held him at arm's length. He clawed at my arms and tried to kick me; but without much success.

"Of course you must be Pharaoh!" I said mockingly. "You are so dignified, so noble. I wonder if you'd look more Pharaohic up-side-down?"

I pretended to drop him, shifted my grip and caught him by the ankles...then held him head downwards while he squealed with rage.

"It's lucky you're not wearing your crown, little Pharaoh, or it would fall off! Poor little Pharaoh! He is so stupid that he has to break the tablet on which he cannot write. So stupid that he cannot remember the words of courtesy. What shall I do with you? Drop you into the lotus-pool, or swing you over the wall into the river? Or shall I set you on your feet again, and see if you have remembered how to be a pleasant little boy...or perhaps you cannot remember because you never knew?"

I set him down. He looked rather red in the face; and I

think for a moment he was too surprised to speak. Then he gulped and said:

"You will be sorry when the soldiers take you away: my grandmother will tell them what to do with you, and she is much cleverer than my father. They'll make copper rods red in a brazier and then drive them down your ears, and then they'll take splinters, or specially long thorns and stick them up your nose and under your finger-nails. And they'll drop heavy blocks of stone on your feet, so that ever afterwards people will laugh when they see you try to run...your feet will be flatter than a duck's!"

"What a dear old woman your grandmother sounds! She must be *very* old to have had time to learn such polished hospitality! In the part of Egypt I come from, guests are treated quite differently. They have all the things they most like to eat, and they don't work unless they want to, and they sail boats, and take their throwing-sticks down to the marshes and have exciting adventures."

For a moment he looked interested; then asked suspiciously, "What sort of adventures?"

"Oh, it wouldn't be any use telling *you* about them: your grandmother obviously isn't the kind of person who'd let you have adventures. You will always have to stay at home with her and do what you're told. How could you do anything else, when she thinks of such unpleasant punishments?"

"*I'm* not afraid of her: she wouldn't punish *me*."

"Then it must be very dull for you. No punishments... and I suppose no rewards either. If no one takes any notice when you're tiresome, does anyone take any notice when you're *not*?"

"I'm *never* tiresome," he said grandly. "Sometimes I have to punish people because they disobey me: but I'm never *tiresome*. I'm much too important to be that. I'm the Royal Heir!"

He watched me narrowly, to see whether I was at last impressed by the enormity of his behavior.

''So you said before...but I find it no easier to believe now than I did when you first claimed it.''

His lip trembled, ''I *am* the Royal Heir! I am! I am! I AM!''

''When I see a quail-chick come out of an ostrich's egg I will believe that you are the son of Pharaoh. If you *were* Pharaoh's son we should be sitting together, perhaps in that pavilion, and you would be telling me how the Royal City has changed in the seven years since I last came here; and I would be telling you stories of battles, and of what the people in the Land of Gold are like, and of the adventures I used to have when I was your age.''

''What's your name?''

''Ra-ab Hotep.''

''I've heard that name before.'' He looked puzzled. ''Ra-ab Hotep....I've heard my father speak that name. Are you—The Oryx?''

''I am.''

''Oh!'' He kicked the gravel and looked embarrassed. ''I didn't really mean that about having my grandmother put you to the torture. Don't tell my father I said that, will you? He doesn't like my grandmother. He thinks she's cruel... and she thinks he's a fool.'' Then he looked up with a rather sly smile. ''If you don't mention my losing my temper I won't tell anyone you laid hands on me. It's death to raise a hand in anger against the Royal Person: so if I don't tell, I shall really have saved your life, and you will always have to be my friend. If we're friends you can tell me about your adventures.''

''I'll tell you about the adventures first, and then we'll see if you still want to be friends.''

I told him stories of things Kiyas and I had done when we were children. How we used to pretend that everyone except us were the Asiatics and how sometimes we had gone out by ourselves at night, even to specially forbidden places like the marshes.

When I had finished, he made no comment for a moment and then said thoughtfully, ''I wish I had a sister like Kiyas. It's rather dull sometimes being disobedient, when you have to do it all by yourself.''

''You'd like Kiyas and she has a daughter who is very like her.''

''Could she come to stay with me?''

''I don't think she'd enjoy being here...and anyway your grandmother wouldn't allow it.''

''No, I don't suppose she would,'' he sighed. ''She doesn't realize that it's dull having no one except grown-ups to talk to. I don't mean that *you're* dull,'' he added hastily. ''You're my friend, so it doesn't matter about your being older than me. If I *did* persuade my grandmother to agree, couldn't you come to live here? And then Kiyas and her daughter could come to stay with you.''

''I've got too many people to look after...hundreds of them, and they wouldn't like it if I went away. I've got a wife; she's very beautiful, and she likes adventures just as much as Kiyas does; and I've got a son who's two years older than you are, and a daughter who's two years younger. It's a pity you don't know them; you'd enjoy it in the Oryx.''

''Couldn't I come to stay with you? If I got my grandmother's permission?''

''I don't believe she'd ever give it.''

''No, I don't suppose she would...even if I made myself extra disagreeable. I can be *very* horrid when I try,'' he said engagingly, ''and I quite often *do* try because everything here is so dull. Even when I pinch people they pretend I'm only tickling them; so I pinch much harder to try to make them squeal...and they do sometimes, though not often.''

''Are you any good at keeping secrets?''

''Secrets? Oh yes, I'm *very* good at that. The palace is full of secrets. Sometimes it's quite difficult to remember which of them I'm supposed to know and which I can make people uncomfortable by asking about. It's a secret that my mother died because she had another baby. Then, when the baby died, that was another secret I wasn't supposed to know. They told me that Ra had come to take it to the country where my mother lived. But I knew that it wasn't Ra. It was men who came to take it away in a box because it was dead. It had a proper funeral as though it were grown-up. I hid in this pavilion and watched the funeral barge going upriver. But they still kept on with their silly secret. You were wrong when you said Pharaoh's son wouldn't lie; it shows that you aren't used to living in a palace. Everyone lies here. My grandmother lies the most...that's why she's so important. Only stupid people tell the truth; they have to, because they aren't clever enough to think of anything else to say.''

''I suppose you wouldn't feel comfortable among stupid people...you being so clever. That's a pity, for otherwise we might arrange an adventure which would lead to your coming to the Oryx.''

''Oh, I wouldn't mind them being stupid,'' he said fervently, ''not if they were your kind of stupid. That sounds rude, but I didn't mean it to be. It's nice when you tell me something, for I don't have to try to guess what you really mean, you just say what you are thinking.'' He sighed. ''Sometimes being clever is so difficult that it hardly seems worth the trouble. Do you *really* think we could make an adventure which would take me to the Oryx?''

''We could if you were very good at keeping a secret. You wouldn't be able to tell anyone about it, not even an attendant or a scribe...and least of all your grandmother.''

He wriggled closer to me in his excitement. ''What would I have to do?''

''First of all you would have to be pleased when your father says he is going to take you on a Progress to the North.''

His face fell, ''But I thought the Oryx was in the South; and it wouldn't be a real adventure if I just went to your home with Father on a Progress. I would have to sit beside him and listen to dull people making speeches, and then smile and smile while people brought me presents I didn't want... they're never any better than the things I've got here; at least sometimes they are but then I'm not allowed to keep them.''

''What kind of things aren't you allowed to keep?''

''Well, a fisherboy once gave me a tame rat. I'm not sure he would have given it to me unless I had asked for it, and even then he mightn't unless his mother had told him to. It bit me a little until it got used to me, and then it would sit on my shoulder and eat food I held between my lips. Father let me keep it all the time we were on the Progress, but when we got home it knew nobody but me liked it and it was frightened, so it got rather cross. One morning it was dead in its box...I believe somebody poisoned it. It's quite easy to poison people, you know; so long as you've got the right thing to put in their food. Sometimes they just go to sleep and don't wake up again, and sometimes they have a terribly bad pain inside first. One of our servants died a short time ago....That was another of the secrets I wasn't supposed to know. I was told that he had been bitten by a snake, but I overheard two of the servants whispering...I had climbed that tree over there, and they stood underneath it and never knew I was hidden by the leaves. They said that my grandmother's foreign physician had poisoned him. I don't know if that was true, but I expect it is, because he is a *horrid* old man. He was brought to see me when I had a pain inside. It was a bad pain and they thought I was dying...I didn't tell them that I had eaten a lot of pickled cucumbers. My grandmother says that pickled cucumbers always give little boys bad pains; but I didn't know until I tried that she was telling the truth *that* time.''

''Are you very fond of your grandmother?''

He looked surprised and then said emphatically, ''Of *course* I am. She is the only person who loves me...she has often told me so. Father doesn't love me because he hated my mother and I remind him of her. And of course the servants can't love me because they are only servants, and the scribes are frightened of me because if they don't manage to teach me anything they will get punished. I once had a scribe whom I *did* like: he taught me a lot without my noticing it, just like playing a very interesting game....I remember now that it was he who told me about you and how the Oryx had helped to make my father Pharaoh. I told grandmother that he must be a kinsman of mine, without either of us knowing it, because I loved him as though he were my elder brother... she says no one can love you unless they are a blood relation. She was angry with me, and said that to be affectionate to a servant betrayed my Royal Blood. So the scribe went away and I never saw him again. That's why I'm so specially careful not to learn anything from the other scribes....But you haven't told me yet how I could come to the Oryx.''

''You can't know a secret until it is ready, any more than you can enjoy an apricot until it is ripe. When our secret *is* ready it will turn into a journey and the journey will have a boat in it for about eight days, and then we shall both be in the Oryx.''

''I must go now,'' he said, ''or they will miss me: it is *very* seldom I manage to get away by myself. Shall I see you tomorrow?''

''Perhaps not tomorrow....''

''You are my friend, aren't you, Ra-ab Hotep?''

''Always your friend.''

''Good-night, Ra-ab Hotep. You won't forget our secret, will you?''

''I won't forget.''

# Scalp-Lock

I had decided that it was wiser not to tell Senusert that he was going to the Oryx lest in his excitement he betray our plans to his grandmother, or, should he at the last moment feel reluctant to leave her, refuse to come with us willingly. I left the City on the Royal Barge and Amenemhet took this opportunity to discuss with me some of his plans further to improve his administration. Senusert was told not to disturb us; this annoyed him, though in the presence of his father he dared do no more than sulk. He refused to eat anything at the evening meal, and I saw him try to trip up a servant who was carrying a wine-jar, and then grin at the man's discomfiture when some of the wine spilt on the table. Senusert looked at me to see if I had noticed, but when I showed no sign of being impressed, he relapsed again into sulks. At sunset he was sent to bed in the small cabin, under the raised platform where Pharaoh usually reclined.

''He can be taken to your boat before dawn,'' said Amenemhet, ''then at least you can have some sleep before commencing the unpleasant task which you have so nobly undertaken. If you cannot report to me in due course that Senusert has undergone a thorough change of character, I shall disinherit him; unless the Gods take this necessity out of my hands. Though, as I have often admitted to you, I take no interest in women, I have provided that should he never become suited for co-rulership, then Egypt shall not lack an heir of my body. I shall not take the mother of my other son to be a secondary wife unless I definitely decide that he shall rule after me: this is again a union of expediency. Her blood is noble, her body strong, her temperament placid; and, so far as I have ever been able to discover, she is not actuated by any desire for personal advancement. Her child is only five years old, but, though he resembles myself physically, he appears to have a tranquil nature and should make a kindly if undistinguished ruler; an adequate figurehead through which the Eyes of Horus would continue to rule Egypt."

"It will not be enough for the next Pharaoh to resemble Amenemhet only in his person," I said. "The Eyes of Horus chose you as a leader, not because they wished to rule in your name."

"Perhaps in Senusert they will find such a leader. His is a strong character, he would never be content to be a puppet, for in him I see much of his grandfather, Men-het. Haven't you seen it, Ra-ab?"

For the first time I realized how strongly the boy resembled the great warrior whom I had watched die after the Battle of the Six Hundred....

"Yes, Ra-ab, I can see that you recognize the likeness. Perhaps that is why I feel a stranger to my son. He reminds me of the man who had cause to call me the Usurper, the man from whose dead hands I took the Crook and Flail. Was I right, Ra-ab? Am I a greater Pharaoh than Men-het would have been? He knew the joy of life and he was a mighty warrior....And I—who knows what I shall prove to be in another twenty years! The future belongs to you as much as to me, Ra-ab; I have failed with Senusert, but if you succeed, then the conflict between his grandfather and I may be resolved at last, and in the boy the two of us shall rule Egypt in peace."

Just before dawn the next morning I picked up the sleeping boy and carried him to my own boat. He stirred and opened his eyes for a moment, then settled into deeper sleep. I sat in the bows with him across my lap, for I did not want him to wake until we were out of sight of his father's barge.

He looked such an ordinary little boy. And because of his great destiny, he had so many difficulties to overcome, so much to learn. He was only a child; and yet one day he might be the Father of Egypt, bringing contentment, or sorrow to his children, wielding great power far beyond the span of his own life.

The oars swept back and forth in perfect rhythm, and already the eastern hills were dark against the morning. "Anubis! Teach me to refresh myself from the waters of memory so that I may understand the mind of this child, and help him to grow in your image. Let him desire above all things to become one with the Gods, and to remember that only the wise can teach the foolish, that only the strong can give courage to the weak; but that he who is never foolish learns no wisdom, and he who has known no weakness can feel no strength."

The boy stirred, and then sat up. He woke abruptly, as children sometimes do without being disturbed.

"Ra-ab, you didn't forget! It was a *real* secret! And yesterday I thought you had forgotten your promise, and that you were only a friend of Father's who was going on the Royal Progress. Oh, Ra-ab Hotep! You ought to have told me that it was only a part of the secret; and then I wouldn't have been so specially horrid. What is the first adventure going to be?"

"First, we must have something to eat, and then you must promise to keep under the awning until we have passed the Royal City. Your grandmother, and other women of the palace, don't approve of little boys having adventures; and if they see you they will try to get you back, and you'll have to go on being dull."

"They *mustn't* see me, Ra-ab Hotep! Hadn't I better hide now?"

"No, it will take us another hour before we are in sight of the walls. Are you hungry?"

"Very hungry! I was last night too; but I didn't eat anything because everyone was hoping I would and I wanted to show I was cross.

"If you're cross with me I shan't mind at all if you don't eat anything. In fact, since anger and food fight in the belly, it is better to refuse hospitality to the second before the first has departed.''

''Won't you *mind* if I don't eat anything, Ra-ab Hotep?''

''Why should I? You're a better judge of the emptiness of your own belly than I am. And if you enjoy feeling hungry, why should I deny you that pleasure?''

''But I might get ill if I didn't eat!''

''You'd have to go on being cross for several days before it did you any harm; and then you'd cure yourself by eating. You'd soon get tired of feeling hungry.''

''Won't your wife mind either....And won't my attendants get worried if I don't eat?''

''No, they won't mind either....And the only attendant you'll have is my old nurse, Niyahm. She's very fierce when she's cross, but if you take the trouble to be nice to her she'll soon get fond of you.''

''Is she obedient?''

''Obedient? To you, do you mean?''

''Yes, of course.''

I laughed. ''Try giving her an order; and see what happens. I've never dared to, and neither has Meri. But if you ask her politely, she nearly always does what you want.''

''But I can't *ask* people, Ra-ab? I'm the Royal Heir. People *have* to do what I want.''

''Ah, but you're not the Royal Heir any more...not unless you prove yourself in the Oryx to be a suitable person to be Pharaoh.''

''I think that's a silly kind of joke, Ra-ab! You *know* I'm the Royal Heir, and I can't help being Pharaoh unless I die before Father.''

''Wearing the Double Crown doesn't make a man royal, even though his family has been royal for many generations. You've got to grow wise and strong, so that people will *choose* you as their leader; choose you not for *who* you are but for *what* you are.''

"But *who* I am and *what* I am are the same thing! I'm the Royal Heir."

"But they are *not* the same thing. You have been born a son of Pharaoh; but perhaps he has other sons he may choose instead of you."

Senusert grinned. "Oh, you've been listening to the stories from the women's quarters! My grandmother told me that Father had another son. He's three years younger than me, and his mother is not even a secondary wife! Pharaohs often have lots of children, but they are never very important unless they are born of the Royal Wife like I was. If Pharaoh took another Royal Wife, then there might be a chance, a very *small* chance, of my not being chosen Co-ruler. But grandmother says that he'd never risk having to spend the rest of his life with a woman."

"Yet the other boy is just as much the son of your father as you are, Senusert. How do you know that he will not find more favor than you do?"

"It wouldn't really matter if he did. Grandmother said that if he was chosen he'd die. She didn't say *how*; but she's good at arranging that kind of thing. I expect she'd do a magic: the kind with black goats in it. And he'd just get thinner and thinner until one day he'd be dead. She says she can do that to anyone who offends her. Sometimes I wish she wouldn't tell me about that kind of magic just before I go to sleep! It gives me such awfully horrid nightmares. Do *you* know anything about magic, Ra-ab?"

"Yes, quite a lot....And you will go to our temple to be taught about it. Nekht-ahn will decide whether you are to be trained as a priest. Once, the Pharaohs were always priests; did you know that?"

"I don't want to talk about priests now. I want to talk about the Oryx. When shall we get there?"

"In seven or eight days if the North Wind favors our journey."

"Couldn't we go faster than that?"

"No, it would be too hard on the rowers."

"Couldn't I whip them? Then they'd go faster! Father won't let me whip his rowers; but grandmother says that shows he has got a weak character. She say's he's afraid that if he whipped the rowers they might hit him with their oars and hurt him! Why don't you whip your rowers, Ra-ab? I'm sure *you* have never been afraid of getting hurt, because you're a warrior."

"I don't whip them because I find no pleasure in hurting my friends. And if they aren't my friends, then why are they rowing a boat for me?"

He looked astonished. "How can you have rowers for *friends*, Ra-ab, when you're a Nomarch?"

"That is one of the things you will learn in the Oryx."

"If the rowers were *not* your friends, could you whip them?"

"Only if I wished to find myself an oarsman."

"But who could make you an oarsman?"

"The Gods: they find no difficulty in placing each of us in the situation which provides that experience we have shown ourselves to be lacking."

"But grandmother says that once you've been born royal you never come into a lesser caste. They never have *royal* rowers, Ra-ab."

"Another thing you will learn in the Oryx is that your grandmother has given you wrong information on some important subjects."

For a moment he looked shocked. Then he giggled and said. "Ra-ab, I *knew* you were the bravest man in Egypt. No one else would dare to say a thing like that about my grandmother. I'm telling you a very private secret. Sometimes I don't believe that she's as clever as she thinks she is! Promise that you'll *never* tell anyone I said that, or something very dangerous might happen to me almost at once....Tell me more about what's going to happen in the Oryx."

"The most important thing that you will have to remember is that while you are living in my house no one must know that you are any relation to Pharaoh. I shall tell them you are an orphan of a kinsman of mine who lived in the Reed. The only people who will know who you really are, will be Meri and Ameni and Beket. You will be treated as though you were also my son, and you must see that you never betray the obligation of one whom I honor by calling kinsman.''

''Do you mean I'll have to behave as though I was an *ordinary* person?''

''You *are* an ordinary person, Senusert...in my opinion. I hope that the day will come when I honor you for your wisdom, but until then you will have to prove that you are worthy of friendship.''

''Won't even the servants do what I tell them?''

''Why should they? Unless you have shown that you are worthy to be obeyed.''

''What will happen if I pinch someone?''

''You will learn what it feels like to be pinched. No, Senusert, you needn't remind me of the law which decrees death to anyone who raises a hand against the Royal Blood. If you doubt that your blood is different to any other I suggest that you prick your finger. You will find that it is as red and as wet as that which flows from a worker in the quarries...or from a water-rat.''

For a few minutes he looked disheartened, and hung over the side of the boat, staring down into the water. I lay back on the striped cushions and pretended to sleep. After a time he came and sat beside me cross-legged. ''Ra-ab,'' he whispered, ''are you awake?''

''What do you want?'' I said, and yawned.

''*You* won't forget that I'm the Royal Heir, will you, Ra-ab? I mean you won't let people be horrid to me?''

''Not unless you have been horrid to them first. You're going to enjoy being in the Oryx, unless you deliberately spoil things for yourself. You'll try to enjoy it, won't you, Senusert?''

"I'll *try*," he said fervently. "After all, it will only be a though I was disguised; like Hanuk used to be when he was making Egypt safe for me to rule."

He began to laugh, "Ra-ab, I'll *prove* I'm going to join in your adventure—I'll cut off my scalp-lock and then no one will know I'm a prince!"

He sat still while I hacked through the plait of hair with my hunting knife. Then he dropped it over the side of the barge and watched it swirl away on the current.

# the Boy and the prince

Senusert was surprisingly docile on the journey, but I knew this mood was unlikely to last once the sense of adventure began to wear thin. I had impressed on him that though his rank was known to my family, they would ignore it; yet I think he was startled when Meri, who was waiting to greet us at the landing-steps, kissed him on the forehead as though he were a most ordinary little boy. As we walked up to the house, Beket and Ameni came running along the path to meet us. Ameni and Senusert eyed each other warily, rather like dogs who have not yet decided whether to fight or be friends, Beket, whom Meri had decided was too young to be trusted with so important a secret, thought that Senusert was an orphan, and by the way she smiled at him I knew she had already decided that he needed cherishing as did the animals which she took under her protection.

She demanded to ride on my shoulders, and I saw Senusert's mouth begin to droop at the corners, as it always did when he ceased to be the center of attention. She must have taken this as a sign that he was homesick, for she smiled down at him and said:

"You come with me and I'll show you my puppy," adding in an outburst of generosity, "You can have him to sleep in your room until you have an animal of your own."

I could see that he had no intention of accepting this invitation, which he obviously considered beneath his dignity.

"You can go with her," I said. "She can stay up and share the evening meal with us, so she will tell you when it is ready."

He hesitated, and then decided it would be unwise to argue. Ignoring Beket's offered hand, he followed her reluctantly across the courtyard. Now that I was alone with Meri and Ameni I told them in detail why Senusert had come to live with us. Meri flamed to the boy's defense:

"I think it was horrible of Amenemhet to say such bitter things about his son! Anyone, especially a child, would be warped if they had to live with the Babylonian. How dare she terrify him with stories of black magic! It's amazing he's as normal as he is. Oh, Ra-ab, I'm so thankful you rescued him!"

"What do you think he's really like?" asked Ameni, more cautiously.

"I like him," I said decisively, "and by 'him' I mean his essential character. His manners, except to those he considers his equals—he is gracious enough to acknowledge me to be one—are deplorable. He is so conceited that it is sometimes difficult not to slap him; and he is a most accomplished liar. But in spite of all this I repeat that I already feel a very real affection for the essential Senusert."

"I think he's a horrid little boy!" said an indignant voice behind me. I turned to see Beket, clutching her puppy in her arms, standing in the doorway.

"What has he done to you?"

"He was *disgustingly* rude to my puppy! He said she wasn't a real breed of dog and was only suitable to a hovel! I don't know what a hovel is, but it must be something nasty or he wouldn't have said it. I told him that she was a very special kind of dog and that her mother belonged to the

Keeper of the Vineyard. Then we quarreled and he went off by himself and I came to look for you. Can he go away soon?'

"I'm afraid not, Beket. He has come here to live with us."

"Have we got to keep him *however* horrid he is?" she asked, appalled.

"Yes, so we had better teach him to stop being horrid."

She sighed. "That will be very tiresome...worse than trying to teach Niyahm not to be difficult about beetles."

"You had better go to look for him," I said to Ameni, "and then take him to see Niyahm."

"I'll stay with you," said Beket firmly. "Nehri's coming here tomorrow; Mother arranged it while you were away. Perhaps he'll be able to teach Senusert to be nicer...I'm always less tiresome myself with Nehri than with anyone else." Then she added as an afterthought, "Except you of course."

Senusert gave up claiming to be the Royal Heir when his first few attempts had met only with pitying incredulity. I had explained to all the servants who were likely to come in contact with him that they must help me to cure his ill manners. So unless he made a request instead of giving an order, he was ignored...sometimes to his extreme discomfiture. Several times during the first month he went hungry from the table, having ordered a servant to fetch him a certain dish, and on finding this brought no response, being too proud to ask for it with civility. Then for two days he refused all food. It was Niyahm who blunted this weapon, having seen that it had begun to worry Meri.

Niyahm came into the room when Senusert had again sat through a meal with his food untasted. "Poor child!" she exclaimed, turning to me in pretend indignation. "Fancy trying to make him eat when he's not well! I have made a special brew that will soon cure him...a nasty taste it's got, but he'll soon feel better."

Then to him, "Come along with me, dear, and I'll promise that by tomorrow you'll feel as hungry as the others."

Senusert scowled at her, "I'm not coming with you!"

"Go with Niyahm," I said.

"I refuse!"

"The poor child is too weak to walk, you'll have to carry him," said Niyahm.

He clung to his stool with both hands, "I won't go. I won't be carried. I'm going to stay here!"

Niyahm put her hand to his forehead. "Feverish! He doesn't know what he's saying."

In spite of his furious protests, I picked him up, stool and all, and carried him to his room.

Niyahm, who was thoroughly enjoying herself, asked me to stay until Senusert had drunk the brew she had prepared. The taste must have been exceedingly disagreeable, for he coughed and sputtered before he managed to swallow it. Then we left him alone.

"Nothing in it but a little gall to make it bitter." said Niyahm. "But I think it will cure his lack of appetite!"

I am thankful to say that it did.

Nehri, who in a few years would be Nomarch of the Hare, knew Senusert's identity and was exceedingly helpful during those first difficult months. Senusert, who considered himself too grand to play with Beket, now found that unless he was willing to join the pastimes of the older boys in a subordinate capacity, they would have nothing to do with him. At first he pretended to prefer his own company, but when at the evening meal they discussed the events of their day—accounts which I am sure lost nothing in the telling—he found it increasingly difficult to remain aloof. He had been so used to receiving servile obedience from everyone, except his grandmother and Pharaoh, that it must have been difficult for him to take orders from boys not much older than himself. He found that when he was in a good mood they took care to show that they enjoyed his company, but that when he was disagreeable they told him to run away and stop being a nuisance to his betters. He frequently threatened them with tortures which would be inflicted on them by his grandmother... at which they jeered until he was reduced to tears of helpless fury.

Finding that he could make no impression on Ameni and Nehri, he turned his attentions to the outdoor servants, hoping, no doubt, that they would not dare to tell me what he was doing. They had, however, been told how to deal with him. He emptied a jar of dirty water over a gardener asleep in the sun. The gardener woke up: Senusert found himself floundering in a shallow, but exceedingly muddy pool. He pelted with rotten figs a woman working in the vineyard... and spent three hours washing the fruit stains from her tunic, while her husband sat on the bank of the irrigation channel to see that he was not idle.

Meri took no part in this drastic treatment, for after considerable thought we had decided that I should represent an authority he must learn to accept, while she must be the symbol of the affection which, because it is born of Ra, is the highest of all authorities. No matter how he had behaved during the day, Meri went to his room to tell him a story before he slept. Even though he knew he was in disfavor with the rest of the household, he found that this made no difference to his relationship with Meri.

Sometimes there were tears in her eyes when she left his room.

''I'm so *sorry* for him, Ra-ab! There is such a lot of himself which he has got to fight against. When I kissed him tonight he threw his arms round my neck and whispered, 'Tell Ra-ab that one day I'm not going to be horrid any more. There are two people inside me; the boy you love and that filthy little prince who can't help making people hate him! When I'm the boy, I know the prince is my enemy. Then suddenly I'm the prince again, and *he* thinks that the boy you

117

come to talk to every evening is weak and silly...so weak that people will laugh at him.'

"I held him tightly in my arms, 'But they never laugh at the boy...it's only the prince who behaves like a fool.' He thought for a moment and then said, 'But the prince doesn't believe that...he stills thinks that no one is important unless their orders are obeyed without question.' So I said, 'Ra-ab always tells you why he gives an order...he never expects you to obey unless you understand the reason for it.'

"He hugged me again and then whispered, 'That's why the boy loves Ra-ab nearly as much as he loves you. That's why the prince still fights against him, because the prince tries to pretend that he's as wise as Ra-ab Hotep.' "

## awful Royalness

I was tired, for the weather was oppressively hot, and I had been in Audience from early morning until nearly sunset, as it was the day on which I received the half-yearly tribute of the tenth part. I was standing at the window of the Room of Seals, watching the evening sky, when I saw a bedraggled procession coming furtively toward the house in the shadow of the garden wall.

First came Ameni, a smear of blood across his cheek. A few paces behind him walked Beket, her hair plastered with mud, holding something carefully between her hands. Some way behind her limped Senusert, and as he drew nearer I saw his cheek-bone was bruised and oozing blood; and his mouth twisted by a split lip.

I went out to meet them. "What have you been doing?" I asked Ameni.

"Nothing important. We had meant to go and help bring in the cows to be milked; then we changed our minds and didn't bother to go so far. Beket found a toad, and she wants it to come live in the garden. I don't think it much likes being a pet toad, but she *would* bring it."

"It does want to come," said Beket firmly. "It's *entirely* a garden toad, and was feeling very lonely and lost by itself in a ditch."

"What happened to your tunic?" I asked her. She was wearing it in a roll round her waist and it looked like a very abbreviated kilt.

"The shoulder-part broke," she said vaguely. "One moment it was there and the next it wasn't; so I had to wear it like this to stop myself tripping over it."

"What's happened to Senusert's face?"

"Oh, he's just bumped himself a bit; nothing that matters. He hasn't knocked out a tooth or anything," said Ameni.

Senusert had been deliberately loitering, but he was now within earshot. When he heard Ameni's explanation, he burst out:

"He's telling a lie, Ra-ab! I didn't bump myself. He hit me...very hard! I wish my father knew what he had done, for then he'd send him to live with the Barbarians. He *deserves* to live with the Barbarians!"

"Did you hit him, Ameni?"

"Yes, I did: and I'm not at all sorry. The only reason I didn't tell you was because he'd asked me not to say anything about it. But if he wants to look a fool it's his fault, not mine."

He turned to Senusert, "All right; you tell Father what happened and if you add any lies I'll bruise your other cheek...and then you won't look so lopsided."

"We were just arguing—at least Beket and I were arguing—when Ameni came and threw me down on the ground. Of course I had to defend myself...that's how he got his scratch. Then, before I could get up, he hit me...twice!"

Beket, who was standing beside him, suddenly stretched

119

out her hand and gave him a sharp pinch on the thigh. He yelped; she giggled, and then dodged behind me, still clutching her toad which had almost managed to escape.

Senusert, his eyes full of angry tears, wailed, ''Look what she did to me! I wasn't doing anything to her, and she pinched me so hard I'll have a bruise.''

''I *didn't* pinch you for nothing,'' shouted Beket. ''I pinched you for telling lies about Ameni. And the next time you're horrid to Ameni I'll pinch you again, till you've got lots and lots and lots of bruises, so many bruises that you'll be black all over and have to go live in the Land of Gold because you'll be as black as they are.''

''There seems to be a considerable difference of opinion as to what actually happened,'' I remarked to Ameni, ''and as you are the eldest, perhaps you will tell me about it.''

''Well, I suppose it was really Beket who started it,'' he said uncomfortably. ''Senusert and I wanted to go to help with the cows and she wanted to come with us. When we were crossing a ditch she saw a toad and insisted on stopping to play with it. We didn't like to leave her there, because she's a bit young to be by herself and we were quite a long way from the house. Senusert got impatient and gave her a push so that she fell in the mud. So she bit him; it was really quite fair because it was a *hard* push. Then he tried to drag her out of the ditch by her tunic, but it broke and she tumbled backwards and went head first into the water...it was mostly mud...that's why her hair looks so funny. When I'd tidied her up a bit she discovered she'd lost her toad, so we had to waste a lot more time looking for it. I caught it eventually and, when I was giving it to her, Senusert snatched it away and held it up by one leg, which must have hurt it a lot. Beket got angry, and rushed at him and tried to bite him. So he gave her a frightfully hard pinch. Then I forgot about him being smaller than me and I hit him...twice...perhaps a bit harder than I meant to. Then Beket and I decided it was rather late to go to see the cows so we came home.''

''You had better all come to my room and get tidied up before Niyahm sees you.''

''Could we go to the garden first to see my toad settled?'' asked Beket anxiously.

''Yes, we'd better, for I expect your hands are a bit too hot for him. We'll find him a nice cool place where he can get his breath back.''

''Perhaps you'd better carry him,'' she suggested, ''my hands *are* a bit hot.''

The toad was looking rather flabby and his throat was palpitating violently. The garden had just been watered, and we found a comfortable place for him under the wall. He hopped a little way, then stopped, and in a moment or two snapped at a fly and seemed to forget his troubles.

''There,'' said Beket contentedly, ''I *knew* he was a pet toad.''

She slipped her hand into mine and trotted along beside me to the house. I washed the raw places on Ameni's and Senusert's faces and smeared on some healing salve.

''Do we go to bed now?'' asked Beket. ''Or are you going to give judgment on us?''

I pretended to consider the point very seriously before replying. ''Judgment? Certainly! I'll begin with you, Beket. Why did you want the toad?''

''Because he was a *pet* toad?''

''Why was he different to any other toad?''

''Because the moment I saw him I said to myself, 'I've always wanted a pet toad and this is it.' I didn't say, '*a* toad,' I said '*pet* toad,' so it must have been one.''

''You didn't ask the others if they minded going toad collecting instead of helping with the cows?''

''No, why should I? The cows are always there, but the toad was a special occasion.''

''You didn't think of asking whether they'd mind changing their plans to oblige you?''

''I may have *thought* of it, but I didn't do it, because

**121**

they would have been almost sure to say they *did* mind...
and I'm not nearly so fond of cows as I am of toads.''

''Did you know you were being tiresome?''

''I knew I was being just a *little* tiresome.''

''If you had said, ''Please, Ameni and Senusert, will you
help me catch my toad, and as soon as he's in a safe place
I'll come and watch your cows,' don't you think it might
have saved a lot of trouble?''

''I think it might. Anyway I'll try it another toadish
time.''

''Thank you, Beket,'' I said gravely. ''I should be most
grateful if you would...and very interested to hear what
happens.

''Now, as you have agreed that you were tiresome, it
cannot have been altogether a surprise when Senusert tried
to pull you out of the ditch...other, and perhaps more subtle
arguments have failed. Therefore the fault that the tunic is
torn is yours, and tomorrow you will ask Niyahm to teach
you how to mend it.''

''*Me* mend it?'' said Beket, appalled by such a suggestion. ''It's not really *worth* mending, there's such a little
bit of it left.''

''A number of people spend a lot of time making and
mending your clothes, so you may as well learn whether
mending is an interesting thing or not. If it isn't I should try
to be a bit more careful; if it *is* you can tear your clothes as
often as you like, for you will enjoy mending them. Before
going back to Niyahm you can bathe in my toilet room, and
Senusert can get the mud out of your hair.''

''*Not* Senusert!'' said Beket firmly. ''He'd get water in
my eyes: he'd do it *deliberately*.''

''If he does,'' I said, ''I will wash his hair, and there
will be water in his eyes...also deliberately. Do you hear,
Senusert? I shall be in here while you are washing Beket,
and if you are wise you will give her as little discomfort as
possible. You had better start now. You will find every-

thing you need in there, and you can use the towels with the birds embroidered on them.''

As soon as we were alone, Ameni said ruefully, ''I'm afraid I hit him rather hard. What should I do to make up for it?''

''I think the balance is already restored...or soon will be if the sound of splashing water is not accompanied by squeals.''

''I *did* try to remember not to hit Senusert any harder than I meant to, but I was pretty irritated by the time it became necessary to hit him. It wasn't a duty; I *enjoyed* it.''

''What part did you enjoy most? The realization that by your own strength you could hurt someone else?''

''No, it wasn't as complicated as that. He'd been having an attack of grandness all day, and a good deal of 'I'm Pharaoh's son pretending to be one of the common people, deigning to behave as if I were your equal.' So it was very satisfactory to show him that he is only a very ordinary boy, who sits down and howls if you hit him too hard....Perhaps that's not quite true: when I saw him pinch Beket...after all she's *much* younger than we are and not really at all tiresome considering her age; I should have liked to pinch him much, *much* harder than he pinched her. Then I remembered that only children pinch, so I hit him instead.''

''I'm afraid Senusert will have to be hit a few more times before it is no longer necessary for him to receive such an education. Do you think he'll sulk as long as he did last time?''

''I don't think he will. He was better after Beket pushed him into the lotus-pool, than he was after I dared him to walk along the vineyard wall and he fell off it. And another thing which show's he's getting better is that the day after you punished him for cutting up one of Beket's pet worms, I saw him putting a stranded worm back on the flower bed...and he wasn't doing it to show off, because he didn't know that anyone was watching him. Another good thing was that the last time her puppy was sick he wiped up the mess without

**123**

being asked; which is all a great improvement on his awful royalness when he first came here.''

''I am very grateful to you, Ameni, for what you are doing to lighten one of the most difficult tasks I have ever been given. Had we failed with Senusert, a future generation of Egyptians might say that the Watchers had deserted them.''

## Sudden Death

Though I frequently sent to Amenemhet detailed reports of Senusert's improvement, he never expressed a wish to see his son. Nearly two years after Senusert had come to the Oryx, I received a message from Pharaoh saying that his Vizier was about to visit me, bearing news of importance. I was surprised that the Vizier should be employed as a carrier of messages, and decided that the real purpose of his visit must be to see how the character of the Royal Heir had improved.

The Vizier had been a member of the household of Amenemhet's father, and, though I had only met him on formal occasions, I knew him to be a man of excellent judgment.

The children shared the evening meal with us, and I was relieved that Senusert showed no signs of relapsing into one of his, now very infrequent, moods of ill-temper. He had acquired some of Beket's attachment to animals; and the gazelle, which I had recently given him, followed him wherever he went.

They had been on the river all day, being taught by my master-boatman how to sail. They had taken fishing lines with them, and, to honor their prowess, the fish they had caught were served to us that evening.

When the children had gone to bed the Vizier said to me:
''The Oryx is famed throughout Egypt for its wisdom:

never was fame more justified, for it has given Egypt an Heir worthy of her.''

''You are pleased with the boy's progress?''

''Pleased? What a narrow word to describe so wide a gratitude!''

''I am glad that your report will relieve his father's anxiety. You came here for that purpose?''

''Only indirectly, I came to bring you news which Pharaoh preferred not to trust to an ordinary messenger. You need no longer watch the boundary for spies sent by Senusert's grandmother. She died, suddenly—thereby making the original purpose of my visit unnecessary.''

''How did her death affect your purpose?''

''I was coming to tell you that she had at last discovered that Senusert is here. She was coming to the Oryx disguised as an exile, thinking so to betray your boundless hospitality for the unfortunate. She had every confidence that she would be able to reassert her influence over Senusert once she was able to see him again. I was to tell you that the boy should be closely watched, even though that might seriously interfere with the freedom of his education.''

''You say she died...suddenly? Do you know from what cause?''

''Such deaths are not uncommon: only the opportuneness of its occurrence made her death at all remarkable. One might almost describe it as a case of divine intervention. The Gods are not always so willing to adjust their plans for the convenience of mortals.''

I knew that had he wished he could have told me more. His face was bland and his manner confidential, but I knew that it would be useless to ply him with further questions.

His visit was of necessity brief, for his office gave him small opportunity for leisure. We parted with many expressions of mutual esteem, but my curiosity remained unsatisfied.

I said to Meri as we walked back from the river, ''I don't

125

believe that the Babylonian died a natural death. The Vizier has well earned his name... 'Father of Discretion.' He would never sow the seed of suspicion except deliberately.''

''Do you think that he murdered her, or that she killed herself?'' asked Meri.

''I think it unlikely that she killed herself: why should she when her plans to come here were already made? Neither do I think that the Vizier killed her.''

''Oh, I didn't mean that he had done it himself, only that he had suggested it to someone who was capable of turning such a hint into reality.''

''Do you think that the boy will be very distressed when he hears about it?''

''No, Ra-ab, I don't: not now. I think that in his heart he will be enormously relieved. His fear of her is much less than it used to be when he first came here, but he still sometimes says, 'Promise that you won't tell my grandmother?' She used to be a source of strength which she misused, the one who could enforce his childish threats. Now he has come to recognize that a woman like Kiosostoris must always be our natural enemy.''

That evening I told Senusert of his grandmother's death. He stood quite still, his face expressionless. Then he said, ''I don't mind, Ra-ab. It's a terrible thing to say about someone who loves you; but I don't *mind* that I'm not going to see her any more...I almost think I'm glad. Is it wicked to say that, Ra-ab?''

''How can it be wicked to be honest with yourself? It is sometimes meritorious to pretend that you are happy when you are sad, if by doing so you can stop your companions sharing a sorrow which it is not in their power to lessen. But there is no virtue in pretending sorrow you do not feel. If you love her, you should not grudge that she is gone to Ra's country; and if you do not love her, why then should you regret that she has left the country in which *you* live?''

''I wonder how she died, Ra-ab. Do you know? Was

she ill a long time? Did she have a lot of pain?''

''She died in her sleep: there was nothing frightening about her death, Senusert. It was only that one morning she didn't have to wake.''

''I'm glad that it wasn't one of her own magics that killed her. Nekht-ahn told me that the kind of magics she used to do—were very dangerous to the person who made them. I thought one of them might have turned back on her so that she died; as though she had tried to hold a cobra by the tail.''

Trying to change the subject, I said, ''Do you wish that you were still living in the Royal City, instead of being one of the common people?''

''No, Ra-ab, I *never* do. You won't send me away, will you? I am getting better, honestly I am. I only very seldom get attacks of what Ameni calls my 'awful royalness.' I can feel them coming on, like the shivers before a fever, and I try very hard to stop but sometimes I can't. I often try to think of myself as only 'me,' not as the son of Pharaoh, or even as your kinsman, but just someone—who hasn't even got a name. Then I get frightened, as though I was going to disappear. I know it's silly, but sometimes I dream about it. At the beginning of the dream I am wearing a prince's scalp-lock and standing beside Father. It is some kind of Audience, for there are hundreds and hundreds of people looking up at us. Then the faces go blurred, dissolve into mist and vanish. I put out my hand to touch the side of the throne, but my hand goes right through it; and the next moment I am alone, standing in an enormous room without any pillars. I am getting smaller and smaller, until the lines between the paving-blocks look as wide as ditches, as canals, as a cleft between great cliffs...And I fall into it and get lost; and I go on falling for ever and ever. Then I'm suddenly awake, and to stop myself being frightened I say 'Pharaoh is your father, and one day you will be the Father of Egypt. You must be grand and important and not afraid any more.'...Why do I have that dream?''

"Perhaps it is because you still think of yourself only in relation to other people—a crowd of faces turned toward you, the throne beside which you stand. When those things disappear, you are afraid of finding yourself alone because you relied, for your valuation of yourself, on things which had no importance in reality. Though ten thousand people turn their faces toward you, they cannot add even a thumb-joint to your stature, and though your blood is of the Royal House, it cannot add to the nobility of your heart."

"Can't you stop me having that dream?"

"I will try but you must help me. Though you are already grown strong enough not to heed the protection of rank, you are still uncertain of your own strength. You must grow confident in your own leadership within the limits which your character justifies. The plan which I will suggest to you is not entirely my own; the original idea belongs to Ameni.

"You have already been several times to the Exiles' Village. There, as you know, are the children who have come with their parents from other Nomes. When the parents are an undesirable influence on the children, they are temporarily separated from them...until each can benefit from the other's company. Some of these children go to live in a house similar to the one in which live our orphans; others share the homes of people who are willing to take an extra child into their family.

"The Exiles' Village is in the north of the Nome. The estate for those children who cannot be allowed to mix with others until they have learned our habit of life, is in the south. There are six children, recently arrived, who have to make the journey south. I'm going to put three of them in your charge, and the other three will go with Ameni. Each of you will have to lead his three in the way you consider best.

"The journey should take you five days. At this season you can sleep outdoors and I will provide you with a pack donkey to carry food. Neither you nor Ameni must say that you are my kinsman. It is not an easy task I am giving you,

**128**

for these children are wild and undisciplined. You will have only the strength of your own character by which to control them; for you must not threaten them with punishments other than those you can enforce without outside help. During the whole journey you will be responsible for their behavior and should they damage grain or other crops, you will have to make good the damage.''

"But, Ra-ab, suppose I can't stop them breaking the laws? Suppose they don't listen to me? How can I make them obey me?''

"Ah, Senusert, that is for you to discover! How will you rule Egypt if three ordinary children won't accept you as their leader? The owner of a dog is responsible if, unprovoked, it bites someone. The parents are responsible if their son becomes a thief. Is it then so surprising that the future Pharaoh should be held responsible for three out of so many thousands of his people?''

# leadership

I had frequent news of how Ameni and Senusert were faring with the exiles' children, though neither of them knew this; and in fifteen days I heard they had left the farm where they had spent the night of their homeward journey. Beket and I decided to go out to meet them, and she said that two of her pet goats wanted to come with us. She had taught them to be surprisingly obedient, and except when they felt that a patch of herbage looked too promising to be passed untasted, they followed us like well-trained dogs.

"I do wish Mother had let me go with Ameni and Senusert,'' said Beket. "She ought to realize that girls of eight are quite as old as boys of ten and twelve. I'm tremendously excited to hear how they got on. I'm sure I should have been much better at it than they were, because of my being able to look after animals. It's no use telling a goat not to nibble Mother's plants; you have to make it believe that grass and unimportant shrubs really taste much nicer. Some people make being good sound so awfully dull...people like Niyahm, I mean. *You* make being good a kind of adventure, which is why I'm so much more obedient with you than I am with anyone else...even with Mother. If I ever meet someone as good as you are, I shall marry him at once."

"Thank you, Beket," I said gravely. "I am very honored."

"I'm not just saying it to be nice; it's *true*. You are a very special person, and so beautifully un-old."

Then, before I could find a suitable reply to this generosity, she cried out, "Look at that naughty goat! He's got into the garden."

She ran down the road, and tried to drag the goat away from a plot of lettuces. The woman who owned them came out of her house, still holding a twist of the dough she had been kneading.

"My goat is very sorry," said Beket apologetically, "but he has absentmindedly eaten four of your lettuces. He says he would like me to do something for you to show he's sorry. Would you like me to help with your dough? I know how to do it, and my hands are clean...at least fairly."

I had waited in the shadow of a straw-stack to see what Beket was going to do, and the woman did not know I was there.

"Come into the house and I will give you a cup of milk," she said amiably, "then you can shape some of my bread for me."

After a few minutes Beket came out of the door...looking back as she walked down the path and waving to the woman who smiled at her through the window. As soon as she had rejoined me she said:

"Such a very nice woman she was: two babies already and

she expects another before the second harvest. And she's got two gray cats, and her husband is very fond of melons and radishes, and he cut his leg very badly when he was making the straw-stack, but now it's healed. She thinks Ra-ab Hotep is an even better Nomarch than his father was. She said that if I could have stayed longer she would have given me a loaf because I helped with her baking; but I explained that my father was waiting for me. She said that I ought to have brought you in too, as there was always food in the house for a hungry traveler. So I told her that you couldn't because you had to look after the rest of the goats. And she said that her father was a goat-herd too, so we belonged to the same caste and were almost kinsmen...which no doubt was why I was such a nice child. Then she said I could come to see her whenever I liked, and I said I would.''

We had brought some food with us, and sat down to eat it under a tree. Beket was soon absorbed in throwing crumbs to a quail, and at last it became so confident that it ate from her hand before flying away. Since she was a baby she had had this power of making animals fearless of her, and though she had been a particularly contented baby, with a smile for everyone, I have seen her attack Niyahm like a wild-cat for deliberately treading on a beetle.

She often spent hours lying on the ground watching insects; and her descriptions of their adventures were as exciting as though she was telling me of a lion hunt. Niyahm frequently complained to Meri of Beket being allowed to keep in the nurseries worms, toads, a rat with a broken tail and a varied collection of beetles. But any attempt to remove them sent Beket rushing to me to demand that I give them my protection. In spite of Meri's sighs and Niyahm's bitter mutterings, I had always agreed with Beket that she had the right of extending the sanctuary of the Oryx to anything she chose.

Suddenly Beket called out, ''There they are! There, just beyond the trees!''

I looked up to see Ameni and Senusert trudging along the

road toward us. They both looked very cheerful, though Senusert's cheek was colored with the olive green of an old bruise.

"Tell us all about everything!" demanded Beket, jumping up and down excitedly. "Senusert first, because his face looks as though he's had the most adventures."

"It's not worth seeing now," said Senusert, "but it was lovely when it was new...though I never saw it at its best because there wasn't a mirror until we reached the overseer's house."

"Was it somebody much bigger than you, or only smaller and quicker that hit you?" asked Beket.

"About the same size, and much quicker...but there were two of them. I'll tell you about it when I get to that part of the story. The three children I got were two boys and a girl—brother and sister, and the other boy was a kinsman who lived with them. I had to collect them from their parents. Even before I reached the house I heard a frightful uproar...a man and a woman quarreling and then the sound of a slap and a child howling. Then the woman opened the door and said rudely, 'Fancy sending a child to take my three on a journey! I suppose I've got to do as I'm ordered, for every time I argue they say that if I don't like it here I can go away. Wicked it is of them I think, not giving a poor woman the right to grumble in comfort without threatening to send her away to live with a lot of black people! Mind you take care of them, and don't lead them into trouble; or Oryx or no Oryx, I'll cut off your ears...even if they kill me for it!'" Her husband interrupted her, saying, 'No ears would be a blessing with you in the house: your tongue is more trouble than scorpions in the thatch!'

"The children looked very clean, and each clutched a bundle tied up in a blue cloth. After they had finished saying good-bye, they followed me quite willingly to where I had left the pack-donkey. For a while they trudged along beside me without speaking. Then one of them asked me which

Nome I came from, and when I told them that I lived here, he said, 'Oh, we thought you were an honorable rebel like ourselves...that's why we've been doing what you told us.'

''The girl was the same age as Beket, but thin and undersized; she soon got tired, so I said she could ride between the panniers on the donkey. The elder boy—who wasn't her brother—thought it a good joke to hit the donkey so that it shied, and the girl fell off and scratched her leg. She made such a fearful fuss that it was difficult to be reasonably sympathetic. She was too frightened to get on the donkey again, so we had to go even more slowly.

''The eldest boy had a blister on his heel...at least he said he had, and he demanded to be allowed to ride the donkey. I explained to him that he was too heavy while the panniers were still full, but he insisted. I let him get up on its back, because it had started to bray, and as I heard another donkey answer I knew it would probably bolt if I let go the halter. It did too! He clung on until they were nearly out of sight, then he fell off into the ditch. The other two screamed with laughter when they saw him covered with mud. He trailed along behind us, muttering to himself and saying that his leg was broken. I didn't take any notice, because he forgot to limp when he thought no one was watching him.

''There were storm-clouds in the west, so, as I thought it might not be good for the girl to sleep out in a field, I stopped at a farm and asked if they would give us shelter for the night. I said that we had our own food with us, but the farmer insisted on our sharing their meal. After we had eaten, I asked him what we could do in return, and when he found that I knew how to groom oxen he let me do his pair. I told the boys that they could clean out the stall, but they refused; so I said that unless they did they would go hungry. They laughed at me, and said I seemed to have forgotten that they had already eaten and so had no need to earn their food. I went to where I had put the panniers and took out some food, saying it was their share for the next day, and gave it to the farmer's geese.

"They didn't believe that I intended to see they went hungry, and when the following evening I took from the pannier only sufficient for the girl and myself they demanded to be given their share. I refused to give it to them, saying that, as they had refused to repay the farmer for his generosity, they could hardly expect me to be generous to them. At first they whined and said they were starving...I hope they felt like it! Then they tried to take food by force; and we had a fight, which is how I got the bruise. But they hadn't been trained in fighting like I have, so in the end I won.

"That night we stopped at another farm, and this time they offered to be helpful without being asked. The elder boy was much the most difficult. He started to throw stones at some ducks, and wouldn't stop even when I shouted at him. So I threw stones at *him* and the girl joined me, while her brother stood jeering at the sight of his kinsman running up the road and yelling to us to stop. He sulked all that day, but he didn't throw any more stones.

"They all seemed surprised to find that when we needed anything, I asked for it and it was always given willingly; and that in return I expected them to join me in doing something to show our gratitude. We saw cucumbers growing in a field and the girl said she wished we dare risk stealing some. The elder boy agreed, and said it was unfair that the owner had so many cucumbers when we had none. But when I said, 'Go and ask the owner,' they thought I was joking; until they saw that as soon as I asked we were each given one. They helped the man weed his field and didn't even grumble.

"The same kind of thing happened three times; once it was some lettuces we wanted, and another time melons. Gradually they realized that it is easier to ask for a favor than to steal...and much less worrying. They found it pleasant to be liked and made welcome instead of being chased away. Their parents had never bothered to make their lives interest-

134

ing, and had ordered them about until it became natural to them to rebel against any kind of authority, without even questioning whether it was true or false. They kept on asking me to tell them more about the Oryx, and they all said it sounded a very interesting place to live in. After that they weren't any trouble and they even stopped quarreling among themselves.''

''Now let Ameni tell his story,'' said Beket.

''Mine is not really worth telling, because it wasn't at all exciting. I had three boys, and I was told they had caused a lot of trouble in the Exiles Village. So I went to them and said that the overseer didn't want to give them permission to go to the south of the Nome, because he thought they were too stupid to make the journey. They were very indignant, and said they had been promised permission to go there, and that they were to be taught a craft. I looked surprised and said, 'Oh, but I thought you didn't want to be taught anything.' They then said that this was a monstrous injustice, that they had as much right to be taught as anyone else and that if they were given the chance they would soon show that exiles were just as clever as the people of the Oryx.

''I promised to try to persuade the overseer to reconsider his decision, adding that I thought it very unlikely that he would. I left them for a while, and then came back to say that the overseer had been inclined to grant permission, but had been unable to do so as he had no one to send with them as a guide; so they would have to wait until someone happened to be making the journey. They looked very disappointed and asked how long I thought they would have to wait, and I said probably for a month or two. Then I added, as though the idea had just occurred to me, 'I'm starting for the south tomorrow. If you want to come with me I can show you the road, but we shall have to go without official permission, and if you break any of the laws of the Oryx I shall get punished for offering to guide you.'

''They assured me fervently that they wouldn't break any

laws, and they didn't; so we had a very uneventful journey.

"They considered it their right to be taught, and the more I told them about our customs, the more they wished to hear. They were like merchants, trying to find out the secrets of another's trade. One of them is going to learn how to be a potter, and the other two are to be apprenticed to the builders-in-stone; it seems that in their own Nome these are considered the most important castes.

"I'm afraid my story is very dull," said Ameni apologetically, "but nothing at all interesting happened...not even a fight!"


# Obedient Monkeys

I had recently appointed an overseer to the new stone-quarry, and was going over the tallies with him, when Meri came to the Room of Seals. I saw that she was worried, so I told the overseer that I would hear the rest of his report the following morning. As soon as he left us I asked Meri what had happened.

"It's Beket: you'll have to talk to her, Ra-ab, I can't do any more. Niyahm was *your* nurse, and Beket is *your* daughter...and I'm tired of defending them from each other! Either Niyahm must stop trying to look after the children or Beket has got to be more tactful with her."

I put my arm round her shoulders. "My love, I'm distressed that you are worried; and comforted that the cause is nothing more serious. When you came in you looked so upset that I thought at least a pestilence had broken out!"

Then I realized that I should have expressed myself with more tact. To Meri this quarrel between Beket and Niyahm had become very important; therefore it *was* important. 'I'm sorry," I said, "it was stupid of me. Tell me what

Beket has done and I'll see if I can find some way to reason with her.''

'I'll send her to you...but I know what will happen. You will try to be cross with her and to look stern, but, by the time she's finished, you will be saying to yourself, 'She's *just* like Kiyas only more so.' And then you'll feel as though you were ten years old again; and you and Beket will be fellow conspirators, thinking of new ways to outwit the grown-ups!''

I felt rather guilty; for though the picture Meri drew was exaggerated, I recognized that a few of the lines were, perhaps, a faithful reproduction.

''You are wrong, Meri, if you think that Beket can influence my judgment. You have often said that it is essential to judge a child as though one were a child oneself. As a grown-up, the things which Beket does may be very tiresome...and even dangerous; but, through the eyes of Ra-ab as he was twenty years ago, her actions are not only understandable but fill me with pride that I am her father...even though that pride is sometimes mingled with exasperation!''

Meri tried to look severe. ''Now *you're* doing it, Ra-ab: twisting serious things so that they seem trivial; and worse, making them look funny! I have scolded Beket and I think she is almost apologetic. If you go and make a joke of it she will be just as naughty by tomorrow.''

''What has she done?''

''It's your fault as much as hers: I told you, years ago, that she mustn't be allowed to bring every animal she has suddenly grown fond of into the house. Toads, and frogs, and rats...two gazelles...they were quite reasonable pets, even though they did eat some of my favorite plants. Then there was that horrible little crocodile you let her keep in the lotus-pool...''

''It was a very *small* crocodile.''

''Yes, but it would have grown; in fact it was growing. I admit that I was thankful when it died, even though Beket wept for hours. She has got five dogs; three of which seem to be constantly having puppies...I suppose that's reasonable for a child who is fond of animals. But is it necessary for her to have four monkeys, with the most disgusting personal habits? To keep three lizards in a box under her bed? To keep a snake in her water-jar?''

''It's not a poisonous snake.''

She stood up and stamped her foot. ''Ra-ab, sometimes I could slap you! You make me look unreasonable, when it's *you* who are being unreasonable. Beket is my daughter too; she is ten, nearly grown-up. She's not interested in clothes, or houses; she's not even interested in the fact that she's growing beautiful! She would have done a lot better if she had been born a hound-boy. I gave her a lovely room on her last anniversary...and now it's unrecognizable. Legs chewed off the furniture, and the curtains I had embroidered for her are torn into strips. And what did *you* do! You deliberately went and gave her a leopard. If she had found it herself it would have been bad enough; but you *gave* it to her!''

''I know I did, Meri,'' I said miserably. ''But you see, when I saw the cub I was not grown-up at that moment; I was the Ra-ab who had so desperately wanted a leopard, and not been allowed to have one. I knew just how much Beket wanted it, because it was a desire that I had experienced; and part of me was *still* experiencing it. Meri, can't you remember how *happy* she was when I gave it to her? And I'm sure it won't hurt her: she's got a kinship with animals which they all recognize. Don't you remember when you first saw her with the cub? I brought you to her room, for it was to be a special surprise: the leopoard was curled up in her arms, purring like a cat. Don't you remember how happy she was?''

Her face softened. ''Dear Beket!'' Then she said firmly, ''No, Ra-ab, she's not always 'Dear Beket.' Those animals of hers are as intelligent as demons, and when she's annoyed with anyone she tells them, and I'm sure they understand.

This morning one of the women servants grumbled to Beket...as well she might, for the monkeys had been eating fruit and had scattered pieces of rind all over the room. I admit that Beket helped to clear it up, but the woman went on grumbling, and Beket said to her, 'Be careful, or the monkeys will hear you!' I suppose they did; because they went to that poor woman's room and tore her best wig to pieces and threw all the rest of her things out the window!''

I felt the corner of my mouth twitch, and with a great effort of will drove away a smile. ''I admit that monkeys are sometimes destructive, but I don't think it would be just to blame Beket for their behavior...any more than it would be just to blame you for what Beket does.''

''I'm *sure* she told them to do it. As soon as I heard about it I went to find her, and she was sitting in the fig-tree at the end of the garden; the two largest monkeys were on each side of her with their arms round her waist, and the other two were sitting on a branch opposite. She was talking to them and they were chattering back to her. I *know* they were telling her what they had done, and that she was praising them! She had been feeding them with pieces of honeycomb, and her hands were disgustingly sticky. When I told her what the monkeys had done, she pretended to be surprised, and then she said to them, 'What naughty little monkeys you are! Haven't I often told you that you must *never* annoy people on purpose!' And she said it in exactly my tone of voice, but it was all done very politely, so I couldn't even be formally angry with her for being impertinent...though she knew as well as I did that she deserved to be scolded!''

''I think you are being rather unfair, Meri. You are remembering the more inconvenient aspects of Beket's really remarkable power with animals, and forgetting the amount of good it had already done. When she first asked that a place be built where sick animals could be brought to be cured, you wished to discourage the idea. It is very seldom that I disagree with you, and even more seldom that I am glad to have done so. But I think you must agree that Beket's idea has proved more than justified. So many sick animals have been cured now that she has fifteen boys whose sole duty it is to care for them; and in addition there is a physician and a young priest of Ptah who devote all their time to healing their younger brothers. I hope there will soon be a similar community in every Nome, devoted both to sick animals and to improving the welfare of animals generally. When all this is weighed in the scales against the trivial inconvenience of the destruction of a servant's wig, I think you will find my attitude of tolerance is fully justified. I also think that a visit to our treasure room would convince you that to replace anything which one of Beket's animals may inadvertently damage is not beyond the limit of our resources.''

There were tears in Meri's eyes, and I was instantly contrite. ''Forgive me for being unkind: it is not that I don't understand how difficult it is to keep all the currents of a great household smooth and unruffled. I will tell Beket to try to keep her animals from annoying the rest of the household... but to her they are like children: and parents seldom realize that the cries of their new-born are not music in the ears of all who hear them!''

I picked Meri up and set her on my knee. ''Let us forget the difficulties caused by our daughter and remember only the peace between ourselves.'' Her cheek was cold and smooth under my lips. Then she relaxed and leaned back against my shoulder.

''I know that I am being mollified,'' she said, and her voice was warm. ''I was determined when I came to you that I was not going to leave this room until I had made you promise that Beket must send away her leopard, and that the other animals must either have an enclosure built for them or in some way be kept out of the house.''

''Let's think of all that another time.''

''You mean, 'Let's *not* think of all that...at any time.' ''

''Perhaps I do.''

"Perhaps you are right; and it is I who am foolish. I may be growing like the woman who kept her house in such a perfect order that her husband couldn't live in it. Do you remember her, Ra-ab?"

"Yes, I remember. Her husband was a cow-herd wasn't he?"

"Yes, she used to make him eat his meals on a bench outside the door, in case he brought mud into the house. She came to me when he refused to enter the house at all, and said he preferred to sleep with the oxen. Do you think I'm getting like her?"

I pretended to look at her very critically. "As yet I cannot see the slightest resemblance. Should I ever see one I will immediately inform you; and I will have my bed carried out to one of the stalls which were built for the noble bulls which came from Heliokios's herd. It would not, I think, be fitting for a Nomarch to share the quarters of a lesser breed of cattle."

"No, Ra-ab, I'm being serious. I always think of you and me as ideal parents: we realize our children are themselves and that we only provided bodies for them to wear. I know that all we can do is to teach them how to cultivate the virtues they have already acquired, and to become strong enough to attain those virtues which they still lack. Why should my daughter be like me? Her face is like mine: but why should her thoughts be mine because of that...if another woman and I wear tunics made from the same roll of linen does that make us twin-sisters? I reproach Beket because she has not all my virtues; and forget to reproach myself because I have not hers."

"My very dear, you and your daughter share many virtues; beauty and courage, and truth, and laughter. And one day she will be wise, as you are wise; for both of you give love and so receive it."

141

# fear in the marshes

I had promised the children, including Nehri who was staying with us, that I would take them down to the marshes at dawn, so that they could show me their progress with the throwing-stick; but I found only Ameni and Senusert waiting for me in the courtyard.

"Where's Nehri? Isn't he coming with us?"

"He decided he didn't want to come," said Ameni. "He's gone off somewhere with Beket, and asked me to tell you."

"But I thought they were both coming."

"He doesn't really like wild-fowling," said Senusert. "He has always pretended he does, because he thought it was necessary for a Nomarch to be good at that kind of thing. Beket only used to come with us because she doesn't like to be left out. She told Nehri last night that she hated to see birds killed. He looked surprised, and then admitted that he didn't like it either. They decided that they didn't mind killing crocodiles...Beket of course added 'except *special* crocodiles,' because she hasn't forgotten the one she used to keep in the pool. Then she said she couldn't come to the marshes because she had heard that a cow belonging to one of the farmers on the western boundary of the estate was ill, and she wanted to go to find out what was the matter with it. Nehri said at once that he'd go with her...either he's as interested in animals as she is, or else Beket is growing up!"

I realized that Beket *was* growing up. Kiyas, at the time of the Blue Death, had been the same age as Beket was now. Then it had taken Sebek to show me that my sister was no longer a child, and now Nehri was playing a similar role.

Ameni had already spent two seasons at the House of Captains, and I decided that Senusert should join him there after the Inundation. While we were walking down to the marshes, I thought it a good opportunity to mention the further plans for him which Meri and I had discussed the previous day.

"Senusert," I said. "I have thought of yet another way by which you may be trained to fulfill the obligations of one of the Eyes of Horus. You are often present while I give Audience, and are already showing remarkable ability in the judgment of petitioners. But accurate judgment can only be gained by experience, and because of the great part you will have to play, which will of necessity cut you off from intimate contact with the common people, I want you to learn as much of their hearts as possible before you become Co-ruler. It is not sufficient to know of their way of life only through your mind; you must in some degree share their experience, know the conditions under which they work, understand their hardships and their pleasures. On a Royal Progress, even though your people know that they may bring their difficulties to you as they would to a near kinsman, you will always be separated from them by the difference in rank. Therefore I have decided that you shall spend twenty days working as a member of some of the principal castes. You may, for instance, live as a fisherman, a small merchant, a field-worker, and a man paying his tribute by labor. You agree with my plan? Think well before you answer, for it will be a hard one to follow."

Senusert's eyes shone with excitement. "Oh yes, Ra-ab, of course I do! Roidahn has often told me about how, before the Dawn, you and Hanuk used to go about Egypt in disguise. He said that is why your Nomes were so happy,...because you made your disguise so convincing that it almost became reality. Can I too go disguised? It wouldn't really be a fair test if they knew I was your kinsman."

My heart warmed to hear him say "your kinsman" instead of the "Royal Heir." Every day he was becoming more a son of the Oryx, and I knew that when the time came for him to return to his father, Meri and I would feel as though our son had gone to live in a distant city.

Ameni, who had gone ahead of us, came back carrying two widgeons and a mallard. ''You had better stop talking if you want to get any birds,'' he said. ''They are coming in fast now. I think something must have been along here and disturbed them, for they are very wary.''

He crouched, and pulled me down beside him. ''Look! Teal—seven of them.''

The birds made a fluid pattern against the morning sky. They may have seen us, for they veered away to the north. I was glad; and realized why Beket had not wanted to come with us.

Ameni must have caught my thought, for he said, ''I'm glad you and Mother decided, as a thank-offering for me being saved from the crocodile, not to allow birds to be snared in the Oryx. It is a filthy kind of death...waiting for a danger from which you can't escape.''

He shuddered, and then laughed at himself. ''It makes me sweat to think of it...even after three years!''

The memory evoked by his words was so vivid that it seemed as though I lived again through that terrible experience....

Meri screamed in her sleep. ''Crocodile! Crocodile! Ra-ab, save him! I can't reach him! The mud's too strong: I can't run! Ra-ab, go to Ameni! Crocodile!

I thought she was only having a nightmare, so I took her in my arms and kissed her gently to wake her, saying, ''Don't be frightened, Meri. You're awake: you are safe with me. Don't be frightened, it was only a dream. You called to me, and I heard you, and now you are safely back in our room.

A shaft of moonlight fell across our bed and I could see that her eyes were wide open. She stared at me without recognition, then put her hand up to her mouth, and before I could stop her, bit her knuckles to try to stifle a scream.

''Meri! Meri! You *must* wake up! You're safe with Ra-ab, *safe!*''

144

Suddenly there was recognition in her eyes: she knew me but the terror remained.

"You'll be all right in a moment," I said soothingly. "You've had a bad nightmare, but now you're awake."

She began to tremble, and her teeth chattered so violently that she could hardly form her words. "It wasn't a nightmare: it was a true dream. Ameni is in terrible danger...not a dream danger, it's happening down here. I've *got* to remember where he is or we shan't reach him in time!"

She covered her eyes with her hands and her body grew rigid.

"Crocodiles! I couldn't get to him because of the mud. He's struggling to get away but he can't move. He's shouting for you, but nobody can hear him...it must be somewhere in the marshes."

"Where, Meri? *Where?*"

"I don't know: I can't remember! Oh, Ra-ab, I can't remember! I know there was something...."

Frantically I implored Anubis to help her to remember.

"It's beside the river...a little further along, the bank curves out and there are some things sticking out of the water...I think they're stakes. Yes, I can see better now. There is a tree on the bank; a white, dead tree."

"It's all right, Meri! I know: there's a sycamore that was struck by lightning, and the stakes belong to an old fish-trap. I can get there in less than an hour."

I thrust my feet into a pair of sandals, and fastened my kilt as I ran down the passage to Ameni's room. I still had a desperate hope that Meri's dream had been only a nightmare. I knew how violently I had clung to this hope when I received the shock of seeing his room empty.

I ran into the outer courtyard, shouting for the guards to join me. I sent one of them to fetch javelins; another to tell the physician to follow us, and to bring litter-bearers with him.

Then I set off, running harder than I had ever run before,

145

the soldiers pounding along the path behind me. Should I take the path to the river and then follow the bank, or risk the shorter way, by which I might get lost in the reeds? The game-tracks were narrow and winding and there was only the moon to guide me...I decided to take the shorter way, and shouted to one of the men to stay where the path forked, to lead the physician and the others with him by the longer, but much surer, path.

Sometimes the dead reeds underfoot gave a firm surface on which to run; then would come patches of soft mud which slowed us down. It was as though at each step I had to drag my feet from the hand of a giant who clutched at them. The water was black as basalt, and in some places the reeds were so high that I could see only a narrow strip of sky above me, and had to follow the twisting tracks blindly, until an opening let me take a fresh bearing from the moon.

When I knew I must be getting near the river, I shouted, ''Ameni! Ameni, where are you?'' Then I paused to listen for an answer above the deafening clamor of my heart. The third time I thought I heard an answering cry, ahead of me and to the right. I plunged on, thrusting my way between the reeds which seemed to claw at me like demon cats. Suddenly I crashed through the last of them and reached the river bank.

''Ameni! Ameni, where are you?''

''Here!''

I recognized his voice; the surge of relief was so intense that it was almost physical pain. ''It's all right, Ameni!''

Above the sound of my running feet, I heard ''Quickly! Oh *quickly!*''

I saw the dead tree, livid in the moonlight. Below it the bank was steep as a cliff: until I reached the edge of it, the mud-flat below was hidden from me. Then I stared down at a scene so terrible that I knew why Meri had awakened screaming.

Ameni was lying head downwards, sprawled on his back. His foot was caught in something, and his hair just brushed the mud at the foot of the bank. He was staring at a crocodile, whose mouth was opening to crush his head between its jaws.

There was only one way to save my son. I must hurl my javelin into that open mouth. Time seemed to stand still: slowly, very slowly, the jaws widened. In the brilliant moonlight I could see the toes of the crocodile's forefeet flex as it slid forward...slowly, so very slowly.

My hand came back, level with the ear; weight on the right foot....''Swing the body smoothly, the spear must be one with the arm.'' I could almost hear the voice of the Master of Javelins. ''One day your life may depend on your skill with the throwing-spear. One day you'll thank me for making you work so hard.'' So much more than my life depended on it now! ''Forward...smoothly...the hand must be one with the spear....''

I saw the haft jutting out of the open mouth. The crocodile reared up and slipped sideways: the threshing tail flashed past Ameni's head. In its struggle it had turned over on its back. I crouched on the top of the bank. ''The bank is about ten cubits high and the light is bad''...I jumped: to land astride the belly of the monster.

I thrust my hunting-knife deep into its throat and dragged on the handle. Slowly the thick skin slid open: blood spurted over me.

I stood up, feeling suddenly faint. The soldiers had arrived; one of them was holding Ameni in his arms. Ameni was saying, ''You needn't hold me. I'm all right. I was setting a snare for a water-rat, I wanted to give one to Beket. Then I slipped and fell head first down the bank, which wouldn't have mattered, but my foot caught in part of the snare....I had made it so well that it wouldn't break. I managed to pull myself up by a bush, but it came out by the roots before I could get my foot out of the loop.''

I walked a little way along the bank to find a pool where I could wash. I stank of the filth from the crocodile's belly, and retched before I could get my body clean.

The physician said that Ameni's ankle was not broken but badly sprained. Ameni protested that he was all right and could easily walk home, so I pretended that the litter had been brought for me and asked him to share it so that he could tell me about his adventure.

"It was very lucky you heard me shouting," he said. "Somehow I knew you'd hear, though I kept on telling myself that I was much too far from the house for it to be any use shouting to you. I think I must have fainted or something silly, a little while before you came. It was when I first realized it wasn't a log, but a crocodile that was moving very slowly toward me. I thought I could see Mother; she was running to me, and then she sank up to her knees in mud and couldn't come further. I could hear her crying out, 'I'm coming, Ameni! Don't be frightened. Ra-ab will come to save you!'

"Then she disappeared and I realized I had only imagined her. It was queer though, for the crocodile was crawling toward me, and suddenly two large birds alighted on its back and stood there screeching and flapping their wings. It tried to snap at them, but they kept just out of reach. They circled round and round above its head. Then it turned and lumbered off toward the river and I thought it had gone. It came back again, but the second time it wasn't nearly so bad, because as soon as I saw it come out of the water I heard you shouting to me....The first shout, not the second."

"What kind of birds were they?"

"I don't know: that's the odd part about it. They were very large...about as big as pelicans but more the shape of heron. I think they must have been white, for they seemed to shine in a funny sort of way...I suppose it was the moonlight. Do you think they were *magic* birds, Father?"

"I'm not sure, Ameni; but I rather think they must have been."

"So do I," he said drowsily. He leaned back against my

148

shoulder, and I felt his tense body begin to relax. Before he fell asleep, he said, "I hope they were magic birds...it's very comforting to have a magic looking after you. Do you think I'll dream about the crocodile if I go to sleep?"

"No, you won't dream about it. The same magic which sent the birds to protect you will let you have only the best kind of dream adventures."

## Royal Tomb

After discussing the matter with both Meri and Senusert himself, I decided that as he had already lived as a fisherman, a potter, and a stone-worker, he should now spend a month with the men who were building the Royal Tomb. Meri and Beket came down to the landing-steps to see him start on his journey; for although we had made our farewells to him before he joined the grain-barge on which he was going north, they wanted to watch until it was out of sight.

"Are you sure we've been wise to send him so far away?" said Meri anxiously. "He's only fourteen, though he's tall for his age."

"If he gets into any serious difficulty he will receive immediate help; for, although he doesn't know it, the overseer under whom he will work is in my confidence."

"Do you think he'll get enough to eat?" said Meri, still anxious.

"He'll get the same as the rest of the workers; and if it is not sufficient, the sooner he finds out about it the better. I wonder whether he will decide to build a pyramid even bigger than his father's, or, after he has discovered what it is like being one of the men who build it, he will design for himself a most insignificant tomb."

"I've already decided what kind of tomb I'm going to

149

build,'' said Beket firmly. ''My sarcophagus will be sunk in the floor, so as not to get in the way, and the door of the tomb will always be open, and round the walls will be feeding troughs, with hay-racks above them, so that any animal who happens to be passing can go in and have a good feed. If it likes being there it can stay as long as it wishes...and if I own any treasure when I die I shall say it is to be used to provide for hay and things, and for someone to keep the drinking-pool at the door always filled with clean water. I think it's silly to have a tomb unless you can make it *useful*. If it was silly enough to stay in there after I was dead, I'd much prefer to have animals for company than a lot of wall-paintings to look at and dull things like furniture. I wonder if poor Senusert will be cross with his father for wanting such an elaborate tomb, and if he'll have any exciting adventures?''

I also wondered: though not until Senusert returned did I hear about them.

''The journey north was interesting,'' said Senusert, ''and often quite exciting because the current was flowing fast. I'm very glad I went by river, for it taught me that as soon as I have the chance I must design a better kind of barge. There will have to be more of them than there are at present, for each will carry a smaller load and have more living-space for the people who work them. There were only three people besides myself in this one, and yet there was hardly room for us to lie down unless we climbed on the grain-sacks. Two of the men were only a little older than me, but the steersman was twenty-four, married, with two children.

''He showed me a row of notches he had cut in the steer-ing-oar, one for each day he had been separated from his wife. He said he was going to try to find work which wouldn't take him away from her, but that it was going to be difficult as his family had carried cargoes up and down river for four generations. I asked him why his wife didn't come with him, and he said that she wanted to, but that there wasn't room for more than four people on the barge, and in any case she couldn't leave the children.

"Then I asked him why a new kind of barge couldn't be built with room for a man to take his family; and he said it could easily be done though it wouldn't be able to carry quite so much cargo. He said it would never happen, because it didn't matter to Pharaoh that a man was parted from his wife. I wanted to tell him that Pharaoh would mind; but I couldn't, because I thought it would make him suspicious of me. But I did say that if he came to the Oryx, work would be found for him which would allow him to stay with his family. I told him that the son of one of your overseer's was a friend of mine and would arrange it.

"I've got another idea about how to make the lives of the barge people happier. There ought to be houses at regular stages along the bank, just as there are wells every two thousand paces on the Royal Roads. In front of each house would be a landing-stage where barges could moor for the night, while the crews could land and have a hot meal and a chance to talk to others who were making a river journey. It is very difficult to cook properly on a barge, and they're not supposed to tie up unless the weather is too unfavorable for any progress to be made.

"When I left the barge, I went, as you told me, to the house of the overseer. He sent me to join a group of boys, all about my own age, who were going up to the pyramid the following morning. We spent that night in huts on the outskirts of the village. Most of the others had come on foot and were tired, so they didn't talk much; a few of them had never been away from home before and were very apprehensive. I think it will take a long time before tribute by labor will be anticipated without fear. The stories of what their fathers, and their fathers' fathers, suffered under the Old Rule, are still too vivid to be easily discounted.

"It took us most of the next day to reach the place where we were to start work, and instead of finding huts to sleep in, there were only shallow trenches, covered with matting. When one of the boys saw these, he said, 'As we've come here to build a house for Pharaoh to sleep in when he's dead, I think he might have given us a better place to sleep in while we're still living! His tomb looks like a palace and our house looks like a tomb!''

''We were each given a cup, a food-bowl, and two strips of coarse wool cloth, which could either be used as covers while we slept, or else one was wound round the waist and the other worn over the shoulders instead of a cloak. The trenches were not so uncomfortable as they looked, for they kept off the wind and were quite dry...but there were four people to each of them so there was no privacy. One of the boys with me snored, and another twitched in his sleep like a dog having a hunting dream.

''We arrived after dark, so we didn't realize until the next morning how unfinished the pyramid is. The foundations are complete, but the outer walls are not yet more than about twenty cubits in height. I believe the tomb-chamber is finished, but only special workmen are allowed to see it, in case we should betray the secret of how it is to be closed. I once heard Father talking about this: I think he is going to seal the passage by granite plugs instead of drop-stones. The inner chambers are stone, of course, but the outer walls, which are six cubits thick, are of mud-brick, and between them and the inner chambers there will be a core of rubble. I'm not sure whether the whole thing will be faced with stone when it's finished...perhaps Father hasn't decided yet.

''There must have been four or five thousand of us. There were very few women...about fifty old ones who baked the bread, and some girls who lived in a shabby little house beyond the pits where the bricks are made. I think perhaps they were concubines of a low caste, though they seemed to take no notice of anyone except themselves and had no fine clothes or ornaments.

''At dawn we took our food-bowls and walked in line past

a man who was serving soup from a large tub. It was mostly hot water with a few vegetables floating in it, and with it we had a piece of bread. I spent all the first day chopping straw which was then taken away to be mixed into the mud...chopping straw sounds very easy, but it isn't after you've been doing it for several hours; you cut your finger if you get careless, and the sharp ends of straw stick into your hands, and get under your fingernails. By noon I felt as though I'd been doing it forever! Then we were allowed to rest for an hour. We could go to fetch a drink from the water-jars...there were plenty of those and the water was clean and fresh...but we didn't get anything more to eat. Some of the new workers had brought food with them from their homes, but it didn't last very long.

"The next day I helped to press the mud into molds. It comes sliding down a wooden channel from the mixing troughs, and as soon as a mold is full it is carried away and left until the mud has hardened enough to be turned out without losing its shape, and then the bricks are sun-dried until they are nearly as hard as stone.

"The days were terribly monotonous; making bricks so exactly like each other that they always seemed to be the same brick. I began to feel like a fly caught in honey, struggling very hard but never getting any further. It was *dead* work...not because we were building a tomb, but because there seemed no hope of us seeing what we were working *for*. The fisherman only has to wait until his net is hauled in to see how Nut has rewarded him for his labor; and in less than a moon the farmer sees the seed he has sown begin its journey to the granary. To produce food, or to weave linen, is to help to sustain the living; it is to share in the life of the Earth. Even to make roads, along which men can travel to seek new friends...that too is alive. But why should men labor, day after day, to bind the stalks of dead corn into clay robbed of its fertility, to build a house which will never warm the cold body that will be its only occupant? Why, Ra-ab, *why?* Why should men build tombs to their own glory?''

''So that they shall remain as records from which men of the future may gain wisdom from the past. Your father knows, as well as you do, that at death the spirit is free of the flesh and takes no thought of its disposal. His tomb is important because it will remind men of the nature of Amenemhet. If he is renowed for wisdom and justice, other men will prosper by following his stature; even if he was false and corrupt, then might wiser men, through his example, avoid the same pitfalls. That is one aspect of the Royal Tombs, but there is another, as necessary even though more material. During the Inundation, thousands of people throughout Egypt cannot carry on their ordinary work because their fields are flooded. Unless by their work through the rest of the year they have gained the right to so long a rest, they might grow discontented if they remained idle. That is why it increases the welfare of our people if work be provided which can be undertaken by unskilled labor when their usual occupation is impossible.''

''But couldn't they build roads instead of tombs?''

''Once they used to do so; but now the Royal Roads are completed and their maintenance is the duty of the Nomarchs through whose lands they pass. I think it is good for men sometimes to work for the future instead of for immediate result: a day cannot be valued until a man can think in centuries.''

''They don't *know* they are working for the future, Ra-ab. Even I didn't understand...but now that you've explained I see why Father wants so great a tomb. But the purpose of its building should be explained to the workers. None of them even know what it is going to look like when it is finished, and by the time the cap-stone is in place many of them may be grandfathers. I think scribes ought to make drawings of how the men of the future will see what we are building; so that we may know where the water-channels will flow and where the avenues are to be planted. Then the work would be alive, and we would gain security from the permanence of the creation in which we shared.''

''That is a wise judgment; are there any other changes you will make when your tomb is being built?''

''This pyramid may take thirty years to complete, yet no effort has been made to provide more than the most temporary shelter for the workers. The food is sufficient to keep them in health, but they seldom get the things they really enjoy...beer, or garlic, or radishes. On their rest-day they should get different food, and there should be story-tellers to entertain them when they have finished the day's work. If a wife wishes to go there with her husband, that should be permitted...for there is plenty of work which women could do. Many of the older men grumble that they have been separated from their wives, and it is one of the things which makes them dread tribute by labor. If the time ever comes for me to build a tomb, I shall try very hard to see that it is not dull for the builders. Did you know that Father was going to visit the pyramid while I was there?''

I nodded, and he went on, ''It's funny, but I think seeing him make a Progress while I was standing in the crowd has cured me of the nightmare of being lost because I was only 'me.' He was coming to inspect the tomb-chamber, and the workers were given a holiday. Early in the morning they began to line the road along which he would pass. He was in an open litter of eight bearers, and he wore the warrior head-dress. I knew that to him I was only part of a great blur of faces; and that the crowd to which I belonged saw him as completely remote from themselves: someone who had never been angry, or tired, or hungry...impassive as a god statue; an object of devotion, a link with the Gods; but never a man who shared emotion with themselves. One day the crowd may see me like that; but because of you, Ra-ab, only a part of my heart will be in the Royal Litter, and the rest will stand beside its brothers in the crowd, and smile at my 'awful royalness.' ''

# Spawn of Set

Senusert was usually present when I received petitioners in Audience, and at the end of the day I used to discuss each judgment with him, explaining the threads I had followed to reach a decision.

''Before you give judgment, Senusert, always try to think as the petitioner thinks, for only then can you understand the seed from which his actions sprang. A knowledge of events in themselves is not enough; you must know the motive for them, and the cause of the motive. It is the cause which is the most important of all, for unless this is removed the motive remains, and similar actions will almost inevitably follow. It is not enough to punish the action, you must try to cure the unbalance which made that action possible. Today we heard evidence of the actions of a thief; now we must decide how he may best be cured. We know he has recently come to our Exiles' Village; that though he has been supplied with everything he needs, he steals whenever he has an opportunity. Yet in hearing what he steals, we find that they are things which seem to have no value except to their original owners. He took from a neighbor's house a bunch of dried flowers, kept because they had been a love-gift; from the store-room of the Village overseer two empty wine-jars, each of which bore an inscription saying that they were a gift from my father in token of honorable service. Then he stole corn from the granary, measure by measure, and buried it under the floor of his house. It was already spoiled when it was found, for that portion of it which had not grown moldy had been eaten by rats. Then he took a polished bone on which a linen-weaver's baby cut its teeth. Curious things for a man to steal, Senusert, but sufficient to give an indication as to why he became a thief.''

''What did they tell you?''

''A bunch of dried flowers; wine-jars which were the gift

of my father; grain, stored by me against famine; a baby's plaything. What have they all in common?''

''The flowers were dead; the wine-jars empty; the grain spoiled; the bone...I suppose the bone was also dead. Did he then so despise himself, that, even though he couldn't help being a thief, he took things which were useless except to one so insignificant as he thinks himself to be?''

''That is sound reasoning, but in this case incorrect.''

''Then did he steal things which people would most mind losing; because he wanted to prove that they were hurt by a trivial loss and therefore weaker than himself?''

''That again is sound reasoning, but not a true interpretation of the facts. You have forgotten what else you have heard about him: that he came from the Sycamore; that he came alone; that his parents died when he was a child...or so he says; that he has no brothers or sisters, nor has he a wife. He has been here for nearly half a year, yet he has made no friend. Now can you guess why he steals such curious things?''

''I think I am beginning to see. He is lonely: he is frightened of loneliness. He longs for friendship, even though he may not realize it, yet he has made no attempt to find a friend. Why? Perhaps because he has a secret which he feels a close friend would discover; a secret which he is desperately anxious to hide.''

''Good, Senusert; very good. Go on.''

''Although he won't admit it even to himself, he wants a friend so desperately that he is driven, perhaps almost against his will, to steal what he thinks will never be given to him. He takes the dead flowers, because he knows, or guesses, that they are cherished as a love token...perhaps he thinks they may be a talisman which will bring love to him. Then he steals the wine-jars because they were a token of honorable friendship; yet he steals them when they are empty, for he wants a friend who will love him in spite of his secret, not because his suspicions are lulled by wine.''

157

''You may be right there; though I think it more probable that he took empty jars because wine should be drunk in company, and to possess wine is bitter when you have no one with whom to share it. Go on, Senusert.''

''He took the bone from the baby, because it represented the baby...the security of family life.''

''You left out the grain hidden under the floor.''

''Oh yes, that was the third thing. Isn't that another symbol of security; protection against future famine, famine not only of food but of friendship? The four things together make up the pattern of the life of a contented man. Flowers; the love between man and woman; wine-jars, the gift to a respected member of the community. Grain which is in the gift of the Keeper of the Granaries, the man who can give food to the hungry; the protector, instead of the friendless outcast. A bone which represents a child...the next generation to which he can hand on the security, the honor, the love, which he has now acquired.''

''You have read the signs as I read them. Now see whether your judgment of what should be done to cure him is also the same as mine.''

Senusert paused before answering, and then said with conviction, ''He longs for friendship, yet dare not seek it. Why? Because he has a secret which makes him go in fear. He will never lose that fear until he has found a friend to whom he can tell the secret; only then will he be free.''

''Again I agree with you. And I think that you may prove to be the friend he needs. He is in one of the rooms of the House of the Petitioners. Go to him tonight, wearing clothes which will lead him to think you come from the same caste as his own. Say that you are to share his room while you are waiting for me to receive you in Audience. I leave it to you to discover a way by which to gain his confidence. You may find it necessary to pretend that you are also a thief or a fellow exile. Use any means you can think of; and remember that your mission is as urgent as though you were a healer-priest, and he suffering from a pestilence which is in your power to cure.''

Senusert came to me early the following morning. His voice was husky, and his eyes looked as though he had not slept.

''Come and have a swim before you tell me what happened,'' I said. ''You look as though you need it; and it's going to be very hot again today.''

He grinned ruefully. ''You'd better dive first, for my head feels so hot that the pool might start to boil when I get into it! I found our patient was so morose that I told him I had succeeded in bribing one of the soldiers to bring us a jar of beer. He brought mead instead. I think it must have come from your store-room, it was so strong! At first my companion refused to share it; and when he did, he insisted on my cup being filled as often as his own. Unless his head is made of granite, I'm sorry for him this morning...nearly as sorry as I was for myself until a few moments ago!''

The cool water revived him considerably, and, as it was very pleasant in the garden, I sent for fruit-juice and a bowl of curds so that we could have the first meal before going back to the house. Only when he had finished eating did he continue his story.

''I suppose we must have drunk more than half the jar of mead before he began to talk. His speech was thick, but after a while it grew exceedingly fluent, and words poured out of him like water through a sluice. His father was a priest of one of the Set temples, somewhere in the North, and his mother was the daughter of a temple guard. She was afraid that if it were discovered that she was going to have a child, either she, or the baby, or both, would be killed. So she fled from her Nome and went to the Sycamore, to seek refuge with a distant kinsman of her father's. But though the family to whom she went gave her shelter, they did so very grudgingly, and when she died, soon after the baby was born, I think they were very sorry it didn't die too. They gave him

159

just enough food to keep him alive, and because they thought the son of a priest of Set was accursed, they would not let him speak to their own children or play with the children of the village. They even made him sleep in a store-room some distance from the main dwelling.

"He must have been terribly lonely, for even the work he had to do did not bring him into contact with people. When he was only a young boy he had to work from dawn till sunset, deepening irrigation ditches and breaking new fields; and at the end of the day he had to groom two pairs of oxen before he was allowed to rest. He was often beaten...his back is still marked with old scars.

"The only person who ever spoke to him was a girl who lived with her widowed mother on the other side of the village. She became the sole object of his affection, and he was convinced that she returned his love. When he was sixteen, he gave her a bunch of moon-daisies on the Festival of Min to show that he wished to ask for her in marriage. She threw down the flowers, stamped on them, and then ran away laughing. It was on the Min Festival of the following year that someone took compassion on him and asked him to join in the village feast. They gave him beer, which he had never tasted before; and he must have drunk a lot of it, for when he began to feel dizzy he thought they had tried to poison him. He attacked his companions with a knife and wounded one of them in the shoulder. He was disarmed, and the headman ordered his kinsman to give two goats as compensation to the wounded man.

"His kinsman shut him up in the store-house for twenty days, with only dirty water and raw grain to eat. He was very ill after that, he said, with an affliction of the bowels. Anyway he wasn't strong enough to do as much work as they expected of him; and, whenever he disobeyed, they starved him again, until he was so weak that he was forced into obedience.

"Soon afterwards the daughter of his kinsman married and

had a baby. One day, when it was about three years old, it was playing in the field where he was working, and it fell and bruised its leg. He carried it back to the house. The mother screamed when she saw him holding the child, and said that by touching it he had brought it under the influence of Set. When he tried to explain that he had only brought it back to her because it was hurt, she spat in his face, and cursed him, saying, 'You, who were born the child of Set, defile everything you touch. The house which you enter is unclean, and he who calls you friend proves himself to belong to the Caverns.'

''That's why he came to the Oryx. He had heard that we accepted outcasts, and, believing himself to be evil, he was bitterly disappointed to find that our people belonged to Ra; for he had thought that among the children of Set, to whom he imagined all outcasts belonged, he would at last find a friend.''

Senusert broke off and laughed, ''I hope that he is still feeling as friendly toward me as he did last night. When he was sure that I was not going to cringe away from him, he was not certain whether I was as evil as he was, or whether he had deceived himself about his own character! He kept on saying, 'I don't mind who you are, or where you come from. Spawn of Set you may be, and your house may stink of crocodiles. But you're my *friend!* Anyone who denies it has got to fight me! My arms are as strong as an ape's, even though I'm not so tall as some people. I'll be a good friend to you, and I'll never be particular as to what you do. If you want a man killed, well, I'll help. If you want to poison one of your relations...well, I'll help. A friend, that's what I am. A *friend!*' Then he went to sleep with his head on my shoulder, and snored so loudly I was nearly deafened!''

''You have done excellently, Senusert. It is interesting to see that we were right. Each theft *did* point to the motive and the motive led you to what had caused it. The flowers; cherished, not thrown down as his were. The empty wine-

161

jars; instead of one filled with beer that led to conflict. The grain hidden under the floor; so that he would never starve if he were shut in there as a prisoner. The plaything of a child; which he can touch as though it were the child itself and yet do it no harm. What shall we do with your new friend?''

''He was right when he said he had strong arms. I should know that well enough, for he hugged me when he said I was his brother and nearly staved in my ribs! I think he would make a good oarsman, and it is a companionable life. I told him that your chief steersman was a friend of mine and would have him trained to take a place in one of your barges. I even told him that one day he might row in Pharaoh's barge!''

He stood up and stretched his arms above his head and laughed again. ''It is very good to be alive, Ra-ab. My head has stopped aching and the sun is warm. This is another day in which to find new friends!''

# PART THREE

# Domestic Scene

As the steady beat of my rowers brought me round the bend of the river, I saw a small boat coming toward us under full sail. Then I recognized the solitary occupant as Beket. She hailed me, and the steersman altered course toward her; she furled the sail and let her boat drift on the current until we drew level. I was not surprised to see her, for she had often come to meet me on my return from a river journey. Usually she came with me in the barge while her boat was towed behind us; but this time she asked me to sail home with her.

"Please come with me, Father. There's something terribly important that I want to talk to you about."

Not until I was alone with her, and the barge had again set course down-river, did she tell me what was the matter.

"Father, you've *got* to help me: I know you hate disagreeing with Mother, but this is one of the things we understand and she doesn't. It's about my leopard: he scratched Niyahm. It was entirely her own fault; she tried to drag him out of my room by the scruff of his neck, instead of asking him to follow her. So of course he got cross and tried to push her away with his paw...I suppose he had forgotten that his claws are so sharp. It wasn't a very deep scratch, though it bled rather badly. Niyahm made a tremendous fuss, and Mother was sent for; she got a healer-priest, and though he assured Niyahm that her arm will soon heal, she is convinced that it's poisoned and that she will never be able to use it properly again. Mother was very angry with me for saying that it was Niyahm's own fault; she told me to go to my room and stay there until you got home, and my poor leopard has been shut in one of the storerooms, and Mother says he's going to be sent away. Please, Father, don't let her do it; you *must* make her understand that it wasn't really his fault.''

''It was my fault really, Beket, for having given him to you. I suppose your grandfather was right, and your mother was right...a leopard isn't a suitable pet for any child...even one who is so specially good with animals as you are. What if he had scratched Nekht instead of Niyahm? Nekht might have been crippled.''

''He wouldn't have scratched Nekht: Nekht loves him nearly as much as I do. Niyahm has always hated him, and so she deserved to get hurt.''

''You can't be sure he wouldn't scratch Nekht...the boy's only eight, and sometimes small children hurt animals without meaning to.''

''My leopard is much more intelligent than Niyahm; he knows what people mean. Animals are much more reliable than humans; they don't get muddled up with words, they know what people feel. Even wise people like you and Roidahn sometimes only hear what people say and not what they really think. When feelings get turned into words they sometimes get distorted. You've got to *feel* what an animal's telling you, and it feels what you're telling it. That's why I can talk to them and they can talk to me...words don't matter; they can hear what I'm thinking.''

I sighed. ''It's all very difficult, Beket. I believe I understand how you feel, but I also sympathize with Meri and Niyahm.''

''You oughtn't to sympathize with them: they are being deliberately stupid. Perhaps Niyahm isn't being deliberately stupid: she was born like that and has never grown out of it. But Mother could understand if she would only try: she isn't the kind of person who should be blinded by unimportant things...like furniture and clothes and terribly clean houses. She's getting more like that every day, and you've got to stop her. The Watchers are meant to teach people to be happy, yet she'd rather have me sitting in a disgustingly tidy room, wearing a new tunic and being entirely miserable and no use to anyone, than learning important things about animals...things they really need people to know about, and being happy and useful...even though I might look rather dirty. She's even getting a special kind of voice to talk to me in; as though I wasn't her daughter or even somebody she liked. She talks about my animals as though they weren't really people at all. I said to her the other day, 'I think your servants are very tiresome.' And she scolded me for talking like that, and said that I must never say 'servants' as though they were all the same, because they were individuals just as much as she and I were. Of course I knew that! I'd only said it to try to teach her how rude it was to talk about animals as though they were no more different than grains of sand...I expect grains of sand are different too, if only one had the sense to see it. Do you remember how tiresome Senusert used to be when he thought of himself as separate from the "common people?" You used to tell him that he would never be really royal until he recognized his kinship with everyone. Mother recognizes her kinship with *people*, but she won't recognize that she's a relation of my leopard just as much as she's a relation of the gardener. She used to tell me stories about the plants being my little sisters: they were true stories too in a way, but I don't think she realized it. It's easy enough to be a sister to a lotus...which only wants to grow in its pool and is no trouble to anyone; yet she thinks it's grand to deny that I have any kinship with a leopard or a monkey...just because they don't happen to behave as she thinks they should!''

I forgot that I was a Nomarch who ruled over the welfare of thousands. I was a man desperately trying to think of a way by which he could make peace between his wife and his daughter, and yet keep it with them both. ''Beket, are you sure you aren't being almost unkind to your animals by making them live in a human environment? Wouldn't they be happier living in the wild state, instead of having to adapt

165

themselves to conditions which must be unnatural to them?''

She looked at me as though I had said something which deeply shocked her. ''How *can* you say that, Father! Have I ever made an animal stay when it wanted to go away? Have I ever tied them up or put them in cages? They have always been free. I have never, never tried to persuade them to stay if they wanted to go. I have never made them into prisoners!''

''Of course you haven't! I'm sorry, Beket...forgive me for asking such a stupid question. But couldn't they have a special house built for them, so that they wouldn't be inconvenient to people who weren't wise enough to understand them?''

''I suggested that to Mother, but she wouldn't listen. I wanted her to let me build a house where I could live with them, but she said it was a ridiculous idea. Mother wouldn't like it if Nekht had been sent to live in a house all by himself just because he cried when he was a baby and kept people awake. She knows Nekht needs her, but she won't believe that my animals need me. They require to be loved and to have someone they love: that's how they grow. I talked a lot about it to Nekht-ahn, and he agrees with me. He said, 'Human beings are to animals as the Gods are to us: they are different rungs of the ladder between the sand the the stars.' I expect water-weed thinks fish are a kind of God; the weed is tethered by its roots and can only move a little way in the current: the fish suddenly appears and then vanishes. And I expect the fish thinks that a bird is a kind of God; for the fish dies when it comes out of the water, but a bird is free of the air. That's why I can't betray my animals, any more than Ptah can betray me. If I *did* betray them I should cut myself off from the Gods as well as from humans. I should be dead, really dead...even though my body went on walking about and other people thought I made most intelligent conversation about things I knew weren't of the least importance.''

''I do sympathize with you, Beket; and I think you're

right. But you must try to understand people who are not yet aware of all their links. You are too young to remember the first people who came as exiles to the Oryx: they made some of our people very unhappy, and I nearly sent them away. It was your mother who persuaded me to give them another chance...try very hard to give her another chance to understand you. It isn't easy to keep a great household contented, but she nearly always manages to do so; even when she herself is tired, when she would like to be able to allow herself to be irritable. I'm sometimes very tiresome too, Beket; I make plans for how people shall be taught to be happy, but I often forget to make allowances for my plans not working. Meri is more tolerant than I am, and wiser."

"Sometimes she's much, much stupider!"

"Aren't you and I often very stupid too?"

"You're not: you're the wisest man in Egypt. Even Senusert agrees to that, and he's going to be Pharaoh."

"I don't feel very wise. I know that somehow I've got to make a plan by which you can keep your animals and yet not disturb the household; by which Meri will not feel I am joining you against her: and by which Niyahm will not again be hurt either in her person or her feelings!"

"I'm sorry about Niyahm, really I am. If only she hadn't made so much fuss I should have been even sorrier. She squealed much louder than Nekht did when he fell out of the tree and cut himself so badly."

We were opposite the landing-stage; and as Beket furled the sail she said, "Mother's coming along the path to the water-steps. Promise you won't let her make you send my leopard away?"

"I can't promise, but I'll try very hard!"

I can never remember feeling more ineffectual than I did when I went to my room late that night. Meri and I had disagreed before, but until now we had never parted without reaching an understanding. I was torn between my loyalty to her and my loyalty to Beket. I tried to show Meri that to part our daughter from her leopard would amount to cruelty: but Meri remained obdurate. Her final words were ''I have allowed myself to be persuaded too often, Ra-ab. Now I have come to a decision and nothing you say will make me change it. Niyahm has been hurt...fortunately not seriously; but it might just as well have been Nekht. I refuse to risk his life just because you will not take a reasonable view of Beket's excessive affection for an animal which is an entirely unsuitable pet. You enjoy the feeling that you understand the children better than I do. Fortunately you have me to protect you from the probable consequences of this over-sentimentality.'' Meri and I then accused each other of having no sense of proportion. Neither of us had...or we should not have allowed a small disagreement to grow into a quarrel which was agony to us both.

Meri had sent Beket to her room as a punishment for having disobeyed her orders to remain there until I reached home. I went down to the store-room in which the leopard had been shut-up. The door was open: Meri had no right to send the animal away without first getting my agreement! I was so angry that I nearly went to Beket's room to comfort her, but realized that this might seem a betrayal of my love for Meri.

I went back to my own room and tried to sleep. Dawn found me still awake. I tapped on the shutters of Meri's room, but though I heard her moving about they remained closed and she would not answer me. My eyes ached with sleeplessness, and I went down to the swimming-pool and dived again and again until my head felt less as though it were filled with millet-porridge.

I decided that this ridiculous feud must cease, and I went to Beket's room, intending to ask her to help me find a way of ending it.

Her room was empty. On the bed, which had not been slept in, was a clay tablet, with my name at the top above several rows of hastily formed writing-signs.

''You and Mother are unhappy because of me. Watchers must be happy. I shall be safe and happy where I am going. I will send a messenger to tell you when I have arrived. Leopard, monkeys and dogs go with me. I will send for the other animals.—BEKET.''

My first reaction was of anger against Meri. She had driven my daughter out of my house!...Without pausing to consider that her unhappiness would be as great as my own, I burst into her room. I could see that she had been crying, yet even this did not make me soften my bitter news.

''You will no doubt be glad to hear that in future your household will no longer suffer disturbance by Beket.''

''What do you mean?'' Her voice was sharp.

''She's gone: you will probably never see her again.''

''She's gone! Where?''

''She has run away, because she knew she had become the source of strife between her parents. Where she has gone I don't know. I can only pray that she will find shelter with people who will treat her with more consideration than we have done.''

''We must find her at once, Ra-ab, and bring her back. Something terrible may have happened to her. She may be lost...or drowned.''

''There can be nothing more terrible than receiving unkindness from a person you love. We both love her, but we made her unhappy. Now she is gone.''

''*Do* something, Ra-ab! Don't just stand there talking! Send people to look for her...to the marshes, the river... everywhere.''

''I shall not send after her.''

''And why not?''

''I shall try to treat her with the consideration with which she treated her animals: she always left them free to come and go as they pleased. When she can find it in her heart to do so she will come back; until then we can only pray that she will not always think of our home as a prison.''

Meri put her hands over her face, and I knew that she was crying bitterly. My anger left me; I felt cold and alone.

"Meri," I said hesitantly. "Meri...we mustn't quarrel any longer. That's why Beket has gone away...so that we shouldn't quarrel."

"I have failed her, Ra-ab. I have failed both of you. I have been cruel and selfish and ignorant...and I only did it because I loved her and wanted to protect her. I suppose I was jealous that you understood her so much better than I did; because she was the only person who has ever been able to come between us. Ameni and Nekht have always been *our* children, but she has always been so much more yours than mine. Please, Ra-ab, will you ever be able to forgive me?"

"Oh, my dear, it is I who should be forgiven." I took her in my arms, and her tears were salt on my lips.

"Do you think she'll be safe? Oh, Ra-ab, do you think anything terrible will happen to her?"

"No, I'm sure it won't," I said, with a conviction I was far from feeling. "She will probably come back tomorrow, perhaps even today. She may have gone to Roidahn, or to join Ameni and Senusert at the House of the Captains."

"Couldn't you send messengers to anywhere you think she might be; not to *look* for her but just to ask if anyone's seen her?"

"Yes, I will do that immediately. Try not to worry, Meri, I expect we shall have news of her before tonight. She may have gone to Kiyas. I will send down to the river to ask if any of the fishermen have seen her."

"Tell them to find out whether her boat is at the landing-stage. If it is gone we shall know she has followed the river. Is it windy today?"

"No, there is only a light breeze, so she can't have gone far."

"You go and send out the messengers: tell them to be swift. And I'll go to question the household servants, in case any of them heard her go."

I held Meri close; she was no longer crying, but she was trembling as though with fever. "What shall we do when she comes back...today or tomorrow?"

"I'll tell her I am so very sorry I was horrid, and ask her to forgive me. Then I'll ask her to help me find a way by which we can all know peace together. Pray hard, Ra-ab, pray very hard, that she will want to come back to us very soon and know that she will be received only with love."

## nomarch's Emissary

The following afternoon I had news: a fisherman had seen Beket on a grain-barge going up-river. It had cargo for the Hare, so I guessed that she was going to Nehri. When I told Meri, she said:

"Your rowers can overtake the barge by sunset; you must start at once and bring her back."

"I have already told you that I am not going to bring her back."

"Ra-ab, that's nonsense! It's not safe for a child to be alone...and what would Nehri's mother think if Beket were to arrive there, unattended and uninvited!"

"To your first two objections I must answer that she is not alone; the steersman of the barge is a Watcher, and she will be perfectly safe in his care. She is thirteen in years and older than that in character. As to what Sebu will think...mind you I am not sure yet whether she is going to them; I am afraid that we must accept whatever Sebu chooses to think of us."

"But it will bring dishonor to the Oryx!"

"It cannot do so unless we deserve dishonor...and it is probable that we do, for a happy child does not run away from its parents."

"How can you say anything so cruel, Ra-ab? Last night

171

we wept together, and now you are trying to make me even more unhappy about Beket than I am already.''

''Last night you remembered only that you loved Beket, and regretted that you had not shown her sufficient understanding. Now she is only the daughter who is being inconvenient, who is doing something which will bring you discredit. Before you and Beket can love each other, you must see her as she *is*, not as you wish her to be. I know that it is hard for you to have a daughter who differs from the image you created in your heart before she was born. You want to give her toys, and clothes and lovely rooms. You want to share the pleasures that she should feel for being beautiful. You want to see yourself in her, both as a woman wise in maturity and as Meri the girl who still waits for her husband. Meri, you are wise, and generous, and very dear to me; but you must learn to give people what they want, instead of only giving them what you yourself would wish to receive. You expect Beket to love the jewels you give her, though to her they are dead metal; yet you have never tried to love her monkeys, for to you they are only a source of disturbance in your household. It needs great wisdom to know the needs of those you love: the desert tribes will barter gold for a handful of salt, but if you give salt to a man dying of thirst he would think you mocked him.''

A tear trickled down her cheek, and she brushed it away with her hand. ''I was proud of being generous, and now you have made me feel that I only give away things that I don't want.''

''Then my words have been traitors to my thoughts: you would give your last handful of millet to any hungry stranger. And I have never known anyone who has a greater power of knowing the hearts of others. I think the only reason why you found it difficult to know Beket's heart is because you take it for granted that your daughter should be like yourself. With your mind you know this is

172

not true, yet you still believe it...and in so doing follow the heresy that man can find immortality through his child. Niyahm embroidered your dress, but do you *think* like Niyahm because you are wearing it? We made a body for Beket; and now we are sorrowful because she has proved you a fool who expected her soul to be a reflection of your own.''

In extreme anxiety I waited for further news of Beket. Although I had convinced Meri that our daughter was going to the Hare, I was by no means sure whether this was true. I had sent two soldiers to follow the barge, with orders to inform me immediately if she should go farther than the neighboring Nome. On the seventh day after her departure, a runner arrived to announce that an emissary from the Nomarch of the Hare would reach me before sunset. I was virtually certain this would concern Beket, but thought it best not to tell Meri until my hopes were confirmed.

Late in the afternoon, a carrying-litter escorted by twenty soldiers wearing the insignia of a Nomarch's bodyguard entered the outer courtyard: obviously the emissary was someone of importance acting in an official capacity. The emissary proved to be Tet-hin-an, Nehri's uncle, who had ruled the Nome of the Hare until, three years previously, the boy became Nomarch. Tet-hin-an was short of stature and inclined to stoutness, but the laughter-wrinkles round his eyes were a true indication of his character.

''It is not often that I travel in such state,'' he said, ''but my young nephew insisted that everything be done with proper formality. I was lucky to be allowed to come with a bodyguard of only twenty; if Nehri had not been so impatient for me to start, he'd have sent me looking like a Royal Progress!''

''Would it be to display undue curiosity if I were to ask the official purpose of your most welcome arrival; or must that be delivered with all formality?''

He looked round to make sure that his attendants were out of hearing, then said, ''There is no need for formality between you and me, Ra-ab. I had to pretend to be formal so long as the men could hear me; otherwise it would look as though I didn't respect the boy's wishes. He's a good boy, even though he does take himself rather seriously. I expect you and I did when we were young...perhaps you still do, but wait until you're as old as I am, and then you'll begin to enjoy the full humor of life!''

''Then I can take it that you do not bring bad news?''

''Bad? No! On the contrary; best thing that could have happened. I thought of sounding you on the subject years ago, but decided that if Nehri knew what I was doing it might make him change his mind. Young people are sometimes very contrary, and won't believe that romance and expediency can sometimes be found in the same bed.''

''Romance?''

''Yes. Surely you know all about it?''

''Am I right in thinking you are talking about Beket?''

''Of course! That's why I've come to you. I am the official emissary between Nomarch and Nomarch, asking that the Oryx shall honor the Hare, by giving in marriage Beket, Daughter of the Oryx, to Nehri, Nomarch of the Hare... there is a lot more of that kind of thing, all very formally set out on ivory tablets which the scribes were working on until an hour before I left home. I wish you had been there, Ra-ab, to see me receiving my orders! First I was told that everything must be done strictly in accordance with precedent; but when I asked what I should say if you refused to sanction the marriage, Nehri forgot to be aloof and shouted, 'Then you can tell him that Beket is here and she's going to stay here. We both want to get married and we shall take the Oath before Ptah whether he likes it or not!''

''What did his mother say?''

''In her heart she is delighted, for she has always hoped for an alliance between the Nomes. She told Nehri that he ought to wait until Beket is a little older; but when they pointed out that she is the same age as Nefer-tathen was when she married Pharaoh, Sebu couldn't think of another objection. I can almost hear her saying, 'My dear daughter, so young, so happy...just the same age as the Royal Wife at *her* marriage.' My sister is an admirable, if rather unimaginative, woman, and you can be sure that she will be very kind to Beket. She was devoted to the boy's father and is zealous for his happiness...and no one who saw Beket and Nehri could do anything but rejoice with them. I am an old man, but it made me feel young again.''

He chuckled, ''I think Nehri has loved Beket for years; that's why I was sure my news would be no surprise to you. When they came up to the house—he had been out in his sailing-boat and met the barge on its way to the landing-stage—they were hand in hand and looked as though they were walking through the Fields of Ra. She was wearing a very crumpled tunic, and the hand that wasn't in Nehri's was holding a rope which led a leopard. Four large monkeys were ambling along behind them, followed by five dogs and a goat...yet she looked like a Queen leading a Royal procession.''

For a moment I did not answer, fearing my voice would betray my emotion. I had been so sure that in a few days Beket would come home to me; and that this time Meri and I would make her really happy. But now I wasn't going to have the chance. She had gone to the man who would make her happy where I had failed. Then I realized how selfish I was being. Only a few days ago I had said to Meri, ''You must always give people what they want; not what you wish to give them.'' Beket wanted Nehri: how ungenerous it would be if I were to make her unhappy because I wished her to receive happiness only at my hand.

''You have told me all I need to know before I give my sanction to this marriage. Beket is happy, and if Nehri were a fisherman, my answer would still be that, so long as my daughter rejoices in his company, he is my son.''

# magic of ptah

Meri, to my relief, put no obstacle in the way of the marriage, though she was momentarily distressed that Beket wished to stay with Nehri's mother until after the ceremony. But when I said that it was wise that Beket should get to know her new kinswoman; and that, as Nehri was Nomarch, it would be according to tradition for the marriage to take place in his Nome instead of in ours; any lingering doubts she may have had were dispelled.

''At last Beket will appreciate beautiful clothes,'' she said contentedly. ''She will need even more than I did, for when we were married you were not yet Nomarch. I shall give her some of my bracelets, and Neku must design some more for her; and of course she will need head-dresses and necklaces as well. Then she must have her own furniture: I will have it painted with animals, for that will be sure to please her. You must look at the tallies of the things Father sent with me, and she shall have twice as much. Shall we travel by road or water? I think we should go by river, for we shall have so much to take with us.''

After a great deal of thought, Meri decided that Beket's wedding dress should be of white mist-linen embroidered with little blue hares, and that Neku should design jewels of silver and lapis lazuli for her to wear with it. Meri chose all our gifts to Beket, leaving to me only the selection of the treasure which would be given to Nehri in Beket's name. But there was one gift I chose myself: two young mouse-deer, small as hunting-dogs, which had been brought from the Far South by one of the men I had sent there to search for medicinal plants. I looked after them myself, and soon they became accustomed to being handled. They were clean and gentle, very intelligent and affectionate. Meri soon grew fond of them; she let them come into her rooms whenever they wished, and often helped me to feed them. I had a little house made for them, the size of a large chest: one side of it was barred, and it had a handle at each end so that it could easily be carried. It was in this that they usually slept, so that, when they were taken in it down to the boat, they would not be frightened.

Sometimes I wondered whether Meri became so absorbed in the gifts for Beket to try to make herself forget how we missed the sound of our daughter's voice. Often, in the middle of talking on an entirely different subject, she would suddenly say, "Beket is going to be very happy," as though trying to reassure herself.

I knew that she was secretly worried lest Beket had stayed in the Hare only because of the estrangement. She tried to hide this fear from me, yet often unconsciously betrayed it. I remember her saying:

"As soon as I met you, Ra-ab, I was impatient to leave my home. Even if I had been much closer to Father than I was, I should have wanted to leave him, so that I could be alone with you. Do you remember what a terrible waste of time it seemed having to wait until we were betrothed?"

"I am glad that Beket had the courage to refuse to be parted from Nehri," I said. "Do you remember how we hated leaving the island on the evening we told each other of our love? If we had not had to work for the Watchers I should never have let you go back to the Royal City. Do you remember how I wanted you to come to the Oryx with me at once?"

"It will be different when Ameni wishes to marry," she said, "he won't have to go away from us....He doesn't seem very interested in women, does he?"

"That's what they used to say about me. Yet have you found me take too little interest in you?"

"You are my most perfect husband: even if I could remember all the hundreds of times I must have been married during the "long years" I should still say so. You have only one fault...you make me pity all other women because they are not married to you."

It was two months later, seven days before Beket's fourteenth birthday, that we started on our journey to the Nome of the Hare. With us came Ameni, Senusert, Nekht and a hundred of our friends and kinsmen, together with their attendants. The boats, of which there were twenty, were garlanded with flowers and gay with pennants.

Nehri was on the landing-stage to meet us, and said that, by his mother's request Beket had agreed to wait for us at the house. It was only a short distance from the river, so we went on foot along a wide avenue, lined with festival mats flying the white and blue of the Hare alternately with the yellow and white of the Oryx. A laughing, excited crowd had gathered to see us, and, even if I had known nothing of Nehri, they would have shown me that he was well loved by his people. He was telling Senusert how greatly he and Beket had been honored by the magnificence of Pharaoh's gifts. I smiled to myself to hear the two boys talking so informally, each so conscious of his young dignity. I thought of them returning covered with mud from some adventure which had included crossing a marsh or an unexpectedly deep ditch; or pummeling each other at the height of a quarrel. I realized that Ameni was thinking along the same lines, for he whispered to me, "How very Royal we are all being!" He grinned, "Do you think Beket will expect me to place her foot on my forehead in sign of humility; or will she be content to leave that privilege to the Royal Wife?"

Sebu was waiting to greet us at the top of the steps which led up from the outer courtyard; but to my surprise there was no sign of Beket.

"I wonder where she is?" I said to Ameni. "Surely she hasn't grown shy!"

"If they have made her lose her self-confidence I shall carry her off home: and if knocking Nehri down isn't sufficient, the two Nomes had better go to war!"

I began to feel anxious. Why wasn't Beket here? Why hadn't she come down to the landing-stage? Was she afraid

178

of meeting Meri...did that mean she still felt bitter toward her mother? I wondered if Meri was worried; but when I looked round I saw she was laughing at something that Tet-hin-an had just said to her.

Sebu was a tall, spare woman, looking older than her forty years. Her life had not been happy: as a young woman she had lost both her daughters in the pestilence, and a few years later her husband had been killed in battle. She had been well content to leave authority in the hands of her brother, though I felt sure she had kept herself fully informed of everything that was done in the name of her son.

I saw Nehri raise his eyebrows in an unspoken question. She shook her head, and said something to him in a low voice...I only heard the words, ''She won't listen...soon, I think.''

We were all puzzled at Beket's absence, but no one had the courage to ask outright where she was. At last, Meri, trying to make her voice sound casual, said to Sebu, ''I hope that Beket is well?''

''Her health matches her happiness; both, may the Gods be praised, are perfect.''

With this we had to be content, and Sebu led us into a long room which opened on one side to formal gardens that flowed down to the river.

''You must be impatient to see Beket,'' said Sebu. ''But she will be with us in a moment. The dear child was so excited that I told her to rest before your arrival. They must have forgotten to wake her, and I expect she is delaying to make herself beautiful for you.''

I saw Meri look at Sebu with a new respect, and could almost hear her thinking, ''You must be a very remarkable woman, if you have made Beket so interested in her appearance that it has become more important to her than greeting her parents.''

We were served with wine, or cool fruit-juices; and girls, who wore blue tunics and wreaths of convolvulus, offered little cakes on alabaster dishes. I knew that Sebu was growing increasingly impatient at Beket's absence, though she tried to conceal it with a bright flow of conversation. To try to put her at ease, Meri said:

"I think it is *so* wise of you to let the child sleep. She will have told you that there is little formality in the Oryx, and she has never been respectful of the hours."

Sebu took this as an indication that we no longer thought it necessary to wait for Beket. "As all of you will wish to rest after your journey," she said, "it would perhaps be best if I take you and your husband to your apartments and Beket can join you there."

We followed her through three communicating rooms into a wing which ran west from the main building. Having made sure that we had everything we required, she left us.

"Ra-ab, what *has* happened to Beket?"

"That's what I'd like to know! It can't be anything serious or Nehri would have told us at once. I watched him carefully to see if he was angry that she wasn't there; and I think he was watching me to see if I was angry."

"You don't think she is trying to avoid us, do you? Not you, but me, I mean? Do you think she hasn't forgiven me for being so horrid?"

"Of course she's forgiven you...and there wasn't anything to forgive."

"I love her so much, Ra-ab...much more than even you realize."

"I know you do, my very dear."

Suddenly she caught hold of my arm, "Ra-ab, what's that!"

I listened, and heard a moan of pain, rising to a wail.

"Ra-ab, somebody's ill. Perhaps it's Beket, and they're trying to hide it from us!"

I tried to give my voice an assurance I did not feel. "No, I'm sure it's not Beket."

"But it might be. Oh, Ra-ab, I'm frightened!"

"I'll go and find out what it is."

"I'll come with you. It came from over there. We'll go that way; I expect all the rooms open on the garden."

Again I heard the wail, and broke into a run. I pulled open the door of a room next to those allotted to us. The shutters were closed, and for a moment I could see nothing outside the shaft of dazzling sunlight which shone through the open door. Then I heard Beket's voice:

"Shut the door or you'll frighten her. Tell someone to go to fetch Nehri. He must come here at once. She is very ill."

Beket was crouched beside the bed on which lay her patient. She was looking down at a dark face, puckered with pain, from whose lips came a pitiful whimpering. "Hurry!" she said imperiously, "I told you to fetch Nehri!"

Then she looked up and saw us. "Oh, I'm so glad you've come! Sebu will be cross because I wasn't there to meet you...or she would be if Nehri ever let her be cross with me. You understand, don't you? I couldn't leave her while she's in pain."

"Of course you couldn't," said Meri. She knelt and put her arms round Beket. "Ra-ab can go to find Nehri and I'll stay here to help you. She's having a baby, isn't she?"

"Yes, but it seems to have got stuck. I was with her sister when her baby was born, but then it was quite easy. She wanted me to hold her hand, but she wasn't in this awful pain."

"I wish Yiahn was here," said Meri. "But he let me help him when some of our women couldn't have their babies easily, so I may have learned enough to be useful." Then she glanced up at me, "Ra-ab, go and fetch some hot water, very hot, and some cloths...heat may help to relieve the spasms. And get me a flask of oil. You will find it in my toilet chest."

I decided that this was more important than fetching Nehri, and, being fortunate enough to meet a servant who was carrying a jar of hot water to one of the other guests, it was only a short time before I was back.

"Wring out one of the cloths in the water," said Meri. I did so, and very gently she laid it on the contorted belly. Then she asked for the oil and poured some of it on her fingers.

"Hold her hands tightly, Beket, I am afraid this may hurt her. If the baby is pressing against a bone I may have to try to move it. Ra-ab, hold her feet in case she struggles."

The frantic whimpering broke out again. "My poor, poor dear," said Beket in an anguished voice. "You will soon be better. Mother will make you better."

"It's going to be all right," said Meri. "I can feel the baby's arm. Give me some more oil, Ra-ab, and press very gently on the pit of her stomach. Now I can feel it's head... it's coming down into my hand."

Again a shrill wail of pain. And Meri's voice saying triumphantly, "Look, it's all right! It's alive! You needn't hold her now; it doesn't matter if she struggles, and I don't think she will. Give me a cloth to wrap the baby in, it mustn't get cold."

"Isn't it *lovely!*" exclaimed Beket. "He's much more beautiful than his cousin was. Look at his lovely little hands!"

The baby set up a curious shrill squealing. "Ought he to go back to his mother, or shall I look after him?" asked Meri.

"She's not ready for him yet."

"If you like, he can sleep in our room. Look, he's not at all frightened of me."

A little black hand curled round Meri's finger. There were tears in Beket's eyes. "Oh, Mother, you're so much, much more lovely even than I thought you were."

We all embraced each other; and I was so happy that I was grateful to the semi-darkness which hid the tears in my eyes. I had been so afraid that Meri and Beket might find it difficult to open their hearts to each other again; that meeting in an atmosphere of formality might have made a constraint between them. But the Gods had been very generous, and allowed no barriers to grow between these two women whom I so dearly loved, arranging for them to meet where the magic of Ptah, which is manifested at every birth, allowed them to see each other as they really were.

The baby gave another shrill cry, and a muffled shout seemed to echo it from the garden. Beket exclaimed, "That's the baby's father. I told them to keep him shut up until his baby was born...I wonder who let him out."

The door swung open. The father looked very suspicious; but when Beket said to him, "No one is going to hurt your family," he sprang on the bed-place and crouched down beside his wife. She snuggled up to him and he patted her consolingly.

"I'll let him see his son," said Meri.

"You had better let me do it," said Beket. "He's not very friendly except to people he knows."

"He won't mind me. He knows that I'm his friend."

She put the baby in the crook of it's mother's arm. The father leaned forward and snuffled it affectionately, and the mother put her free arm round her husband's neck.

Meri slipped one hand in mine and the other in Beket's. "Two families," she said happily. Then she smiled up at me. "He looks nearly as proud of his baby as we were of Beket."

"Oh, Mother, I'm so happy! I was such a fool not to understand that you loved monkeys as much as I did!"

"Nor did I...until you taught me to open my heart to them."

183

# younger brothers

No one who heard Meri talking to Sebu would have guessed that once she had found animals a disturbance to the household. I had presumed that Sebu would have known why Beket came to the Hare, but I found that she did not. When I told Beket how grateful I was for her loyal secrecy, she said ingenuously:

"It was Nehri who told me not to tell his mother the real reason; he told Sebu that he had implored me to marry him, but had not said anything to her in case I refused. She was a little shocked at my over-eagerness in coming in person instead of sending an emissary, but she was pleased to think how my action honored her son. Nehri told me that she wasn't very reliable about letting animals live in the house. Of course he didn't have to ask her permission, he is the Nomarch; but she could make it difficult for him by being unamiable. We decided that if she knew how Mother shared her views it would make her feel more justified!"

"Then why did she take so much trouble to try to conceal from us the real reason why you were not there to greet us?"

"Nehri told her that you and Mother might be offended. We knew you wouldn't, when you knew what I was doing; but he said it would be wiser to explain privately."

"Were you sure, before you went to him, that Nehri loved you?"

"Oh yes: we both knew it since we were children. Perhaps that's why we never said it in words; we were both so sure that the other one knew it too. It was obvious that one day we should marry each other, but I didn't realize I was grown-up until I saw how much easier it would be for everyone if I was with him instead of being at home. I am afraid that when I first came here I was still angry with Mother, but Nehri soon made me see how tiresome I must have been to her. It wasn't her fault that when I was young I didn't value *things*, only animals and humans; and that I just went on in my own way without trying to make her see my point of view. As soon as Nehri and I started to choose furniture, and saw the linen being woven, which would be used for curtains in our own rooms; I realized that things could be important, not in themselves, but because they are the background against which one lives. It was the same about clothes: as soon as I wanted to be beautiful for Nehri, I knew why Mother thought clothes important. They were part of the expression of her love for you, and were a joy in which she wanted me to share. When my leopard chewed up some matting specially made for the floor of our sleeping-room, I knew just what Mother felt when my animals spoiled her things. It wasn't the *things* that mattered, it was what they represented.''

''Did Sebu welcome your animals as warmly as she welcomed *you?*''

''I think she was rather startled when she first saw them, but she tried not to show it. The only time she was really cross was when the leopard got into her room and knocked over her toilet chest. Most of the things in it got broken. She sent a message to say that she would not join us for the evening meal; and she told Nehri to have her informed when the last of the animals had taken up residence in the house—so that she could move into their quarters, and hope to find there peace in which to sleep undisturbed. It was only by making him laugh that I prevented him from having her bed moved into one of the empty ox-stalls...he said it would teach her not to make requests which she didn't wish to be granted. There was rather a coldness for a day or two between her and us; but she soon got over it. It was that row which gave Nehri the idea of building a new wing, where, when we feel like it, we can live with the animals without giving trouble to anyone.''

When I saw this new wing, I thought how typical it was of Beket and Nehri that this should be the first thing they built together. It would have been customary for a Nomarch to have added a new banqueting-hall, or a new wing, to his house, to mark the occasion of his marriage; but what they had done must have been unique. Between the main house and the Court of the Animals was a series of rooms opening on a walled garden. Here all the pet animals were free to come and go as they pleased, but no human might enter without express permission.

"It will be so beautifully private for us," said Beket contentedly. "Whenever we get tired of being formal, we have only to come here to forget that we have so many responsibilities. One of Nehri's personal attendants used to be a hound-boy, so he can look after us."

The floors were tiled, and I noticed that all the furniture was plain and solid and could be replaced as often as necessary. The bed-place was a wide shelf high in the wall, presumably so as to be out of reach of all save its rightful occupants.

Beket was delighted with the mouse-deer, and soon they followed her wherever she went.

"They may like to share a room with the monkeys," she said, "but they will have to decide for themselves; animals like to choose their friends just as humans do. My leopard's favorite companion is an old Hoopoe bird, which Nehri has had ever since it was a fledgling with a broken wing. At night it perches on the edge of the leopard's sleeping-box, and they eat out of the same dish. Then there is a horned lizard and a rat; they have decided to share the same burrow. The only serious fight was between one of my dogs and Nehri's young jackal. They mauled each other quite badly before we could separate them: they still haven't decided to be friends, but both pretend not to notice when they see each other."

She pointed to a large pond, not yet completed, in the middle of the garden. "Nehri's going to get a baby hippo to keep there; I've always wanted to have one. The heron will like paddling in the water, and so will some of the others."

That evening Meri said to me, "How much wiser Nehri is with her than I was. No one could help loving her; but I am so grateful to the Gods for finding a husband who understands her so well."

"Do you think he will always be so eager to do everything she wishes?"

"I don't think he's just doing it to please her; they both want the same things. They are as happy as two children content in a game."

"They must remember that Nomarchs are not children. It is unsuitable for them to be so absorbed in something which has no bearing on their work of administration."

Perhaps Nehri sensed this unspoken criticism, for when he was showing me his vineyards later that same evening, he said:

"I had always found myself happier in the company of animals; but until Beket and I discussed why this should be so, I did not realize how much we could learn from them. We have seen how animals which one would think are natural enemies can come to live as friends. Beket never tries to make an animal change its essential character, but she has taught them to find their kinship through having a mutual object of affection. A cat and a dog may obey an ancient impulse to be antagonistic, but they will no longer do so when they both love the same master; for love is stronger than instinct. When men love Ra, even Egyptians and Asiatics can be brothers! Because Beket loves animals they do not fear her; having no fear they can love her; loving her they can love each other. Unless our people love Beket and me, we can never fulfill our true role, which is to make our people love each other through the link we make between them all. Be it the love from animal to man, or from man to God, the link from the younger to the wiser will unite also those of the same age."

"With that I am in complete agreement: the only thing I question is whether it is necessary for you to spend so much of your time with your younger brothers."

"It is necessary for us, because we have still much to learn from them. You cannot learn from animals who are kept as captives, any more than you can keep your scribes imprisoned and expect to profit of their knowledge. Only a few days ago, the father of one of my young nobles came to me in great distress, saying that his son wished to marry the daughter of a foreign merchant, and asking me to threaten him with my displeasure if he continued to thwart his parents. I said that before I could give judgment, the two who wished to marry must be seen by my priest of Anubis. The priest told me that the link between them was a true link, and that it was right for them to continue their journey together. It was difficult to convince the father; perhaps I should not have been able to restore peace to that family unless I had been able to show him the leopard and the Hoopoe bird, and say to him, 'Consider the animals, for they are often wiser than men. They do not allow themselves to be deceived, as we sometimes do, by difference of caste, or color, or tongue. Does the lion boast of his tawny majesty to the singing-bird, or deny the beauty of her feathers because she cannot roar?' "

When Nehri took me to the temple, where in a few days he and Beket would take the Oath before Ptah, I was interested to see that the statue in the sanctuary of Anubis was not in the form of a jackal, but of a man with a jackal's head. I remembered that I had seen Anubis represented in this way in one of my father's papyri, scribed before the oldest pyramids were built. When I commented on this to Nehri, he said:

"That statue was placed there by my father. If he had not been called to the Watchers, he might well have become a priest, for he remembered more than passed in the waking day. I was very young when he died, but the scribe who taught me had been his close friend and often spoke of him. Through the scribe, I came to see, not the Nomarch and the warrior, but the man who had dreamed dreams."

Then Nehri went on, "My great-uncle, who, as you know, was Nomarch under the Old Rule, was suspicious of everything which gave pleasure, saying that Set gilded the nets in which he snared mankind. He allowed no vines to be planted, nor were there dancing-girls or harp-players in his time. He was just, according to the limits of his vision, but he was a bleak man, who could find no warmth even in Ra. He tried to make my father believe that everything which could beguile the senses was evil, and told him stories of the country through which a man passed on his way to the Underworld. There were flowers there, but each hid a poisonous spider; there was lush grass, which whispered with snakes; there were young and lovely women, but when a man took one of them in his arms it was to find her flesh was soft only because it already crawled with maggots. So the boy became assailed with fearful night-terrors. He had been taught that his uncle's authority was absolute; second only to Pharaoh, whom he felt sure was still more bleak and incomprehensible. He was too proud to tell anyone of his fears, until at last, when they became unbearable, he spoke of them to the scribe. The scribe told him to seek peace through Anubis: and gradually the night-terrors gave way before the light of true-dreams. The words of his uncle could no longer inspire fear and were recognized as the worthless utterances of a man of narrow heart.

''In sleep he saw a wide horizon, and went among people who laughed and sang and were beautiful, who gloried in each other, and rejoiced in their strength; and yet were most pleasing to the Gods. While awake he had to be obedient to his uncle; he was not allowed to choose his friends, and as those chosen for him were distasteful, he preferred his own company. That is how he came to learn so much of animals, for they gave him their friendship without thought of expediency. Each time a new link was created between him and an animal, so did he find a new link with Anubis. He realized that when men say, 'Such and such a man is evil because he behaves like an animal,' it shows that the speaker is evil and despises his body which he should have honored in the name of Ptah.

''My father knew that a child must grow strong on milk before it is ready for wine. Only a fool demands that the strength which the milk gave him be taken away, for if that were granted, he would be a starveling, too weak to lift the wine to his lips even though it were a royal vintage. So also does a man who denies the strength he learned as an animal become too feeble to seek further wisdom. That is why our statue of Anubis is in this semblance; so that all who see it may remember that Gods are born when men and animals together have given strength to the spirit.''

Nehri showed me not only his personal estate, but many other parts of the Nome; while, to Meri's delight, Beket willingly agreed to stay at home to arrange the final preparations for the wedding festival.

I was greatly impressed with the magnificence of his herds: never had I seen oxen more sleek, or cows with such rich udders; and the sheep had sound feet and long, fine fleeces. Nowhere did I see a beast in poor condition. I was delighted to see this practical aspect of Nehri's ideal. Once, as a young man, I had visited a noble in the North, who prided himself on his kindness to animals. No meat was eaten in his household nor was any animal killed within his boundaries. There I had seen an ox, blind with age, lying helpless in its stall: flies had gathered on its festering sores, undisturbed by the feeble quiver of its hide. I had asked that I might be allowed to set it free of its pain, and only the courtesy due to a guest saved me from being reviled as a monster of cruelty. Even courtesy had not prevented my host from exclaiming, ''I regret that I must deny the favor you ask. I regret also that any man should wish to attack a beast which is too weak to defend itself.''

I told this story to Nehri, and he said, ''It is sometimes difficult to make people realize that there are occasions when to allow others to continue to suffer pain is as though one inflicted pain upon them. It is for the Gods to call men to their kingdom, but the Gods have given us responsibilities toward animals, so that we may learn how one day to become Gods to men. We betray both ourselves and the Gods, if, through fear of exceeding our authority, we refuse to take our proper responsibility. I know that sometimes my guests, who have heard how animals are honored in this Nome, are surprised to find meat at my table. Some of them have even cried out, 'How can you bear to eat animals when you call them your brothers?' There are always people who confuse love with false sentiment. I explain to them that should Min, of his wisdom, decide that my cows and ewes should have but one male to a hundred females, then there would no longer be meat served in any household of the Hare. The cows give milk to our children, and in return, when they are too old to calve, they are given all they require for their contented age, just as though they were warriors too old to fight. So are our sheep honored for the gift of their wool. When age prevents their days being pleasurable to them, or if they should become afflicted by a disease for which as yet we have not discovered a rapid cure; then they are given a swift and painless death.

''But should all the bulls and rams be allowed to mature and live out their normal span, soon all the herds would go hungry, for there would not be sufficient pasture. The finest of them are kept to sire new herds, and there are some of my strain in nearly every Nome; the rest are sent on their journey when they are a year old. Why should it cause them pain that the flesh which they no longer use is of benefit to those who have been their friends?''

He laughed. ''Though this to many would sound blasphemy, I think that another instance of the wisdom of beasts is that they would prefer that the body which once was of use to them should be of use to others, rather than that it should be wasted in a sarcophagus!''

In the Nome of the Hare, each town, and most of the larger villages, had an estate to which sick animals were taken, either to be cured or to be released from a body which had become a prison. Great care was exercised that they should never die in fear, for the seers had said that the places where, under the Old Rule, animals had been slaughtered, were gray with terror. This terror was immediately sensed by those who came after, and it added to the shameful record of the priests of Set, and to those men of ignorance who had worn priestly robes, that this grayness was most intense in places where the temple bulls had been sacrificed.

At each estate there was a healer-priest, and men trained both in the use of herbs and with the knife. Here all herdsmen, and others whose work brought them into contact with animals, had to be trained for three months before taking up office or entering into an inheritance.

The strain of several breeds had been improved by mating those specially selected; and, because of this, many thousands of animals now found their bodies more pleasant to live in. The food suitable to the requirements of each kind had been studied, and considerable tracts of land were under new fodder crops. In pastures which had no shade-trees, thatched shelters had been provided. Many new water-channels had been cut, and shallow wallows dug so that an animal could seek relief from flies by rolling in the soft mud. So greatly had the yield of wool increased that the Nome now had work for three hundred extra weavers, and many hundreds of cubits of fine woolen cloth were available for barter each year.

The health of the people had been greatly benefited by the increased quantities of milk, cheese, butter and curds, both from cows and goats, which had been added to their food. In addition, all could now eat fish. To make this possible, Nehri had provided all villages which were distant from the river with large artificial ponds kept fresh by water from the extended irrigation channels. These were kept stocked with fish, and were of great value to people who in the old days had never tasted it except when salted; for transport had been too costly when so large a proportion stank before reaching its destination.

Everything I saw made me yet more grateful to the Gods

for finding Beket a husband so near to my heart. I told this to him on the morning of the day when he became my son before Ptah. He answered:

"If you see wisdom in my Nome, it is because I learned wisdom in the Oryx. If in me there is any virtue, it is because Beket has taught me the meaning of love."

Their love for each other shone like living rays upon all who saw Beket and Nehri on the day of their marriage. Tethin-an had been wise when he said they looked as though they walked together through the Fields of Ra. Happy were the crowds who lined the road to the temple to watch their Nomarchs pass; and even the white oxen, who walked in the procession with garlands round their necks and gilded horns, might have been blessed by Hathor; and perhaps they were. Many hundreds joined in the great feast, which lasted far into the night. Jar after jar of wine was opened, and when one group of singers fell silent others took up the song. Yet the Nomarchs of the Hare shared more than wine with their people: they shared with them their joy.

## the GReat RIVeR

I knew that Nekht often found solitude a necessity, but though it was quite usual for him to spend all day in the marshes, he seldom forgot to tell Meri when he did not expect to be home until late. So, on a day when he had left the house at dawn and by early evening had not returned, I went to the river hoping to find him. I took the path down-stream, and when I was nearing the fishermen's huts, I saw Nekht coming toward me. He looked tired, yet curiously exalted. I felt he had news of importance for me, and with difficulty resisted a desire to question him. I pretended that I was surprised to see him, for I did not wish him to think that we had been worried by his absence. Meri and I both knew that only selfish parents make their children wear fetters, even the fetters woven of affection. ''Don't do that, or your Mother will be worried,'' those words are so often inscribed on the bars of invisible prisons!

For a time Nekht walked beside me in silence. Then he said, ''Let's sit down on the bank and watch the river. There is a water-rat with a young family in a hole near here. If we sit very still she may bring them out to play; she did yesterday, and the day before.''

He picked up pieces of dried mud and threw them down into the water: so I knew the rat was only an excuse and that he was trying to find words in which to tell me something. ''Father, I know you never remind me that I'm still young, but I want you to try specially hard to forget I'm only ten. I have done something which may sound awfully conceited... you may think I oughtn't to have done it without first consulting you or Roidahn. But I know I had to do it alone, and that it was right.''

''I have always told you to follow your own authority, haven't I, Nekht? You and I are both Watchers, and I'm not so foolish as to think that wisdom can be measured in years.''

''This morning I woke at dawn, and I knew that Dudu, the old fisherman who has lived alone since his wife died last year, was going to die today. The important thing was that I had to be with him when he died, because there was something I could do for him...something I could do better than anyone else. The ten-year-old part of me said that I ought to tell you or Mother, so that you could come with me, or send one of the priests instead; but the *real* me said that if I did, it would be the act of a coward...the responsibility was mine and I had to take it alone. I nearly left a message to say I had gone to watch birds; then I realized that a lie is not becoming to a priest. What I was going to do was the work of a priest...it sounds a terribly conceited thing to say. You *do* understand, don't you?''

I reassured him. ''Of course I do, Nekht, and I am very honored that you trust me.''

''First I went to the headman, and asked how his people were. I was careful not to let him think I had any special reason for asking, and he took it for part of the ordinary greeting, saying that there was neither discontent nor sickness among them...so I knew he didn't know about Dudu. Dudu's hut is about two hundred paces away from the rest of the village, and is screened by some tall reeds, so no one noticed me going there. Dudu was asleep. He was breathing very slowly, and I saw the same mist round his head as I have seen before...Do you remember how I told you that Nehri's mother was going to die?''

''Yes, I do...and that was not the only time.''

''Well, when I saw that, I knew I had been right to come to him. He lay so quietly I was sure he wasn't in pain...at any rate his body wasn't. But I wasn't sure whether he'd return before he died, so I went and filled the water-jar in case he woke up thirsty. I tied some leaves together to make a fan, so that I could keep the flies away from him. It must have been nearly noon when he opened his eyes, looked at me, and said, ''You have come! You promised that you would take me across the River. My wife will be waiting for me on the far bank; but I must go to her; she is not a Steersman of the Boat.' Then he smiled and his eyes closed.

''I knew he was still alive because I could hear him breathing; the breaths were slower and louder than they had been before. I lay down beside him with my hand in his, because I knew I must leave my body and join him. Almost at once I found myself standing with him outside the hut. There was a path leading down to the water, and a boat was rocking gently in the shallows. It was a river; but it wasn't this river: it was much wider, and, though it was evening on our bank, the far side was shining with a curious pale light, warmer than moonlight yet I knew it was not the sun.

"It seemed a very ordinary kind of boat, but I knew it belonged to me, and that in it I had made many journeys on that river. Dudu sat in the stern and I took the oars. It was very easy to row, as though there was a current which carried us across, but I had to keep rowing to set the course.

"As we left the bank I noticed that Dudu was wearing his best tunic, though I couldn't remember him putting it on. He looked very old. He was nearly eighty, but he hadn't wanted to go live with the old people and had been happier in his hut. Everyone in the village used to give him part of their catch, and in return he mended their nets.

"In the middle of the river the mist was so thick that though he was sitting right in front of me I could only see him very indistinctly. Then the mist thinned out, and as we drew near the far shore the pale light flooded everything. Going through the mist must have made Dudu young; not very young, perhaps about thirty. His skin was smooth and firm instead of being wrinkled, and his hair was very thick and black. There was a flower in his forehead-thong, and he was wearing a kilt of the Watcher's colors, and on his feet were sandals with turquoise studs.

"A woman was waiting for him. I wondered who she was, for he had said that his wife would be there to meet him, and I knew she was over seventy when she died. But this woman was young, wearing a garland of white and yellow flowers. It was silly of me not to realize at once that she had grown young too. Dudu sprang from the boat, splashed through the shallows and took her in his arms. I remember turning the boat round; then the current must have caught it for I didn't have to row. I woke up before I reached the mist....

"Dudu was still breathing. I saw that I couldn't have been away more than a few minutes, because sunlight was coming through the window, and before I lay down I had noticed the position of a shadow it made. But I was quite sure that Dudu would never come back to his body: it was quite empty, though it still had enough life stored up to keep it breathing for a little while. There was nothing else I could do for him, for I knew he was safe with his wife. So I tidied up the hut, and then I picked flowers from his little patch of cultivation, and put some of them in a jar on the window-ledge, and the rest at his head and feet. I wanted everything to look cheerful in case any of his friends should want to come to say good-bye to his body. Folded away in a small chest, I found the tunic he had been wearing in the boat; and under it there was the kilt of fine linen, and the sandals with the turquoise studs...both very old and worn. His body died so quietly that only the sudden silence told me that it had stopped breathing. I carried water from the river to wash him in. He was a very thin old man, so I could lift him quite easily. I combed his hair, and he had died with his mouth shut so he looked very serene and peaceful...but I remembered to tie up the lower jaw so that his mouth wouldn't fall open. I dressed him in the blue tunic, because he had chosen it to wear in the boat while he was still old. Then I went to ask the headman to arrange for Dudu's body to be buried, and to tell his friends that he had gone across the River.''

''I am very honored in my son,'' I said. ''Both your mother and I have recognized your wisdom, and Roidahn says that when you become initiate he will make you his heir to the Horizon of Horus: then you will be his son as well as mine.''

''It's only sometimes that I'm a priest, Father; usually I'm a very ordinary boy...and I'm not at all clever at learning the things scribes try to teach me. Nearly all the time I'm Nekht who was born ten years ago; and then I find myself being somebody much older, who knows things that Nekht doesn't understand. I talked to Roidahn about this feeling, and he knew exactly what I meant. We were walking through a bean-field at the time, and there were some yellow lupins growing beside a ditch. He picked one, and showed me how the little flowers of which it is made do not open at the same time, though, until the flower-spike is complete, the seeds do not ripen. He said, 'Each lupin is made of many flowers, and each spirit is made of many lives.' Then he picked off one flower near the top of the spike and one of several rows below it, and said, 'These are quite separate in themselves, yet they are both part of the same whole. The central stalk, to which all the flowers are joined, is your spirit: nourishing each flower and in turn receiving life from it; and through the stalk, each has contact with every other. One flower is Nekht; another a man through which your spirit gained experience two hundred years ago, and a third may represent a woman born of your spirit before the first pyramid was built.' Then he said, 'Always remember, Nekht, that even if you feel "I can't do this, it is too difficult," your spirit has the wisdom of many I's, for the spirit is the source of all wisdom which is yet available to you. Therefore instead of saying, "I, Nekht, powerless," say "May Nekht be sustained by the wisdom gathered by other parts of me which belong to the same whole."'

"That's what I did, Father, when I woke up this morning. Nekht only knew he had to go to Dudu; but when Nekht got there, 'I' knew how to do what was necessary. A single experience like this is very little to go on, and it may sound conceited to talk about it yet, but I believe being a Steersman is a faculty which all priests used to have, though in our time it is not recognized. There may be some people, perhaps many of them, who can cross the River alone, or who have friends already on the far bank who can come to our side of the River to collect them. But others, perhaps because they are too young in spirit or have not yet learned even a little magic, need someone from their own side of the River to take them across. Dudu must have known this while he was asleep, and that is why he sent for me and called me 'Steersman of the Boat'...I believe that's an official title, like 'Priest of Anubis,' or 'Lord of the Hawk.' I don't know which is our special God: I'll have to ask Roidahn about that, but I think we may belong to Osiris."

''Nekht, what do you think happens if a man who is in need of a Steersman dies alone?''

''I expect a Steersman would go to him in sleep...or perhaps there are special people on the other side of the River who come to ferry across those who have no friend to make the journey with them.''

''Then it doesn't matter if there are few Steersmen among us.''

''Oh, but it does, Father! You have often said that people mustn't be afraid of taking responsibility, that they mustn't leave everything to the Gods. It is *our* job to see that people cross the River safely; every priest should also be trained as Steersman. Think what a difference it would make to people if they could be told exactly what their dead were doing. It's not enough just to be told that those you love are in the Fields of Ra...at least it isn't unless you can remember having been there. If I died tomorrow wouldn't you want to know what I was doing the day after? I'm sure Mother would, and so would Beket.''

''Yes, my son, it would help the pain of physical separation. But even without that knowledge I hope I would try not to spoil your freedom by my grief.''

''Then you will help me to learn as much as I can?''

''Of course; it is already arranged that you will go to the Horizon of Horus to begin your priestly training at the end of next year.''

''You've got to do more than that, Father. You have got to allow me to train in my own way; even if it should mean my *not* going to the temple.''

''I will talk with Roidahn before coming to a decision.''

''Whatever he says, you have got to give me the chance to work in my own way...at least until I've found whether I can do anything worth doing. I want you to let me be alone with people who are dying, when it is certain that the healers and physicians can do no more for them. If I find that I can't help them, that I am not really a Steersman and could only pilot

199

Dudu because there was a link between us which I don't yet know about…then I will train as a Horus priest.''

''It is a difficult promise to make,'' I said slowly. ''The dying are not the right companions for a boy, even for a boy who is also a priest. When the afflictions of the body release their hold on a man at death, they may attack those who are with him. Your mother would never forgive me if I allowed you to expose yourself to unnecessary dangers.''

''Would you have obeyed my grandfather if he had forbidden you and Kiyas to look after our people when they were afflicted by the Blue Death? I too have people whom I must look after: and they would still be my responsibility even if you and Roidahn were to disinherit me.''

## Steersman of the Boat

At first Meri was very reluctant to give her consent for Nekht to be alone with the dying.

''I wouldn't mind if he were older, Ra-ab, but surely it would put too great a strain on him while he's not even eleven? I am glad that he is to go into the temple, for there his faculties will be allowed to develop among people who know how to look after him. I wouldn't mind so much if he didn't say he wanted to be alone…surely we can make him see that he must wait until he is initiate, or at least has been a temple pupil for two or three years, before he is ready for this.''

''I should agree with you entirely had he not been so insistent. But he spoke with an authority which I felt I had no right to over-rule.''

''Ask Roidahn to talk to him. He will be able to make him realize that he is being over ambitious.''

''I saw Roidahn yesterday. After he had heard the story,

he said that he could not give me an answer until he had found out whether Nekht had brought back an accurate record. Roidahn lay down and covered his eyes with his hand. After a few moments he said, 'It was a true record; even to the smallest detail. We must honor the authority in the voice of Nekht.''

''But surely Roidahn doesn't wish Nekht to spend his time with the dying? Oh, Ra-ab, don't let that happen! Let him go on being happy and young, and enjoying things.''

''His experience with Dudu doesn't seem to have made him unhappy. He is in the vineyard now, and if you listen you can hear him singing. Does his voice sound as though he were burdened with too heavy responsibilities?''

''No,'' said Meri doubtfully. ''And this morning he swam with me in the pool, and told me about an adventure he had yesterday. He and two herd-boys rode on the cows which they were bringing in to be milked...he *seems* quite normal and happy, but...''

''Meri, aren't you being over-anxious? When you were his age you had some of the faculties of a priest of Anubis... and have you forgotten how we used to meet each other on the other side of the River?''

''No, of course I haven't forgotten, Ra-ab. But those were *happy* things.''

''Is death not happy, save in our imagination? I have seen many people die, Meri, in battle and by pestilence. I have never known any who were afraid of death when they saw him face to face, even under the Old Rule when people had been taught to fear. I think that even if Nekht had no inward wisdom to sustain him, he would still benefit from the peace of the dying: and if he can share in their freedom, then will he be most blessed. I have told Nekht that should he again wake with the knowledge that there is someone waiting for him to act as their Steersman, he is to tell me; and I have promised to give him every possible assistance. He said he would do so, and asked that when I next heard that someone was dying—

someone to whom I did not think his presence would be an intrusion, I would give him the opportunity to be with them.''

About a month later after this conversation, I heard that the eight-year-old daughter of a man who worked on my estate had been seriously injured. The Priest of Ma-at had seen her, and said that she was dying and would not regain consciousness. She had been helping her father to clean out an ox-stall. The ox was stung by a hornet and lashed out suddenly, kicking the little girl on the back of her head. I sent for Nekht and told him what had happened, and at his request we went immediately to the house to which she had been carried.

The child was lying as though in deep sleep, her breathing hardly perceptible. I asked her father whether he would permit Nekht to sit with her for a little while, and said that I would wait with him in the garden. This he agreed most willingly to do, for I could see that he was finding it difficult to contain his grief and was afraid that any outbreak of emotion would disturb the peace of the dying.

It was nearly an hour later when the door opened and Nekht came out to join us. He was pale, but perfectly composed. He went up to the father and put a hand on his arm.

''Your daughter is with a boy of about her own age,'' he said calmly. ''When last I saw them they were walking together through a rich pasture, playing on reed-pipes. Beside them skipped a young goat. She asked the boy where you were, and he said, ''He's asleep in the house over there.' Then he pointed to a white house set among shade-trees on rising ground, and went on, 'You will see him this evening when he wakes up. He often comes to see us, because our mother lives here. He still has to go away sometimes, but not so often as he used to, and soon he will live with us all the time. Then I shan't have to be a child any more—I only do it to please Mother, and to stop her being so lonely while she's waiting for him.''

I saw the man was deeply moved, and I asked him, "Does anything Nekht has said hold any special significance for you?"

The man nodded; there were tears in his eyes. "I had promised my daughter a kid to play with, and then I thought it would only be one more animal to look after, so I didn't bother to get one for her. And I said I would make her a reed-pipe and teach her to play it....I meant to do that when next I took her down to the river."

"Had she a companion who is now dead?"

"She had a twin brother, but he died when he was four days old. Her mother died the following year...it is curious that she should be living in a white house on a hill. She always said this part of the country was too flat. She came from much further south. I have never been there, but she told me that there are many hills. We had been married ten years before the children were born. I used to work on a trading-barge, and was often away from home. That is why she wished for children...to be company for her."

"They *are* company for her," said Nekht firmly. "And when you go to sleep it is as though you open a door into the white house where she lives."

"The boy is there too?" he asked eagerly.

"All three are there, and soon you will join them."

"I'll remember that...somehow, even if I wished, I could not disbelieve it."

Nekht smiled up at him. "I must go now," he said. "I promised to help a friend of mine make a fish-trap. But I will come and see you tomorrow." He paused at the end of the garden to wave to us; then ran off down the road.

The man stared after him, and said in an awed voice, "He is only a boy, yet he spoke to me like a priest. He was right: I am not going to be unhappy, even during the time I must wait to join them."

It was nearly dusk when I head Nekht whistling on the path up from the river, and went to meet him. His kilt was torn and there were smears of mud on his cheek. He was carrying a string of fish, and it was difficult to realize that he was the same boy who, only a few hours earlier, had spoken with the authority of a priest.

"My fish-trap *does* work!" he called out excitedly. "I only finished it a little while ago, and look...it's caught three fish already! I want you to lend me a scribe who can make a drawing of it, because I want to send one to Beket. She'll want her people to use it, because it's so much kinder to fish."

It was not until we were finishing the evening meal that he referred to the child's death; and then only when I asked him about it.

"I don't think she needed me at all," he said diffidently. "In fact, I'm sure she didn't; but I'm glad I went, for it seemed to make her father a bit happier."

"Didn't you help her cross the River?"

"No, and so far as I can remember there *wasn't* any river. I lay down beside her, just as I did with Dudu; but instead of staying a separate person, as I did with him, I seemed to become the girl herself."

"I know what you mean. I have had such an experience in sleep. When you are helping anyone it is sometimes necessary to share in their experience so closely that you almost become one with them; on waking you think their experience was your own."

"That must have been it," agreed Nekht. "Everything happened as I said it did; except that the girl walking with her brother seemed to be me....I knew not only what she was doing, but how she felt. She was very happy and excited, yet nothing seemed at all unfamiliar. She knew the boy almost as well as I know Beket, so she must often have met him in her dreams. I knew a lot of other things as well, but I didn't tell them to her father as I thought they would confuse him.

"For instance, I learned that it is possible to sleep both here and on the other side of the River: whichever side you belong to is your waking world, and you remember the other side as a dream, though perhaps this is only true of people who are young in spirit. It was quite true what I told the man, that when he slept it was like opening a door into the white house; but when he wakes 'down here' he doesn't disappear in the dream world...he just lies on a bed and goes to sleep. I think he must have some skill in magic; for he made a second body so that his wife can see it sleeping and so not realize that she is dead while he is still alive. He has to make it afresh every time he comes back here, and it's rather tiring to do...that's why he tells her sometimes that he has to go away on a journey, so that she doesn't worry about him while he has a rest from doing magic.''

''Why doesn't his wife realize she is dead?''

''I found that out too. I think she must have been rather a silly woman while she was alive, for nothing would make her forget the frightening stories she heard as a child under the Old Rule. She thought that if she was wicked she would go to the Caverns, and that if she wasn't, she'd lie safely in her sarcophagus. When she died and found that everything was quite ordinary, it never occurred to her that she was dead; and her husband thought it would be kinder to leave her like that until he was dead too. The boy who was born as her son is older in spirit than she, but there is such a strong link of affection between them that he spends some of his time as the little boy she loves to look after, and only when she has put him to bed is he free to go on with his real life. That's why he said, 'As soon as Father is here all the time I shan't have to go on pretending to be a child.' ''

''Did the girl also go there every night?''

''No, only occasionally. But the mother was quite happy about it, because she had been told that the girl had been adopted by a rich kinsman and could only come home to visit her. The mother isn't bothered by time as we know it; for her days pass much more quickly than ours do...I'm not quite sure why. I'll have to find out about that later.''

"Was it a real goat? Where did it come from?"

"It wasn't a sleeping, alive goat, but one the boy had made to amuse his sister. That's why it was so tame and could talk. Sometimes being dead feels a little strange at first, so people give you things you specially wanted...just as Mother always put people's favorite flowers in their rooms when they came to stay with us, to make them feel at home.

"Do you think there wasn't a river for her to cross, or just that you didn't happen to remember it.

"I'm not sure yet; but I can't help thinking that I should have remembered if the River had been there...because everything else was so vivid. One moment I was lying beside her on the bed-place, and then I began to think it was I who couldn't move. I tried to sit up, but couldn't make my body obey me. I drew a very deep breath, as you do before making a dive: then my body wasn't heavy any longer, and I knew it was perfectly easy to stand up, so I did. I thought it was silly to stay in bed in the middle of the day, so I walked across the room and opened the door...I remember the feel of the latch-string quite distinctly. But outside the door there wasn't the garden I expected to see, but a path leading up-hill through meadows. I wanted to find out where it led, so I followed it. The boy was coming down to meet me; and by that time the path wasn't at all strange, and I had forgotten about the garden which I had expected to find outside the door. I have told you what happened then. The last thing I remember is running up some steps which led to the white house. I knew my mother was waiting for me, and I was pleased and excited to see her...but only as though I had been away for two or three days. Then I woke up as Nekht, and realized that the 'I' he had been thinking with belonged to the girl whose body lay beside me. I knew the body was dead, even before I touched it and found that the heart had stopped."

He paused, and then added, "I don't know why Mother was worried about me seeing dead bodies. They are no more frightening than empty wine-jars. Of course, I shouldn't like to be with a body which was dead and neglected, because decay is always rather horrid.''

We had been eating cold, roast duck. He picked up a leg and began to gnaw the last shreds of meat from it. ''People are silly when they think that anything which isn't actually alive is *dead*. 'Dead' means when the spirit is free forever of that particular body; but the body has enough life stored in it to be clean for a time. Only when the life is used up does it begin to decay. There was life in the flesh of the duck I am eating, there is still some left in it even after it has been cooked; and it is that which increases the life in me. If I had eaten it the moment the stored life has been used up, it would have done me no good; and if I had eaten it when decay had begun, it would have done me harm...for decay, which is the opposite of life, would have used up some of my life-store to neutralize it. If there had been more decay in it than there was life in me, I might have died.''

''How long does the stored life last after the spirit has gone out of it?''

''That depends...the more energy a body uses, the more life it requires. A stranded fish begins to decay more quickly than a cut cabbage, because the fish-body needs more life each moment than does the cabbage-body, and, in proportion, is able to store less. Then there is another reason: a cabbage is in rhythm with the full sunlight, so even in the heat of the day it is not working at more than its usual speed. But a fish is specially adapted to the cooler water, and immediately it is exposed to the warmth of the sun the rhythm is greatly increased, and the amount of stored life which ought to keep its body unchanged for several hours is used up in a much shorter time. Sunlight always increases the flux of energy, which is why meat lasts for several days in cold weather, though in high summer it must be eaten almost at once....''

He selected an apricot from a bowl of fruit, and added, ''I found out about all this because I thought it would make

Mother less anxious. I knew she thinks that fever-demons look for someone new to attack as soon as the spirit has left their host. But she's wrong; they are quite satisfied with what they have got to feed on until they have sucked out the last drop of life. There is nothing sinister or unpleasant in death, but only in decay.''

He looked rather embarrassed and said, ''But of course you know all this, or you wouldn't have made the law which decrees that all refuse must be burned or buried before the fever-demons start looking for something else to feed on.''

''I made that law, but you have given me a much better reason for it than I had before.''

''I know that I haven't found out much yet,'' he said fervently, ''but you *will* let me go on finding things out in my own way for a bit longer?''

''What I have heard today has convinced me that you can see your own path, and that instead of being led in search of wisdom you can guide others toward it.''

## Incredulous Woman

Six months later, Nekht came to me before the first meal and said, ''Father, you remember the man whose daughter I was with when she died?'' I nodded, and he went on, ''I want you to come to his house with me. If I've dreamed true, he died during the night.''

''Tell me your dream.''

''I was walking along the path which I knew led to the white house on the hill, but this time I wasn't the little girl; I was myself. I was waiting for someone; just as the boy had waited for the girl. I didn't know who it was until I saw a man coming toward me. Then I recognized him. He said, 'I had no illness to warn me that I was going to die, otherwise I should have sent to your father and asked that you might be with me when I made the crossing. But I see that though I thought no one had heard me, you did not let my call go unanswered.'

"I was surprised that he wanted me, for I knew he had made so many journeys there. He must have guessed what I was thinking, for he said, 'It is not that I find death unfamiliar; in fact it is most restful no longer to have to take elaborate precautions to make my wife think that she is still on Earth.'

" 'Then why did you send for me?' I asked.

" 'Because I need your help to prove to her that she is dead. Since our daughter died I have been trying to persuade her to adopt a wider horizon, and in this both the children helped me. But though I love my wife, I fear she is very stubborn; for though I do things which on Earth would be called miracles, she accepts them without surprise, or considers herself the victim of her own imagination!'

" 'What kind of magics have you done?' I asked.

" 'All very trivial,' he said...and somehow he reminded me of one of Neku's apprentices being over-modest about an early sculpture. 'I covered the whole of the house with a vine, and when she saw it, my wife said, "How glad you must be that you agreed to our moving to a part of the country where the soil is so fertile." She picked a bunch of grapes, and, after tasting them, decided that they must ripen a few days longer before they were ready for pressing. So that night I removed the vine, and when she came out of the door, she found twenty wine-jars, all of them sealed with clay—except one, which was open for her to taste the vintage.

" 'First she praised me for my diligence in pressing the grapes so quickly, and then she began to scold me for cutting down the vine and burning it while she was asleep.

" 'Then I changed all the colors of the flowers, so that one morning they were all red, another morning they were yellow, and a third blue. She was quite surprised after their

209

third change, and I ventured to say, ''I never knew a thing like that could happen on Earth.'' I thought that might make her a little suspicious as to where she was; but she said tartly, ''That, dear, only shows how little of Earth we know. Leaves change color in the autumn: why shouldn't flowers change color in the night?''

''' '''Ordinary flowers don't change,'' I expostulated, ''...not poppies, and lupins, and moon-daisies.''

''' '''What a silly thing to say...when you've just seen them do it! Don't let it worry you: I expect it's due to something in the soil.''

'' 'Then I decided to do a bigger magic, and for this I had to get someone to help me. Perhaps it was you—I don't remember. I made her twenty years younger!

'' 'For a day or two she never noticed the change, for, luckily, she had never worried over her health; so she has felt perfectly well since she died. So I made her a large silver mirror in which she could see herself...and all she said was, ''It's the first time I've noticed that my herbal wash I make has all the powers my grandmother claimed for it.'' Then she embraced me and said, ''I rejoice for you, my dear husband; for we have been married over twenty years, and we have been so happy together that I have not aged, even by a day.''

'' 'After that she was so occupied in making more of her herbal brew...and as often as she cut her plants they grew afresh, for I had arranged that when I first made them...that soon the house was cluttered with jars of it, which, she said, would soon bring us a fortune. And when I asked why we wanted a fortune when we already had everything we required, she scolded me for being so improvident.'

''I was so sorry for him,'' said Nekht, ''it must be so disheartening to have your magic ignored! I was trying to think of something comforting to say, when he asked me:

'' 'I suppose you have noticed that I also am looking younger?'

''I had to admit that until he mentioned it I had not noticed the difference, but he certainly looked no more than twenty.

" 'I only changed myself last week. I was fifty when I died, so I've been quite successful.' Then he added sadly, 'I thought I would be able to take her back to the time when we were betrothed, before she became so set in her ideas. But she was determined that my appearance was due to her grandmother's brew, and that my ardor came from the same source! She admitted that she must have added a new ingredient which her grandmother had overlooked. I hope you will understand that I should not have troubled you in this matter unless I had already tried everything in my power.'

" 'I am most honored that you should ask me to help,' I said, 'but it seems that you are better at magic than I am. Can you suggest anything you would like me to try?'

" 'I think the chief trouble is that she knows me too well. Magic is a thing which is usually more credible if practiced by strangers from far countries. Perhaps it may be allowed to the nobles, but to her it seems too improbable for the common people. She has, however, a tremendous admiration for your father; in fact I know that she ascribes to him the divinity which most people allow only to Pharaoh. If you could disguise yourself as Ra-ab Hotep, and come as an honored guest to our house, she would regard with the most proper awe any magic which you cared to do for us. If Ra-ab Hotep told her so, she might even believe that she was dead.' ' "

Nekht smiled up at me, "Making myself look like you wasn't at all difficult, and I thought I would seem most impressive in ceremonial dress, such as you sometimes wear in Audience. The man went ahead to tell his wife that she must prepare to receive the Nomarch, and I followed him. I thought I ought to behave ordinarily at first. I drank a cup of the wine she gave me—it was very sour, so I don't think while he was alive he can have been knowledgeable about vintages. I was wondering how I was going to convince her she was dead, when it suddenly occurred to me that she might have heard of it as Crossing the River; so, until she *saw* a

211

river, she would never believe that she had already reached the far bank.

"I made a tremendously strong mental picture of a wide river flowing at the foot of the garden. Then I went to the door and said—in what I hoped was a very impressive manner, 'Though I am Nomarch of the Oryx, you are my kinsman. In life you are under my protection, and in death there shall you be also. The time is come to leave this ordinary country and to enter the Boat of Millions of Years. Beyond the mist is the Shining Land, and to that place will I be your Steersman.'

"I led the way down the steps and across the garden to a boat waiting at a landing-stage. The man and the woman and their two children followed me. I saw that she kept firm hold of her husband's hand, but she was eager rather than apprehensive. I heard her whisper to him, 'It seems almost a pity we are going to die—just when we have earned so much treasure.' And he answered, 'We shall have no need of that kind of treasure: in each other we shall find riches.'

" 'Happiness,' she answered. 'Yes, that is the only thing worth having. I'm glad we are dying, for in time my grandmother's unguent might have lost its power: now we shall always be young.'

"When we reached the middle of the River, she said, 'I never knew that to die was to walk into happiness.' And I asked, 'You know that you are dead?'

"She smiled, and answered, 'Have you not told me that I am? And do I not rejoice in the knowledge?'

"Then she turned to her husband, and they embraced and I woke up.

" 'I don't remember seeing the children in the boat: I suppose that as soon as they knew that their mother didn't need their protection any more they went on with whatever they wanted to be doing.' "

Then, without waiting for any comment from me, he

said, ''So you see why I want to go to find out whether he's dead?''

''I'll go to tell your mother where we are going: then I'll come back to you.''

''Can we take our food with us instead of waiting to eat it here?''

''Certainly, if you wish. But why, if he is dead, are you in such a hurry?''

''Partly because it's a chance to prove that I dreamed true, and partly because the man had a cow and there will be no one to milk her.''

We traveled by litter and arrived within the hour. The cow was lowing in her stall, and the shutters of the house were still closed. The door creaked on its hinges as I pushed it open. A shaft of sunlight shone through the doorway to the bed-place, where a man lay with a smile on his dead mouth.

''So it *was* a true dream!'' whispered Nekht. ''I...I think I'll go and milk the cow.''

## the half-Brothers

Senusert had been staying with Kiyas and Hanuk in the Jackal, and on his return he said to me:

''Hanuk was telling me more about the journeys he used to make in disguise before the Dawn. I realized that although I have lived for a time as a member of most of the principal castes, I have always filled a role already prepared for me and the people with whom I worked accepted me as one of themselves. Now I want to learn how Egypt receives a man of no caste; who has no village he can speak of as his home, who is without the background of kinsmen. I think I ought to take every opportunity of judging the authority of the different Nomarchs.''

''I am sure that compared with the time before the Watchers came to power the administration is as sunlight to the murk of a crocodile's larder.''

''Yes, Ra-ab. But you and Roidahn have always told me that only by ceaseless vigilance can tranquility be maintained. Many exiles still come to us: would there be so many if all Nomes were like the Oryx? You are not sure of the North: remember, they accepted my father only because it was expedient. They did not fight oppression as did the men of the South; nor have they worked so wholeheartedly to keep Fear in exile.''

''You wish to go to the North?''

''Yes, and to the Royal City. Perhaps as a beggar in the servants' courts I shall come to know more of the worth of my father's nobles than I shall ever discover when I take my place at Court.''

So Senusert, soon after his sixteenth birthday, left the Oryx and was away from us for four months.

The news he brought home with him more than justified his decision to make the journey, and proved that Meri and I had been right to overcome our very considerable anxiety in letting him go.

''If I become Pharaoh, Ra-ab,'' he said, ''and I have a son, he too shall go nameless among my people before I allow him to become Co-ruler. I have brought with me a tally, more than two hundred names, of people who should no longer be allowed to hold their present authority. Two hundred, in a hundred and thirty-four days! I should have been appalled to find so many had I not asked for charity only from those who had never been Watchers. Seventy of those names have proved to me how vital it is that one day Nehri should become Vizier, for then the overseers of every state would be directly responsible to him; both for their people and their herds. It is curious that some people who would be horrified at neglecting a child are callous to their animals. Sometimes those who were generous to me with food, had goats which looked half-starved; and a man who gave me a pair of sandals because he noticed that the thong of mine was broken, had an ox with a disease of the hooves which must have caused it considerable pain.

''When I came to the Royal Nomes I went to the kitchen-quarters of the houses of the nobles. They never refused food to me, and usually I shared the meal of the lesser household servants. Apart from three estates where the servants were unduly apprehensive of their master's temper, or suffered from a mistress too particular about trivialities, I found nothing disquieting to report. When I reached the Royal City I thought it would be interesting to go to the Palace. It was the first time I have ever entered the servants' courts, for I was never allowed to go there in my grandmother's time. I offered to pay for food with labor, and said that I had some skill as a gardener. Rather to my surprise, I was allowed to work in the private gardens. Once my father walked past me, so close that I could have touched him; but I prostrated myself and he did not recognize me.''

Senusert looked up and his voice took on a new note. ''It was in the garden that I first saw my half-brother. Did you know that he now lives in the Palace; that he occupies the apartments that used to be mine?''

''When last I heard of him he was living with his mother, not far from the House of Ramios.''

''I was told they had only recently come to the Palace.''

''Did you find an opportunity to speak with him?''

''Yes. While working in the garden I heard him cry out, and found he had been stung in the hand by a poisonous spider. I sucked the wound, and then treated it as Yiahn had taught me. He was grateful, and asked how I, a gardener, had learned such effective measures. I told him that I had not always been a gardener, but had once worked for a man who made elixirs of herbs.''

''What did you think of him?''

''I liked him, Ra-ab. He is not so tall as I, but in some

215

ways more closely resembles my father, though his brow is wider and his eyes are gray. I pretended to take him for the Royal Heir, and asked, 'How soon will it be before you become Co-ruler?' He replied, 'My father, Pharaoh, has not yet decided. He has another son, older than I am. His name is Prince Senusert, and his mother was the Royal Wife. Some people think he will rule instead of me.' 'Senusert...' I said, pretending to be puzzled, 'I have never heard of a Prince Senusert.''

'' 'Quite a lot of people have forgotten about him,' he answered. 'I think he is in a temple being trained as a priest. Once, Pharaohs always used to be priests, you know. They wanted me to go into a temple, but Tet-hen—he is my father's high-priest—said I might take several lives before I was ready for Initiation.'

''Then I asked what Senusert was like. He hesitated before answering, and then said, 'I don't know. I have never seen him: he hasn't lived at the Palace for a long time. I once heard one of the servants say about me, ''Let Ptah be thanked; he is not like his half-brother!'' So I don't think they can have liked Senusert. I asked my mother about him, but she said it wasn't fair to listen to servants' gossip...and that if Senusert had been a horrid little boy it was his grandmother's fault.' Then he stopped and said, 'I don't know why I'm telling you all this.' So I said reassuringly, 'You let me cut your hand and suck out the spider poison, and that has made us blood-kin for seven days. So you can say anything you like to me without its being disloyal, and I can do the same to you.'

'' 'Does it?' he said, looking rather bewildered. 'I didn't know.' But he accepted it, for I expect he wanted someone to talk to just as much as I did when I used to live in the Palace; someone who treated him as an equal. So I took the risk of asking him why his mother hated Kiosostoris, who had been dead for years.

'' 'I don't know; she has never told me. But until Kiosostoris died, my mother was always frightened of something happening to me. I was never allowed to be alone, and Mother always slept in my room...except when she came here, which was very seldom. My mother doesn't want me to be Pharaoh. She says I should be much happier as a secondary prince.'

"Then I asked if he thought he would be Pharaoh, and he said, 'I don't know. It depends entirely on what Father decides. I don't see him very often; but I don't think he likes Senusert or he wouldn't have sent him away. Mother is frightened of what may happen to us when Senusert comes back. She says that if he has been trained as a priest some of the nobles will dislike him more than they dislike Father.'

"I said, 'Do the nobles dislike Pharaoh?' He looked very uncomfortable, and said hurriedly, 'I should not have said that...you must forget I ever said such a thing. You understand? Forget it at once!' I laughed, and said reassuringly, 'It is already forgotten. You need not be afraid; are we not blood-brothers for seven days?'

"I did not see him again; but, because of what he had told me, I went North the next day, to try to find out more in the kitchen quarters of the Nomarchs and the more powerful nobles. There is little strength in a blade of grass; but with many grasses you can make a strong rope. From chance phrases, even from the inflection of a voice, though alone they were not important, I learned that there is a strong faction in Egypt which is hoping that my half-brother will become Co-ruler. They want him because they think he will be easily influenced by those who have their personal interest at heart, rather than the welfare of the country. Although the tribute which the nobles now pay is smaller than it was under the Old Rule, they would rather see their wealth go to emblazon the Court than used to increase the comfort of the common people. They resent the simplicity in which my father lives, and would like once again to see the Royal Treasure squandered on those lavish displays which were supposed to mollify the people under the Old Rule. They would prefer to go to a temple where, provided their tribute was lavish, they were promised the favor of the Gods, than to be told, as they are by our priests, that no one can enter the Fields of Ra except by the value of a heart burnished by his own exertions. They are less convinced by a priest who in complete simplicity can cure their sickness, than they used to be by those who masqueraded in the temples, and whose ritual was a lamp which burned no oil of truth.''

''But why, Senusert, are the nobles dissatisfied? Under the Old Rule they had to bribe the tribute-gatherers so heavily that sometimes they had to pay three times the value of the 'tribute of the tenth part' so as to secure their tenure. Now they have a security they never before enjoyed: the people are content, the army is strong...they have nothing to fear, either within our boundaries or from foreigners.''

''They have themselves to fear, Ra-ab. A man can no longer hold authority unless it continues to be justified in his own person. I can understand how great a change this is, perhaps even more vividly than you. I used to think that because I was the Son of Pharaoh I did not have to observe the laws as did other people. I thought the Gods had already made their choice by assigning me to such a birthright. I did not have to work for my position; I did not have to make any effort to be worthy of it; I was Senusert the Prince. You stripped me of that false strength and made me grow strong in myself. It was only to Senusert the boy that you gave love, and trust, and friendship. It made no difference to you from whose loins I sprang. Senusert was the name of a friend...or of an enemy; and it could not be enhanced by any title which was justified only by temporal position. A warrior who believes in his invincibility only because he has a spear while the enemy is unarmed will always resent the order which bids him fight with bare hands. In time the warrior may become grateful for that order, but not before he has learned the strength of his own muscles. The weak man who knows that he cannot

218

stand alone will always hate the man who exposed his weakness. That is why some of the nobles hate my father...and hate the Eyes of Horus who gave him the Crook and Flail. They can no longer say, 'These lands will belong to my son because he is my son,' for now they must add, 'if he proves himself worthy to administer them.' They must question not only their own integrity, but that of their heirs, and, worse than that, Ra-ab, they must permit their own authority to be questioned...and only a wise man can with composure allow that to happen!

''There have been a few instances when Amenemhet has had to show the power of the Flail. Men who in the early days of the reign owned great estates which they had held for several generations now find themselves reduced to the rank of field-workers. Only a wise man would have been able to say, 'Pharaoh is just; for my people are happier under their new master.' And the Watchers do not condemn the wise.''

''You think that the dissatisfied faction wish Seneferu to become Co-ruler in your stead? Why? Do you think there is anything in his character which justifies their belief that he is venal?''

''He is not corrupt, of that I feel sure; but he has not had the special training necessary to make him invulnerable to other men's opinions. He is sensitive to criticism, and so cannot hope to remain impervious either to flattery or to the reverence in which Pharaoh is held. It would be natural for a young man to wish for more lavish entertainments than are at present to be found at Court; for even the most loyal in the Royal City are disappointed that my father shares so few pleasures with them. I am sure that Seneferu has a warm nature which will respond to affection even when it is superficial. He would never inquire closely into the conduct of a friend's estate...he would forget the Flail, until in time the Crook also had lost its power. They will laugh with him, and flatter him, and use him; and in time perhaps destroy both Egypt and themselves.''

219

''Have your forgotten that our laws decree that no one shall hold authority which is not justified in his own person?''

''It would be difficult for the Watchers to lead a rising against a man so well liked by his people. People will always make excuses for their ruler unless they hate him. They hated my great-grandfather...very bitterly: and that hatred doubled the number of your arrows. Corruption which is masked by the smile of a kindly, though foolish ruler is, by a long measure of time, more dangerous than the most bitter tyrant. The cruelty which the tyrant practices is a seed which comes quickly to maturity and poisons the sower, who must eat his own harvest: but the stupidities of a well-meaning fool sometimes lie fallow for many years, and like all plants of slow growth, they put down long roots which only arduous toil can clean from the field.''

''In less than a year, Senusert,'' I said, ''you will have to leave the Oryx and return to your father. I know that Amenemhet has already chosen you to be his Co-ruler, and he will declare you to the people on his twentieth anniversary.

''He may still change that decision.''

''He will never do that, for if he did so it would be to deny the wisdom of the man who made him Pharaoh: Roidahn, to whom he gave the title, 'Lord of the Horizon.' You will be Pharaoh, Senusert, not because you are the son of Amenemhet, but because you are the Pharaoh of the Watchers; in you they will see the truth for which they stand.''

To my intense emotion, he knelt on one knee and took my hand between his, as though he were a servant taking the Oath of Fealty. ''If I become Pharaoh, and all the people of Egypt are my children, I can never hope for a son who will give me such love and honor as I give to you and Meri, who are my father and my mother in Horus.''

# amulet of Ra

The Vizier, whom I had not seen since he came to the Oryx to tell me of the death of the Babylonian, came to Hotep-Ra shortly before Senusert was to return to the Royal City. I joined him at Roidahn's house, and during the first evening he spoke only of matters concerning general administration. Though he must have known that I had not seen Pharaoh for a long time, he preferred to assume that I was in constant communication with Amenemhet. I was anxious for an opportunity to find out whether he considered Senusert's estimate of the strength of his half-brother's following either too hopeful or too apprehensive; but only by circuitous means was I able to lead the conversation in this direction.

"I consider Prince Seneferu to be an honest and amiable young man," said the Vizier. "I seldom have occasion to speak with him, but he is well liked in the Palace, and he shares with the nobles of the Court the pleasures in which Pharaoh no longer permits himself to indulge."

"Do you think that Amenemhet is unwise to become so much of a recluse?"

"It is not for me to give an opinion of Pharaoh's conduct, but if he were an ordinary man and therefore open to criticism, I might say that he is foolish...perhaps foolish is too strong a word, to withdraw himself completely from those who might be his personal friends. His judgments continue to be admirable; the laws of the Watchers continue to be meticulously carried out by the officials: yet sometimes I wonder if it is enough for a man only to be just and incorruptible? I once heard Roidahn say that a man who has forgotten he is a man cannot be a priest...."

"You suggest that Pharaoh has forgotten his humanity?"

"That is too direct a question for me to answer. Prince Seneferu has not inherited his father's austerity; he has the faculty of treating others as equals without losing the dignity of his rank; but he is impulsive, and I think that if he had to choose between a plausible rogue and a cold man of upright heart, it is into the hand of the rogue he would give his Seal.''

''Though this warmth is in some ways an admirable quality, it might be disastrous in a Pharaoh,'' I said.

The Vizier pretended to be surprised. ''Pharaoh? Why should Seneferu become Pharaoh? No one should know better than you, Roidahn, that Prince Senusert is soon to be declared Co-ruler with his father.''

''Sometimes, my friend, truth and discretion cannot drink from the same cup. When one of these must thirst, it is the tongue of discretion which must continue to know drought.''

He smiled, and the eyes under the full lids were no longer wary. ''The air of Hotep-Ra opens the mouth of a man even so tortuous as myself! Forgive me for having taken you upon so long a journey when our destination was so close to both our hearts.'' He laughed, ''You see that even in my apology I try to conceal the honey of my meaning in the bee-hive of parable!''

Then he went on, ''As I told you when I last came to the Oryx, I hoped that after the death of the Babylonian, Amenemhet would no longer hold himself apart from his friends. I have tried by every means in my power to discover what has caused him to change, and had he ever failed to uphold our traditions I would have considered it my duty to inform you and Roidahn. I may have been partly responsible for Prince Seneferu and his mother going to live in the Palace: I hoped that their influence might make Pharaoh remember his humanity. But he continues to behave as a man haunted by something I do not understand. He is kind, and even indulgent, to Seneferu, but the boy is not close enough to his heart to be able to do what I hoped he might find possible. It is not altogether surprising that even the nobles who have always been loyal to our cause regret that the Palace, which used to be the center of their lives, is now no more than a Hall of Audience. Seneferu is their only link with the Royal

House: they think that if he ruled, their own luster would again be increased.''

''Are there not some of them who hope for more than luster?''

''I have already said that Seneferu would never denounce a rogue who was his friend. They think, and perhaps not without cause, that he would be easily influenced; that he would be content if his wide avenues were lined with festival masts when he went on a Progress, and would not pay very much heed to the narrow alleys which once were thought beneath the dignity of the the Royal Footstep. It is known that Senusert is being trained to follow his father, but not that he is in the Oryx. It is widely thought that he is in a temple; and many expect that when he takes up the Crook and Flail further austerities will be imposed on the Court.''

''Will there be any open hostility when he is declared Co-ruler?''

''No. The respect in which Amenemhet is held is too strong for his decision to be questioned...openly.''

''Then what have we to fear? As soon as Senusert has had a chance to show his quality, surely he will be most thankfully acclaimed?''

''By those who look to the Horizon...but not by those who think their own navels the center of the universe!''

''You have come to warn me against...what? Let us have it in plain words.''

''I warn you to keep Senusert well guarded. If he should die, Seneferu would take his place...without bloodshed, without question.''

''You think there will be an attempt to murder him?''

''Murder can be subtle. As the Royal Heir, Senusert will lead the Army into battle...and a warrior does not always die by the spear of a foreign enemy. Warn Senusert to be constantly on guard against his half-brother; not to take into battle men who are known to be partisans of Seneferu, and to have as his cup-bearer a man whom he can trust with his life.

Urge him to choose a wife...a wife who will be accepted as the Royal Mother. An heir would be a strong shield against Seneferu; for Senusert could appoint you and Roidahn to be the child's guardians.''

''Then your suggestion is...?''

''That it would be greatly to the interest of Egypt if Senusert is married *before* he returns to the Royal City.''

After consulting Roidahn, I decided that the Vizier's conversation must be reported in full to Senusert; but before doing so I discussed it with Meri.

''Ra-ab,'' she said, ''you must impress on Senusert that though he seems to be faced with the same problem as was his father, he must never marry for expediency.''

''Even if the Vizier is right, and by refusing to take a wife he would endanger Egypt, his position is not the same as was Amenemnet's. He can make a free choice, and it is only necessary that Roidahn and ourselves approve of the woman who will become the mother of his children: of this Pharaoh has sent me his personal assurance.''

''How can Senusert remain loyal to the ideals of the Eyes of Horus if we ask him to betray his own heart? Remember what you said to Kiyas. If it had not been for you she might have been content with a marriage which would never have brought her the happiness she has found with Hanuk.''

''Would a woman who really loved Senusert mind being a secondary wife?''

''Ra-ab, if you had married the Daughter of the Hare, I should have willingly become your concubine...but I think *she* would have been unhappy. Are we going to ask Senusert to deny himself the happiness which we have taught him to demand as his right? Is the boy we have trained so weak a man that he must shelter behind a child who is not yet conceived?''

''You think I should conceal from him what the Vizier has suggested?''

"Senusert is a man, not a boy any longer. He must make his own decision, and we must provide him will all the facts from which to make it. We must not influence his choice, for it may alter the course of his life." Then Meri smiled and said, "To you, my Ra-ab, I am always honest, and if he tries to marry a woman only because he thinks it is his duty, I shall use every means to make him change his mind!"

It was with great reluctance that I told Senusert what I had learned from the Vizier. I gave him a clear and full account of our conversation, looking out of the window as I did so because I deeply feared to see his face cloud with sorrow. I turned to see that he was serene, and his eyes joyous.

"Ra-ab, I knew by your voice that you hated to tell me all that. You feared that you were offering me the choice between duty and happiness. Yet, had you but known it, you brought me glorious news! I thought I should not be allowed to marry until I had become Co-ruler, and that I should have great difficulty in persuading my father to let me take a Royal Wife who had not been selected by himself. Now you say that I can marry as soon as I like, and that my father will approve the marriage if both you and Roidahn give your consent. That consent I know you will give, for have you not always told me that true nobility is not born with the blood?"

The relief his words brought me was so intense that for a moment I did not answer lest I betray my emotion. "You have found the woman you love? Why did you not let Meri and me share in your happiness?"

"Because I thought I should have great opposition from my father, and I did not wish to add this burden to the many you carry."

"What is her rank?"

"The most suitable of all for a Pharaoh to marry: she is a priest."

"Who is she? Does she belong to the Temple of the Horizon?"

"No, she does not live in the Oryx."

"How did you meet her?"

"When, as a beggar, I was returning from the North. I had a cut on my foot which would not heal. I was very lame, and after crossing the northern boundary of the Jackal I stopped at a house to ask for shelter. Whether the poison spread, or whether I had another fever, I am not sure, but I became very ill. I was afraid I should have to tell my real name to the people who were looking after me, and ask them to let Hanuk know I was within his boundaries; but they told me their daughter was initiate of Ptah in the temple which Hanuk built soon after he became Nomarch, that she was coming to visit them, and would arrive the following day. They had given me a room in the servant's quarters, but the woman and her husband both treated me as though I were their son. When I thanked them, they said, 'If we had done less, why should the Gods remember us, for we would have proved ourselves traitors to their laws.'

"They were very proud that their daughter was a healer-priest; they told me that when she was a small child she would hold a sick bird between her hands until strength came back to its wings and it could return to the air; of how she could take away fever, and bring sleep even to those in great pain.

"As soon as I saw her I knew that I should always bless the lameness which brought me to her home."

"And I bless it too: for with you I can now share joy instead of sorrow. We must go to tell Meri so that she can rejoice with us."

She was even more deeply moved than I had been, and after she had embraced Senusert, she said:

"Even when your wife is Pharaoh with you I shall still think of her as my daughter. Together you will be winged, as they were winged who held the Crook and Flail when the temples of Egypt were as an avenue of torches. Senusert, you must go tomorrow to bring her to us. I am so eager to see her! We will begin the wedding preparations immediately, and work so hard that it shall take place within sixty days. You will take the Oath before Ptah at the Horizon of Horus; and the Jackal, the Hare and the Oryx will share in the rejoicings.''

Senusert looked a little troubled. ''Meri,'' he said, ''I don't want to disappoint you, and if you think it necessary I shall of course agree to your plans...but *need* I have an important wedding?''

She laughed, ''Surely you have not become shy? Don't you want to let your people have the privilege of seeing your bride?''

''It may sound foolish...but you know how I dread leaving the Oryx for the formality of the Court! The years are going to hold for me so many festivals. So many times I shall have to be a figure-head at ceremonies. When I take the Oath before Ptah I want to be Senusert who is your son, not Senusert the heir of Amenemhet, not Senusert the man who is soon to become Co-ruler.''

''How well I understand,'' I said warmly. ''I remember how difficult it was to pretend that the elaborate preparations Meri made for our wedding were worth the hours we wasted apart from each other! If the choice had been mine we should never have been separated for a moment which we might have shared!''

''Would you mind, Meri,'' he asked, ''if only you and Ra-ab—and of course her parents—know of my secret until I can declare her as my wife? Do you remember how, when I was a little boy, you told me that on the morning after you and Ra-ab were married you pretended that the clearing on the river bank, where your pavilion was set, was a little island under the protection of Nut, and that you were going to live there forever? I should like Ptah-kefer and I to have such an island of quietness to remember, so that those few days may remain as an amulet made in the name of Ra, which at a word will always be able to change the formality of a royal banquet, or the monotonous ceremonial of the Court, into a man and woman alone by the river. That amulet will make two Pharaohs forget that they can never be free of the responsibility of holding the Crook and Flail, and will allow them to remember that they hold a higher rank than the Double Crown...the rank of lovers. The time may come when, to lead my armies, I must be parted from Ptah-kefer; but above the heavy rhythm of marching feet I shall hear the quiet lapping of the water which greeted us when we woke together in the dawn. Even if we live to be very old, we shall only have to smile at each other to remember...and to be young.''

# pRincess ptah-kefeR

Before giving his consent to the marriage, I had expected Roidahn to wish to see Ptah-kefer; but when I asked him if he wanted the girl to be brought to him, he smiled and said:

''Has Senusert forgotten that when he told me of what he experienced in the guise of a beggar, he mentioned that he had spent a few days in the Jackal on his way home? He tried very hard to make his voice sound casual, but when he mentioned that the daughter of the people who had succored him was a priest who had healed his sickness, it was obvious that he felt for her much more than gratitude. I have spoken of her to Hanuk's high-priest, in whose temple she was trained, and everything he told me made me glad that Senusert has made so wise a choice. On Earth she and I are still strangers, yet I know her well. When she wears the White Crown it will not be for the first time.''

''What do you know of her mother and father?''

''Though it is a matter of no importance, the two who call her daughter are but foster-parents. They know nothing of her history and think her family died in that pestilence which broke out in the Reed soon after the Dawn. They found her lying in a small cedar-wood chest, the lid open, under a shade-tree on the boundary of the Reed and the Jackal. It was two or three years before they lost their fear that she might be claimed and taken from them.''

''Why would a child be abandoned even if the parents died in the pestilence? The outbreak was not serious enough to cause any disorder; only a few villages were affected and there were less than a hundred dead.''

''I too thought the story unlikely, but as I did not want to arouse comment by making inquiries, I found out all I needed to know by using the faculty of Anubis. I read Ptah-kefer's memory, though the events which I recorded occurred when she was a baby and so she has no recollection of them in her waking mind. Her father was a noble of the Reed, and her mother his favorite concubine. At the time of Amenemhet's accession, he was suspected of being unworthy to continue in his office, but we had not sufficient evidence to decree his exile. Two years later he proved himself incompetent to hold any authority under the Watchers, but he was given the opportunity of going into voluntary exile. It was thought that both the concubine and her six months old daughter accompanied him out of Egypt: the concubine went, but she loved the Two Lands so dearly that, rather than condemn the child to a life among foreigners, she gave it into the care of a servant who was to take it to a kinsman who lived in the Nome of the Tortoise.

''The nurse was afraid that if it were known that the child was the daughter of an exile, she might be punished for helping a member of a family which had incurred Pharaoh's displeasure. You must remember, Ra-ab, that this was in the early days, when there were many who had not lost their fear of authority. On her way south, the woman became ill of the pestilence. She tried to continue on her journey, leading a donkey in whose panniers were the baby and the cedar chest.

She must have known she was very ill—perhaps she realized she was dying. She put the baby in the chest under the tree and rode on in search of help. She must have had a sudden seizure; she died alone and unrecognized; was buried and forgotten.''

''Which story shall be told to the people?''

''Neither. It should be sufficient for everyone that Ptah-kefer is both a priest and the beloved of Senusert. When he returns from the Oryx, at his side will be the woman who is his wife, the Princess Ptah-kefer.''

To bring happiness to Senusert, Meri and I were very willing to enter with him into a small deception. He wanted us to go to the Jackal, not as Nomarchs but as his parents. We were to travel in a manner suitable to a couple who owned a few fields and a small herd of cattle.

''If they saw you as Nomarchs before they had a chance to know you, they might be embarrassed,'' he said. ''They are not noble except in their hearts; they thought me nameless, yet they treated me as their son. I must go gently with them, for if they knew the circumstances to which I had been born they might treat me as a stranger!''

''Surely Ptah-kefer knows who you are!'' exclaimed Meri.

''She knows that we love each other, and that there were reasons why I could not tell her where I came from or who I am. She assured me that nothing could make any difference to our love, and reminded me that even wise men break laws, and that all of us have left the Causeway at some time in our long history.''

''Does she have no suspicion who you are?''

''She may think I am a thief, or even that I had to leave my village because I killed a man. But she looks to the horizon, to the future we shall share. She said that all yesterdays belong to the dead years, and that a burden need no longer be carried when again we turn our faces to the Sun.''

''She was willing to marry you without knowing anything

about you, not even where you came from?''

''When I asked her that, she said, 'We come from the Gods, and we shall return into their company. Can you measure the Road to the Horizon in thumb-joints, or our ten thousand years in little yesterdays?' ''

So on the twelfth day of the fourth month of the Sowing, Senusert, Meri and I went to the Jackal. I wore the kilt and woolen cloak of a prosperous husbandman, and Meri was dressed in a manner suitable to his wife. Her only ornaments were a necklace of rough turquoise, strung on a plaited linen thread, and two armlets of copper.

Senusert permitted us to travel by litter until we came within about a thousand paces of our destination. Then we went on foot, with a pack-donkey carrying the few possessions he had allowed us to bring. A girl was coming along the road toward us, and when I saw Senusert's face I did not have to ask whether she was Ptah-kefer. He ran ahead and took her in his arms; then they stood hand in hand waiting for us to join them.

She was not so tall as Meri, yet the beautiful proportions of her body gave an illusion of height. She gave us the greeting between kinsmen, and I saw that she had the serene and fearless eyes of a true priest. I was amused to notice that she was trying to put us at our ease; it was obvious that she believed us to belong to a caste inferior to her own, and was afraid lest we be embarrassed. Did not her father own a thousand by a thousand paces, have a herd of cows, and a bull already famous enough to be sought as sire for other men's herds? Did he not have a house of six rooms, with separate quarters for the three women who worked in the house, and the four men who helped in the fields?

She tried to end our ''shyness'' by showing how deeply she honored our son. Many children in the Oryx had been called Meri or Ra-ab, so I knew that our names would cause no comment. Her mother was waiting for us by the outer door, which led directly into the main room.

"This is Meri and Ra-ab, Mother," said Ptah-kefer, and then Senusert turned to us and said, "The name of Ptah-kefer's mother is Nia, and of her father, Beras."

Nia told us that our host had not known the hour of our arrival and was busy with some duty on his estate. While we were waiting for him she gave us mead and sweet cakes, and talked of matters which she thought likely to interest us: the prospects of the next harvest, whether any of our animals had suffered during the winter, which had been unusually cold; whether we lived near enough to the river to get fish, and, if not, had our village a fish-pool?

Before her husband joined us, with profuse apologies that he had not been there to greet us at the door, Senusert and Ptah-kefer had found some excuse to wander off together. Soon afterward Nia took Meri to see the room we were to occupy.

At first Beras did not mention Senusert, but instead talked of how under the Old Rule he had been a Leader of a Hundred, and had been severely wounded during a border skirmish which ended his usefulness as a warrior. This farm had been his wife's inheritance from her mother, and during the last fifteen years they had prospered and been able to acquire more land.

"I hope you feel assured," he said courteously, "that both my wife and I have given our warm approval to the marriage of our daughter. Your son told me, very frankly, that he had no name or position. But he is young and healthy, and if he wishes to become a farmer I will make over a third of my property to my daughter on her marriage day. At the death of my wife and myself all that we have shall be theirs."

"I too will try to help them," I said. I saw this troubled him: he paused for a moment, as though searching for words which would not hurt my pride, before saying:

"I want you to believe that it would bring joy to my wife and myself to help your son. Soon he will be my son also. It happens that the Gods have been generous to me, and to do for our children what I have suggested will be no hardship. I understand from Senusert that you have fewer possessions than I have—though in those treasures which a man can carry with him when he goes on the long journey I feel sure you are much richer than myself. Your son must never feel indebted to me, so perhaps it would be as well if he thought they received an equal portion from us both...that the shares are not equal must remain our secret. Will you not allow me this privilege, for I am an old man and it would give me great happiness?''

To refuse this offer seemed so grave a dishonesty, yet to accept it was to deceive him. What was I to do? I was saved having to make an immediate decision by Ptah-kefer coming into the room to tell us that the evening meal was prepared.

I was only alone for a moment with Meri, but she whispered to me, ''They have decided that you must be a very hard-hearted father to have turned your son out of the house! I couldn't explain without betraying Senusert's secret. Of course Nia didn't say it directly, but it was obvious what she was thinking.''

''What did you say?''

''She was praising Senusert, saying how handsome he was and how proud I must be of him. Then she added, 'It is a pity that men sometimes forget that they too were impulsive when they were young. You are his mother, and I am sure you are never angry with him. It must have been terrible for you until he was allowed to return to his father's house.' ''

Having heard this, I was not surprised when Beras said to me later in the evening:

''I have never inquired what caused Senusert to come here nameless and apparently without a friend. He must have done something which greatly angered you, otherwise you could not have denied your son, even when anger was in its first heat. Are we not perhaps sometimes unduly harsh with our sons because we have decided that they shall become like ourselves...or rather as we consider ourselves to be? My father was not a warrior; he was a merchant in the chief city of the Leopard. He told me that as a soldier I should always be poor, and when I insisted, he said that if I left his house I should never return to it.

"I never did return; nor did I hear that he was dead until he had been in his grave for three years. If there is still in your heart a trace of anger against your son, I beg you to recognize that it is a stranger who has entered your courtyard as a thief to steal your happiness. I repeat that I have no wish to know what Senusert did; but are you sure that you would be angry with him if you knew the motive which made him act? He may have stolen, but do you know *why* he stole? He may have killed a man, but are you sure he did not consider it to be an act of justice?"

"I see that in you my son has a most loyal friend!"

"I took him into my house because he was in need. Had I denied him, why should the Gods remember me when I am in trouble? He was a stranger, yet both my wife and I felt that it was familiar to have him under our roof. He was in pain, and his pain became ours, as though we were indeed of one flesh. When with my daughter he found love, we again knew the happiness of young lovers. Though I wish to give my possessions to Senusert because he has made my daughter happy, because I love him as a son, there is yet another reason why I wish him to be my heir...a reason which I do not fully understand. I feel that if I were undecided whether to turn to the right or to the left, he would be able to tell me which path to follow: if I were afraid, I would be strong in his presence, and if I were dying I would wish him to act as my Steersman."

"You think that my son, who came to your house as a beggar, who must have deeply angered his parents for him to have been friendless and alone, yet has such character that you accept his judgment without question?"

"I do," said Beras fervently. "You may call me a fool for seeking wisdom from a boy of eighteen, but he has a quality I have never before seen, except in rulers such as Amenemhet.''

''And you would trust your daughter to him, even without knowing who he is or whence he comes?''

''I have already done so.''

''What if he does not wish to stay on your land? He left my house; why should he not leave yours?''

''That is for him to decide. One thing only shall I ask of him: that where he goes there shall my daughter go also, for if they were parted she would know bitter sorrow.''

''He has often talked to me of distant countries. What would you say if he took your daughter to live in the Land of Gold, or even became a trader with the people of Punt?''

''Wherever he goes she can work beside him. Is she not a healer-priest? And are there not sick people to be succored in the name of Ptah in every land which Ra sees on his journey across the sky? I am old, and selfish, and therefore I hope that it is in this Nome that she will work; but who am I to judge whether Ptah wishes Egyptians to be healed by her, or men whose skins are of a different color, and whose language I do not understand? But they will understand *her* language, for all men and all animals, even the plants and the rocks, are fellow kinsmen of Ptah, in whose name she brings them life.''

''I am very honored by what you have told me. We are two men no longer so very young, yet let us for a moment imagine that we are magicians...as perhaps we often pretended when we were children. I have heard that the Eyes of Horus boast that one day there will be no one in the Two Lands who has not the widest scope for his talents, nor will there be one overburdened by a task too great for him. It is not always easy to assign each man his task; even the most fruitful branch may break if the crop is too heavy for its growth. If the decision were yours, to what position would you assign Senusert?''

''I would give him wide authority. Tomorrow I should

have him declared headman of our village, and soon the people themselves would make him the overseer of the town.''

''Why stop at a town,'' I said, as though in jest. ''Why not make him the Nomarch?'

''If I thought that Hanuk and his wife could be improved upon I should gladly put Senusert in their place. But they are so well beloved that I would not deprive them of their office even to advance my son.''

''There are other Nomes than the Jackal. Would you make him Nomarch of the Oryx?''

''As you come from the Oryx, of that you should be a better judge than I. But from all I have heard, Ameni will be a worthy successor to Ra-ab Hotep, and no Nome could ask for more.''

''There are other Nomes. Shall we make him Nomarch of one of them?''

''You may jest,'' he said angrily, ''but if you do, I shall claim to be a better judge of your son than you are yourself. I *would* make him a Nomarch, even though his father is only a farmer like myself—and has never even been a warrior in his youth!''

I got up and put my arm round his shoulders. ''My friend, one who is so wise in the weighing of men's hearts must no longer waste that talent even on such admirable fields as your own. Pharaoh has need of men like you, for even in our time they are rare. You are not deceived because a man is poor, nor will you be deceived because he is rich. You are not afraid to uphold your judgment, even when it must seem that the one to whom you speak has had greater opportunity of knowing the facts than yourself. That is the quality which is required by those who hold the Ivory Seals of Pharaoh. Pharoah will not forget.''

For a moment he looked puzzled, and then he laughed, ''For a moment you looked so serious that I forgot we were speaking in jest. Although I am held in authority in the little world of my fields and am acknowledged as overlord by my seven servants, even when I fling the net of my thoughts most widely I do not imagine that Pharaoh has ever heard my name, or that if he had he would remember it.''

''Pharaoh will never forget your name. He will not have the opportunity, for you will always be one of his closest friends.''

''Me, a friend of Pharaoh!''

''A man is not usually the friend of one who claims to be the father of his son!'' I said smiling. ''But I am a friend of Pharaoh, and I can tell you the name of the man who will rule after him, the name of our next Pharaoh, in whose hands the Crook and Flail will be held in the name of Ra.''

''I don't understand. Why do you mock me?''

''I do not mock: his name is Senusert, and Ptah-kefer will be the name of the Royal Wife.''

# PART FOUR

# the new Direction

Though Beras and his wife willingly agreed to be my guest in the Oryx, I could not persuade them to accompany us to the Royal City for the ceremonies attendant upon the declaration of Senusert as Co-ruler.

"Are you sure, Beras," I said, "that you will not change your mind and come with us to the Royal City?"

"Quite sure, Ra-ab. I do not doubt that Senusert would make me one of his overseers, though it is too much to expect that he would give me one of the Ivory Seals."

"That would not be too much. I did not speak lightly when I said that Pharaoh has need of men like you."

"Perhaps, where my own capabilities are concerned, I am a better judge even than Pharaoh. I am old, Ra-ab, and content with my fields. My wife would not be happy if she had to learn the usages of ceremony, which are unfamiliar to us both."

"They are easy to learn. She must not allow her diffidence to set a limit to your power for Egypt."

"It is not diffidence: she is only trying to protect me from being tempted beyond my strength."

"Am I your tempter?"

"No: he is the man I was thirty years ago; the young soldier who imagined that one day he would be a captain, and raised to the rank of noble, and enjoy a great estate. Then, as I have told you, I was wounded in the right arm, and ceased to be useful as a warrior. It is curious that I had never imagined the possibility of being crippled: either I would become a leader of warriors, or die in battle. I had little interest in the occupations of the soldier in time of peace: I always longed for battle in which I hoped to find advancement. At thirty I was still alive, but hating the body which had deprived me of ambition.

"It was my wife who taught me that there are enemies for a man to fight when he can no longer throw a spear or flight an arrow; adversaries more worthy of our strength even than are the Asiatics. In time, the corn growing in my fields became a people I must protect. Through me they can withstand the silver arrows of the clouds which the shout of thunder looses on their ranks. Through me they can contain the siege of the long heat; it is I who provides the water which saves their citadel. I can outwit the spies Set sends among them, the blight, the maggot and the rat. Corn is the treasure I bring home to Egypt, a treasure richer than any victor's spoil; for my arms are turned against the common foe of all mankind.

"There may be others to whom I can teach this secret; warriors who think their hearts broke with their swords. Let them come to my house—perhaps in the future I may need more rooms built for them. I will tell them stories which have known many camp-fires down the generations. They will acknowledge me as one of themselves, for they will see the scars of my old wounds. Though they are weary when they come to my door, when they go forth again they will see that their pennants, which they thought forever furled, still stream out on the wind of their clear future."

While in the Royal City, I was able to see Seneferu and form my own estimate of his character. It was obvious that he felt no jealousy toward his half-brother; indeed, far from being envious, he seemed to have profound sympathy for him.

"I wish I could do something to help Senusert," he said warmly. "But Pharaohs, and I suppose Co-rulers also, do not seem to want help from anyone. I am sorry for Ptahkefer. She is very gay and beautiful, but I expect that when she becomes the Royal Wife she will never go to banquets or enjoy the festivals.''

''Why not?''

''My mother lives almost entirely alone, except for her personal attendants. It would not be fitting for her to seek entertainment which her husband does not share. Pharaoh is always much too busy for entertainments.''

''He need not be.''

The boy looked startled. ''Are you suggesting that my father is wrong to live so austere a life?''

''That is for him to decide. If he is too tired after carrying out his work, then of course austerity is a necessity to him, to conserve his energy.''

''You mean, that if Pharaoh were young and strong, he could go hunting, and enjoy the pleasures of ordinary people?''

''Of course: he is a man like other men.''

''I didn't realize that,'' he said slowly. ''I suppose I always thought that everything my father did was necessary. Do you, Ra-ab Hotep, enjoy yourself in spite of being Nomarch?''

''I do more than that; I enjoy being Nomarch! Work is unpleasant only when it is uncongenial, and what I have to do is most exciting.''

''Exciting?''

''Yes. Would it surprise you that a sculptor is excited when at last he sees the granite on which he works taking the shape which he has so long held in his mind? The Oryx is my block of granite. The rough shape of the statue could already be seen before my father handed me his sculptor's tools. Each time I am able to bring happiness to one of my people it is as though I freed another chip of stone and so brought the final vision nearer its fulfillment.''

''Don't you do it because it is your *duty*?''

''Our first duty is to Ra. Ra decrees that we shall always act out of love; and to act out of love is to be happy.

Therefore it is our duty to be happy.''

"I thought duties were unpleasant; something we had to do because the Gods demanded it."

"What a strange paradox! That we should make ourselves unhappy because we had been told to be happy!"

"Won't the Court be so dull now that Senusert shares the Crook and Flail?"

"It will depend on your conception of dullness. His part of the Palace will be like any other house where a man welcomes his friends."

"Who will be his friends?"

"That you will discover for yourself."

"Will they all be nobles?"

"I should think that very unlikely. The Eyes of Horus are as near kinsmen; they are chosen not by rank but by quality. So you need not be surprised if at a banquet given by Senusert you see a man whose father was a field-worker seated in the place of honor."

"Will they be nice to my mother?" he asked anxiously. "Do you think Ptah-kefer will go to see her sometimes? My mother is often very lonely. She knows that my father is unhappy and would like to comfort him, even though it was only by a very ordinary kind of comfort...like being allowed to bring him wine when he is tired, or stroking his forehead when he is restless and cannot sleep. He never allows anyone to do things like that for him; I used to try when I was younger...the Vizier told me to, but though my father was kind to me and gave me everything I asked for, I always knew he was eager to be left alone. Senusert says you are one of his oldest friends. Ra-ab Hotep, couldn't you tell him it is the duty even of Pharaoh to be happy?"

Little did Seneferu know how much I longed to do that! But, though Amenemhet received me most graciously, expressing his profound gratitude for the way in which I had educated his son, the easy friendship which used to exist between us had vanished. He asked what favors he could grant me in return for what I had done for Senusert: I might have been a high priest, being asked how much tribute should be given in honor of the God in whose name my temple had been dedicated. He inquired about the welfare of my children, but I knew the subject held no real interest for him. He might have been asking how my herds had multiplied, or whether I was satisfied with the level of my granaries.

Meri and I attended the banquets given in honor of Senusert, and at all of these Pharaoh was present. Yet he never asked me to come to his private apartments; where once Meri and I had been welcomed as his closest friends.

It was Meri's suggestion that we should go to see Seneferu's mother, Nantani, at the house to which she had returned when Senusert brought his bride to the Palace. The house might have been occupied by one of the minor officials of the Court; the garden was more extensive than usual, but there was nothing else to distinguish the rank of its owner.

Nantani's son did not resemble her except in the color of his hair, which was tinged with red. She was thin, almost emaciated, yet her face was unlined and her eyes clear and brilliant under the level brows.

''I am grateful for the kindness you have shown to my son,'' she said, after we had talked for some time of trivial things. ''As a mother I wish that it had been he instead of Senusert who grew up in the Oryx, even though that would have meant my being parted from him.''

''But you also would have been so welcome,'' said Meri impulsively.

''I could not have left his father, even though there is so little I can do for him.''

''I am sure that you do much more than you realize,'' I said.

''You are kind to say such a thing; but it is not true. I have given Amenemhet a son, and my love; perhaps one day he may be ready to accept more from me. I used to think it was only because he had buried his heart with Nefer-tathen that he was so remote. I am afraid that I used to hate her, before I came to realize that our love for the same man made us sisters. Sometimes I think that I am nearer to her now than I have ever been to anyone. Amenemhet once told me that you and your wife taught him how to open his heart. I have wept, so many tears, because I have not your power. I think he trusts me: I have tried so hard to prove that from him I need nothing save affection.''

She turned to Meri. ''Should I have been wiser if I had pretended that I wanted the things, which were all he had to give me? He wanted to build me a great house; but when he brought me the scribes' plans, I said that I would prefer to remain here, where I was born. He had jewels specially designed for me to wear; and I said I would prefer it if he used the gold for his people. I think, in his heart, he used to be glad that I wished to live secluded. Sometimes—not very often—he used to come here alone, at night. We were still lonely when he thought of his body as a leopard whose hunger I could appease; but there were times when he slept in my arms, and if he cried out in a troubled dream he was comforted when I held him yet more close.

''You must be wondering why I speak of things so intimate to people I have met only today. It is not easy for me to speak, for I have acquired the habit of silence. For years I have lived on the hope that should Amenemhet despair in his loneliness, he would turn to me for comfort and I should not fail him. I want you to promise that should it be possible for him to turn to you, he will not lack a friend.''

''Why should he turn to us, when he has you?''

''I may be summoned by one who will not wait on the pleasure even of Pharaoh.''

''If you are ill, you must let us help you. In the Oryx there are men so skilled that death is content to wait at their command.''

She smiled the calm, serene smile of a woman without

fear. ''I would have come to you, asking that Yiahn might help me with his knife…yes, Tet-hen told me of Yiahn. But this is a sickness too deep even for him to exorcise. It is jealous of my life, this little death which houses in my body like an unborn child.''

''You are not afraid?''

''Afraid? How could I fear death, when I have not even been afraid of life?''

## Royal heir

Three years later, the Vizier came to the Oryx on his way to the First Cataract, where he was to open, in the Name of Pharaoh, a stone-quarry which had been unworked for centuries. As it was customary for any Bearer of the Royal Seal to stay with the Nomarchs through whose lands he passed, I attached no particular importance to his arrival. So I was surprised when he said:

''I am glad of this opportunity to discuss with you certain urgent matters.'' He paused, and then added with deliberation, ''I have reason to believe that I shall shortly find myself unable to continue my work—owing to ill-health.''

He was only fifty-five years of age, and appeared to be at the height of his powers, so I said, ''I find it difficult to believe that there are not many years in which you will continue to work for Egypt. If your body has recently given you cause for anxiety, I suggest you remain here as my guest, so as to avail yourself of the skill of those who heal our people at the Horizon of Horus.''

''I did not say that I am ill: only that, in the immediate future, I expect to resign from my duties, for reasons which will be attributed to failing strength.''

''Surely you have not fallen under the influence of some

foreign soothsayer, who pretends to be able to foretell a future which he says is not in your power to change!''

''In thinking that, you do me an injustice, Ra-ab Hotep. It is my duty to serve Pharaoh. When I can no longer do so in a manner which pleases him, my last service will be to relieve him from the embarrassment of my dismissal.''

''Dismissal! How could he dismiss one who is renowned for his loyalty both to the Royal House and to the Watchers!''

The Vizier sighed. ''Loyalty is not enough when one's master has ceased to believe in one's integrity. I know that to you I can speak in confidence, for you have always been Amenemhet's friend. For some reason which I do not understand, Pharaoh no longer trusts even those who are most faithful to him. He acts like a man fearing assassination. Once there were guards only at the gates of the Palace; now there are always chosen members of the Bodyguard outside every room which Pharaoh enters. Even this would not be significant unless taken in conjunction with other indications, and of these there are many. He is giving increasing authority into the hands of Senusert: this has my full approval, for Senusert is already a greater man than his father has ever been. But what is the motive for this? I think it is because it provides an excuse for Pharaoh to dismiss all those who were once in some degree his intimates, replacing them by men chosen by his son. He still believes that people can feel personal loyalty to Senusert, and that through this they may withhold enmity from their Prince's father.''

''Is that why Ameni was made Captain of the Bodyguard? I always thought he was rather young to be given so great a position, even though, as the leader of three expeditions, he has proved himself a wise and courageous warrior.''

''Ameni is worthy of his rank; otherwise Senusert would not have chosen him, even though they are as brothers.''

''Senusert chose him?''

''Yes: Pharaoh avoids making any decision which can

safely be relegated to his son. I think he is afraid of being attacked because he is Pharaoh. He is trying to merge into the background so that Senusert becomes the central figure on the stage: the central figure, who would suffer if there should be revolution.''

I was horrified to hear him talk so calmly of revolution. ''Who would revolt against a rule which has brought peace to the Two Lands!''

''It would not be a successful rising...for it is against the will of the great majority of our people. I warned you, before Senusert became Co-ruler, that there is a faction in the North who would like Seneferu to wear the Double Crown.''

''Have you warned Senusert?''

''Yes; he keeps himself fully informed, and he is convinced that his half-brother is not a source of danger so long as their father is alive.''

''And when Pharaoh dies?''

''Senusert has promised to guard himself, though he refuses to take the danger seriously. He says they are friends as well as half-brothers; that they have nothing to fear from each other.''

I was alarmed for Senusert....Though had I been able to see seven years into the future, I should have known that Senusert's judgment was wiser than mine. Rather than become a focus of unrest in the North, Seneferu fled into voluntary exile when news was received of Amenemhet's death. The Princes were on an expedition against the barbarians of the Western Desert; and to Ameni, his only confidant, Seneferu said:

''If Senusert had guarded his heart against me, I might have listened to the voice of ambition which urged me to become Pharaoh in his stead. But he trusted me, and once he saved my life in battle at the risk of his own. Now I can best serve him by my absence. I shall be lonely for Egypt, Ameni, until I make a life for myself among the foreigners. Perhaps when I am old I shall ask leave to return...and I know that

Senusert would welcome me as though we had been parted only for a day, instead of for half a lifetime.''

But this knowledge was hidden from me: for I could not unroll the papyrus on which it was scribed with the slow reed of time.

Before I had time to voice my apprehension, the Vizier continued, ''I discussed with Senusert what I believe to be Pharaoh's attitude toward me. At first he was reluctant to agree that my decision was well founded. In fact, before he did so, I had to state that I would not continue in my office when I no longer received the trust of which I know myself to be worthy. For twenty-two years I have worked for Egypt. I have seen those who were once called rebels bring peace to a land which had become divided against itself, even in families and in persons. I have done my work, and am content to go into honorable retirement. All that remains is for me to consult you as to who should be appointed in my stead.''

''Has Senusert expressed any preference in the choice of the new Vizier?''

''Yes; were the decision his alone, he would appoint the Nomarch of the Hare. Nehri is your daughter's husband and you have known him since childhood. What is your opinion?''

I longed to say that some other man should be chosen. Nehri and Beket shared a rich happiness with their people. Why should the Hare be deprived of the presence of its Nomarch? Why should Nehri accept responsibilities, which though wider in scope, were so impersonal in character? If Pharaoh could betray a man who had served him faithfully for more than twenty years, why should he trust Nehri? His unwarranted suspicion might destroy what Beket and her husband had created, a tranquillity which was shining and complete.

Perhaps I failed to conceal my thoughts—or were they so natural to a father that it needed no insight to know them?

''Senusert told me that unless you agree, no word of this

plan is to reach Nehri. Senusert knows that he is asking for a great sacrifice; the happiness of the Nomarchs of the Hare cannot be increased by honors.''

Surely I had the right to protect my daughter? Was not even Senusert himself warning me to do so?

''Hear me a little longer before you give your decision, Ra-ab Hotep. Believe that it is not easy for me to ask a young man to take up a burden which has proved too heavy for me to carry. Ptah-kefer asked me to tell you how greatly she longs for Beket and Nehri to join them. The Prince Senusert needs friends at his side nearly as much as he will when he is Pharaoh. In the Royal City, there is only Ameni who knows the Senusert of the Oryx: to the other nobles he is always Co-ruler, even though he treats them as his equals.''

The voice of the Vizier was unwarmed by emotion; yet I noticed he clasped his wine-cup so tightly that the knuckles showed white under the wrinkled skin. ''Egypt needs a Vizier whom the future Pharaoh can trust as he would a Brother in Ra. *Egypt*...not only Senusert.''

''You have deprived me of the weapons with which I hoped to protect the peace of my children.''

''Then I may go to Nehri? To ask whether he will agree to be declared my successor, in the Royal City on the first day of the third month of the Harvest?''

''That is in sixty days...must it be so soon?''

''I dare not strain Amenemhet's failing confidence any longer.'' Then, very gently, he asked, ''Ra-ab, may I go to the Hare?''

I hope I did not show how much it cost me to say, ''My barge shall be ready to take you there—at dawn.''

# Ceremonial Masks

Though Nehri and Beket had to occupy their official residence when in the Royal City, I gave them my estate of the Two Winds, so that within two hours they could reach a home which would give them an illusion of being in the Hare. Six months after Nehri's appointment, Meri and I went there to stay with them. We arrived earlier than our fore-runner had anticipated, and found Beket swimming in the pool with her three children. The eldest girl, and her brother, two years younger, scrambled out of the water and came running toward us; the youngest, who was within a few days of her third anniversary, favored us with a smile, and then paddled off to the far end of the pool without taking any further notice of us.

Nehri came home soon after the children had gone to bed. He and Beket disliked being parted as did Meri and I; so when his duties necessitated his spending the night in the Royal City she always accompanied him. I was thankful to see he did not seem oppressed by his responsibilities, and realized that I had been unduly apprehensive. Their happiness did not depend upon environment, and, provided they were together, I think they would have found tranquillity even among the barbarians.

"Nehri," I said, "I rejoice to find that formality has not been too heavy a yoke for you to carry."

He smiled, "It might have been, if Beket and I had not made it a kind of game. It was Beket who taught me to recognize that the measured phrases and elaborate ceremonial of the Court is a disguise, which people have worn for so long that they have come to believe in it. We try to discover who is hiding behind the mask. Sometimes the real person peers out like a furtive animal glimpsed for a moment in the tall reeds. Is it a water-rat, or a wild-cat—that quick shape which you only saw out of the corner of your eye? Turning those talking statues into human beings is rather like teaching animals, long hunted, to gain confidence. What makes it more exciting is, that until almost the last moment, you never know the nature of your quarry. Sometimes you bend down thinking to tickle a kitten behind its ear—to find a leopard's teeth through your hand. Or you may go out to hunt crocodile, and find the ripples were caused only by a baby hippo browsing in the shallows."

"I hope there are more hippos than crocodiles!"

"In the North it would be unwise to bathe without first inspecting the water with due care."

"You mean the nobles favor Seneferu?"

"If they recognize the qualities of Seneferu it shows that they are not altogether without wisdom; but if they think he will agree to become a gate through which they can escape their responsibilities it shows that they have not the wit of the great saurians."

"Then you consider that the anxiety of the old Vizier was unfounded?"

"It was justified in so far as there will always be men who prefer to work against, rather than for, the community. If a man gives in the name of affection, he himself is enriched. But should he refuse to follow the great law of Ra, he must hoard his poor possessions; pride, and power, and ancestry...that pitiful treasure with which some men try to defend their loneliness."

"Are there many such men in the North?"

"Yes, and there are also some in the South. Is it very surprising that when animals live each in a secret lair; whenever they hear the reeds rustle, they flee from the noise without even pausing to inquire whether it might be their mate in search of them? When men take off their masks, they recognize their brotherhood; but until then they remain separate; wary and suspicious, savage in their fear."

"The older nobles may perhaps resent having to acknowledge the authority of a Vizier so much younger than themselves.''

''I think at first they welcomed the change; they believed their years had brought them power, and that it would be easy to outwit me.''

''They soon found they were wrong,'' said Beket. ''They were so surprised, the old ones, to find that we were not impressed by their false dignity. They had heard of the Nomarchs of the Hare; and I think stories about me must have improved in the telling. The first time we stayed with the Ibex—his house is near the sea on the boundary of the Western Desert—he had expected me to bring all my animals with me. A courtyard had been set aside for them, with food of different kinds sufficient to feed a herd. I think he was disappointed to find me so ordinary!''

''I should hardly call you ordinary, Beket,'' I said with a smile.

''Oh, but I can be when I try. In three days you are coming with us to the City, and then you will see that I can be as ordinary as anyone else.

The House of the Vizier was second only to the Palace in magnificence, and when our carrying-litters passed under the pylon of the outer courtyard, a bodyguard of a hundred, wearing the Royal colors, lined the way to the doors of the great entrance. Nehri and Beket had preceded us earlier in the day, and, as they were occupied with official duties, we were conducted to our apartments by the Steward of the Household. Even in the bedrooms there were elaborate wall-paintings, and the ceilings were supported by pillars.

''I am glad I didn't remember how oppressive such magnificence can be,'' I said to Meri, ''or I think some other Vizier would rule instead of Nehri.''

''I thought Beket might be different after living here, but I am so glad she hasn't changed. Did she say anything to you about Amenemhet? I never mentioned him, for I know how

251

she cherishes the time when she can be with her children and forget the City.''

''She has not spoken to Pharaoh, except on the occasion of Nehri's official appointment as Vizier.''

''And Nehri?''

''He is the Vizier; yet in all official matters he refers, not to Pharaoh but to the Co-ruler. Senusert ascribes this to Amenemhet's wish to make the transition of rulership as smooth as possible. The new officials are to regard Senusert as the supreme authority from the moment they take office. Only those who have long been in Amenemhet's service— and of these few remain—still take their orders directly from him.''

''If he feels like that, why doesn't he give the Crook and Flail to Senusert? It is not unusual for Pharaoh to abdicate in favor of his son; and surely, if Amenemhet finds the burden of rulership too heavy for him, he should have the courage to admit it.''

''Roidahn told me that he had suggested such a course to Amenemhet. The suggestion was made in friendship, but it was received in hostility. Amenemhet replied, 'Only at my death shall I relinquish the Crook and Flail. Those who wish them to pass to other hands must look to death to be their emissary.' ''

''Amenemhet said that to *Roidahn?*''

''He caused those words to be scribed; and sent them enclosed with the formal acknowledgement of the tribute from the Horizon of Horus.''

''I shall talk to Ptah-kefer about him,'' said Meri decisively, ''Senusert is too loyal to his father to say much, even to you; but women are quicker to recognize when discretion is no longer valuable. Yes, I shall certainly talk to Ptah-kefer. It is ridiculous that Senusert—*our* Senusert—should be troubled by a father who seems to be making things difficult for everybody.''

I smiled, ''Will you promise to tell me when I am

becoming a trouble to Ameni?''

''Of course I shall—only it will never happen; for we are not afraid of growing old, and it's fear that makes people tiresome.''

That evening, some of the more important nobles attended a banquet which Beket was giving in our honor.

''I am afraid most of them are very dull,'' she said. ''But you and Mother can play the game of 'Who is behind the Mask?' ''

Beket did not need a mask to be the wife of the Vizier. I caught my breath when she entered the room where her guests were assembled. She was poised as an opening lotus; her dress was of green mist-linen pleated to her feet, her jewels were of gold and malachite, and in her hand was a spray of sesemu flowers, also of gold. On each side of her walked a leopard, the twin daughters of the one she had taken with her to Nehri. They were mild and intelligent as cats: the lamps struck high-lights from their burnished skins, and sparks from their gold collars.

''She is—magnificent!'' whispered Meri.

Each guest in turn came forward to be presented to us. I wondered what they would have thought had they known that their hostess, so proud, so dignified, murmured without moving her lips a prelude to the formal words of introduction.

Of a tall woman, languid, her voice warm as a purring cat; she said, ''Monkey, who always snatches food from its neighbor.''

As the woman greeted us, I thought, ''Monkey—why is she like a monkey? Surely something feline would be more apposite?'' It was only later that I recognized the depth of Beket's wit.

I saw this woman gather men about her, while in the background the wives concealed their annoyance. None of the men were desirable of her, except in that they belonged—or she thought they belonged—to someone else. A servant passed, carrying a dish of fruit. She took a fig, sniffed its

253

warm scent, and, hoping to look even more provocative, laughed up at the man beside her. Her small, white teeth bit into the fruit—fruit that was sweet because it was a symbol of that which grew beyond the wall of her garden.

I looked up and saw Beket watching me. Our eyes met, and I knew she was thinking, "Wasn't I right, Father?"

A moment later she had a chance to speak to me without being overheard. "Can't you hear her chattering? But she is well-trained; she doesn't pull the wigs off people who annoy her."

"I prefer *your* monkeys," I said, "who have not forgotten how to swing by their tails."

A man, perhaps sixty years old, wearing the heavy wig fashionable in his generation, was approaching us. "One of our most respected tortoises," murmured Beket. "Perhaps you could persuade him to peer from his shell, and even to take some refreshment at your hands."

He was indeed a tortoise! To try to lure him beyond the meaningless phrases of formality, I offered many topics for his delectation; but none served to inspire him with any desire for original thought. He had a genius for asking questions which required only the most dull and factual answers. What was the level of my granaries? What did I consider to be the best strain of cattle? What were the prospects for the next harvest? At last I realized that he considered those Nomes which did not join the Royal City to be no more than outlying farms, valued only for such produce as was useful to people like himself.

He owed his position to the name he had inherited, and to an inborn lack of initiative which had prevented him doing anything sufficiently positive to merit either praise or condemnation. His value to the community could at best be only that of antiquity: a tree which is cherished for its age although its boughs are no longer fruitful. He, I think, had borne no fruit, even in youth. Yet it was obvious he thought the Nomarch of the Oryx to be no more than a prosperous farmer, who out of courtesy should be put at his ease. I recognized that a few of the company had a very real affection for Beket: the others were duly impressed by the Wife of the Vizier, she was so polished, so very beautiful. I thought of the Beket I had seen yesterday; running through a bean-field with her children, hair streaming in the wind, her feet naked to the warm earth. Yet Beket was alive even in this coffin of ceremonial; even when surrounded by people of whom many were almost indistinguishable from the likeness which would be painted on the mummy-case.

# fear in the palace

Not long before we returned to the Oryx, Senusert made the yearly Progress to the Northern Garrison. He usually took Ptah-kefer with him on such occasions, but she was within two months of the birth of her second child and so had preferred to accept Beket's invitation to stay at the House of the Two Winds. With her she brought her son, the young Amenemhet. He had already become firm friends with Beket's children, and Ptah-kefer told me that he was never happier than when playing with them.

''He is so like Senusert,'' she said fondly. ''Sometimes I think he *is* Senusert, and that those miserable years with his grandmother never happened, because I am his mother as well as his wife.''

Then she added slowly, ''I hate the Babylonian, Ra-ab! Sometimes I think she resents us living in the rooms which once were hers; that she too thinks my child is Senusert grown young again, and is trying to take him away from me.''

''Even a woman who is also a priest is sometimes the prey of fancies when her body is occupied in making a child,'' I said gently.

"Yes, women are foolish, and are prey to fancies; even the wisest of them—though I am not very wise. You are right, Ra-ab; my apprehension, it is not strong enough to be called fear, has increased since this child stirred in my womb. A leopard is never so fierce as when defending her cubs. Why has a woman less than her usual power when defending her unborn child from fear?"

"Perhaps it is because each of us has only a certain vitality available. If we use that vitality in the way of a priest, the body must make do with what remains. I am not myself greatly experienced in such matters, but many priests have told me that magic is more exhausting, even to the body, than is physical labor. Your body is willing to live on less vitality than it really requires, but it will not let the child go hungry. To prepare for birth, the unborn must gather strength, and for a time its mother must become its willing servant. The child has the first demand, and only the vitality which it does not need is free for the mother to expend elsewhere."

"You are very comforting, Ra-ab. I shall look forward to the time when I am again the Ptah-kefer who does not shrink from shadows; but instead can take a light in her hand, and drive them away—to see them, like all shadows, flee from a light which gives them challenge."

I knew Meri wanted to talk to Ptah-kefer alone; so, making excuse that I had promised to play with the children, I left them together. When Meri came to find me, I had already said good-night to the older children, and was telling the little Amenemhet the story of the quail-chick, a story which had been the favorite of Ameni when he was the same age.

The sky was soft with dusk as Meri and I left the nurseries, to walk through the garden, hushed and cool after the heat of the day.

"Have you and Ptah-kefer decided who is to hold the Crook and Flail?" I asked.

"If the choice were ours, Senusert would be declared Pharaoh tomorrow."

"Is Ptah-kefer thinking as a priest, or as a wife?"

"We talked as women who love Senusert. He refuses to admit that his father is showing himself inadequate as Pharaoh. Senusert says that it is only generosity which makes his father dismiss the old officials, and allow the Co-ruler to appoint new ones in their stead. He even pretends that he will do the same when his son is old enough, so that young men shall rule in their own generation. Then Ptah-kefer told me how glad she was when Ameni became Captain of the Bodyguard, for now he is always with Senusert when they go on expeditions."

"Does she think he is in danger—Senusert, I mean, not Ameni?"

"She is afraid for him, of that I am certain. But whether it is Amenemhet she mistrusts, or Seneferu, or something else, I couldn't quite understand. She became evasive when I tried to make her be more definite."

"You think it is more than the anxiety natural to a woman with child?"

"I think so, but I am not sure, Ra-ab. I asked her whether there was any hope that Amenemhet would change his mind about abdicating, and I found that she did not know that Roidahn had made any such suggestion. She was so startled that she cried out, 'Of course he wouldn't abdicate! To him it would be the final acceptance that he had failed Egypt. I think that is a fear which never leaves him, that he will be— or perhaps has already been—unworthy of his trust.' "

I knew that Meri was deeply troubled. "There is fear in the Palace, Ra-ab. Amenemhet is afraid—of what? Ptahkefer is afraid—not for herself but for Senusert and her children. There was fear in the Palace when we stayed there years ago, when Ameni was a baby. But there oughtn't to be fear there now; not now, when the Babylonian is dead."

Soon after Egypt had rejoiced at the birth of his second son, Senusert asked that I visit him in the Royal City as soon as it was possible for me to do so. The message added that if for any reason I could not make the journey, he would come to the Oryx, so secret and immediate were the matters which he wished to discuss.

Within three days I had started north, and Senusert's own litter-bearers met me at the royal landing-steps. I was conducted straight to his personal apartments, and, as soon as we were alone, he told me why he had sent me so urgent a summons.

"I regret having had to ask you to make this sudden journey, but when you have heard my news I am sure you will see I was justified, and that I dared not trust it even to the most faithful messenger. I am Co-ruler, and my oath of allegiance to Amenemhet is more binding than any other similar oath in all Egypt. Yet it may not be possible for me to keep that oath, and yet remain loyal to the laws of the Watchers."

"When two loyalties conflict, you must always choose the higher," I reminded him.

"I know: that is why I must tell you that I think my father is...mad!"

"Are you the only one who suspects this?"

"How can I tell? I have not dared to discuss it with anyone except my wife. A month ago my father was afflicted with a disorder of the bowels. Ptah-kefer asked to be allowed to heal him. This he grudgingly permitted, and within two days he was restored to health. He has never treated me as an intimate, though he listens to my suggestions with apparent interest, and has at no time questioned my judgment. Often, as you know, he lets me give Audience in his stead; in fact he seems eager to let more and more authority pass into my hands. Till a month ago I should never have questioned his sanity, even though he seems afraid of all human contacts. But the day before I appealed to you for help, help I most desperately need, he summoned me to his apartments, and, as impersonally as though he were describing an architect's plans for a new village, he told me that a plot to kill him had failed only because Ptah-kefer's exceptional powers had prevented the poison being effective. It was only then that I realized that he had been brooding as to the cause of his brief illness.

"I asked him for the names of those he believed to be conspiring against him, but he refused to give them to me. All he would say was, 'To name an enemy is to believe that those whom you have not already recognized as enemies are your friends: it is easy to die at the hand of a friend, for you are not protected against him.'

"I tried to expostulate, but he took no notice and went on, 'I shall not tell you the names of our enemies...your enemies and mine, or you will trust those whose names I have not spoken. I am an old man of wide experience; and I command you, I, Amenemhet, Pharaoh of the Two Lands, command you, to trust no one, even those whom you imagine to be most faithful. A man has only one friend he can trust: himself. Only one who will not betray him: himself. Only one in whose company he is at peace: himself. Be not deceived by your wife or your son; be not deceived by your mother or your father: be not deceived by your grandparents or your grandchildren: be not deceived by friendship. Only then need you fear no one.

" 'Be not deceived by a smile of greeting; for then you will not hear the whisper of the assassin. Be not deceived by generosity; for then you need not fear the thief. Be not deceived by words of kindliness; for then you will not be destroyed by falsehood. Be not deceived by any act of friendship; for then you will never cry out, "I am forsaken!" '

"Then he said, 'Pharaoh has spoken! You may go.'

"I tried to argue with him, but he would not listen. Instead he gave me a papyrus on which he had scribed this terrible advice. 'Read it,' he said, 'many times; before sleeping, and when you wake, so that my words brand your memory like a rod of hot copper which sears flesh beyond

259

healing. That is the greatest heritage I can give to you, my son: the strength to be alone, always alone.'

''Something must have happened to him, Ra-ab, of which we know nothing. He continues to administer the laws, yet this is his considered advice to his son, the son he has appointed as the next Pharaoh. It is a negation of everything in which the Eyes of Horus believe. We know that only when a man gives love to his fellows can he receive it from the Gods. We know that he who remains separate is as a grain of corn which never enters the ground and gradually loses its power of growth until it becomes sterile...perhaps forever.

''No act of cruelty or injustice has ever been recorded against Amenemhet: before the Forty-two Assessors he could say: 'That I have not done, that law I have not broken.' Yet the greatest of all laws he denies; which is that man should give love unsparingly as the Sun gives out heat. To be separate is at last to know the ultimate cold of a dead moon, dark and insensate in the eternal night.

''Why has he shut himself away, Ra-ab? Why? Is it because he has some secret of which he is so bitterly ashamed that he tries to close it in his heart, even if that heart must remain closed also against all happiness? Has he betrayed a friend, and known such bitter remorse that he dare not again give friendship? Has he killed someone with so little justice that he dare not receive life?

''I have tried so desperately hard, Ra-ab, to give him sufficient confidence to speak freely to me...but it is useless. Three times, to my knowledge, he has opened his heart to you, and there is a chance, a very slender chance, that he may do so again. If you demand Audience with him he cannot refuse you, but there is little hope that he will admit you to his private rooms, for he did not do so even when you brought back to him his son. Yet if you ask to see him alone, not as Pharaoh and Nomarch but because you are both Eyes of Horus, I think he will not dare to deny that right.

''He is afraid of the Eyes of Horus, Ra-ab, for he even

warned me against them. He said, 'Remember, Senusert, that the Eyes of Horus made me Pharaoh, yet if they judge me unworthy they would without hesitation take from me the Crook and Flail. You have been trained by them; therefore they will be reluctant to admit that they have failed with you. But do not trust too much in that reluctance; for if they ever decide that some other man would wear the Double Crown more in accordance with their traditions, then you would die...and a magnificent sarcophagus will conceal their failure.''

## The Unseen Guest

Senusert's face told me before he spoke that my journey to the Royal City might be to no purpose.

''He won't see me?'' I was less asking a question than stating a fact.

''No. At first I thought there was hope, for he said, 'Ra-ab wants to see me?...He was always my friend—Ra-ab...' Then he laughed, that terrible cold laugh I have come to dread, and said, 'Why should I trust Ra-ab? You and he are Brothers in Horus; you love Egypt and Egyptians...you do not love Pharaoh. The Watchers made me Pharaoh, and when they are ready they will make a new Pharaoh. Take care, Senusert, lest they deceive you as they have deceived me...deceive you so much that you think yourself a stronger man than you are, and take up a burden which is too heavy for you to carry.'

''He is so terribly alone, Ra-ab! Is there nothing we can do to help him! He is like a man dying of thirst: yet who flings down the cup because he thinks the water in it poisoned; or like a man with a pestilence, afraid he will contaminate his fellows. The people have not yet realized what has happened to him; he carries out all formal ceremonies...and afterwards he says to me bitterly, 'There is neither good nor evil in a statue; it is only a symbol of power. That is why, my son, I have become only a symbol of rulership. In the early days of my reign I erected statues of myself in many Nomes, and on the anniversary of my taking the Crook and Flail, my people put flowers and fruit before them as though they were God-statues. Those statues will never fail the people, for they see their ideal held safe for them in stone. When I have still further subdued my spirit I shall be as worthy as a statue to receive their honor: I shall be without virtue, and without the power to do harm. Once I hoped that my voice would be the voice of Egypt, and my strength her protection. They must never know how unworthy I have proved myself, how small a man holds this high office. My enemies think that I shall betray Egypt; but the wise farmer husbands a little grain against a time of famine, and even when his children cry for hunger he does not break the seal on this last store until it becomes vital. I too have a last store on which to draw in my extremity: only a friend can know a man's heart; only a friend can see beyond the mask he turns to the world. I have found the courage to deny myself all friendship: I shall continue to live entirely alone. My body will perform the ceremonials necessary to Pharaoh; and my tongue has so long been trained in the formalities that it will continue to be my faithful servant until the final breath.' "

There were tears in Senusert's eyes, and his voice broke on the last words. Then he went on, "The only time he gains an illusion of happiness is when he is choosing the furnishing of his tomb. I have seen him stroke an alabaster vase as another man might caress the curve of a woman's shoulder...and whisper to one of his canopic jars, 'Soon we shall be free to enjoy each other in the long security of my pyramid. No one will ever disturb us again: for the drop-stones are heavy, and if they should be passed...though I think it impossible... there are false passages which lead to shafts down which a thief would fall and perish. He would never find me: I shall be at last alone; secure forever from both friends and enemies.'

''He is always warning me against friends, Ra-ab. He even tried to make me send Ameni away. I told him that nothing would make me betray Ameni, and he laughed at me and said, 'I drink to the brave son who is so sure that he will never become like his father! Even when I was older than you are I believed in friendship: but now I am wiser. I know that if I allow any man to become my friend he will see my heart, and seeing it he will become my enemy.' ''

''Can the priests do nothing for him?''

''He will not see them. He only goes to the temple to make ceremonial offering.''

''How many of the people close to him realize his torment?''

''Very few: and those say nothing. He sits in Audience to receive tribute; he still has every plan for new buildings, new roads, brought to him for sealing. The Army tallies go to him, and his judgment in these matters is as clear and just as it has always been. Except for festival banquets, which he occasionally attends, he always eats alone. He has never been fond of formal entertainments, but when I was a child I remember that he liked a friend, or perhaps two or three, to share the evening with him. I doubt if even the people who used to share those hours with him realize that others no longer come to the Palace. Each thinks he has offended Pharaoh in some way, or that he has grown tired of their company...so they never mention it. After all, the people do not think less of the Gods because the Gods do not ask them to share a cup of wine.''

''I have been seven days in the City, and have heard nothing to suggest that any of the nobles are offended at not being asked to take more part in the life of the Court. And of you, everywhere I hear praise; of your courtesy, your bravery, your generosity, the quickness of your wit.''

''I am very glad, Ra-ab, that I have thus been able to repay a little of the happiness which I found in the Oryx. You taught me to be happy: that is why it is easy for me not to make people disappointed. Father's happiness lasted such a short time, and the memory of it only makes the present more bitter by contrast.''

''Are the servants curious to know why he lives so much alone?''

He paused before answering, and then said reluctantly, ''They don't realize that he does.''

''Why?''

''I'm frightened that one day they will discover that his guests are—invisible.''

''What do you mean?''

''You remember that there is a door leading into the garden from his private apartments, by which his personal friends used to enter the Palace? That entrance was originally made so that the Eyes of Horus might come to visit Pharaoh at any time, without their presence arousing suspicion or jealousy. For a long time I thought the door was still being used; for I heard voices coming from his room after the servants had taken away the food. Then one night I realized that there was only one voice, his own. Either the persons who answered him always spoke in a whisper...or else there was *no* answer. The next time I heard him talking, I waited in the garden to see who came out through the private door. But no one came out...and when I went back to the house I found him alone.''

''You mean he talks to himself?''

''Either to himself...or to some uneasy ghost who returns to visit him.''

''Is it so surprising, Senusert, that a man should talk to a ghost? If Meri were to die before me, I think she would know that I was lonely for her physical presence...and when she came to comfort me, should I not speak to her in words as well as in thought?''

''A spirit who comes in love is not what I mean by a ghost.

You would never be afraid of Meri; you would never mock her; you would never cry out that she was powerless to hurt you...and that even when you too were dead you would still be beyond her power, because you had sworn to spend eternity in your tomb.''

''You have heard him speak like this?''

''Yes; many times. I have a hard request to make, Ra-ab. I want you to spy on my father—though to do so is to risk death. If he knows what you have done he will have you killed. And even the Co-ruler could not defend you from Pharaoh. I would not ask you to do this unless I knew it was the only way by which you could judge if there is any means by which he might be cured. I could repeat what I have overheard...but that is not enough; you must hear the quality of his voice before you can hope to find what has caused this desperate sickness of the soul.''

''How shall it best be done?''

''There is a strong trellis outside the room where my father entertains his invisible guest. High in the wall there is a grating, and by climbing the trellis you can hear all that is said inside the room. It is dangerous, for he is always uneasy with suspicion; at the slightest sound he might dash out through the private entrace...and if he did so he would see you before you could get away. There are always guards within call. He is terrified of being spied on...and those he suspects may be killed before they have a chance to make any explanation. There have been spies...though only in his imagination. The lover of one of the woman servants was trying to get out of the Palace early one morning without being seen. He heard a guard coming and hid behind some bushes...which rustled and so betrayed his presence. Father heard him being taken...and ordered that he be killed immediately. It was from the woman that I heard the truth. She begged me to intervene for him...but I could do nothing: his body had already been thrown into the river.''

The night was very still. I waited in the little pavilion on the river walk, watching for the light which Senusert would set in his window if he should hear his father begin to talk with the unseen presence. Three nights I had waited in vain. Each time I had slid down the rope into my waiting boat and returned by the water-steps to the house where I was staying.

It was the dark of the moon but the stars were brilliant. Shapes of trees stood out against the denser darkness of the Palace. A light flowered and flickered in the window I was watching. Twice, then a third time, it passed from side to side. I knew then that I must climb the trellis; and again I asked Ra that I might make no sound.

A bat swerved out of the vine, its squeak sounding loud as the challenge of a sentry. Gradually I let my full weight be taken by the wooden rods, and stealthily began to mount. Until my head was level with the grating I could hear nothing: then, quite suddenly I could hear as clearly as though I too were in the room. Amenemhet's voice sounded calm and steady: he might have been speaking to me, as he had so often done. Every few moments he paused...as though he listened to an answering voice.

"Now we may talk together undisturbed; for the servants have gone and will not return unless I summon them. I must apologize for a small discourtesy: you will have to drink from my wine-cup, for they have forgotten to leave a second one. The wine is rare, and smooth upon the tongue. You see I remember your taste....Are you still looking for your grandson, that little boy whom no one but you could love? The scribe loved him though...but you had the scribe killed. It was impertinent for a scribe to love the son of Pharaoh.

"It took you a long time to find out where the boy was hidden...nearly two years. He had forgotten you by then; forgotten that he was tied to you because he was afraid of being lonely. But he had found other people to love, people who didn't hold friendship at such high purchase as did his grandmother.

"You had a very pretty plot by which to get him back, didn't you, O Daughter of a Foreigner? Your spies told you that I had sent Senusert to the Oryx, and that you would not be allowed to cross the boundary into that Nome. It was a clever scheme of yours to gain entry to the house of Ra-ab Hotep by pretending to be a woman unjustly condemned to exile by the Reed. You would have begged Senusert not to betray you, saying that you had come to him only because you were starving for love. He might have believed you: even though he is my son he is overtrustful. Gradually you would have got him back into your power, and would have destroyed him, just as you are trying to destroy me.

"I knew that you had planned to leave for the Oryx on the morrow: but you thought I was deceived by your story that you wished to return for a while to the Summer Palace. You were pleased when I asked you to have the evening meal with me on that last night...here in this room. You took it for a sign that your deception of me was complete.

"I chose the meal myself, for the rules of courtesy decree that the guest who goes on a long journey shall be sustained by the best that his host can provide. Even you admitted that the quails were roasted to perfection, that the cream and honey, crushed almonds and orange buds, had never before been blended with so rare a subtlety. With them we drank a wine paler than this: do you remember? You asked if I would give you a jar of it to take with you to the North. I promised that you should have two of them...and I kept my promise. As you have seen, there is one jar at the head and one at the foot of your sarcophagus.

"The wine we are now sharing is of the same vintage that we drank when you had finished eating apricots. You had five apricots: you are surprised that I remember every detail of our little meal so clearly? But, you see, it was not a meal like other meals. I was not only a host watching his guest eat apricots...for when you had finished them you would drink the second wine...the wine that since then has been kept only for Pharoah. I wondered, 'Will she take another apricot before she drinks?' What would you have thought if I had said, 'The moments of your life could be measured in apricots, each little stone is like one of the great steles which marks a day's journey on a Royal Road. And you have come to the end of your journey: for I have sworn that with this Flail I will defend my people from their enemies.' Their enemies...do you understand? You are Pharoah's enemy: you would destroy his son. You are Egypt's enemy: you would destroy Pharaoh.

''You turned to look at me before you went away. Do you remember how I was standing at the far side of this table, and there was a lamp between us: we were divided by the light, yet both of us were in shadow. You put your hand up to your throat as though you had suddenly found it difficult to swallow: and you said, 'I shall not see you tomorrow, Amenemhet; but I shall think of you on my journey. And I shall not forget the wine.'

''And then you went away—holding yourself very upright, as you always did. Even when you were old you carried yourself like a young woman, and a princess.

''I was not sure how much you meant by those last words...the last anyone heard you speak. Yet I must have understood them: for I was not surprised when you came back to share another evening with me. You are a very patient guest, for night after night you come here, and night after night I drink the toast we drank together. Always you expect that at last there will be that same slight bitter taste in my wine as there was in yours...that tomorrow there will again be the sound of lamentation in the Palace...though this time it will not be your name that they cry, but mine.

''You think that when I have no longer this ageing flesh to protect me I shall be your prisoner. But you are wrong, O Foreign Woman whose daughter I have loved! My priests are strong; and they shall place such seals upon my tomb that none shall enter it...not even fiends of Set...not even you!

"When I am dead you shall wander alone, and no one will give you shelter. You may come back to this room, and no one will see you: you may tap on the shutters of my room, and whisper, 'Amenemhet! Amenemhet! I have returned!' Yet no one will hear you. You may make the lamp flicker, and though a man may shiver in a sudden draft...no one will notice you. I am the only mortal with whom you share a secret: and you have no other causeway of return...not love, not truth, nor a heart's gratitude. And hate can build no causeway from the tomb, save to the one you hate...and who hates you."

Then I heard he whom I loved, my friend, walk from the room and go away, alone.


# City of the Dead


Tet-hen and I went on foot to the City of the Dead. On this occasion I dared not confide even in my own litter-bearers, for to share with them so dangerous a secret would be unjust when they were not vital to our plan. We were both dressed as merchants, wearing sleeved robes and head-cloths of blue linen, for it was necessary that Tet-hen's shaven skull should be concealed. I led a pack-donkey, for the things we required were too heavy for us to carry.

Toward evening we reached the outskirts of the last village on the road which led to the tomb of Amenemhet's guest. We let the donkey graze on a patch of rough herbage beside the road, and ourselves sat down on the edge of an irrigation ditch to wait for dusk.

"This is a desperate venture for a High-priest and a Nomarch," I said to Tet-hen.

"And the need is desperate."

"You think this is the only way to break the link which binds him to her?"

"As we cannot approach him, and the Gods have not answered our prayers for his deliverance, we must take even this road to set him free."

"I have made our plans carefully. Tonight there will be no guard on the tomb, for the man whose turn it is to watch will receive a message, just before he starts for the City of the Dead, telling him that his son, who is working on a Royal Road, has been taken suddenly ill. The messenger will tell him to go straight to the Overseer's house, which he should reach about midnight. This should protect him from any accusation of complicity should it be noticed that the tomb has been opened."

"You think we shall be able to enter the tomb without great difficulty?"

"Senusert showed me the plans from which it was built. There are only two chambers, and the outer passage is not closed by drop-stones, only by doors. The doors have been sealed, but I have brought with me both the seal and the clay with which those we must break can be replaced. The inner door is of cedar-wood, and I have brought tools with which to knock away the wedges that hold it fast. Have your brought everything you will need?"

He smiled, "My will; my Gods. What more does a man need?"

"A lamp...to comfort his mortality! And I have brought it with me."

"You don't need a lamp to see a ghost, Ra-ab."

"I know: but sometimes a light will hide a ghost you do not want to see!"

"You must not be disappointed if we find no more than the bones in mummy-wrappings. It is unlikely that the soul is still held to the body, but it is not impossible. I have known it to happen; and if the soul will not obey my authority which bids it depart to dwell in peace, then must the body be destroyed. The Babylonian has power, Ra-ab; it will not be easy to set her free. You realize that this may prove to be the most dangerous encounter you have ever undertaken? If she, and her friends, prove to be stronger than we are: then we shall die...more surely than if there had been poison in *our* cup.''

In a field on the other side of the road a plowman was singing to his placid oxen. Their hides glistened like water in the warm light; their heads swung in gentle rhythm as they plodded slowly forward across the rich earth. I tried to hold my thoughts to that most ordinary scene: tomorrow I could see it again if I wished, tomorrow Tet-hen and I would be walking back toward the Royal City, our work accomplished. Why was I so afraid? Magic was not unfamiliar to me, though Ra-ab was not trained in the way of a priest. Once I had fought to make Amenemhet Pharaoh; now I must join another battle, so that in his hands the Crook and Flail should remain undefiled. I had seen many dead: people who had died in peace, in pestilence, in battle. Had I not watched Yiahn at work? Had I lost the courage of the younger Ra-ab, who saw his kinsman so carefully embalmed?

''Providing that an embalming was perfectly performed,'' I asked Tet-hen, ''would it be possible for a soul to re-enter its own body? Re-enter it so that for a time it could again walk in the flesh?''

''That was once held to be possible, but only by an ignorant priesthood.''

''Why is it not possible? I know, of course, that it is not permitted for anyone to possess the body belonging to another; but why cannot one use one's own body?''

''At death the link between the body and the soul becomes too tenuous for life to flow through it in sufficient strength to move anything so dense as matter. The soul should separate from the body at the moment of death; and it always does, unless the will of the person who inhabited the body is joined to it by an impulse so powerful that the soul will not recognize its freedom. You remember your own experience with the slave who was still chained though he had been dead for fifty years? The link between soul and empty flesh is of the same substance as the chain worn by that slave: both are made of thought, and thought is reality.''

''You believe that the Babylonian returns to her tomb when she leaves Amenemhet? Why?''

''Because her dying effort must have been, 'I shall return from my tomb. Every night I shall go to him, until at last I force him to put poison in his own cup, and he is no longer protected from me by his body as by a shield. Then he will be naked as I am naked, and he will die again, forever...and this time by my hand, by the dagger which on Earth I had not the courage to use.' This I learned while my body slept in the pavilion, and I saw her come out by the private entrance to Amenemhet's room: I knew her thoughts. After a few paces she vanished. It was then that you heard the guard approaching and woke me in time for us to hide.''

''I wish she had been more material in her thoughts, and then she would have had to walk back to the City of the Dead and we could have waylaid her!''

''I think she can never have imagined herself being required to walk, except for pleasure in the garden. To her it would have been an exercise only permissible to the common people. I have always found that those who have no royalty of character are so *very* royal!''

''Then the only place where you could make her hear you is either in Amenemhet's presence or in her tomb?''

''I fear, though highly unfortunate, that is almost certainly true.''

The evening cloud was coming up from the horizon to meet the sun, and for a moment the water-channels seemed to run with blood. I stood up, ''It will be dark by the time we reach the village. We must go.''

''It is at sunset that the servants leave Amenemhet alone to wait for her?''

"At sunset. He will have filled his cup; and again, as on so many, many nights, the flask which holds the poison will remain sealed. But if we cannot break the link, Tet-hen, then will that seal be broken...and Pharaoh send his own soul into exile."

I tethered the donkey in a clump of trees; they were wild figs, very old and twisted. Four days earlier I had been to the tomb with Senusert, and had memorized the shape of the ground so that I could find my way there in the dark. Tet-hen walked behind me with his hand on my shoulder. The silence roared in my ears. Some small animal—it may have been a rat—scurried across the path: I hoped that Tet-hen could not hear the thudding of my heart.

We reached the small funerary chapel without being seen. The door to it was not fastened: we entered, and the darkness was thick with the smell of dead flowers and rotting fruit. My hands were sweating; it was difficult to hold the fire-stick steady, but at last the wick of the small lamp burned with a clear flame. With my hunting-knife I prized off the seals which secured the door of the outer tomb-chamber. The hinges seemed to scream a protest as they moved. The floor of the tomb-chamber was soft with fine, brownish dust. In it there were no footprints: and I realized that it had been stupid of me to expect to see them.

Tet-hen caught my thought: "No, there are no footprints, Ra-ab, nor will there be any even beside the sarcophagus."

It was difficult to remove the wedges which held firm the inner door, and in my haste I was clumsy. As the door creaked slowly open the lamp flickered, and would have gone out if I had not shaded it with my hand.

Trying to reassure myself, I said aloud, "There is often a draft from a room which has long been sealed."

The outer sarcophagus was of red granite. In addition to the four canopic jars of alabaster, at the head and foot there was a wine-jar, banded with gold and sealed with Amenemhet's cartouche.

Everything was covered with the brown veil of dust. Half seen in the shadows, I noticed a toilet chest of a foreign pattern, and realized that it must be the one which Senusert had told me about when he was a little boy. There were many vases of fine pottery, and other vessels containing food and grain; a box which had been used to hold her necklaces; two ostrich-feather fans, one green, one purple, their color still unfaded; a copper mirror with an ivory handle....

Tet-hen was standing beside me, and suddenly he became tense.

"We are no longer alone," he said quietly.

I felt as though ants were running all over my body, and my tongue was dry as the tongue of a man long dead.

"Put out the light, Ra-ab. I can see her more clearly in the dark."

Never had I so fervently desired to disobey an order, but the authority in his voice could not be questioned. I pinched the wick: the darkness was like a black cloak thrown over my head. I knew there was something standing on the other side of the sarcophagus. If only I could see her; could hear her. But I was deaf, and blind.

Tet-hen's voice: "You are in company, Kiosostoris. I have come in the Name of Ra to set you free.

"No, I am not a tomb-robber who should be sent by the cold gate of torture to the Caverns of the Underworld. I am a priest, Kiosostoris, a *true* priest: and in the name of the Lord of the High Noon I bid you go from this place to dwell no longer in the shadow.

"A strong tree is not uprooted if the leaves of its branches hear a passing wind: why then should I be riven as though by lightning because I hear curses which have echoed in the temples of Babylon?

"Yes, I know you died by poison, but you make your

own death. You are alive now: why do you follow this pitiful masquerade?

"Amenemhet did not take away your beauty: he did not make you old. He may have killed you, but in so doing he gave you life. Can you not accept a rich gift even if the hand which offers it is not beloved?"

Suddenly the darkness was no longer impenetrable. There was a gray mist on the far side of the tomb-chamber, against which, Tet-hen, his hand outstretched, could be seen as an outline against a darkness that was less dense. The grayness began to take shape. It was true that the Babylonian had power! She could make Amenemhet see her; now I was beginning to see her, in spite of my longing to remain blind.

I shut my eyes; only to find that eyelids are no protection against the long-sight. I could see her more clearly now. Horror was cold on my forehead. I had never realized how terrible was the guest for whom Amenemhet waited, night after night. I was not seeing the Babylonian as I had known her; not even as those who had come to take her body to the embalmer had seen her.

She was a mummy. Under the bandages, the ridge of her nose, her forehead bones, the caverns of her eyes, were outlined. There was a slit in the bandages in place of the mouth; and through it I could hear her voice come forth...from a mouth whose tongue was only a strip of flesh dried hard as leather. Her arms were crossed on her breast; and I knew why Amenemhet had said, "You always hold yourself upright." No one has a back so straight as a mummy.

The authority in Tet-hen's voice was like a white flame. "In the name of Ra, and of Horus his son: in the name of Osiris and of Isis: in the name of Ptah, and of Hathor: in the name of Nut and of Min: I bid you rise up from the dead to walk on the hills of the morning in the body of your youth. Put forth hatred from your heart as though it were a scorpion which had hidden in a fold of your dress. See it as something which no longer belongs to you, which has become submerged in the waters of life on which the boat of your years now travels to the sea. The Gates of Life are open before you, and the link of death which your hatred has made is thin as the spinning of a spider. Break that thread, and the doors swing open: keep it, and you remain closed in the darkness of eternal solitude. Ra is the name of the gate of the House, and Horus the name of the lintel: Ptah the name of the bolts which shall be opened in his name, and Hathor the name of the door-sill. Therefore I say to you: in their name depart from this thy tomb; and leave here only thy body which is forgotten, and thy hatred which shall return to the dust also. Enter the House of Ra, and dwell there in peace, in wisdom, and in charity.''

I thought then that I should see a woman raised from the dead, as once I had seen Katani. But from the slit in the mummy-wrappings, which was the mouth of Kiosostoris, I heard come forth the curse which is inscribed on the portals of the Caverns in the blood of bats which nest in the bellies of dead vultures: the Curse of the Black Ram.

Tet-hen's voice was urgent, ''Ra-ab, don't let her make you hear! Call on the name of Horus...so loud that you cannot hear anything else...Horus!''

I tried to shout: but my throat seemed empty, as though my body too had been embalmed. Inside my head I shouted, ''Horus! Don't let me hear her! Horus!''

I dug my nails into my palms until I felt the blood run between my fingers, a sharp physical pain which dulled the sound of her searing power, but could not altogether shut it out.

''Horus! Don't let me hear her! Horus!''

On and on droned the curse, more venomous than serpents...obscenity after obscenity, corruption on corruption. Then came laughter; laughter beside which even the horror of the curse was insignificant.

After the laughter her voice continued: ''No one shall make me obey him: I belong neither to the living nor to the dead. I do not belong to Ra or to Set. That is why I am free, both of Gods and of men: even of men who speak to me in the Names of the Gods. I shall not depart from here until I have taken my revenge. Even the Gods are but creations of man: I am neither God nor mortal. I belong to neither company; neither can have me in their power. Only when I have fulfilled my oath, that he who killed me shall himself be killed, and also in my presence; shall I be content to sleep—a long sleep from which there is no waking. You who disturbed me, soon you will die, for I have cursed you. But there will be no quiet sleep for you: *your* bones will not be sweet in spikenard.''

Tet-hen's voice was urgent, ''Ra-ab, you must open the sarcophagus!''

By a tremendous exertion of will I managed to break the thongs which were binding me in the power of evil. Suddenly the darkness was again impenetrable. I was able to say, ''I can't do it unless I have a light.''

''Then kindle one.'' His voice was steady, though it sounded as though he was very tired. I groped for the lamp: the dust was hideously soft under my searching hands. Panic touched me like the wing of a bat. What if I never found the fire-stick? ''You may not be able to open the door: you may be trapped here—forever.''

''Steady, Ra-ab!'' My fingers touched the fire-stick. I had to spin it several times before a flame kindled. Twice the lamp flickered out, but at last it burned clearly. I stood up, holding the lamp in my hand.

Tet-hen's face was glistening with sweat, but his eyes were fearless. ''Our protection is stronger than her curse, Ra-ab. Ra is always stronger than Set unless you forget Horus his son. You must move the lid of the sarcophagus. I will protect you while you are doing it. You must hurry, for we have much to do before dawn.''

He stood behind me, his hands outstretched, protecting me from an enemy that to me was again invisible. The lid was held down by a thin layer of plaster which had set nearly as hard as granite. With difficulty I managed to chip enough of it away to insert a knife-blade, and then the tapered edge of a strong lever. The lid began to move. I had brought wooden wedges and rollers to put under it. The lid was so heavy that I felt as though the muscles of my back and arms would crack. It was all I could do to hold it up with my whole strength. I said to Tet-hen, ''You will have to put in the rollers.''

He did so, and I tied a rope round the lid and slowly dragged it back.

The inner coffin was of wood, painted in the likeness of she who stood watching us prize off the lid. The scent of myrrh and bitumen poured out. The bandages were as I had already seen them; but on this head there was a wreath of gold and enamel flowers; on this breast were three necklaces of rose-quartz and carnelian.

I lifted out the body: it was very light, even for so small a woman. Except for a few brown stains, perhaps where the spices had seeped through the bandages, the linen was as white as on the day it had been woven.

''Carry her into the outer room, and then return here. We must close the sarcophagus before we leave.''

Then I saw him sway on his feet. ''No, Ra-ab, we must return here *after* she is freed.''

''You said, 'By fire'...a fire might be seen if we were to kindle one anywhere near here...and it will be death for both if we are discovered.''

''It will be death for us both if we stay. I am near the end of my strength. Do I need to tell you that the Babylonian is very powerful? Carry the mummy outside, Ra-ab; and I will follow you.''

The same laughter, fainter to my ears, but still terribly audible, swirled like smoke through the room. I saw Tet-hen's hand go to his throat as though he were fighting for breath.

278

"Put your hand on my shoulder," I said. "We have got to get out into the clean air." He nodded, unable to speak. I felt immeasurable relief to be again under the stars. I had decided where we must burn the body: in a tomb which had been abandoned when half finished because of a fault in the rock. Part of the shaft had been excavated, and in it the light of a fire would be hidden from anyone who passed farther away than ten or twenty paces.

I put down the mummy, and said to Tet-hen, "Will you be all right here alone...with *that*, while I go to get the oil and the brazier?"

"Yes, but hurry. I don't think she has realized what we are going to do...yet."

I was reluctant to leave him, but I knew we must not waste any of his energy, for soon it would all be needed. I took the risk of being heard and ran back to where I had left the donkey.

# mummy-ðust

Tet-hen was waiting for me at the edge of the excavation. "Ra-ab," he said urgently, "we have forgotten to bring the canopic jars. Everything must be burned, there must be nothing left with which she could make a link. You must fetch them, for I shall need all my vitality for what I have still to do."

I put down the things I was carrying and ran off through the darkness toward the tomb. I knew that Kiosostoris would be waiting for me beside the empty sarcophagus. I halted by the outer door to light the lamp, and its thin flame was like a sword in my hand against the shadow. As I entered the tomb-chamber the flame flickered: it was much more than the light from a lamp, it was a symbol of my will which she was trying to quench. In the darkness she would conquer, but so long as the oil burned, my strength would prevail. I shielded the lamp with my hand: the stillness was profound, yet the flame flickered as though someone were trying to blow it out.

A sudden impulse made me open the chest which stood beyond the sarcophagus. It was filled with dresses, their pleats dry and brittle with age. I touched the flame to them: for a moment a thread of fire curled like a little gold snake, making a girdle for a ceremonial dress of blue fine-linen. Then the myrrh and spices in which the clothes were packed leaped into sudden heat. The tomb-chamber was flooded with orange light, and so fierce was the heat that the cedar-wood chest split open like a lotus of fire.

My fingers were clumsy as I broke the seals on the first of the canopic jars. The bitumen had set hard as the alabaster... I should not be able to draw out the heart or the lungs, the brain or the viscera. I should have to break the jars...but there was not time...no time while the fire was spreading. A voice spoke to me....

''*She* has lit the fire, Ra-ab...the fire will be her torch to summon the guardians of her tomb....''

I knew it for the voice of my friend, yet not Tet-hen. ''You must put out the fire, for when it reaches the outer door the cedar-wood will burn and the keepers of the City of the Dead will come to take you...and you will die the death of a tomb-robber.''

There is nothing which will put out the fire. Her toilet chest is of wood; it will burn as fiercely as the rest. There is nothing....''Your kilt will burn: it will not smother the flames, it will only feed them.''

Then I heard myself saying aloud, ''The wine, you fool! Amenemhet's wine, which he gave to fulfill his promise. Break the seals!''

The wine-jars were fully three cubits high. I lifted the first from its stand. As I broke the seal the room lived with the scent of the grape. Smooth and golden, the wine splashed on on the flames. They hissed, like snakes recoiling; then flared up again. But when the second jar was empty the room was in darkness.

Twice I had to stumble through the black smoke to bring out the canopic jars. Should the tomb ever be opened it would no longer be possible to conceal that it had no occupant to guard. I did not wait to seal the outer door...that must wait until I was free to return...if I were ever free.

Deep in the excavation, abandoned with the rest of the working, was a slab of dressed stone, shaped like an altar. On it lay the mummy of Kiosostoris.

Tet-hen had slit open the bandages. Her naked body was a tribute to the art of the embalmer. She had always been thin: now the skin clung a little more closely to the delicate bones. Even the paint on her eyelids had not lost its color; but her lips were puckered as though the fruit of revenge was bitter even when the taste of it was fresh in her mouth. Her talon finger-nails were sheathed with gold, and the pointed breasts were capped with silver sesemu flowers. Her body retained a curious quality of youth; as though she had died, not as a woman of fifty, but as a girl.

"Even her body looks alive."

"She has kept it so. As soon as I unwrapped the bandages I knew that she would never be free so long as it was in existence."

"Why?"

"Because she has created a fresh link between it and herself. Once it lived because she dwelled therein: the link was broken at death, but she has woven a new link; she has used it to keep herself bound into the narrow circle of her life as Kiosostoris, and even the flesh has taken on a semblance of immortality. She had not the power to throw off the bandages or to raise the lid of the sarcophagus...and I doubt if she has ever wished to do so. But she has made the body of death the garment of her soul; in it she has lain quiet, content to dream as though the mummy wrappings were smooth linen on her bed-place in the Palace.''

In horror I exclaimed, ''Then for years she has been buried alive!''

''You forget that her lungs do not need air. This body has no lungs, they are in the jar you are holding. Or does it contain her heart, which needs no blood; her bowels which neither fear nor pity can move, or her brain which no longer commands her body to her will? Amenemhet tried to kill her, and the women of the Palace wailed that she was dead. The embalmer worked on her body for forty days, and her tomb has been sealed for many years: yet it is you and I who are going to kill her, Ra-ab. We are going to burn her alive. She will not feel it; yet she will defend herself to the utmost of her power.

''Light the brazier, and keep it fed with the oil I have charged in the name of Horus. See that each particle of what I hand you is completely consumed. She will take desperate means to make you falter, to quench the fire, to let even a finger-joint fall into the sand to be forgotten. Only when her body has passed through the fire, my fire, will it be no more than dust. Give me your dagger.''

He took it, and held the blade in the newly-kindled flames. ''In the name of Horus let this blade be tempered to my will. It must kill, that life may be given; it must sear, that the sick may be healed: it must sever, that there may be growth: it must destroy, that there be creation.''

Then Tet-hen went to the foot of the corpse: and I knew that at its head there stood the woman to whom this body still belonged.

''Kiosostoris! You have died and were set free: but you have made yourself a prisoner. Therefore you shall again enter this body, so that when you leave it by fire it shall be to return into life. I, Tet-hen, Son of Horus, command you in the Name of my Hawk to enter this body: you shall breathe, though you have no lungs; your heart shall beat, though you have no blood in your veins: you shall hear me, though your ears are stopped with myrrh: the smoke of your bones shall enter your nostrils, though they are closed with bitumen.''

He took the heels of her narrow feet in the palm of his hand. "Many times, many thousands of times, you have left your tomb for the Palace of Amenemhet, where whispers still echo which were born of hatred. Many times you walked to the room to which came the spies you set upon your husband, and upon your daughter, and upon Pharaoh...and upon other spies. And your feet have carried you on all these journeys, and been obedient to you.

"Do you remember that before you were known as 'The Babylonian,' for then you lived among people of the same race, these feet ran through the gardens of your father when you were still a child...before you became ambitious? Do you remember your foster-sister, and the tame gazelle which you allowed her to share? You had forgotten her. Remember, remember that you loved her, that you still love her even though she has been dead so much longer than you.

"Do you remember your mother? You hated her: but it was from her that you inherited such small, fine bones, and that quiet face by which so many people have been deceived. These feet have carried you along the gentle paths of a child, to a foreign court...to Egypt. Everyone who heard your footsteps has been sorry: your husband, because he thought you were a fool; your children, because they feared that even your affection had tentacles which sought to smother them; your servants, because you had not the gift of benevolent authority; Pharaoh, because he knew that the sound of your feet echoed his own loneliness.

"But there have been three times when your footsteps were awaited with joy: by the gazelle, whom you never failed to care for when you were a child; by a servant of your father's house who had been your foster-mother—you comforted her when she was dying, and with her last breath she blessed you; by a beggar beside a road, somewhere in the Land of Cedar on your way to Egypt—you gave him gold when he had hoped only for a handful of corn. He never forgot you, and on your bounty he raised two sons, who always remember your name in their dawn prayer.

''Your feet, because they were three times blessed, shall no longer walk in the way of a prisoner!''

Tet-hen then raised the dagger above his head. Swift as a plunging hawk, he cut down to the thigh bones; in a few moments the tendons were severed. Into my hands he put the legs of the Babylonian.

The flesh of thigh and calf was smooth as the skin of a living woman. Cold sweat rolled down my face as I fed the long, slender legs into the brazier. The toes bent upwards as though she were trying to draw herself to her full height. The flesh charred quickly: the smoke was thick as oil.

Now Tet-hen was holding her two hands in one of his.

''In these hands you have so often held out a poisoned wine-cup to Amenemhet that poison is more familiar to them than malachite. Many have died at your hand, and, though their blood never touched your fingers, the stain is upon them. Your hands have held treasure which was unclean, and with it you have tempted those, who, had they had strength to resist, might still be living in contentment. Your hands have destroyed many bright-winged insects, for that gave you more satisfaction even than tearing the petals from a flower: both were symbols of the women you meant to destroy when you became the Royal Wife. You used to give them names...do you remember? The names of women you thought Men-het had favored, women more wise, more incorruptible than yourself. When you destroyed a number of flowers or insects to which you had given their names, you found that the women sickened: and you began to discover your power for evil. It was amusing to hear that someone you disliked had begun to fail in health, to lose her comeliness... even though you were not able to tell her of the little pile of butterflies' wings, and the heads of moths, kept in the box on whose lid was her name. It was not always a woman; sometimes it was the name of a man who had displeased you with his indifference. Do you remember the soft feel of a moth's head before you crushed it? And how it left a smear like mummy-dust on your finger-tips?

"Do you remember how the handle of the whip you used upon the backs of your servants grew slippery when the thong cut so deeply that the blood spurted? Do you remember the feel of earth under your nails as you severed the roots of plants which your husband had admired? You were jealous of him, even though it was not love but only admiration that you craved.

"But I have not forgotten that once your hand was cool on the forehead of Senusert when he had a fever, and for a little while you forgot that he was the Heir through whom you hoped to rule Egypt, and remembered only that he was a little boy who called to you through the darkness. You sat by him all night: your hands brought peace to him, and they were gentle. Those gentle hands you shall carry with you: the rest shall be cleansed by blood, in my fire."

Again the knife fell. I held the stumps of the severed arms upright in the brazier; pressing them down against the heat, which slowly, so very slowly, consumed them. The wrist-bones were thin and brittle...the long, narrow hands of Kios-ostoris. Suddenly they opened, curled back, as though they took the posture of a ritual dance. Then the fingers reached forward into talons, the golden nails glittering like fresh blood in the light of the fire.

I tried to tell myself that it was only due to tendons contracting in the heat: but the slowly moving fingers had the terrible fascination of a cobra whose head sways from side to side before it strikes.

I knew by Tet-hen's voice that he was nearing exhaustion.

"Your body has given sorrow to many; but to your foster-mother it brought contentment, for her own child had died, and in you she saw the fulfillment of her pain. Your body has been to you a faithful servant; neither inconveniencing you by weakness nor importuning you by its desires. But have you been to it a generous mistress? No, you have repaid its fidelity as though it was not a friend but only a slave whom you despised. You have permitted it no indulgences: when it wished to swim in the sea, you said that would not be becoming to your dignity; you grudged it even the benison of cool water. When you were fifteen, it bade you let it find fulfillment in the arms of a noble of your father's court: it implored you not to marry Men-het, for it found the body of a foreigner abhorrent. Yet you forced it to lie with an Egyptian; and when it protested you listened, but would not let yourself be guided by its voice. Your hatred grew, and to that hatred you gave heed; and plotted against the man whom you had chosen as the father of your children. Yet your body was stronger than you, for twice it refused to bear the child which it considered a violation of its privacy. It avenged itself on you; for a dead child is most agonizing to bear. You punished it for its disobedience with purges and salves which you had obtained from the foreign physician. Do you remember how your belly revolted against the mouse steeped in honey which he had advised; and against the broth of viper's eggs which he said would protect you against poison?

"You had learned to listen to your body by the time your daughters were born; you shared in its protest, and yet the children lived. Your pitiful body has so many reasons to hate you! It has never known the caresses of a man which it desired, or stirred with a child which it rejoiced to conceive. It has not suffered from gluttony, but it has received so many other needless pains at your command...for you thought that the secret cultivation of endurance would increase the power which you so ardently desired. Your body has brought comfort to no one, and it has aroused not even desire. Even when you no longer needed it for a garment you would not let it rest, and you in your turn have become its slave. Now at last it shall be set free of its obedience."

Then his voice took on a new quality, and he said to me,

"Break the canopic jars, and feed what they contain into the brazier."

Before I did as he commanded, I thrust the hands of the Babylonian deep into the fire: for a moment they remained upright, palm to palm, as though in supplication. The brittle skin flared in the heat, and the finger-bones fell apart as beads fall when the thong of a necklace is broken.

I had to use a heavy stone to break the jars. Their contents were no longer recognizable; all had been absorbed into a mass of resins. I turned to see that Tet-hen had cut the trunk into three pieces. The body-cavity had been filled with sweet gums, and the smell of myrrh was almost overpowering. The heart and the viscera burned with an intense flame, flaring up with such heat that had I not drawn back it would have seared my face. I expected at any moment to hear the shout of a guard...surely now that the fire was leaping so high its light must be clearly visible beyond the excavation?

Her belly was smooth as the skin of a living woman: even the breasts were still taut...like the breasts of a dancer who has never borne a child.

"It is nearly finished, Ra-ab. Remember, everything must be consumed...even a finger untouched by the fire might provide a new focus for her."

He set the head upright on its neck in the center of the stone slab. The eyelids were closed, but it seemed as though they were about to flicker open.....Surely she is not dead; she is only feigning sleep?

"Kiosostoris, hear me! The head which bound you to Earth is about to be consumed in my fire, even as your body has been consumed. Only those thoughts which were dedicated to Ra, even though you denied his name, shall you remember. The hands, and the blood upon them, are consumed; and the body which you betrayed is consumed also. The feet which you led among the thorns, having forsaken the Causeway; they are as dust. You died in the palace: but by your own will you were born again in your sarcophagus.

That half-life is ended: when this head falls into ash, the last link shall be severed. You shall be born in a new body, in a new time, in a new country. The woman Kiosotoris you shall forget; until you have gained sufficient wisdom not to be endangered by the lust for power.

"Unless you can destroy me, you must acknowledge Ra to be stronger than Set. In Ra's service you shall be born, and the stench of the Caverns of the Underworld shall be an abomination to your nostrils; and you shall forsake the ways of evil; and you shall again follow the Road to the Horizon.

"I, Tet-hen, in the Name of Ra, and of Horus his Son, challenge you! Prove yourself stronger than I...or accept peace at my hand! Destroy me, or be healed by me! Blind me, or see because of me! Make me deaf, or hear the voice of truth, and be no longer deceived by Set. Hear my challenge, Kiosostoris! Either destroy me, or accept my command; and accepting, go into freedom!"

I could see Tet-hen's arms outstretched in front of him, and the head of the mummy resting upright on its neck; but I realized that these were only the symbols of two embattled powers. I shall never know how long it was before Tet-hen's hands fell to his sides, and, in a voice exultant but very weary, he said, "She is free, Ra-ab. You may burn her head."

I held it, staring down at the closed eyes and quiet mouth. Against my palms I could feel the small, proud ears. The modeling of the skull was delicate, and the skin was smooth over the temples.

Gently I rested the head on the red embers. The hair caught, and for a moment she wore a crown of fire. Did I imagine it, or did the eyelids open, and eyes full of life and intelligence, eyes no longer cold and arrogant, look up at me?

Did she cry out as she felt the fire lap against her mouth? Or was it only air sucked by the heat out of the empty skull?

# narrow victory

Anyone who entered the deep shade afforded by a group
of stunted trees, about three hundred paces from the road to
the Royal City, would have seen two men in the sleep of
exhaustion. I did not wake until moonrise, and for a
moment thought that what I had experienced with the Babylonian had taken place in the Underworld. I rolled over and
saw Tet-hen lying beside me. Beyond him our pack-donkey
cropped contentedly at the thin pasture.

Tet-hen stirred and opened his eyes. ''We have been
victorious, Ra-ab. The spirit to which Kiosostoris was only
one of many successive souls does not know of anything
learned by the Babylonian, nor will the record of her life be
available to it, perhaps for millennia.''

''Then Kiosostoris has died more than an ordinary
death?''

''For a time, yes. When you and I die, Ra-ab, the
change will be imperceptible, except in so far as our bodies
are concerned. You could, if you wished, continue to be
only Ra-ab Hotep, just as I might decide to be limited by
the small knowledge of Tet-hen. There would of course be
wider fields open to us, even as there are now when we are
asleep. The love which you hold for Meri is not born of
your knowledge of her only as Ra-ab, for that is but one
thread of the hundreds which together make the gold link
between you. For her you have the love of father to son, of
daughter to mother; of sister to sister, and of warrior to
brother warrior. Now you are husband and wife, as afore-
time you have been wife and husband. The link between
you is a link of the spirit as well as of soul and of flesh. A
soul cannot endure through its own substance unless it is
linked by affection to some other soul. That link Kiosostoris
was never able to create. I have lifted from her the burden
of her hate, but she must go naked except for her love, and

289

of that there was so little that it was less substantial than a wisp of cloud.''

''But you have broken all the false links she made?''

''Yes; Kiosostoris no longer has any power, either for good or evil.''

''And will Amenemhet be cured of his sickness? Will our friendship be as it was before she exerted her influence over him?''

''Her influence has gone, but the memory of it remains. I cannot remove part of his memory and leave the rest. If I made him forget Kiosostoris, and that would not be impossible, every detail of the last ten years might be cut off from his waking mind. Because of the position he holds we cannot allow that to happen.''

''Then what can we do?''

''Now that her influence is broken, it should be possible to make him accept as a reality those experiences which made him afraid he was going mad. It was that which caused the change in his character. He is a brave man, Ra-ab; few others could have lived day after day with a phantom which they believed to be an embodiment of their own guilt. That is why he tried to shut himself away from his friends. He believed that because he continued to see Kiosostoris he was being haunted by his own fears, of which her apparition was only a symbol. He, the Pharaoh who had sworn to send fear into exile, was himself the prisoner of fear. Was it surprising that he thought that any man who knew the secrets of his heart would judge that he had betrayed the Oath which he made when he took up the Crook and Flail? How could he say that he had sent fear into exile when it was his invisible companion? He must have been in terror that his priests might at any time be able to see the projection of his fear. His every action was an attempt to preserve the thickness of the mask he must constantly wear so that through it no one should see terror naked in his eyes.''

''How can we best help him?''

"No way is certain, for it is not easy to break down the habit of ten years. I have a plan which, although it holds considerable personal risk to yourself, might prove more efficacious than any other. Tonight, as on every other night, he will wait for the Babylonian. He will be waiting now; and for the first time in a decade she will not come to him. Tomorrow you must wait in the garden until he dismisses the servants. Let him hear your footsteps, like those he has heard so often before: this time the door will open, and he will see, not Kiosostoris, but Ra-ab Hotep, his friend. For me to advise you what to do then is impossible...you must judge his mood for yourself. It will be dangerous, Ra-ab, for if he thinks you have spied on him he may order your death. He has kept up this desperate concealment for so long that when he realizes that you have broken through his defenses he may turn on you with the fury of a trapped leopard. Somehow you must convince him that the Babylonian will never again return; convince him that you honor him for his courage during these terrible years, that though you know his secret your friendship is increased and not diminished. Remember that he is still bowed down under a sense of guilt, and that no man who feels guilty is entirely sane. Only by removing the guilt can you set him free; only when he is free can you say to him, 'Your sins are forgiven in the Name of Ra.' "

The wind had risen, and the garden was sibilant with leaves which concealed the small sounds I made in climbing the trellis to the grating in the wall of Amenemhet's room. I heard the door close behind the servants. For a long time there was silence. Then I heard his voice:

"Where are you, Kiosostoris? For ten years you have never kept me waiting. Am I to be denied even *your* company? Are you tired of coming to me only when I am alone? Shall I see you sitting beside me when I give Audience?"

Then his voice became even more tense, "You are trying to make Senusert recognize you...Senusert, for whose sake I

291

killed you! You will fail, Kiosostoris, just as you have failed with him before. I sent him to the Horizon of Horus, where they are wise in magic. Roidahn will protect him; Roidahn will prevent Egypt again being ruled by a man who is haunted. You think you can attack me through my son, O merciless Babylonian? You think because he is my son he will be afraid of you. But you misjudge him, O foreign woman! You always misjudged him, even when he was a little boy. You thought he would become so obedient to you that I, his father, would despise him and leave him in your care. But I tricked you then, and I will trick you again. You hate Senusert, don't you, Kiosostoris? You thought you could make of him a mask which would conceal your power. But Senusert is strong, and if you attack him he will not be alone. He will betray you to the priests, as I have not dared to do. You are stronger than one man, even though he is Pharaoh of the Two Lands; but you are not so strong as a great priesthood, who are mighty because they have not betrayed their Oath as I have done. They have cast out fear; to them you will only be a trivial enemy, a scorpion to be crushed under the heel of a gold sandal!

"You think that you can make me betray Senusert: make of his loyalty to me and his loyalty to the great traditions, a pestle and mortar between which the corn of his Will shall be ground to dust? You think he will not be able to endure having to choose between breaking the Oath of Allegiance to me, and betraying the Eyes of Horus in whose service he has been trained?

"You even tried to make me hate him because he is stronger than I. You made me believe that he poisoned me because my death was necessary to Egypt, and that his wife only pretended to heal me so that she could mock at my weakness. But you could not make me deny the power of Ptah when I felt it in my own body, and of my sickness I was healed.

"You think Senusert will not be able to choose between

292

me and Egypt; and because of this indecision he will gradually lose his power of judgment until he no longer trusts in himself. You will fail, Kiosostoris, as you failed before...and for the same reason! It is I who will save him. A man must be prepared to die for his son, and though I am pitiful as a Pharaoh I am still a man. Pharaoh will die, and Pharaoh will be born again. Amenemhet will be forgotten, save by those who have the charity to remember his youth; but the name of Senusert will live in the mouths of men down the avenue of centuries which leads to the Horizon!''

I heard him cross the room, and realized he was going to take from the chest the poison with which he had killed the body of the Babylonian. I swung down from the trellis and in three strides had reached the door.

Amenemhet was standing at the far side of the room: in his hand was a little golden jar.

In a voice entirely without expression, he said, ''I can relieve you of what I feel sure must be an unpleasant duty, Ra-ab Hotep. It would be better for Egypt if Pharaoh is not assassinated. I ask from the Eyes of Horus only a little patience: tomorrow they will hear that Pharaoh has died in his sleep. They may find it difficult to join in the formality of tribulation, but perhaps if they try to remember the Amenemhet of twenty years ago they may find it possible to behave in a manner according to custom.''

''I do not come to kill you, Amenemhet, my friend. I come to tell you that you will never again wait for your unseen guest: for she, at last, is dead.''

''It is not necessary to mock with his madness a man who will so soon be beyond all mortal mockery.''

''If you are mad, then I am mad also...and so is your high priest, Tet-hen.''

''What do you mean?''

''A few moments ago you asked me to be patient so that you could die in your own manner: now I ask *you* to be patient, so that you can live, in mine.''

His expression did not change, but he swayed on his feet as though he were going to fall. "Sit down, Amenemhet, and listen as you have never listened before."

"It can make no difference what you say. I have decided what it is necessary for me to do."

"Listen, Amenemhet! Listen! The Babylonian is dead. She did not die by your hand; it is I who killed her. Now she is dead and her power is broken, and her hatred is less than the ashes of her bones which I, Ra-ab Hotep, consigned to the fire."

"Poor Ra-ab, you too are mad," he said wearily. "How have you become infected with my madness? I have been so careful to keep myself apart. Are my thoughts a pestilence, creeping from village to village, bringing death into the nostrils of those who were clean before my coming? Is Senusert mad? Tell me, Ra-ab, I command you, is Senusert mad too?"

"He is sane, as you are sane, as I am sane."

"But I have seen her, night after night I have seen her."

"So has Tet-hen. It would be a bitter irony, Amenemhet, if you were to drink the poison when she has lost her power to tempt you with it. Night after night Kiosostoris came here from her tomb; only her body was dead, and even her body kept a sense of terrible mortality. Tet-hen and I went to her tomb to give her challenge. Together we had a dual strength, but only by the utmost exertion of our powers, were we able to set her free, to set *you* free. That for ten years you, alone, have held out against her, shows that you are as strong as Tet-hen the priest and Ra-ab the warrior. In the name of us both I do you honor: as a man, whose courage is an inspiration, and who is never a fool except when he tries to value his own heart."

"I killed her, Ra-ab."

"All honor to you for not neglecting the responsibility of the Flail. Can a man give life who dare not take it? How can we serve the Gods if we dare not fight against their enemies?

If the King of Babylon brought an army against us, would you think yourself a traitor to Egypt if it was *your* spear which entered his heart? The daughter of the King of Babylon was a more dangerous, a more subtle enemy than ten thousand of her father's soldiers.''

''If I did no injustice, why did the Gods allow her to torment me?''

''Because you hated her so bitterly. Love and hate are as the light face and the dark face of the moon. When two hate with such an intensity as yours, they are linked as closely as lovers; yet instead of creating, they destroy; their seed is sorrow instead of happiness.''

''She won't come back any more?'' It was less a question than the cry of a child trying to convince itself that the night holds no terrors.

''No, my friend. Kiosostoris will never return. Soon you will not be able to remember her, even if you wished to do so.''

''How can I forget her? How?''

''By ceasing to be alone. You must learn to believe instead of to distrust. You must learn to receive friendship and to give it, for with each ray of love which shines from your heart, another thread of hatred which binds you will crumble to dust. You must learn to love as a child learns to walk; even though at first it may seem difficult because of false pride, which will try to convince you that it is weakness to need friends.''

He sat staring in front of him at the white wall. ''She will not come back any more. She is dead. The Babylonian is *dead*...and I, Amenemhet, am alive! Alive!''

He began to laugh; the high pitiful laughter of a man who has been for too long under an unendurable strain.

''You have beaten her, Ra-ab!'' he gasped between gusts of laughter. ''You have beaten her so narrowly in a battle which has lasted for ten years!''

His face puckered like a child's, and he buried his face in

his arms. "Don't leave me, Ra-ab, don't leave me...until I have grown used to being alone."

"You will never be alone any more...neither will your friends who have been so lonely for you."

He groped for my hand and held it against his closed eyes. I could feel the tears rolling down between my fingers. "I am not going to be alone, never alone any more."


## Son of Osiris


Tet-hen had warned me that the sudden termination of prolonged mental strain sometimes leads to physical collapse, so I was not surprised when Amenemhet, beside whom I had watched through the night, was too weak to raise his head when he woke in the early morning.

"You are still here, Ra-ab?" he whispered.

"I shall always be here while you need me."

"It is good not be be alone...." His voice trailed off into silence, and again he slept.

For the next three days he roused only sufficiently to take a little wine or broth. Senusert or I were always beside him, and Ptah-kefer replenished him with life at dawn and at sunset. I was resting, on the evening of the third day, when word was brought to me that Nekht had arrived at the Palace and wished urgently to see me.

The cold hand of fear constricted my throat. Had he come to tell me that Meri was ill...that she was dead?

"Bring him to me!" I shouted to the startled servant.

In a torment of apprehension I waited for Nekht. But when I saw him, I knew that he had not brought news of calamity. He looked tired, but perfectly composed. I embraced him and then asked:

"Why have you made this sudden journey?"

296

"I think you need me here, Father. I was staying with Roidahn, and I had a dream. We both knew it was too important to be ignored."

"Tell me about it."

"I thought that I was in the presence of the God Osiris...it must really have been one of his pupils who is teaching me away from Earth. I cannot remember all that he said to me, but I woke knowing that one who is a Steersman of the Boat has other powers which he can use. Osiris, and those who follow him, can do more than take a man across the River: they can rescue his soul from the Caverns of Set, or from Caverns which are self-created. You need not tell me about the Babylonian, for I have heard of that from Tet-hen...I went to his temple on my way here. I know that in sleep Amenemhet returns to a world which his thoughts during the past years have created. Only he can destroy what he himself formed, and, until he is free from those shadows, he cannot learn again to walk in the sun. Into that hell I shall go as his companion. I cannot slay his enemies for him, but I may be able to tell him what weapons to use against them. Does he sleep nearly all the time, or does he try most desperately to keep awake?"

"He sleeps."

"That is good news. He is a brave man to march alone against his demons. A man who had not such courage would sleep only when terror was less insistent than physical exhaustion."

"What do you wish me to do, Nekht? Your commands shall be obeyed without question."

As I spoke I thought that few parents could have said this to a son of sixteen. Yet it was Nekht, already declared by Roidahn to be the next Lord of the Horizon, whose authority I accepted.

"I must have something to eat, and then sleep. I have traveled here with relays of swift litter-bearers, and for the work I have to do even my body must not be weary. At dawn

I will go to Amenemhet. I shall lie beside him, and you and Senusert—Ptah-kefer also if she wishes—can remain in the room. You may see nothing but two men asleep; but it is possible that our bodies may speak of what we are experiencing. Try to remember every detail of what is said, for it is probable that I shall not have sufficient energy to bring back a complete record, and it may be helpful in deciding how Amenemhet can best be aided to regain tranquillity."

Then, with one of those abrupt changes from priest to youth to which I had become accustomed, "Food for us both now, Father. It will be the first meal I have eaten in a palace. I presume the kitchens offer a wide choice! Do you think they have quail? Or blue-fish baked in vine-leaves? Not that I am particular, I'm far too hungry. And wine, we must drink wine to our new adventure!"

Food was brought, and he attended to it with a vigorous appetite. "I'm glad I'm not a false priest," he said between mouthfuls, "for such people have to pretend not to be interested in worldly matters...hoping that their lack of appetite will be mistaken for a hunger for truth! There used to be a tradition that priests fasted before an ordeal, but that was only necessary when they found it difficult to get free of the body...they could have got the same kind of effect through drinking too much...a different sort of vision of course, but almost as unsatisfactory in the long run. Mother wants to know whether Ptah-kefer would like some more of her special unguent; and she said that if you've got to stay here much longer she will come to join you. Kiyas and the children are staying with her, so she's not lonely, though of course she misses you."

He kept up a flow of inconsequential talk until he had finished his wine. Then he yawned, and putting one arm round my shoulders hugged me affectionately. "It's not worth asking them to prepare another room. I'll sleep on the second bed-place."

He yawned again as he unbuckled his kilt. "Wake me

an hour before dawn. Sleep well, Father...I know that I shall."

Ptah-kefer watched beside Amenemhet during that night, so both Senusert and I could rest. After waking Nekht, who said he would join me when he was ready, I went to the room where Amenemhet was still lying in profound sleep.

"He roused twice during the night," said Ptah-kefer. "He drank some broth with a raw egg in it, but he was too drowsy to recognize me. His heart is not beating any slower, but if you notice a change, or his lips become blue as they did yesterday, send for me at once."

"Don't you wish to stay to see what happens?"

"I should like to, but it would be better if you tell me about it afterwards. I want to reserve my energy in case it is needed: I shall be resting in the next room so that I can come immediately if you call me."

She kissed Senusert, who had joined us while she was speaking, and then went out of the room just before Nekht entered. He stood looking down at the sleeping Pharaoh, then touched him on the forehead, the breast, the soles of his feet, and lay down beside him.

He appeared to fall asleep almost immediately, but for nearly an hour nothing remarkable occurred. Then Amenemhet began to mutter unintelligible words. Gradually they became distinct.

"Why should I tell you, O Son of Osiris, what I am seeing? You are standing beside me and your eyes are clearer than mine....But you are a God, so I must obey your orders even though I cannot understand them...I am a beggar, staring through the window into a lighted room. The family are sharing a meal together. They will not give me anything to eat though they know I am starving."

Then Nekht spoke: "Have you knocked on the door, Amenemhet?"

"It is no use: they would only turn me away."

"Knock, and the door will open."

"I am a beggar. I have nothing to offer them. I would lose even my pride if I were to knock and be refused."

"Knock! The door shall open!"

"It is no use."

"*Knock!* Knock in my name!"

"The door is open! They say that they have been waiting for me. My food is already prepared. They give me an earthen cup: on it is my cartouche to prove that they were waiting for me!"

Again nearly an hour passed before either of them spoke. Suddenly I saw the muscles of Amenemhet's neck stand out like cords, as though he were a dumb man trying to scream. I was afraid for him and nearly called to Ptah-kefer...then his lips parted to let forth a torrent of words.

"The eyes! The eyes! Everywhere I see them...I thought they were only a Hundred of Horus, but there are thousands, hundreds of thousands. The servants are watching me, the soldiers, the crowds. Eyes, everywhere there are eyes: watching to see if I am mad! They know I am mad, and they are waiting to kill me in their own time. Birds are no longer snared in Egypt, for they say that no animal shall die save by a quick, clean death. Why will they not show such clemency to Pharaoh? They are afraid that if they kill me now there may be some among my people who will say that Pharaoh was sane. They are going to let me live on, until my assassin will be praised throughout the Two Lands. They will say that he wrenched the Crook and Flail from the hands of a mad Pharaoh....Which long-dagger that my soldiers wear will kill me? In which cup shall I find poison? Or shall I feel hands at my throat...whose hands? Will they be long and slender with a woman's nails; or have wrinkled knuckles like my Vizier's? Will it be with layers of fine linen that they smother me while they think I sleep? Or will my nostrils be stopped by a woolen cloak in winter? Only the Eyes know: the thousand, thousand eyes of Egypt."

Nekht's voice was decisive as a Captain ordering his men to battle:

"Why are you afraid of the eyes, Amenemhet? They are the same eyes which watched you when in every Nome of Egypt you declared the Laws of the Horizon to your people. The eyes of dead men are closed, but because of you these eyes are open to freedom. Ra-ab Hotep has told you that you are sane: the Eyes of Horus do not lie to Pharaoh. No, Amenemhet, they do not hate you, though you hated yourself. Take in your hand the dagger which you thought belonged to an assassin. Take it! I command you! See, it is a weapon put into your hands by your armies to defend them from foreigners: your armies, who watch to see you lead them to victory. You do not fear that dagger any longer, Amenemhet.

"In your cup there is no poison. It has been filled to your honor. Drink from it! The water of truth is cool in the mouth, Amenemhet. You are not longer parched with thirst.

"The woman's hands do not belong to the Babylonian: they were the hands of the mother of your second son. She was lonely for you; she longed to smooth your forehead when you were weary yet could not sleep. From the other side of death she still waits to give you comfort which once you refused at her hands. The other hands? Yes, they belong to your Vizier; and the knuckles are wrinkled because he grew old in your most loyal service. The hands of a friend, Amenemhet; outstretched in the friendship you were too proud to accept.

"The fine linen? I will show you the fine linen which you feared would smother you. There are many uses for it: tear it into strips to bind the wounds of a man injured in your service. Look, Amenemhet, he is lying at your feet. Listen while he tells you how he was wounded by one of the rebels of the Western Desert. You must cut the arrow-head from his arm and bind it tightly to stop the flow of blood. He does not know that the man who succors him is Pharaoh: yet the gratitude in his eyes belongs to you, gratitude in the eyes you used to fear.

''It is winter, Amenemhet, and you are wearing the woolen cloak you feared would forever stop your nostrils. The wind is heavy with sand, but it is easier to breathe when your face is protected by the cloak. Above the noise of the storm you hear someone coming toward you along the path. It is difficult to see him because of the driving sand. He is much older than you are, and he has no cloak. He is gasping for breath, sucking sand deep into his lungs. He has not your strength with which to fight the storm. You have given him your cloak: the stinging dust makes water run from your eyes, yet you can see that, between the swollen eyelids of the wayfarer, looks out enduring friendship. You are not afraid of the cloak, are you, Amenemhet? You are not afraid of the dagger, nor of the cup, nor of the linen: for with each you can protect your people who gave them into your hands.''

Amenemhet lay so still that only by the almost imperceptible rise and fall of his chest could I know that he still lived. Twice I asked Senusert whether we should call Ptah-kefer; each time he said we could wait a little longer.

Suddenly Amenemhet again began to speak; but now his voice was full and resonant.

''I know my beloved is not dead! Only a little farther along this road is the house where she waits for me!''

''She need not wait, Amenemhet. You will find her where the road turns to the West.''

''They are both there! Nefer-tathen, and the mother of Seneferu. I thought they would be jealous of each other, but they are as sisters. I wonder if they will think I have grown too old? Nefer-tathen laughs and makes me look at myself in a mirror...a silver mirror which I gave her before our daughter was born. I am young! Why did I think I was an old madman whom men called Pharaoh?

''I try to ask forgiveness from my other wife for all that I caused her to suffer. She smiles, and says there is nothing to

302

forgive; everything is forgotten except happiness. They make me promise to come often to see them. I am bewildered: have I not been here before? For a moment I am frightened: shall I again be able to find the road by which I came to them? 'Make me remember! Make me remember the road that leads to you.'

"They are going to show me the road, so that never again shall I lose my way when I try to come here. They walk one on each side of me, hands linked with mine. We come to a pylon: between the pillars are a pair of great copper doors, fallen from their hinges. On both doors and on the lintel, is my cartouche....I cannot remember giving the order for their building...I hear the women laughing, 'You built them yourself, dear husband. See, upon them you have scribed, ''The Pride of Amenemhet''; and with them you closed the Road to Affection. So many people have tried to come to you by this road; men and women and children. Some were nobles and some worked in your fields. We came every day, but you would not answer when we called to you to open the doors. Only you can set them again upon their hinges to shut them fast against us. There are so many waiting for you, if you will but come to us along the Road to Affection.' ''

I heard Senusert whisper, ''Look at his face!'' While we watched, the mask that might have been carved of granite, the mask behind which for twenty years Amenemhet had tried to hide from his people, became warm and alive. The gray skin took on the color of health, and the hard mouth relaxed into a smile.

I turned to see Nekht standing beside me. ''We can leave him now, Father. When he wakes he will know that he is no longer alone.''

# the Road to affection

It was Nekht, Priest of Osiris, who said to me later that evening:

"Until now I did not realize how many willing assistants Set is able to command. For twenty years Amenemhet has been in the Underworld, yet he built his own Caverns. Do you remember Roidahn once saying, 'Make a man feel guilty and he is ready to acknowledge Set as his overlord'? If you looked at the brick of nearly every building in hell, you would find on them, not the Cartouche of Set or Sekmet, but Guilt enclosed with the name of some unfortunate."

"Why should Amenemhet, of all men, have felt guilty? Why should the murder of a Babylonian, whom I would have most willingly killed for him, have so affected Pharaoh?"

"He must have fallen into the habit of guilt long before that happened. His father was Vizier, and although he worked under the Old Rule, I gather that he was a most careful and diligent man. In youth Amenemhet was interested only in things such as lion hunting: no doubt his father often accused him of idleness. The first seed of guilt was, 'I am idle: my father is burdened by responsibility which I have neither the wit nor the inclination to share.'

"Then he met Roidahn and became one of the Watchers of the Horizon: yet he thought he should have done so only because it was his duty to Egypt, not as a new adventure. The second seed of guilt: for he did not realize that it is right for duty to be a new adventure.

"Then he became Vizier and had to play a double role: as one of the Eyes of Horus, and as the trusted counselor of a decadent Pharaoh. It is not pleasant to be in the confidence of someone whom you are plotting to betray. Unless you recognize that when two loyalties conflict you must follow the higher without remorse; you have to armor yourself with hatred, and eventually come to look upon all affection as the temptation to be weak. He decided that if he permitted himself to feel affection toward those whom one day he might have to judge, he would not be able to assess them without bias. There were many people whom under different circumstances he would have made his friends: he used hatred to conceal from himself that they might in the future think of him as a betrayer. Unfortunately he had not learned that hatred and understanding are incompatible; that only with understanding can justice be given, the enemy be rendered harmless and made ready for affection to turn him into a friend. Thus the third seed of guilt was sown.

''He would have preferred to be Vizier to Men-het, whom he liked as a man and respected as a leader, than to become a Pharaoh who might be remembered as 'The Usurper.' He knew that this desire was an unspoken criticism of the wisdom of Roidahn: because of it he felt that he betrayed both Roidahn and Men-het. The fourth and fifth seeds of guilt.

''He married for expediency, thus betraying one of the ideals of the Watchers: the sixth seed.

''He married the daughter of the man who might have been his Pharaoh, and failed to make her happy: the seventh seed.

''Then for a time you showed him that only by love can the bitter harvest of guilt be destroyed. He opened the doors which barred the Road to Affection, and with Nefer-tathen he found happiness and peace. She died, and because he had suffered through affection, he took it for yet another sign of guilt. He saw, even in the love he felt for her, the sign of the destroyer, and so again closed himself against it: the eighth seed.

''In his heart he was glad when his daughter died, for every time he saw her he remembered that had she not been born her mother might be alive. She died of the Summer Fever; but because he desired her death he felt like a murderer: the ninth guilt.

"To justify his sense of guilt he refused to recognize the real character of the Babylonian; through her he made Senusert suffer: the tenth seed.

"But why try to measure by numbers the burden he carried? He felt guilty every time he drew breath, for in his heart he knew that he betrayed himself because he refused to obey the great law of Ra. He believed he was going mad not only because he saw the Babylonian, but because he *wanted* to be mad. For then he could have said, 'My sins must be forgiven me: the mad are not responsible for what they do.'

"I have been able to lift from Amenemhet the burden of his old guilt, but unless he can learn to live by the light of affection he will never know the peace which endures.''

Senusert came to my room early next morning, and before he spoke I realized that something deeply disturbed him.

"Ptah-kefer says that Father is very ill. She has sent for Tet-hen, and they think it may be the Summer Fever, even though the worst of the hot weather is over.''

For the next twelve days none of us knew whether the next hour would begin the Forty Days' Lamentation throughout the Two Lands. Crowds waited in the outer courtyard of the Palace: had Amenemhet seen how much they longed for news of his recovery, he would have known that he need never have feared his people.

Ptah-kefer, or one of the healer-priests, was able to reduce his fever; but in an hour it had mounted again until his skin burned as though he were lost in a waterless desert. Yet there was no sign of delirium which usually accompanies such an illness: he was seldom conscious for more than a few moments, but then he seemed perfectly composed, was obedient as a child and expressed gratitude to those who ministered to him.

Gradually these periods of consciousness became more

frequent until at last he seemed entirely rational. I was in the room when Tet-hen told him that he would soon be completely restored to health. This appeared to distress him, and he said:

"You need not try to hide from me that I am a sick man, for I assure you that I am perfectly able to bear any pains which my body may inflict upon me. My Crook and Flail are safe in the hands of my son: why then should I resent my failing strength? My body is no different to any other man's, and when it has served its purpose no one should weep because he knows that soon it will return to dust."

Senusert found this attitude disquieting, "It is so unlike him, Ra-ab. He has always bitterly resented being ill; even when he had fever he insisted on taking Audience, though had he been well he would have preferred me to do it for him. If at any time I said he looked tired it was to incur his instant displeasure."

We were in the garden, and Nekht was sitting beside me peeling an apricot. He looked up.

"Of course Amenemhet dreaded to be ill when he thought his body was his only protection against the Babylonian. Don't either of you realize why he wants to go on being ill now? He rejoices that he has put off an old burden but is afraid of building a new Cavern. How can he build anything so long as he remains helpless as a child, unable to take any responsibility? He knows that unless he learns to live by the light of affection he will again find himself alone in the dark. It is not easy to change your habits after twenty years—especially when you are Pharaoh. He has made it difficult for himself to find friendship, for he deliberately became remote and austere. Yet while he is ill he can accept tributes of affection and allow himself to display gratitude without hurt to his pride, for he only sees those who know his secret, from whom he has nothing to hide. But when he is well again, he must live among people whom he has always regarded as strangers."

''I believe he's right, Ra-ab,'' said Senusert. ''We must arrange for Father to leave the Palace until he has regained his self-confidence. It need not be generally known that he has left here; so he can forget for a time that he is Pharaoh.''

''Where shall we send him, to the Summer Palace?''

Then, before Senusert had time to answer, I added, ''No, it must to a place which holds no memories for him. Could we take him to the Oryx?''

''Later, nothing could be better for him, but he is not yet strong enough to make so long a journey.''

Then Nekht said, ''Why not send him to the House of Two Winds? Beket is the person he needs. To her he will always be Senusert's father, not the Lord of the Two Lands. If she can make a hawk share its food with a mouse-deer, she should have no difficulty in making Amenemhet remember that he too belongs to the kinship which is shared by all the children of Ra.''

# Land of free people

When, nearly a year later, I broke the Royal Seal which closed a papyrus that a messenger from Amenemhet had given into my hand, I wondered whether it would presage another hasty journey north.

''During the hot weather it is pleasant at the Summer Palace. If Meri and Ra-ab, and Roidahn also, should feel inclined to make so long a journey to honor Amenemhet with their company, then would his heart rejoice. He longs to share with them the tranquillity which he enjoys during the autumn of his years.''

Meri, who was reading over my shoulder, exclaimed, ''Of course we must go! It would be good for both you and Roidahn to rest for a time...you work too hard.''

"Now that Ameni and Nekht relieve me of so many responsibilities I am more in danger of idleness than of overwork!"

Beket's children, who were staying with us, ran past the windows on their way to the swimming-pool. "Couldn't we take them with us?" suggested Meri, "They would love the sea."

"Beket is taking them there later in the year. We will go alone, with Roidahn, for it must be a rest for you too...for a time you must forget the concerns of a grandmother."

Amenemhet was waiting to greet us at the gateway of the Summer Palace. I heard Meri catch her breath when she saw him: for, through some quality of the evening light, he looked young as the man whose brief happiness we had shared so many years ago. Yet he had attained a serenity which even then he had not known: Pharaoh was forgotten, only the man who was our friend remained.

"Senusert's sons have been staying with me," he said eagerly. "They are coming back soon, after they have been with their mother to visit Beras in the Jackal. I am building a boat, Ra-ab, doing the work myself!"

He laughed, and then turned to Meri. "You must help me work in my garden, and so must Roidahn. You will find me a most eager pupil. Beket will approve of my gazelles: they could not be more tame even if it was her voice, not mine, which spoke to them."

He poured wine for us, and then led the way to rooms whose windows opened to the sea.

"There is a view to content a man of any age," he said. Then, scooping up some soil from a flowering plant which stood on the window-ledge, "Earth in my hand; my eyes to the horizon...that is how I found my peace."

Next morning, though it was soon after dawn when I left the house, I met Amenemhet coming back from the garden. He carried an alabaster jar filled with blue convolvulus.

"Do you remember that they were Nefer-tathen's favorite flower?" he said. "These are descendants of the ones we planted together. When I came back here after twenty years. I found that my orders to tend them had been so scrupulously carried out that there was nothing to show they were not the same flowers which my wife and I had watched climb that trellis. I am going to put them in her room. I sleep there now, sleep that often brings me to her door—the road to it has become almost as familiar as the paths of my garden. I never feel alone any more, Ra-ab, either asleep or awake."

Then he took me to see his vineyard. "I shall gather many grapes this year," he said, "even though I was warned that sea-winds are not favorable to vines."

The fruit was already formed among the clustering leaves. He bent to twist off a bunch where the stem was too crowded. "Wine of my own growing will taste better than any that was closed in the wine-jars of Pharaoh. It took courage to plant these vines, Ra-ab."

"Courage?"

"Yes, I flinched from anything which might remind me of the time when I was—separate. When you have drunk from a thousand wine-cups wondering if each was poisoned, it is not easy to plant vines. Now I have grapes of my own pressing with which to fill the cup I raise to Ra, that he may bless the toast I drink to all my brothers." He smiled, "It was another victory for you, Ra-ab, when I could close with bitumen the seams of the boat I am building: to find that bitumen had the brave smell of a quest for new horizons."

"Bitumen?" I asked, for a moment puzzled.

"Yes, bitumen...the warm breath of a mummy who would not die."

"She was freed long ago."

"I was freed also, Ra-ab; by you, who have always been my friend."

"No, it was by Tet-hen."

"It was your friendship which made it possible for him to

310

break the link: your affection which was stronger than her hatred.''

A gazelle jumped over the vineyard wall, paused when he saw me, and then came trotting to his master. Amenemhet stooped down to fondle him; ''Beket gave him to me,'' he said, ''Beket, who gave me peace. I love her as a daughter, Ra-ab. So we are closer than brothers; your daughter is my daughter, my son your son. Was it you, or Roidahn, who had the wisdom to send me to Beket?''

''Neither, it was my younger son.''

He smiled, ''Our relationships are becoming very complex, for Nekht is not only your son, but Roidahn's also. I am blessed in my kinsmen...I, who used to be so lonely. Did Beket ever tell you how patient she had to be with me? What did she say about me, Ra-ab?''

''She spoke as though you were one of her children, who must be cherished to heal him of a bitter hurt.''

''I never realized she saw me like that, but now I see it is true. I was surprised at being received without ceremony: you must remember that I had only met the Beket of ceremonial, the Wife of the Vizier. I was carried straight to my room, and found it strange that its appointments were so simple. There were flowers on the window-ledge—blue flowers. Beket said, 'Mother told me that blue is Nefer-tathen's favorite color.' No one had dared to mention my wife to me since her death. For a moment I was angry; then I realized that Nefer-tathen was a women who waited for me beyond sleep—a living woman. The beautiful mummy for whom I had long sorrowed was only a dress she had discarded.

''Beket's children used to come to talk with me. To them I was not Pharaoh: I was only a guest of their mother's who had been ill and needed comforting. It was when the youngest girl wept for pity because I could not play with her in the garden that I became ashamed of hiding behind my illness. I went out into the sun, and the child taught me to help her weed her private plot. There was earth, rich, clean earth,

311

on my hands and under my nails when Beket found me. I remember thinking that, since I was a little boy, it was the first time I had ever been dirty. 'I am learning to be a gardener,' I said to her. 'Look at all the weeds I have pulled out.' She smiled, 'Soon you will be ready to make things grow. It is not easy to be a gardener, it needs patience, for there is much to learn.' I promised to be patient if she would take me as a pupil: and I thought 'At last Pharaoh is beginning to learn something!'

"Beket would not let me help her with the animals until they had become accustomed to me. For a while they would not trust me—why should they, when I mistrusted myself? The first time one of her leopards rested his chin on my knee, and purred when I stroked him, I knew that I had been accepted into a kinship from which I had long been exiled.

"It was soon after this when Senusert and his wife came to the House of the Two Winds. They too were part of Beket's family. Since his return from the Oryx I had honored Senusert, given him trust and admiration. I was proud that we were linked by blood; but it was through Beket that I found the Senusert whom I dearly love. My grandchildren had never liked me when I was Pharaoh, but now they came to accept me, as did Beket's children, for one of themselves. The first time they asked me to tell stories to them before they said good-night, I knew it was much more important than my Reading of the Laws: for now, at last, I could read the Great Law, of true affection."

Often we would go down to the beach after sunset; there to lie in the warm sand, while the small waves rippled like harp-strings half heard in the distance, and we enjoyed the good bread of conversation. We had been watching a flight of sea-birds crossing the path of the moon, when Amenemhet said:

"I had forgotten that even the far-sighted would become blind if they refused to live by the light of affection, even as the world would die were it forsaken by sun and moon. All light, whether it kindles torches on the wind or points a lamp in some close-shuttered room, belongs to Ptah. When a man tries to use his possessions to separate himself from his fellows, he is a prisoner, a starveling who dare not share in the fruits of the earth. I thought that Pharaoh was right to remain aloof: was he not by tradition a link with the Gods? I had forgotten that the Gods themselves keep open all their links: they can speak in the voice of a brother to a rock, to a blade of grass, to a water-rat. Yet Pharaoh, who was only a man, thought himself nearer the Gods because he would not say 'brother' even to his own people.

''In terrible isolation, my soul began to wither: it became small and hard and brilliant...as are the souls of tyrants. I, who had sworn to bring peace to Egypt, might have been recorded on the steles as 'The Oppressor, the Narrow-hearted.' Down the empty centuries I should have heard the echoes of whips raised in my name; and my weary feet, treading alone the avenue of years, would have kept to the rhythm of muttering crowds who were hungry and afraid.''

I saw that he was deeply moved; and I was trying to think of a way to change the sorrowful trend of his thoughts when the need for this was taken from me by Roidahn.

''You could never have become a tyrant; even if you had longed to do so, even if you had held a hundred times more power than any man yet born.''

''Of course I could have become a tyrant!'' Amenemhet's voice held the indignation of a boy. He heard this too, and began to laugh at himself, laughter in which we joined. ''Couldn't I have become a tyrant, Roidahn? How I wish I had known that! It was a terror which never left my side for twenty desolate years.''

''You might have become a *small* tyrant,'' said Roidahn consolingly. ''Perhaps as the overseer of a minor town in the least successful of our Nomes. No, I doubt if you would have been able to do so even there. But had you wished to go among the Babylonians, I have no doubt that you would have been able to rule them, to their extreme discomfort, within a short time of your arrival in their chief city!''

''You mean that had I remained in Egypt you or Ra-ab would have removed me...perhaps in a manner not unfamiliar to a certain Babylonian?''

''No, it would never have been necessary...and had you only realized that, it would have saved you much needless anxiety! But I see I must explain myself more fully if my meaning is to become clear.''

And in that discourse, perhaps more than in any other, Roidahn gave the secret of the Watchers, who in peace lead men to the Horizon.

''For several years before you were in any danger of becoming a tyrant, Fear had been sent into exile. At first all we could do was to remove physical fear, to convince our people that it was a fact, not only a promise, that there would be no whip-men in Egypt; convince them that we had banished famine and corrupt officials and injustice...and all the other fears which for centuries they had suffered. But then we gave them something much more vital to their happiness: they were no longer afraid of themselves, and so they had no reason to fear any false authority, for unless they suffered a change of heart it could never again arise among them.

''Which is the reason why, my friend, I told you that you would have to go to a place like Babylon before you could hope to be a tyrant. My statement, I assure you, was not intended as a reflection on the strength of your will or the scope of your influence! A country, or a Nome, or a village, is only an aggregate of individuals; just as the individual is an aggregate of many lives of experience. The weapon given into the hands of any tyrant is the accumulated fear which people feel for themselves.''

''I agree that I feared myself,'' said Amenemhet. ''But surely mine was an extraordinary case?''

''Extraordinary only in that it took a dramatic form...it is

314

not given to all of us to be haunted by the mummy of a Babylonian! Yet under the Old Rule nearly everyone was haunted by something almost as unpleasant. Unseen guests sat at many tables, and in each case, hatred had opened the door for them to enter. If husband and wife are forced to live together when affection no longer justifies their close companionship, is it surprising that hatred enters their house? Each thinks that the other cannot see this unseen guest: each thinks in his heart 'It is I who have brought it here.' Yet to conceal this thought from themselves they say in a much louder voice, 'I am innocent! How pitiful I am that I have to live with this monster who has so terrible a familiar! They have made me their prisoner, and I cannot leave—for it would not be according to custom.'

"You feared your unseen guest, Amenemhet. Do you blame others for fearing theirs? Their cure is the same as your own...affection; for only in that name does Ra rise up to bid Set go once more to exile. Your people, Amenemhet, have learned to love themselves; and so they are free to love their fellows.

"They no longer feel guilty if they differ from their parents: they no longer feel guilty if they find no link of true affection with any member of their family: they no longer feel guilty when the link between husband and wife ceases to be strong enough to justify them in continuing to share the same house; nor do they feel guilty if they are poor, or if they are rich. They do not feel guilty if they are sick, for in the temples of our time they find healing both for the body and for the soul; nor do they feel guilty to be in health when others are in pain. They do not feel guilty when they are idle or when they are working, for they know that a measure of both is necessary for contentment. They do not feel guilty because they are young, for they know that wisdom cannot be measured in Earth years; nor do they feel guilty when they are old, for they know that the strength of the spirit cannot be judged by the muscles of a man's arm.

"Greater than all these, Amenemhet; your people have learned that it is most pleasing to the Gods when men are happy; and in learning this they have lost the most terrible of all guilt. Now they can turn their faces to the sky, and laugh, and bless the day when they were born into Egypt, this Egypt which can give no allegiance to a tyrant while her people remember they are free."

## Epilogue

Word that Roidahn was dying traveled throughout Egypt. From the North and from the South, from beyond the Eastern Cliffs and from the Great Desert, a multitude who loved him came to the place where he would bid farewell to Earth.

According to his wish, no tomb had been prepared for Roidahn. He had said:

"Man is born of fire and of water: on a pyre of sweet woods the body which has been my faithful servant shall be consumed, and my dust be given to the river. My only stele shall be the memory of me in men's hearts.

"Instead of lamentation there shall be rejoicing during the Forty Days. Do you not rejoice when the bird with the broken wing can fly, when the exile returns to his home, when the sick are healed?

"Even so shall you share my joy. Put garlands in your homes, and unseal the wine of festival; let the dancers be supple as reeds, and the strings of harps ripple like silver water. Roidahn, your friend, wishes you to share his joy: but if you weep, then will the Fields of Ra be misty with your tears, and Roidahn sorrow."

Even in the last hours his body did not mask his spirit. To those of us who were with him he spoke as a traveler setting forth to a country long familiar, a forerunner who went to prepare the place of our meeting.

He died at sunset. His last words were for Hanuk and Nekht, who stood together at the bed-place.

"I am greatly honored in my sons. Hanuk, who carried the torch I kindled and cleansed the Two Lands from corruption. Nekht, my son in Horus, who, before the clouds which light Ra on his journey have faded from this evening sky, leaving the stars as his sentinels of the night, will have become Lord of the Horizon."

Then he raised his head to smile at all of us, saying, "Because of you I am well content: I go forward to the Fields of Ra, in peace."

# Joan Grant

Joan Grant was born in England in 1907. Her father was a man of such intellectual brilliance in the fields of mathematics and engineering that he was appointed a fellow of Kings College while still in his twenties. Joan's formal education was limited to what she absorbed from a series of governesses, although she feels she learned far more from the after-dinner conversations between her father and his fellow scientists.

When Joan was twenty, she married Leslie Grant, with whom she had a daughter. This marriage ended soon after *Winged Pharaoh* was published in 1937—a book which became an instant best-seller. Until 1957 she was married to the philosopher and visionary Charles Beatty, who is the author of several books, including *The Garden of the Golden Flower*, a treatise on psychiatrist Carl Jung. In 1960, Joan married psychiatrist Denys Kelsey.

Throughout her life, Joan has been preoccupied with the subject of ethics. To her, the word ''ethics'' represents the fundamental and timeless code of attitudes and behavior toward one another on which the health of the individual and society depends. Each of her books and stories explores a facet of this code. As Denys Kelsey has written, ''The First Dynasty of Egypt once knew the code well, but lost it and foundered. Eleven dynasties were to pass before it was recovered, but those were more leisurely times when the most lethal weapon was an arrow, a javelin and a club. We feel that in the present troubled days of this planet, these books must be presented.''

# THE FAR MEMORIES

Ariel Press is proud to announce that it has brought all seven of Joan Grant's "far memory" novels back into print in a uniform collection of books. They may be purchased individually or as a set. The books, and their prices, are:

*Winged Pharaoh.* $14.95.
*Life as Carola.* $9.95.
*Return to Elysium.* $9.95.
*Eyes of Horus.* $11.95.
*Lord of the Horizon.* $14.95.
*Scarlet Feather.* $10.95.
*So Moses Was Born.* $9.95.

These books can be purchased either at your favorite bookstore or directly from Ariel Press (include an extra $1.50 for postage; $2.50 for Canada and overseas).

In addition, Ariel Press has also reprinted three other Joan Grant books: *Far Memory,* her autobiography; *A Lot to Remember,* a memoir of travels and clairvoyant impressions in the Lot region of France; and *Many Lifetimes,* a penetrating study of the impact of earlier lives on the present, co-authored with her husband, Denys Kelsey.

*Far Memory* costs $10.95, plus postage.
*A Lot to Remember* costs $10.95, plus postage.
*Many Lifetimes* costs $12.95, plus postage.

For those who prefer, the entire set of seven novels plus the other three books may be purchased as a set of 10 for $100 postpaid. *No substitutions or deductions are allowed on subscriptions.*

All orders from the publisher must be accompanied by payment in full in U.S. funds—or charged to VISA, Master-Card, Discover, Diners, or American Express. Please do not send cash. Send orders to Ariel Press, P.O. Box 297, Marble Hill, GA 30148.

For faster service, call toll free 1-800-336-7769 and charge the order. Or e-mail us at light@stc.net.